D0813096

The novels of Stephen Leather

Pay Off

The Fireman

Hungry Ghost

The Chinaman

The Vets

The Long Shot

The Birthday Girl

The Double Tap

The Solitary Man

The Tunnel Rats

The Bombmaker

The Stretch

Tango One

The Eyewitness

About the author

Stephen Leather was a journalist for more than ten years on newspapers such as *The Times*, the *Daily Mail* and the *South China Morning Post* in Hong Kong. Before that, he was employed as a biochemist for ICI, shovelled limestone in a quarry, worked as a baker, a petrol pump attendant, a barman, and worked for the Inland Revenue. He began writing full-time in 1992. His bestsellers have been translated into more than ten languages, and *The Stretch* and *The Bombmaker* have been filmed for television. He has also written for television shows such as *London's Burning*, *The Knock* and the BBC's *Murder In Mind*.

Stephen Leather now lives in Dublin.

Visit his website at www.stephenleather.com

The Birthday Girl

Stephen Leather

CORONET BOOKS
Hodder & Stoughton

Copyright © 1995 by Stephen Leather

First published in Great Britain in 1995
by Hodder and Stoughton
A division of Hodder Headline PLC
First published in paperback in 1996
by Hodder and Stoughton

The right of Stephen Leather to be identified as the Author
of the Work has been asserted by him in accordance
with the Copyright, Designs and Patents Act 1988.

A Coronet Paperback

10 9

A CIP catalogue record for this title
is available from the British Library

ISBN 0 340 66068 6

Typeset by Hewer Text Ltd, Edinburgh
Printed and bound in Great Britain by
Clays Ltd, St Ives PLC

Hodder and Stoughton
A division of Hodder Headline PLC
338 Euston Road
London NW1 3BH

For Philippa

It all happened so quickly that it was only after his abductors had shoved the sack over his head and made him lie down on the floor of the van that Anthony Freeman realised he hadn't said a word. He hadn't begged, pleaded or threatened, he'd just followed their shouted instructions as he'd half crawled, half fallen from the rear of the wrecked Mercedes. He was still in shock from the crash and he'd stumbled towards the van as his captors prodded him with the barrels of their Kalashnikovs.

It was like some crazy, surreal nightmare. Only minutes earlier he'd been standing outside the Holiday Inn, hunched into his sheepskin jacket and wondering whether the far-off rumbling sound was approaching thunder or artillery fire. The Mercedes had arrived on time, rattling along the road with its rear window missing and its licence plates removed. The driver was the man who'd picked him up at Split Airport several days earlier and driven him overland to Sarajevo, taking the dirt road used by the Red Cross to ferry supplies to the besieged city. Zlatko, his name was, father to six children, three of whom had died in the conflict. He'd refused to allow Freeman to help him load the bulky metal suitcase into the boot. It had been

1

Zlatko who'd told Freeman the names of the abandoned villages they'd driven by, some of the ruins still smoking in the cold winter air, and it was Zlatko who'd explained that he'd taken the licence plates off the car to give them a better chance of getting through the many roadblocks. There was no way of knowing in advance who was manning the barricades and a wrong licence plate could be reason enough for a hail of bullets.

Zlatko had done everything possible to avoid the truck as it braked, and if he'd been a less skilful driver the crash would have been a lot worse. As it was, Zlatko's head had slammed into the steering wheel hard enough to stun him, and he'd been unconscious when the doors had been wrenched open. The kidnappers had raked his body with bullets from their assault rifles, the noise deafening in the confines of the car.

There were five of them, maybe six. All Freeman could remember were the black ski masks and the Kalashnikovs and the fact that he'd evacuated his bowels when they'd dragged him from the back seat, screaming at him in heavily accented English.

Freeman couldn't understand what they wanted from him. It wasn't as if he was in Beirut, where hostage-taking was a way of life. He was in Sarajevo; it was snipers and artillery attacks that you had to watch out for. It didn't make sense. The sack smelled of mouldy potatoes and something was crawling across his left cheek but he couldn't get to it because they'd tied his wrists behind his back with rope. His damp trousers were sticking to his skin. He could barely breathe and the musty smell made him want to gag.

Freeman jumped as whatever it was that was crawling

around the inside of the sack bit him on the neck. He tried to move, to ease his discomfort, but a foot stamped down between his shoulder-blades and a voice hissed at him to lie still. He lost all track of time as he lay face down on the floor of the van. Eventually he heard his captors talking to each other and the van made a series of sharp turns and came to a halt. Uncaring hands pulled him out. His cramped legs gave way and as he slumped to the ground the men cursed. More hands clawed at his legs and he was carried bodily.

He heard the crunch of boots on broken glass, then the sound of a door being thrown open. The footsteps became muffled and he realised he was being carried across a carpeted floor, and then he heard the sound of bolts being drawn back and he was hustled down a flight of wooden stairs. More bolts rattled and without warning he was thrown forward. His legs were still weak and he fell to the ground, his chest heaving from the effort of breathing through the thick, foul-smelling sackcloth. He heard the door crash shut behind him and the grate of rusty bolts and then he was alone in the cellar, more alone than he'd ever been in his life.

The doorbell rang just as Katherine Freeman stepped into the shower and she cursed. She stood under the steaming hot spray and closed her eyes, enjoying the feel of the water as it cascaded over her skin. The doorbell rang again, more urgently this time, and she knew that whoever it was wouldn't go away. She climbed carefully out of the shower stall and dried herself with a large pink towel. Downstairs the dog barked, but it was a welcoming yelp rather than a warning growl. Katherine checked herself in the mirror. She'd tied her shoulder-length blonde hair up so that she wouldn't get it too wet in the shower and she shook it free. 'This had better be important,' she told her reflection. The last thing she wanted was to go downstairs and find two earnest young men in grey suits asking her if she'd been saved.

She pursed her lips and examined the skin around her neck. 'Katherine Freeman, you sure look good for a thirty-five-year-old broad,' she said, and stuck out her tongue. She threw the towel into a large wicker basket and picked up a purple bathrobe. The doorbell rang again as she ran down the stairs. 'I'm coming, I'm coming,' she called. If it was Mormons, God help them, she thought. Buffy, her golden retriever, was sitting by the front door, her tail swishing from side to side. 'A smart dog would have opened the door,' said Katherine, and Buffy chuffed in agreement.

Katherine yanked the door open to find Maury Anderson standing on the porch. He was wearing a plaid sports jacket and brown trousers and his tie looked as if it had been knotted in a hurry. 'Maury, I wasn't expecting you,' she said, frowning. Anderson said nothing, and Katherine suddenly realised that something was wrong. Her hand flew up to her throat. 'Oh God, it's Tony, isn't it? What's happened? Oh my God, what's happened?' Her voice rose and Anderson stepped forward to put his hands on her shoulders.

'It's okay,' he said.

'He's dead, isn't he?' She began to shake and Buffy growled, sensing that something was wrong.

'No, he's not dead, I promise you, he's not dead. As far as I know he's not even hurt,' Anderson said. His voice was quiet and soothing, as if he were trying to comfort an injured child.

Katherine pushed him away. 'What do you mean, as far as you know? Maury, what's happened? Tell me.'

'Let's go inside, Katherine. Let's sit down.'

Katherine's robe had fallen open but neither she nor Anderson was aware of her nakedness. Anderson closed the door and held her arm as he led her to one of the couches that straddled the fireplace. He sat her down and then without asking he went over to the drinks cabinet and poured her a large measure of brandy with a splash of Coke. He handed it to her and she cupped it in both hands. She looked up at him, still fearing the worst.

'Tony's been kidnapped,' Anderson said quietly.

The statement was so surprising that it took several seconds for it to register. Katherine had been sure that her husband had been involved in a traffic accident. Kidnappings happened to politicians or millionaires, not to the boss of a struggling defence contractor. 'Kidnapped?' she repeated. 'You mean the Mafia or something?'

'No, not the Mafia,' Anderson said. He sat down on the sofa, his hands clasped in his lap. 'Terrorists are holding him hostage.'

'Terrorists? In Italy?' Katherine remembered reading about terrorist groups in Italy who'd killed businessmen, shot them in the head and left them in their cars. Her heart raced.

Anderson took a deep breath. 'He was in Sarajevo, Katherine.'

'What the hell was he doing in Sarajevo?' She took a

large mouthful of the brandy and Coke and gulped it down. There was a pewter cigarette case on the coffee table. She opened it and took out a cigarette. Her hand shook as she lit it.

'He was there to demonstrate our mine clearance system. We were putting together a deal.'

'But he told me he was in Rome. He called me yesterday morning.'

'I know, I know. He flew to Split and then drove to Sarajevo. It's a long story, but the upshot is that he's been taken hostage by Bosnian terrorists.'

'What do they want?' Her voice was wavering and she fought to keep it steady.

'I don't know. All I've had is a phone call. They said we weren't to speak to the police and that we'd be contacted with their demands. If we call in the authorities, they'll kill him.'

Katherine's hands shook so much that her drink spilled. Anderson took the glass from her hands. She grabbed at his arm. 'What do we do, Maury? Tell me, what do we do?'

Anderson looked at her levelly. 'That's up to you, Katherine,' he said. Buffy whined and put her head on Katherine's knee.

'The FBI can't help us?' Katherine asked.

'It's out of their jurisdiction,' Anderson said. 'We'd have to go to the State Department.'

'So let's do that.'

'Katherine, Tony shouldn't even be in Serbia, never mind doing business there. There's a UN embargo.'

'So? Tony's still an American citizen. The State Department has to get him back.'

'Actually, the fact that he's Scottish makes it more complicated.'

'Damn it, Maury. He's my husband. He's got a Green Card. The State Department has to take care of him.'

'There's a war being fought over there. It's a shambles. No one's sure who's fighting who. We're not even sure who the bad guys are.'

'Goddamn it, Maury, what was Tony doing there? What the hell was he doing there?' Her voice broke and she began to sob uncontrollably. She stubbed out the cigarette. Anderson took her in his arms and held her, tight.

'He was trying to help the firm,' Anderson said. 'We're desperate for contracts, you know that.'

Katherine dabbed at her eyes with a handkerchief. 'I can't believe he didn't mention that he was going to Sarajevo.'

'We didn't know until he was in Rome. The Serbs insisted on seeing him on their territory.'

'Maury, this doesn't make any sense. I thought there was an exclusion zone or something around Sarajevo.'

'Yeah, there is. He had to fly to a place called Split and then drive overland. The Serbs insisted, Katherine. We had to do it.'

'We?' Katherine said. 'We? What do you mean? I don't see you out there.'

Anderson ignored her angry outburst. 'We needed the contract,' he said. 'He probably didn't want to worry you. But as you know we're having cash-flow problems and we have to take orders from wherever we can.'

Katherine pushed him away. 'But you said there was a UN embargo? Doesn't that mean we can't sell to the Serbs?'

Anderson shrugged. 'There are ways around all block-ades,' he said. 'There are middle-men in Europe who'll handle it. Everybody's doing it. Not so long ago the Russians sold 360 million dollars' worth of weapons to them.'

'Yes, but we're not Russians,' Katherine said. 'We're an American company.'

Anderson sighed. 'Look, the Russians were selling T-55 tanks and anti-aircraft missiles, serious weaponry. We're just talking about a few mine clearance systems. That's all.'

'But you're saying that the authorities won't help us because Tony shouldn't have been there in the first place?'

'That's right,' Anderson said. 'But you're missing the point. We can't get help from anyone. If we do and the terrorists find out, they'll kill him.'

Katherine closed her eyes, fighting the urge to slap Anderson across the face. 'Damn you, Maury,' she hissed. 'What have you done?'

There were six guards taking it in turns to watch over Freeman, and over his weeks in captivity he'd made some sort of contact with them all. Freeman knew that the psychiatrists referred to it as the Stockholm Effect, when a hostage begins to form a relationship with his captors, but he also knew that there was a more fundamental reason for his need to communicate with his guards – sheer boredom. They allowed him no books or newspapers, no television or radio, and for long periods he was left alone, chained to a disused boiler in the freezing-cold basement.

Four of the men appeared to speak no English at all and communication with them was restricted to nods and gestures, but even their surly grunts were better than the hours of mind-numbing isolation. The fifth man's name was Stjepan, and he appeared to be the leader of the group. He was in his early twenties, thin and wiry with deep-set eyes that seemed to stare at Freeman from dark pits either side of a hooked nose. He spoke reasonable English but slowly and with such a thick accent that often he had to repeat himself to make himself understood. Stjepan told Freeman why he was being held hostage, and what would happen to him if the group's demands were not met. On the second day of his captivity, Stjepan had Freeman's aluminium suitcase brought down into the basement and demanded that he show him how to work the equipment it contained. Freeman had complied, though Stjepan's limited English meant it took several hours. The equipment was then carefully repacked into its case and taken back upstairs. Suddenly, and for no apparent reason, Stjepan had punched Freeman in the face, hard enough to split his lip.

A Sony video camera was brought down into the cellar and Freeman was handed a badly typed script to read. As he struggled with the poor grammar and inept vocabulary of the statement, he realised that the punch had probably been planned in advance to give more authenticity to the video, but the thought didn't make it hurt any the less. Freeman asked if he could record a personal message to his wife and Stjepan had agreed. When he'd finished Freeman was given a plate of watery stew and left alone.

While they waited for a response to the video, Stjepan was an occasional visitor to the basement, and Freeman felt it was because the young man wanted to practise his English. There was no further violence, which reinforced Freeman's belief that the punch in the face had been for effect rather than to punish him, but Stjepan always kept his assault rifle close by and left Freeman in no doubt that he was prepared to use it.

During his hours alone in the basement, Freeman spent a lot of time thinking about his wife and son, and it seemed that the more he replayed the memories the stronger they became. He began to recall events and conversations that he had thought were long forgotten, and as he sat on the cold concrete floor he wept for the life that had been taken from him. He missed his wife and he missed his son.

He lost track of time after just a few days. The basement was without windows and illuminated by a single bulb which hung from the ceiling by a frayed wire. Sometimes it was on but usually he was in darkness. Electricity was as scarce as medical supplies in the war-torn city. His meals came at irregular intervals, so he had no way of knowing what time, or day, it was.

The wait for news of the Bosnians' demands seemed interminable. Stjepan said that the tape was being sent over to the United States because they wanted to deal directly with Freeman's company. Freeman knew that made sense: the US government prohibited the sort of deal he'd been planning to sign with the Serbian forces and he doubted that they would want to negotiate with Bosnian guerrillas. Once Maury Anderson heard that he was in trouble, Freeman knew he'd move heaven and earth to get him out. If anyone was to blame for Freeman's predicament it was Anderson and his insistence that Freeman fly to the former Yugoslavia to find new markets for the minefield clearing system they'd developed. NATO forces had turned him down flat, saying that they were developing their own system, and the only real European interest had come from the Serbian forces. A representative of the Serb military had made contact with Freeman in Rome and asked him to fly to Split for a demonstration. Freeman had wanted to refuse and had called Anderson in Baltimore to tell him as much. That was when his partner had broken the news of yet another US Army contract that had fallen through. The workforce of almost two hundred men was depending on Freeman, and if he didn't come up with a European contract soon almost half of them would have to be laid off. CRW Electronics was a family firm, founded by Freeman's father-in-law, and Freeman knew every one of the employees by name. Anderson had put him in an impossible position. He had no choice but to go.

Twelve hours later he was in a hotel in Split meeting a German middle-man who knew how to slip through the US trade blockade, for a price. Everything had been done in secrecy, including getting the equipment into the country on a mercy relief convoy, and Freeman had no idea how the Bosnians had discovered what he was up to. He'd asked Stjepan, but the man had refused to answer.

Stjepan was more forthcoming on his own background. Over the course of several days, he told Freeman that he had been fighting since Croatia and Slovenia declared their independence in June 1991, splitting the Balkans into warring factions. He was a Muslim and his parents had been killed by Serbs, though he refused to go into details. His sister, Mersiha, was also one of Freeman's guards and

11

more often than not it was the young girl who brought his food and emptied the plastic bucket that they made him use as a toilet. Unlike Stjepan, Mersiha refused to talk to Freeman. At first he assumed that she couldn't speak English, because no matter what he said to her she glared at him as if she wished he were dead, and some days she would put his food just out of reach and later take it away, untouched.

Freeman waited until Stjepan seemed in a relaxed mood before asking him about his sister. He said that she had been particularly hard hit by the death of their parents, and that she could speak some English. Their mother had been a schoolteacher, he said. Freeman asked Stjepan why he had the young girl with him but Stjepan shrugged and said there was nowhere else for her to go.

Mersiha's black hair was tied back in a ponytail and her face was always streaked with dirt but there was no disguising her natural prettiness. Freeman knew that she'd be a lot prettier if she smiled and it became almost a compulsion, the urge to crack her sullen exterior and expose the real girl beneath. He greeted her each time she came down the steps, and thanked her when she put his food close enough for him to reach. He even thanked her whenever she emptied his plastic bucket, and he always used her name, but no matter how pleasant he tried to be, her expression never altered. Eventually he could stand it no more and he asked her point blank why she was so angry with him. His question seemed to have no more effect than his pleasantries, and Freeman thought that maybe she hadn't understood, but then she turned to him, almost in slow motion, and pointed her Kalashnikov at his stomach. The gun seemed huge in her small hands, but she handled it confidently and he watched in horror as her finger tightened on the trigger. He cowered as the young girl's lips parted into a grimace of hatred and contempt. 'I hope they let me kill you,' she hissed, and jabbed at him with the barrel of the gun as if it had a bayonet on the end. She looked as if she was going to say something else but then the moment passed and she regained her composure. She turned to go, but before she went back up the stairs she kicked his bucket to the far side of the basement, well beyond the reach of the chain.

The next time Freeman saw Stjepan he asked him why his sister seemed to hate him so much. Stjepan shrugged and in broken English said that he didn't want to talk about his sister. And he warned Freeman not to antagonise her. Freeman nodded and said he understood, though he wasn't sure that he did. He asked Stjepan how old the girl was and the man smiled. She'd be thirteen years old the following day.

As soon as she came down the stairs the next day, carrying a plate of bread and cheese, Freeman wished her a happy birthday in her own language, trying to pronounce it exactly as Stjepan had told him. She showed no reaction as she put the tin plate on the floor and pushed it towards him with her foot, covering him all the time with the Kalashnikov. Switching back to English, he told her that he had wanted to get her a present but that he hadn't been able to get to the shops. Her face remained impassive, but at least she was listening to him and her finger remained outside the trigger guard. Freeman began to sing 'Happy Birthday' to her, his voice echoing off the walls of his prison. She looked at him in disbelief, a worried frown on her face as if she feared that he'd gone crazy, then she realised what he was doing. When she smiled it was as if the sun had come streaming into the basement.

Maury Anderson's office was like the man himself – showy, pretentious even, and definitely built for comfort. Katherine walked across the plush green carpet and sat down on the imported sofa which curved around one corner of the room. It was the best office in the building, with its view of the woods and fields, and no expense had been spared on its furnishings. It was the office that the company used to impress its clients. Her husband's office was in stark contrast, a small cubicle overlooking the car park with a threadbare carpet, cheap teak veneered furniture and one sagging couch.

Katherine studied Anderson as she lit a Virginia Slim. He was pacing up and down in front of his massive eighteenth-century desk, rubbing his hands together. He was dressed as if he were going to a funeral: a black suit, starched white shirt, sombre tie and gleaming black shoes. 'You said you'd heard from the kidnappers,' Katherine said, crossing her legs.

'Uh-huh,' Anderson grunted. 'It arrived by Federal Express an hour ago.'

Katherine looked across at the large-screen television and video recorder which was normally used to show the firm's promotional films to clients. 'A video?'

Anderson stopped pacing. Katherine had never seen him so tense. She wondered how bad it could be. 'Can I get you a drink?' he asked.

Katherine shook her head. 'Just show me the video, Maury,' she said. She took a long drag on the cigarette and blew the smoke out through tightly pursed lips.

'You'd better prepare yourself, Katherine. He doesn't look too good.'

Katherine nodded curtly and Anderson pressed the 'play' button. The screen flickered and then Tony was there, sitting on a stool and holding a sheet of paper that looked as if it had been torn from a child's exercise book. He was staring at the camera, then he jumped at a whispered command. He began to read from the note.

'I am held by Bosnian forces who are struggling against invaders from Serbia. The Serbs are killing our country like Hitler in Europe.' Tony grimaced at the unwieldy English and looked off-screen. A harsh whisper told him to go on. 'Anyone who trades with the Serbian invaders is an enemy of the people of Bosnia and will be treated so. If I am to be released, you must agree not to sell your weapon to the Serbs.'

'Weapon?' Katherine said. Anderson held up a hand telling her to keep quiet until the end of the message.

'As compensation for breaking the United Nations embargo, you will give the Bosnian forces fifty of the equipment.' Tony broke off from reading and looked at the camera. 'They mean fifty of the MIDAS systems, Maury. They'll want the complete kits.' The man standing behind the camera told Tony to keep to the script, but Tony insisted that he had to explain what was meant so that there'd be no misunderstanding. The off-screen voice grudgingly agreed. 'They also want a quarter of a million dollars in cash, Maury. When it and the equipment is delivered to our contact in Rome, I'll be released,' Tony continued. His voice faltered. 'If this doesn't happen, I'll be killed. This video is proof that I'm alive and well. You'll be contacted within the next few days so that arrangements can be made.'

The screen flickered as if the camera had been switched off and then Tony reappeared, looking directly into the camera. It felt to Katherine as if he was staring right at her and she shivered. 'Katherine, I love you,' he said. 'Please don't worry, this will work out all right, I promise.' His hand went up to his bruised and unshaven face and he smiled thinly. 'Don't let this upset you. I cut myself shaving,' he said. He smiled, and for a moment it seemed almost genuine. 'They're treating me okay, and if Maury does as they ask they say I'll be released unharmed. I think they mean it, so just hang in there. I'll be back before you know it.'

A whispered command made him turn to his right and Katherine got a closer look at his battered face. 'Oh my God,' she whispered. 'What have they done to you?'

'Just one more minute,' Tony pleaded, then he turned back to the camera. 'Don't even think about coming over here, Katherine. It's not safe. They'll probably release me in Split and I'll fly to Europe, Rome maybe. I always promised you a trip to Rome, remember? I love you, Katherine, and . . .'

The screen went blank in mid-sentence. Katherine turned to Anderson. 'Have they been in touch yet?'

Anderson shook his head. 'No, like I said, the video's only just arrived. I'll stay here night and day until they call.'

'He's in a terrible state, Maury.'

'I think it looks worse than it is. They haven't let him wash or shave.'

'Maury, he's been beaten.'

Anderson went behind his desk and sat down. 'I don't know what to do, Katherine.'

Katherine realised she'd finished her cigarette. She stubbed the butt in a crystal ashtray and lit another. 'Do we have the equipment?'

Anderson nodded. 'Sure. We were planning to sell them to the Serbs. They're all ready to go, complete with Serbo-Croat instruction manuals.'

Katherine blew a tight plume of smoke up to the ceiling. 'So we do as they say.'

'You realise that with the cash we're talking about a million dollars, give or take?' Anderson said.

Katherine's eyes hardened. 'And you realise that we're talking about my husband,' she said coldly. 'Give or take.'

Anderson held her glance for several seconds, then he nodded. 'I'll make the arrangements,' he said quietly.

'Do that, Maury,' Katherine said. 'Do whatever it takes.'

Over the weeks of his captivity, Mersiha opened up slowly to Freeman like a flower sensing the morning sun. It started with her wishing him good morning when she came to empty his bucket, and then she began to ask him if there was anything he wanted. He asked for a razor and soap and when she finally brought it to him she sat on her heels and watched open-mouthed as he shaved.

Her English was surprisingly good. Mersiha explained that her mother had been a teacher of languages – English, French and Hungarian – and that before the war she'd spent most evenings at the kitchen table studying. Freeman asked her what had happened to her parents but she'd answered with just one word: dead. She resisted any further probing and Freeman realised that if he pushed too hard he risked damaging their fragile relationship.

Despite her new willingness to talk to him, the girl left Freeman in no doubt that he was still her prisoner. She never got within range of the chain which kept him bound to the boiler, and the Kalashnikov never left her hands. And while she smiled and sometimes even laughed with him, he was always aware of a hardness in her eyes which belied her years. Freeman wondered what she would do if her brother's demands were not met, whether she would still be prepared to kill him. He decided that she would, without hesitation.

The black limousine pulled up almost silently and the back door opened. Maury Anderson could see nothing through the darkened windows but he could smell Sal Sabatino's cologne and cigars. He climbed into the luxurious car and closed the door behind him.

The man sitting in the back seat made even the stretch limousine feel cramped. He sat with his legs wide apart, his ample stomach threatening to break free from the constraints of his tailored trousers. He had a big cigar in his right hand and a glass of red wine in his left. 'This better be fucking important, Maury,' he said. He jabbed the cigar at Anderson, punctuating his words.

'It is, Mr Sabatino. This could be what you've been waiting for.'

Sabatino's smooth-skinned plump face was covered with a thin film of sweat despite the limousine's air-conditioning. He took a long sip of wine and studied Anderson with eyes that looked like they belonged to a dead fish.

'The company's going to need cash to get Tony out. A lot of cash. The banks sure as hell won't give it to us, so it gives me a reason to look for outside investment. And who do I know who wants to invest?'

'How much?'

'As much as you want, Mr Sabatino. With Tony out of the way, I'll be able to approve it. His wife's too upset to even think about company business. She'll leave it up to me.'

Sabatino nodded. A gold crucifix glittered at his throat under his open-necked white silk shirt. 'I want more than just a part of the company, Maury. I want it all.'

'I know that, Mr Sabatino. But this is a start.'

'Just so long as you know it's just a start.' He flicked the ash from his cigar and it sprinkled over the carpet. Anderson made no move to leave and Sabatino raised an eyebrow. 'Is there something else?'

'I don't suppose you have any . . .'

Sabatino put his head back and laughed. He stuck his cigar between his lips and took out a small package which he handed to Anderson. 'Enjoy yourself,' he said.

The limousine pulled away leaving Anderson standing

on the roadside. He could smell the cologne long after the car had disappeared from sight.

Katherine Freeman put Buffy's food bowl on the kitchen floor and as the dog attacked the meat and biscuits she went through into the sitting room and poured herself a drink. She dropped down on to a sofa, kicked off her shoes and lit a cigarette. Her hand trembled as she inhaled. In the kitchen, Buffy's nose banged the bowl against a kitchen cabinet in her eagerness to get at the food.

'Damn dog,' muttered Katherine under her breath. Buffy was pretty much Tony's dog, but the retriever seemed not even to be aware that her master had been missing for more than two months. All she wanted to do was eat, sleep and play with her frisbee. The first thing Katherine intended to do after Tony got back was to tell him how disloyal his dog was. Well, the second thing maybe. Or the third. The telephone rang and she jumped. She took a sip of brandy and Coke before picking it up. If it was bad news, she'd rather hear it under the influence of an anaesthetic. It was Maury Anderson and she steeled herself for the worst as she always did when he called. 'Good afternoon, Maury,' she said, fighting to keep her composure. She realised she was only a step away from screaming.

'Good news,' Anderson said, as if sensing how tense Katherine was. 'The consignment has arrived in Italy.'

'When will they let Tony go?' Katherine asked. Buffy wandered in from the kitchen, sniffing as if searching for more food.

'It won't be long now,' he assured her. 'Their middle-man will inspect the goods, then they'll be shipped over to Serbia. The terrorists have promised to release Tony as soon as the crates are on Serbian territory.'

'Do you believe them?'

'Maybe. But I've got a fall-back position. I've met some people in the security business who say they can help. They've dealt with kidnappings before. If the Serbs screw us around, they'll move in.'

'In Sarajevo?'

'They've got contacts there. Are you okay?' he asked, the concern obvious in his voice.

'I'm fine,' she replied. 'Under the circumstances.'

'I could come around,' he said.

Katherine took a mouthful of brandy and Coke as she considered his offer, but then declined, telling him that she preferred to be on her own. She stayed on the sofa for most of the day, chain-smoking Virginia Slims and refilling her glass at regular intervals. From time to time she looked over at a collection of framed photographs on the sideboard. Two in particular held her attention: a formal wedding portrait of her and Tony under a huge chestnut tree, taken just minutes after they had exchanged vows, and a smaller photograph of Tony and their son, Luke, laughing together as they played basketball, taken just two days before Luke died.

Mersiha sat cross-legged on the concrete floor, cradling her Kalashnikov in her lap as she watched Freeman shave. She tilted her head from side to side like a small bird, and when he shaved under his chin she lifted her head up, gritted her teeth and tightened the skin around her neck as he did.

'Why do you do that?' she asked as he splashed water over his face.

'Shave, you mean? Because it feels better. Doesn't your brother shave?'

Mersiha giggled. 'His skin is like a girl's,' she said. 'Do all Americans shave?'

'I'm not American. I'm Scottish.'

'Scottish?'

'From Scotland. Next to England. The English come from England, the Scottish come from Scotland.' He rinsed his razor in the bowl of cold water.

'But you live in America?'

Freeman nodded. 'My wife is American. What about your father? Didn't he shave?'

Mersiha shook her head. 'He had a—' She screwed up her face as she sought the correct word. '—beard,' she finished. 'He had a beard.'

She fell silent as Freeman used an old green towel to pat his skin dry. 'I'm sorry about what happened to your father,' he said quietly.

She frowned. 'How do you know what happened?' she asked.

There was a hard edge to her voice and Freeman realised he would have to tread carefully. 'Your brother told me,' he said.

'Told you what?'

'That he died,' Freeman said, realising how lame that sounded.

Mersiha snorted. 'Not died. Killed,' she said. 'Killed by

22

the Serbian butchers.' She stood up and Freeman noticed with a sudden chill that she'd slipped her finger through the trigger guard. 'Why do you deal with them? Why do you do business with the men who killed my parents?' Freeman held out the towel to her, hoping to break her train of thought, but she ignored it. 'Why?' she pressed.

'It's hard to explain,' Freeman said.

'Try,' she insisted.

Freeman took a sharp breath as he saw her finger tighten on the trigger. It was hard to believe she was the same girl who only minutes earlier had been giggling and mimicking the way he shaved. 'I have a factory, in America,' he began. 'We make things for the Army. If I don't sell the things we make, the people who work for me won't get paid. They'll lose their jobs, their homes.'

'Why do you make weapons?' she asked. 'Why do you make things that kill people?'

'We don't,' Freeman insisted. 'My company used to make arms, but I made them change. We make other things now. Machines that tell you where mines are buried. My machines help people, Mersiha. They don't kill people.'

Mersiha frowned. 'Why did you come here, to Bosnia? Why don't you just sell to America?'

'Because the American Army doesn't want to buy what we make. The people here do.'

'Not people, animals. The Serbs are murdering animals. They killed my father, they killed my mother, and you are helping them . . .'

'Mersiha, I didn't know . . .' he began.

She waved the Kalashnikov at him. 'Of course you know. Everyone knows what the Serbs are doing. Everybody knows, nobody cares.' Her eyes blazed with a fierce intensity and Freeman was suddenly afraid. 'My parents did nothing wrong, nothing. They were killed because they were Muslims . . .' She frowned as a thought crossed her mind. 'You,' she said. 'You are a Christian, yes?'

Freeman hesitated, knowing that the answer would only antagonise her further.

'Yes?' she repeated.

Freeman nodded. 'Yes,' he said softly.

The barrel of the gun was suddenly still, centred on Freeman's chest. It was as if time had stopped. Freeman was aware of her finger tightening on the trigger, the perspiration glistening on her brow, the small, almost imperceptible movements of her chest as she breathed, the slight parting of her lips, the smears of dirt on the knees of her wool trousers. A myriad images were compressed into a single second, and Freeman had a sudden fear that they would be the last things he saw. His knees trembled and he wanted to say something to her but he had no idea what words to use. 'Mersiha . . .' was all he could get out, but he could see that she wasn't listening. Freeman wasn't looking into the eyes of a thirteen-year-old girl, he was staring at a killer. He thought of his wife, and of his son, and the objective part of his brain surprised him by wondering whether the bullets would hurt.

Mersiha opened her mouth to speak, and Freeman knew with a dread certainty that her words would be the last he ever heard. The words that tumbled out weren't English and Freeman couldn't make any sense of them. Tears sprang to her eyes and her face crumpled. 'I miss my mother,' she said, her voice trembling. 'I miss her so much.'

Freeman stepped forward. He wanted to hold her, to

comfort her, but the chain tightened and he couldn't get close to her. 'Mersiha, don't cry,' he said, but she wasn't listening. Tears trickled down her cheeks and her whole body shuddered.

Suddenly there was an irregular tattoo of loud cracks from upstairs which Freeman realised were gunshots from automatic weapons. Mersiha's head jerked up and then she looked back at Freeman, her cheeks glistening wet. There were more shots, louder this time, and Mersiha turned to cover the door. They both heard screams from upstairs, followed by more shots.

Mersiha took a couple of steps backward, putting distance between herself and the door. There were muffled voices from outside, then something heavy thudded against the wood. The door bulged inward, the hinges screeched, then the thudding was repeated. 'Stjepan?' Mersiha shouted. 'Stjepan?' She stood next to Freeman, visibly shaken.

The thudding stopped. Mersiha looked at Freeman, her eyes wide. 'I don't know,' he said in reply to her unspoken question.

Freeman heard footsteps, running away from the closed door, then silence. 'Get down!' he shouted, and when she didn't react immediately he threw himself on top of her.

The sound of the explosion was deafening. Fragments of the door blew across Freeman's back and then he heard a rapid footfall on the concrete. He looked up. A large man stood in the doorway wreathed in smoke like some sort of demon, an assault rifle in his gloved hands. He was wearing grey and black camouflage clothing and his face was streaked with black and grey stripes so that

Freeman had trouble seeing where the uniform ended and the flesh began.

'Freeman?' the man said.

'Yes,' Freeman replied, his voice little more than a guttural whisper. His ears were still ringing from the explosion. 'Who are you?'

'We're here to get you out,' the man said. He had the bluest eyes Freeman had ever seen. Two more figures appeared behind him, similarly dressed and carrying identical guns. More shots were fired upstairs, singly and with a different sound to the earlier reports. Pistols rather than automatic fire.

'Get up.'

Freeman clambered to his feet, the chain tightening around his waist as he stood up. He reached out to help Mersiha. She was lying on the ground, stunned, her Kalashnikov out of reach.

'Step to the side,' said the man at the door, gesturing with the rifle. Freeman started to obey automatically. The man's voice broached no argument. But as he moved, Freeman saw the man swing the barrel of his gun down towards Mersiha.

Freeman began to shout, but he knew even before he opened his mouth that there was nothing he could say that would stop what was going to happen. The man with the gun had his eyes fixed on Mersiha and his jaw was set tight in anticipation of the recoil. 'No!' Freeman yelled, and he threw himself at Mersiha, trying to push her out of the way, trying to protect her from the man with the killer blue eyes. Bullets raked Freeman's legs and he screamed in agony. Mersiha began screaming too, and Freeman covered her with his body. His last coherent thought was that if the man with blue eyes wanted to kill the girl, he'd have to shoot her through him.

Freeman drifted in and out of consciousness several times before becoming fully awake. His mouth was dry and he could barely swallow and he could feel nothing below his waist. He tried to raise his head so that he could look at his legs but all his strength seemed to have evaporated. A woman screamed to his left, a plaintive wail that made Freeman's heart start pounding. He slowly turned his head to where the sound had come from, but he couldn't see further than the neighbouring bed and its occupant – a man with heavily bandaged eyes. Blood was seeping from under the bandages and the man's hands were gripping the bedsheets tightly. Somebody was crying, and somebody else was moaning, and he could make out hushed voices in a language he couldn't understand.

He managed to slide his left arm up the bed in an attempt to see what the time was but when he finally got his wrist up to the pillow he discovered that his watch had been removed.

He turned his head to the right, looking for a nurse, a doctor, anyone who could tell him where he was and when he'd be going home. There seemed to be no one in authority in the ward, no one treating the sick or consoling the suffering. Freeman lay back and stared at the ceiling. At least he was in a hospital. For a while he concentrated on his legs, to see if there was any sensation at all. He tried flexing his toes and moving his feet, but he had no way of telling if he was succeeding or not. There was no feeling at all.

He heard metal grating and glass rattling and he looked towards the sound. An old woman in a blood-stained blue and white uniform was pushing a trolley full of bottles down the middle of the ward. Freeman tried to raise an arm to attract her attention but the effort was beyond him. He tried to call out but his throat was too dry. Tears welled up in his eyes. It wasn't fair, he thought. It just wasn't fair.

'Tony? Tony, wake up.' The voice pulled Freeman out of a nightmare where he was trapped in a car wreck, covered in blood and screaming. The scream blended into Katherine's voice and when he opened his eyes she was standing by the side of his bed next to a man in a grey suit.

Katherine saw his eyes open and she sat down on the side of the bed. 'Thank God,' she said. 'Tony, are you okay?' She held his left hand and squeezed it.

Freeman smiled at the question. He wanted to say something witty, something to make her smile, but no words would come. All he could do was blink his eyes to show that he understood. Katherine turned to the man in the suit. 'We have to get him out of here,' she said.

The man nodded. 'That won't be a problem,' he said. He was American, his voice a mid-western drawl.

Freeman tightened his grip on Katherine's hand and he shook his head. No, there was something he had to do first.

THE BIRTHDAY GIRL

* * *

The car rattled through potholed streets, past buildings that were pockmarked with bullet-holes and gutted by fire. Electric cables draped over the sides of abandoned buildings like dead snakes. In the distance Freeman heard gunshots, the single rounds of a sniper. He looked across at Katherine and she forced a smile.

The man in the passenger seat twisted around and looked at Freeman over the top of his glasses. 'I can't stress enough what a bad idea this is, Mr Freeman,' he said. His name was Connors and he was with the State Department. He was the man who'd taken Katherine to the hospital and who'd had him transferred to a United Nations medical facility where they'd saved his left leg from turning gangrenous.

'I have to do it,' he said quietly. 'I'm not leaving until I know that she's all right.'

Connors shook his head and turned back to stare out of the window. A shrill whine was followed by an ear-numbing thud as a mortar shell exploded some distance behind them, and the driver ducked in his seat, an involuntary reaction that would have done nothing to save him if the shell had hit the car. Freeman noticed that Connors was totally unfazed by the explosion.

The car swerved to avoid a massive hole filled with dirty water and accelerated around a corner. The motion of the car smashed Katherine's head against the window and she yelped. 'Hey, take it easy!' Freeman shouted at the driver, a bulky Serb who hadn't spoken a word since he'd picked them up at the UN medical centre.

Connors spoke to the driver in the man's own language, and the driver nodded and grunted, but made no attempt to slow down.

'We'll be there soon,' Connors said over his shoulder. He was as good as his word; five minutes later the car came to an abrupt halt in front of a football stadium. The driver continued to rev the engine as if he wanted to make a quick getaway until Connors spoke to him sharply. Connors got out of the car and walked around to the rear. The air that blew in through the open door smelled foul and Katherine put her hand over her mouth and nose. 'What on earth is that?' she said.

'People,' Freeman said. 'A lot of people.'

Connors appeared at the rear passenger door and opened it. He jammed it open with his knee as he assembled the portable wheelchair. The smell was much stronger, and for the first time Freeman became aware of the noise: a distant rumble, like thunder.

Connors and Katherine helped Freeman slide along the car seat and half lifted, half pushed him into the chair. The UN doctor, a thirty-year-old Pakistani, had assured him that eventually he'd be able to run a marathon but for the next few weeks or so he'd have to use the chair. Freeman was just grateful that the pain had gone.

When Freeman was seated in the chair, Connors stood in front of him, his arms folded across his chest. He was a big man with the shoulders of a heavyweight boxer, but deceptively light on his feet. Freeman wondered if he really was a representative of the State Department as he'd claimed. He suspected that he was with the CIA. 'Mr Freeman, I want to take one last shot at persuading you not to go through with this. There's a plane leaving for Rome this evening. You can be back in the States by tomorrow morning. This is no place for you just now. Or for your wife.' The crack of a rifle in the distance served to emphasise his plea.

Freeman shook his head. 'You're wasting your time,' he said. 'I can't leave without knowing that she's okay.'

Connors shook his head in bewilderment. 'She's a terrorist. She'd have killed you without a second thought.'

'She's thirteen years old,' Freeman said. 'They killed her family, did God knows what to her parents, and they would've blown her away if I hadn't stopped them. I want to make sure they haven't murdered her.'

'This is a war, Mr Freeman, and she's a soldier. There's something else you should know.'

Freeman narrowed his eyes. 'What?'

'The rescue operation. Your company funded it.'

'They what?' Freeman looked at Katherine. 'Is that true?'

Katherine shrugged. 'Maury said he'd handle it. He arranged to have the ransom and the equipment delivered to a middle-man in Sarajevo and the man disappeared with it. He called in a security firm. They said that once the equipment had been delivered they'd probably have killed you anyway and that the only thing to do was to bring you out ourselves. They put Maury in touch with some people. Mercenaries.'

'So you see, Mr Freeman, it's your company that's responsible for what happened in the basement. If anyone's to blame . . .'

Freeman pushed at the wheels of the chair and rolled forward.

'Mrs Freeman, can't you . . .?' Connors began, but

Katherine grabbed the handles at the back of the wheel-chair and helped push her husband.

'I've told him what I think,' she said. Connors followed Katherine and Freeman along the broken pavement towards the entrance to the stadium. The closer they got to the entrance the more noticeable the smell became. It was the smell of sweat, urine and faeces, the smell of a thousand people gathered together without adequate sewage or washing facilities. The metal gates that barred their way were three times the height of a man and looked as if they were a recent addition. A smaller doorway was set into one of the gates and it opened as the three of them approached. A young soldier stepped out and spoke to Connors. The soldier nodded and stepped aside to allow Connors inside. Freeman realised that his wheelchair wouldn't go through the doorway. He looked up at the soldier and shrugged. The soldier looked back at him with unfeeling eyes and sneered. He shouted something to two more soldiers behind the gates and they all laughed. The gates grated back and Katherine pushed Freeman inside.

'My God,' Katherine said. 'What is this place?'

'It's a holding facility,' Connors responded.

'It's a concentration camp,' Freeman said, his voice little more than a whisper.

The prisoners were confined to the area that had once been the football pitch; the white markings could still just about be seen in places through the mud. There were hundreds of them, dressed in rags and with their heads shaved. Many of the men were bare-chested; some of them were little more than skeletons with deep-set eyes and slack mouths. A chain-link fence topped with barbed wire ran around the perimeter of the playing area and machine-gun emplacements looked down on the encampment from the stands. Inside the fence were a few makeshift huts surrounded by tents, but most of the prisoners stood or sat out in the open, talking in huddled groups or staring vacantly out at their guards.

Connors seemed oblivious to the suffering and misery. He stood with his hands on his hips and surveyed the camp. A soldier with a bushy beard came over and spoke to him, and they both looked over at Freeman and his wife who were staring at the prisoners with looks of horror on their faces. Connors and the soldier laughed and the soldier slapped Connors on the back.

Katherine looked down at Freeman. 'You wanted to do business with these people?' she asked.

'I had no idea,' he said, shaking his head. 'I didn't know.'

'They wouldn't keep her here, surely? They're all adults.'

Freeman stared at the human scarecrows behind the wire and shuddered. Connors walked back and loomed over Freeman. 'She's not here, is she?' Freeman asked.

'Uh-huh,' Connors grunted. 'She fought like a soldier so that's how she's being treated. They're going to find her now.'

A guttural amplified voice boomed across the stadium from loudspeakers that had once announced nothing more sinister than the half-time score. A skeletal figure stood scratching its chin and stared at Freeman with blank eyes. Freeman shuddered. There was no way of telling if it was a man or a woman. The electronic voice barked again, and as it did the crowds parted. Freeman shaded his eyes with the flat of his hand. 'Can you see her?' Katherine asked.

Freeman shook his head, then he stiffened as a small figure walked towards the wire fence. He looked up at Katherine but before he could speak she began to push his wheelchair forward. 'My God, what have they done to her?' he whispered. Her head had been shaved and they'd taken away her clothes and given her a threadbare cotton jacket and trousers and she was wearing shoes that were several sizes too big for her so that she had to shuffle her feet. She reached the wire and gripped it with one hand as she waved to a guard.

'Is that her?' Katherine asked, horrified.

Freeman nodded, unable to speak. His eyes filled with tears and he reached down to push the wheels of his chair, trying to move faster. Freeman and Katherine got to the fence before the guard. Freeman put out his hand slowly and stroked the back of Mersiha's hand. She looked back at him blankly. Her face was stained with dirt and one eye was almost closed amid an egg-shaped greenish-yellow bruise.

'Mersiha?' he said softly.

She didn't reply, but a tear ran down her left cheek. Freeman looked up at Katherine. 'We're not leaving her here,' he said.

Katherine nodded. 'I know,' she said.

The meeting took place in a windowless office with no name on the door and a sterile air about it, as if it was used only for emergencies, or for business that was supposed to remain secret. Connors was there, but he said nothing. He stood by the door with his arms folded across his barrel chest like an executioner awaiting his orders. Freeman sat in his wheelchair, his hands lying loosely on the tops of the wheels. The two other men had arrived separately. One was American, a State Department official called Elliott who had a clammy handshake and an over-earnest stare and who clearly outranked the now-taciturn Connors. The final member of the group was a Serb, a small thick-set man with a square chin and eyes that never seemed to blink. He made no move to introduce himself and the Americans didn't tell Freeman who he was or why he was there, but it was soon apparent that it was the Serb who was going to have the final say. It was, when all was said and done, his country.

Elliott was shaking his head. 'Out of the question,' he said.

'She has no relatives,' Freeman said. 'No family members to take care of her.'

'She is a prisoner of war,' the Serb said.

'She's a child!' Freeman protested. 'A small, frightened child.'

'Mr Freeman, I can assure you that once hostilities are over, she will be released. This war will not go on for ever.'

Freeman thought he saw the beginnings of a smile flit across Elliott's face, but it vanished as quickly as it appeared. 'And what then? How's a thirteen-year-old girl going to survive on her own?'

The Serb made a small shrugging movement. His eyes were hard and unreadable. Freeman couldn't see what he had to gain by refusing to allow him to take Mersiha out of the country.

'I can take care of her. I can give her a home.' Freeman leant forward in his chair. 'I'm the only friend she has.'

'She tried to kill you,' said the Serb.

'No,' Freeman said quietly. 'Your people tried to kill her.'

The Serb looked across at Elliott. 'Mr Freeman,' the American said, 'have you really thought this through? This girl knows nothing of America, she has no connections with the country, and she is a Muslim. What religion are you, Mr Freeman?'

Freeman was an irregular church-goer at best but he had no wish to be drawn into a religious argument. 'I'll be responsible for her religious upbringing. I'll make sure she has a tutor who teaches her about her religion, and her culture.'

Elliott had a file under one arm, but he made no move to open it. Freeman doubted that the State Department would have a file on a thirteen-year-old girl, and he wondered what was in the folder.

'The girl is a terrorist, and she will be treated as such,' the Serb said.

Freeman's eyes flashed fire. 'The girl has a name,' he retorted. 'Mersiha. Her name is Mersiha. She was with her brother, because you killed her parents. There was nowhere else for her to go. She's an orphan. Now you've killed her brother, she has no one. Where's it going to end? When they're all dead? When you've cleansed the whole fucking country?' His hands were shaking with rage and he had to struggle to keep himself from shouting.

'Mr Freeman, there's no need to be offensive,' Elliott said.

Freeman glared at him. 'Listen to what he's saying, will

36

you? First of all he says she's a prisoner of war and that she'll be as right as rain once the war's over. Now he says she's a terrorist. She's a thirteen-year-old girl, for God's sake. She needs help. She needs a family.'

Elliott nodded as if he understood, but it was clear from the look on his face that he didn't care one bit how Freeman felt. He took a slow, deep breath. 'You had a son, didn't you, Mr Freeman?' The 'Mr Freeman' came almost as an afterthought, as if Elliott was nearing the end of his patience. Freeman didn't reply. The room seemed suddenly cold. He held Elliott's stare and gripped the wheels of his chair. 'Are you sure you want to do this for the best of motives?' Elliott continued. Still Freeman didn't reply. He knew that the State Department official was trying to provoke him, to prove that he was unstable, and that if Freeman did lose his temper they'd never let him take Mersiha.

'There are also problems with adoption, Mr Freeman,' Elliott said. 'The authorities here aren't keen to allow their children to be taken away. They feel that their needs are best served among their own people.'

'In concentration camps?'

'You might also find it difficult to get the adoption approved back in the United States.'

Freeman kept his eyes on Elliott. He had only one card left to play, one threat to use against the hard-faced State Department official and his file. 'If you insist on leaving her in that camp, I'll have no choice but to go public,' he said, his voice little more than a hoarse whisper. 'I'll speak to every newspaper and TV correspondent I can find. I'll go to London and hold a press conference there, and then I'll do the same all across the United States.' He slapped the side of his wheelchair. 'I'll sit in this chair and I'll tell the world how a mercenary with blue eyes and a Virginia accent tried to blow away a little girl, and I'll tell them that the State Department wanted her to be kept in a concentration camp because they didn't want the world to know the truth.'

Elliott studied Freeman, his forehead creased as if he were contemplating a mathematical problem. 'No one will care,' he said. 'Besides, the mercenaries, if indeed they were mercenaries, were acting on your behalf.'

'They'll care,' Freeman replied. 'And you know as well as I do that once it gets into the media, you'll have no choice but to let her into the States. And I don't think it'll be too difficult to prove that they were assisted by the State Department. I'm sure the *New York Times* would love to know what you and Connors are doing here.' He paused for breath. 'Look, this isn't a poker game. I've no reason to bluff. You allow my wife and me to adopt Mersiha, or I go public. One or the other. Your choice. And don't worry about the adoption. I'll go to the best lawyers in the States, I'll pay whatever it takes. Whatever.'

Elliott looked across at the Serb. Freeman kept his eyes on Elliott, as if he could get the answer he wanted by sheer force of will. He didn't see how the Serb had reacted, but he heard Connors shift position behind the wheelchair.

'You take her,' Elliott said. 'You take her today. I'll arrange the paperwork at this end, you'll be responsible for all costs.'

Freeman nodded. 'Agreed.'

'I haven't finished,' Elliott said smoothly. 'You are never to come back to this country, Mr Freeman. Neither is the girl. If the girl leaves, she is never to return. And you, Mr Freeman, are never to speak of this again. To anyone.'

Freeman nodded. He couldn't stop himself smiling. He'd won. He'd played his last card and it had been a trump.

'I hope you understand what I'm saying, Mr Freeman,' Elliott said, his voice suddenly hardening. 'You will not talk to anyone about what happened. In the cellar. At the camp. Or within these four walls. It never happened.'

Elliott stared at him, and Freeman knew that there was more that the State Department official wanted to say. He wanted to tell him what would happen if he broke the agreement, and Freeman knew that it would involve a man like Connors, or maybe a man with blue eyes and a Virginia accent, and he was suddenly scared. Before Elliott could continue, Freeman nodded, almost too eagerly. 'I understand,' he said. 'Mersiha's all I want. Nothing else matters.'

Elliott continued to stare at Freeman, and for a moment Freeman feared that he was about to change his mind. 'Thank you,' he said. He looked across at the Serb. 'Thank you,' he repeated. The Serb and Elliott exchanged glances, then left the room without a word. Freeman turned his chair around to find Connors leaning against the wall with a sly smile on his face, slowly shaking his head. 'You're a lucky man, Freeman,' he said enigmatically.

Freeman opened the refrigerator door and peered inside. He pulled out a carton of orange juice and took it over to the sink. As he poured himself a glassful he looked through the window and across the lawn to the line of trees that separated his property from that of his neighbour. Mersiha was playing with Buffy, throwing a blue frisbee for the dog and laughing each time she brought it back. It was a game Buffy would happily play for hours at a time without getting bored. Mersiha's laughter carried into the kitchen and Freeman smiled. The teenager who was running across the lawn was a far cry from the frightened girl he'd taken from the camp in Serbia almost three years earlier. She was a great deal taller, almost a young woman, and her jet-black hair was thick and shiny.

'Go get it, Buffy!' she shouted. There was hardly any trace of a Bosnian accent any more. The all-American girl. Freeman drank his orange juice. Mersiha saw him and ran to the back door. She burst into the kitchen with all the energy of a SWAT team.

'Hiya, Dad,' she said, hugging him around the waist.

'Hiya, pumpkin. Do you want a ride to school?'

'No, thanks. Katherine will take me later.'

Freeman put his glass in the sink and untangled himself from Mersiha's hug. She picked his briefcase up and handed it to him. 'What time are you coming home?' she asked.

'About six,' Freeman said. Mersiha was always asking him where he was going, and when he'd be back. Bearing in mind her background, he wasn't surprised by her insecurity. In some ways it was reassuring. He had many friends who'd love to have the same degree of concern from their adolescent children.

Buffy stood outside the kitchen door, barking at Mersiha to return to their game, but she ignored her. She looked at Freeman and frowned, deep lines creasing her forehead. 'Is everything okay?' she said.

'Of course. Why?' Freeman was already late but he put his briefcase back on the table.

Mersiha shrugged. 'You look worried. Like the world was about to end and only you know.'

Freeman smiled. 'Everything's fine. I have everything I've ever wanted. A home. A family.' Buffy barked, louder and more insistent. 'And a dog. What more could any man want?'

Mersiha looked at him for a few seconds before she smiled. 'A million dollars?' she said.

'Ah, the American Dream,' Freeman sighed.

'America is truly a wonderful country,' Mersiha said, putting on a thick European accent and then collapsing in a fit of giggles. She picked up his briefcase and carried it out to the car for him. 'Don't forget your seat belt,' she said before he could even reach over his shoulder for it.

'Do I ever?' he asked, buckling himself in. A sudden wave of sadness washed over him and he shivered. He caught himself just in time and managed to keep smiling.

Mersiha saw the change in his face and immediately realised what was going through his mind. She flushed. 'I didn't mean . . .'

'I know, I know,' he said.

'I just meant I wanted you to drive safely, that's all.'

'Mersiha, there's no need to explain, I know what you meant.'

'Yeah, but I don't want you to think that I . . .'

Freeman took her hand and squeezed it. 'Shhhh,' he said. 'I promise to drive carefully. Now go and play with your dog.'

He waved goodbye to Mersiha and backed the Chevrolet Lumina out of the driveway into the road. In the driving mirror Freeman saw her stand and watch him drive away. It had been more than five years since Luke had died in the car crash, but the memory of it still brought tears to Freeman's eyes and he blinked several times. He and Katherine had explained to Mersiha what had happened and why they had no children of their own, and it pained Freeman to see how carefully she tried to avoid the subject. He knew she was trying to protect his feelings, and that made it all the worse. If anything it was he who should be trying to help her. He could only imagine what a tangled mess her emotions must be. There were times, usually when she didn't know that he was watching her, when he saw a look of such sadness cross her face that his heart would melt. He knew that she must be thinking about her real mother and father.

Both Freeman's parents were alive and reasonably well, living in a bungalow in Bishopbriggs, a suburb of Glasgow, and whereas he saw them only once or twice a year, he knew how much he'd miss them when they eventually passed away. And not a day went by when he didn't think of Luke. God only knew how Mersiha had dealt with the loss of her parents and her brother, especially considering the circumstances in which they'd died, circumstances that she had yet to really talk about.

Mersiha was seeing a psychiatrist on a regular basis, but he wasn't making much progress with her. It wasn't that she was uncommunicative or withdrawn, quite the opposite in fact. She was bright, she was outgoing and she was as cute as a button, but she simply refused to tell anyone what had happened to her in the months before Freeman had met her. The psychiatrist, Dr Brown, had said that it was just a matter of time and that eventually she would open up. It would probably happen once she felt totally safe in her new home, Dr Brown had said, and he'd stressed that it was up to Katherine and Tony to demonstrate that she had a loving, supportive family that would always be there for her. That wasn't a problem; they were more than happy to have her. More than happy. She went some way towards filling the void that Luke's death had left, but it was more than that – they couldn't have loved her more if she had been their own child.

Freeman was still thinking about Mersiha when he pulled into the parking lot of CRW Electronics and drove over the painted letters that spelled out his name and title: chairman. Maury Anderson's white Corvette was already in its space and Freeman found him sitting in his plush office reading a computer printout and drinking a cup of black coffee.

'Hiya, Tony, you ready for the inquisition?' he asked.

'As I'll ever be,' Freeman said. He nodded at the printout in Maury's hands. 'Anything I should know about?'

Anderson held the paper out. 'I was just taking a last-minute look at the figures. It's not a pretty picture.' He sniffed and ran the back of his hand under his nose.

'Tell me something new,' Freeman said, scanning the numbers. He knew Anderson was right. The company's financial position was precarious at best and he could see no reasons for optimism. They were due to see their bankers at 11.15 and Freeman was expecting the worst. CRW Electronics was covering its interest payments, but cash-flow projections suggested that this state of affairs wouldn't continue for much longer. Even the time and place of the meeting underlined the way the company's fortunes were progressing. In the good old days of the Reagan arms build-up the bank officials would come to

CRW's offices for lunch in the boardroom, eager to fund their expansion programmes. Now it was a half-hour at the bank's city headquarters with the minimum of hospitality. The next stage on the slippery slope would be Chapter 11, protection from creditors, unless he and Maury could do something to stop the rot. Freeman passed the printout back to Anderson. 'Your car or mine?'

Anderson smiled. 'I think they'd rather see us in the Lumina, don't you? Under the circumstances.' He sniffed again.

Freeman grinned. 'Maybe we should take the bus. Are you coming down with a cold?'

'Just a sniffle,' Anderson said. 'I think it's the air-conditioning. Hey, what do you call a blind elk?'

Freeman shrugged.

'No eye-deer,' Anderson said.

Freeman gave Anderson a half-smile and checked his wristwatch. 'Better we get there early,' he said.

They parked the Lumina in an underground car park close to the headquarters of the First Bank of Baltimore. As they sped up to the top floor, Freeman checked himself in the mirrored wall of the elevator. Anderson chuckled. 'It's like being sent to the principal's office, isn't it?'

'Yeah. I was just thinking that it wasn't that long ago that they were beating a path to our door.'

'They will again, Tony. Once we're back on our feet.'

They were made to sit in the bank's reception area for a full ten minutes, which Freeman took to be yet another sign of the institution's displeasure, but when they were finally ushered into the corporate lending office at least he was able to greet a friendly face, that of Walter Carey, an affable man in his early sixties with whom he'd been doing business since he started at CRW. There was no game-playing with Walter. He walked quickly from behind his desk to shake hands with Freeman and Anderson in the centre of the room and his handshake was firm and dry. He showed them to a highly polished rosewood table, big enough to seat twenty, and waited until they had taken their places before sitting down himself. The office door opened and Walter's secretary, a smiling matron with grey curly hair and surgical stockings, backed in carrying a tray with a pot of coffee and cups and saucers. Walter got to his feet and took the tray from her, thanking her profusely. He was a gentleman of the old school, and Freeman wondered how he'd managed to survive in the cut-throat world of modern banking.

Walter put the tray down on the table as the secretary closed the door behind her. Freeman noticed that there were four cups and saucers on the brass tray – either the secretary had made a mistake or they were expecting another. Without asking, the banker poured coffee for Freeman and Anderson and waved his hand over the milk and sugar, suggesting that they help themselves. He served himself last and waited until they had sipped the hot coffee before speaking, and even then it was to enquire about their respective spouses. Walter stirred his cup slowly, far more than necessary to dissolve the single spoonful of sugar he'd put in. Freeman realised he was waiting for something. Or someone. The door opened and, as it did, Walter's spoon clattered against the side of the cup, spilling some of his coffee into the saucer. Freeman caught his eye and smiled reassuringly. Walter smiled back, but he couldn't hide the apprehension he was obviously feeling. It suddenly hit Freeman that perhaps Walter's position at the bank wasn't as secure as he'd thought. He turned to look at the new arrival.

A tall black man was closing the door, a manila file under his arm. He had broad shoulders, a square jaw and close-cropped hair, and he walked across the office like a male model on a catwalk. He flashed a smile that showed perfect teeth and as he held out his hand Freeman saw a big gold watch on the man's wrist. 'Tony, Maury, I'd like you to meet Lennie Nelson,' Walter said as he got to his feet. 'Lennie's our new VP in charge of business development.'

Nelson's handshake was as firm as Walter's had been, but there was a slightly damp feeling to it. 'Good to meet you both,' he said, handing out business cards. He pulled out the chair at the far end of the table, the one opposite Walter, and dropped the file in front of him as he sat down. 'So,' he said. 'No need for me to ask how business is, is there?' He patted the manila file as if it were a sick child. 'This is depressing reading, but I guess you guys know that, right?'

Freeman nodded, wondering where the conversation was going and knowing that he wasn't going to enjoy the journey. 'We're suffering from the peace dividend, that's for sure,' he said.

Nelson nodded. 'You and every other defence contractor in this country,' he said. He sat back in his chair and unbuttoned his jacket. His shirt gleamed as brightly as his teeth. 'I tell you, when Gorbachev announced the break-up of the Soviet Union, while everyone was cheering and saying what a great guy he was and how it was peace at last, I was on the phone selling defence stocks like there was no tomorrow. People don't look ahead, most of them. They don't think.

If I was in the defence business, I'd have seen the writing on the wall years ago and started diversifying. The margins in the defence business are like nowhere else, but if there's no business, what good does it do you, right?'

Freeman found himself nodding in agreement and saw that Anderson was doing the same. Freeman tried to speak, but Nelson raised a hand and continued unabated. 'I'm obviously not as close to the company as you are, I understand that, but I do have a fresh perspective. I can, as it were, see the wood for the trees. And gentlemen, I have to tell you that the wood is pretty rotten.'

'I don't think that's . . .' Freeman started to say, but before he could get any further Nelson started speaking again. Freeman tried to continue but Nelson simply carried on talking. It was clear that he had no intention of stopping and it was Freeman who gave up first. He looked at Walter and the old man gave him a sympathetic smile.

'The way I see it, your company's problems stem from its inability, or unwillingness, to move into new product areas. From what I've seen of your inventory, the company manufactures nothing but defence equipment. Correct?'

'That's what we do,' Anderson said. 'We're a defence contractor.'

'Exactly,' Nelson said, as if Anderson had made an amazing intuitive leap. 'But unless the Cold War starts to heat up again, only the big boys are going to stay in the game. Smaller independents like CRW are going to be squeezed out. If we were having this conversation two years ago, I'd suggest that you sell the company, but I don't think that's an option any more. To be frank, I don't think you'd find a buyer.'

'Sell the company?' Freeman repeated incredulously.

'What in God's name are you talking about? We made profits last year.'

'You made a pre-tax profit of 330,000 dollars last year. But you made no provision for the write-down of obsolete inventory you're holding. You're carrying missile guidance systems to the value of six million dollars on the books. How much do you think they're worth now bearing in mind the SALT talks?'

Anderson shrugged. 'We might still find a buyer. That's why they've not been written down.'

Nelson looked at Freeman and raised his eyebrows. 'What do you want me to say?' Freeman asked. 'You're right, we're probably not going to sell them, not right now anyway.'

'They were built for a contractor who went under last year. You're never going to unload them,' Nelson said. 'And they're not the only assets that are being carried on the books at way above their market value.' He tapped the unopened file on the table. 'According to the financial projections I've made, you'll be lucky to break even in the current year, and next year you'll be in the red to the tune of 95,000 dollars. Gentlemen, diversification is the key to the survival of your company. And to that end, I have two words for you.'

Freeman grinned. 'Golden parachutes?' he said.

Nelson smiled tightly to show that he'd got the joke, but his eyes remained cold. 'Video phones,' he said.

'Video phones?' Anderson repeated. He looked at Freeman. 'Video phones?'

'Video phones,' Nelson repeated. 'Do you have any idea how many telephones there are in this country alone? More than one billion. And within the next ten years they're all going to be replaced by video phones. It's the technology of the future, and I think CRW is perfectly situated to get in on the ground floor. The video guidance system you've been developing for surface-to-air missiles could easily be adapted to a communications system. Think about it.'

Freeman stared at Nelson in amazement. He couldn't believe that a man more than ten years his junior, a man with clearly no business experience other than the management lectures he'd attended and the textbooks he'd read, should be telling him how to run his company. CRW had its own research team working flat out to come up with new products, and in fact they had already considered expanding their video capability, but it wasn't as simple as Nelson made out. Some of the largest corporations in the world were researching video technology and it didn't make sense to go up against them in the company's present precarious financial position. He was just about to unleash a torrent of sarcasm at the man when he felt a hand on his arm. It was Walter. 'More coffee, Tony?' the banker asked, the concern clear on his face. Freeman realised it was Walter's way of asking him not to make a scene. Walter Carey had been CRW's banker for more than a quarter of a century, and he'd been a pall-bearer at the funeral of Freeman's father-in-law. He'd been a tower of strength, but now he looked like a weak old man, frightened for his job. The two men held each other's stare for a few seconds, then Freeman nodded almost imperceptibly. 'Please, Walter.'

The banker poured, his hand shaking noticeably. Nelson sat back in his chair, tapping his fingers on the manila file.

'It's an interesting thought, Lonnie,' Freeman said.

'It's Lennie,' Nelson said, his smile unchanged.

'It's an interesting thought, Lennie. I'll speak to our development people about it.' Freeman nodded at the file. 'Does that file contain details of the other new products we're developing? The computerised navigation system we're hoping to produce for the recreational boating market? The night surveillance aids we're hoping will appeal to hunters?'

'And our new line of police equipment,' Anderson added. 'We're also working on a sniper identification system which tracks bullets back through the line of . . .'

Nelson nodded and held up a hand to silence Anderson. 'I've noted them. But until they work through to sales, they're just pipedreams. You need orders now to keep your cash flow in the positive. Has anything happened on that front recently?'

'We've a group of Middle Eastern buyers coming over to look at our minefield neutralisation system,' Anderson said.

'How much are we looking at, assuming they go ahead?' Nelson asked, reaching into his jacket pocket. His hand reappeared holding a slim gold pen.

'That depends on how many they want,' Anderson said.

Nelson clicked his pen. 'And how many do you think that might be, Maury?' he asked. 'Ballpark figure?'

'Ballpark? A hundred. Maybe more.'

'Let's say one hundred, shall we? I don't see any reason for being optimistic at the moment. So, that would be in the region of one and a half million dollars, right?'

Freeman nodded. Nelson might be an arrogant son-of-a-bitch but he certainly knew his way around the company's numbers.

'Any other orders in the pipeline?'

Anderson shook his head.

'Well, that'll be a help,' Nelson said, making a few notes on a small yellow notepad. 'But it's not going to keep the wolf from the door for long.'

'Now just one minute,' Freeman said. 'What wolf are we talking about here? The only wolf at our door at the moment seems to be you.'

Nelson smiled, and there was something canine about the expression. 'Perhaps wolf wasn't quite the right word,' he said. He put the pen back in his jacket pocket. 'But I think it is fair to say that CRW is now on the bank's watch-list. We'll be wanting to see you on a monthly basis, and I'd like to be kept informed of any major changes in the business picture. Any new orders, any cancellations, union problems, investment plans . . .'

'You mean every single business decision has to be cleared with you? Is that what you're saying?' Walter flinched and Freeman realised he'd raised his voice.

'It isn't necessary to clear anything with us, Tony. But we want to be kept fully informed of what's happening at CRW.'

'For what reason?'

Nelson leant back in his seat. An inch of starched cotton peered out from beneath the cuffs of his suit and Freeman saw the glint of gold cufflinks. 'The bank has a considerable exposure to your company. With things the way they are at the moment, we aren't prepared to risk that exposure. If you're heading for Chapter 11 or worse, we want to know in advance.'

'You mean as soon as it looks as if we're going under, you want first claim on what assets we have left?'

'We already have that. Most of the bank's recent loans to you were against specific properties owned by CRW.'

'Most, but not all,' Freeman said. 'Is that it?' The First Bank wasn't the only institution which had lent money to the company, and CRW had used various buildings as collateral against other loans. Now he understood what was worrying Nelson. If the company went bankrupt with zero cash and a next-to-worthless inventory, it would be lucky to get half of its investment back; if it foreclosed its loans right away, it would just about break even. But taking its money back would be a self-fulfilling prophecy – the company wouldn't be able to survive without it. Perversely, that would work in Nelson's favour because he could point to the collapse of the firm as a sign that he'd made the right decision in pulling the plug. He'd come out of it as a hero, the man whose shrewd business savvy had saved the bank's millions.

'I think it fair to say that we would be happier if we had more collateral,' Nelson said. 'But CRW isn't exactly rich in unencumbered assets, is it?' He looked at Freeman like a prosecutor grilling a hostile witness.

'There's the land we own near Annapolis,' Anderson said, trying to take the heat off Freeman.

Nelson shook his head. 'Undeveloped. I'm surprised you didn't sell it years ago.'

Freeman felt as if he had to defend himself, even though Nelson had made a valid point. 'It was where my father-in-law built his first factory. He kept it for sentimental reasons long after the buildings were demolished.'

Nelson smiled. 'You won't believe how many times I've seen sentimentality ruin a perfectly good business. Managers can get too attached to a workforce or a product and they fail to take the necessary steps to safeguard their business.' He bent over the table, his body as tense as a sprinter waiting for the starter's gun. 'Being a good manager is like being a surgeon. You have to recognise when the body is unhealthy, and you mustn't be afraid to cut to save the patient. Better to lose a leg than have the patient die.'

Freeman looked at his watch. 'Is there anything else we have to discuss?'

Nelson and Walter exchanged looks. There obviously was something else. It was Walter who spoke first. 'Tony, don't take this the wrong way, but the bank feels that until you're through this period, it might be better if we had a representative on your board.'

'A representative?' Freeman repeated.

'Namely myself,' Nelson said.

'Let me get this straight,' Freeman said. 'We have to report to you each month, and you want a seat on the board?'

'In a purely non-executive capacity,' Nelson added. 'You'll still be running the company. I'll just be . . .'

'Interfering . . .' Anderson interrupted.

'. . . keeping an eye on things. Looking out for the bank's interests,' Nelson finished. 'I hope you'll come to see me as an asset to your management team.'

'Do we have a choice?' Freeman asked, but he could see from the look of anguish on Walter's face that he didn't.

'I understand the board meets next Thursday at three o'clock,' Nelson said. 'I'll see you then.'

Freeman felt like a schoolboy being dismissed from the headmaster's presence. He felt his cheeks flush involuntarily and his stomach churned. There was nothing he could say, nothing that would be productive anyway. He stood up and picked up his briefcase. Nelson leapt to his feet and extended his hand. Freeman felt like turning his back on the young banker but he knew that would be childish. He shook hands with the man, and Anderson did the same. On the way out of the office, Walter patted him gently on the back like a relative at a funeral, wanting to reassure him that life went on, no matter how bad things looked.

Anderson said nothing as they rode down in the elevator and the silence continued as they walked towards the car. 'What do you think?' Freeman said eventually as he opened the car door.

'About the boy-wonder banker?'

'Yeah.' Freeman slid into the car and opened the door for Anderson.

'We're caught between a rock and a hard place,' Anderson said as he climbed into the car and slammed the door shut.

'But at least they're not closing us down,' Freeman said.

'Yeah. But I don't like the idea of Nelson watching our every move.'

'You never know, he might be a help,' Freeman said. He started the Lumina and drove to the car park exit.

'He's barely out of college,' Anderson protested. 'What the hell could he know about running a business? Especially a business like ours.' He slammed his hand down on the dashboard.

'Yeah, I know what you mean,' Freeman agreed. 'But I don't see that we've got a choice. I think you should start looking for alternative sources of finance. See if any of our other banks will take over First's loans. Maybe see if we can bring in new money.' Anderson pulled a face as if he had a bad taste in his mouth. 'Yeah, yeah, I know,' Freeman said. 'But I can dream, can't I?'

Mersiha ran her fingers through the magazines on the table, looking for something, anything, worth reading. She picked up a copy of *People* magazine and flicked through it. She couldn't concentrate on the photographs of movie stars and television personalities and after a few minutes she threw the magazine back on the table. She looked at her watch. It was exactly five o'clock, the time her session was due to start, and Dr Brown was usually punctual to the point of obsession. She wondered if he was having trouble with one of his patients. An unstable teenager threatening suicide, maybe. A middle-aged woman professing her undying love for the psychiatrist, offering him her heart and soul if he'd only take her there and then on the office floor. Mersiha smiled at the thought. Dr Brown was an unlikely lover, a small, chubby man with a receding hairline and small, baby-like lips.

'Are you okay, kiddo?' Katherine asked.

'Sure,' she replied, reaching for another magazine.

'What are you smiling at?'

Mersiha shrugged. 'Nothing. Just happy, I guess. Can we get ice-cream after this?'

'Sure, kiddo.' Katherine went back to reading a dog-eared copy of *Vanity Fair*. Mersiha studied the door to Dr Brown's office. In the three years she'd been attending weekly sessions at the psychiatrist's office, she'd never seen one of his other patients. There were two doors to his inner sanctum: one led to the waiting room where she was sitting with Katherine, the other opened on to a corridor that led to the car park. It was a simple system, but it worked: arriving and departing patients never met.

'Katherine,' Mersiha asked, 'how much longer do I have to do this?'

'Do what?'

'Come to Dr Brown's. It's a waste of time. And money. Think of the money you'd save if I stopped coming.'

Katherine looked at her as if considering the offer, then shook her head. 'When Dr Brown says there's no need for you to come any more, then you can stop.'

Mersiha flopped back in her chair and pouted. 'But I'm going to be sixteen in two weeks.'

'No buts. And don't worry about money. This isn't a matter of how much it costs, it's whether or not it's good for you.'

'It's a total waste of time.' Mersiha folded her arms and glared at the door to Dr Brown's office as if daring him to come out.

Katherine looked across at Dr Brown's receptionist, a heavy-set matron who could be a harridan or sweetness and light, depending on the state of her relationship with her live-in lover, a burly steelworker who wasn't averse to knocking her around after he'd had a few drinks too many. Today she was in a good mood and she smiled sympathetically at Katherine. 'Can I get you a cup of coffee, Mrs Freeman? Dr Brown shouldn't be too long.'

Katherine shook her head. 'No thanks, Nancy.' Before Katherine could go back to reading her magazine, the intercom on Nancy's desk buzzed.

'Okay, Mersiha, Dr Brown will see you now,' the receptionist said.

'Great,' Mersiha said under her breath as she pushed herself up from the sofa.

'Be nice,' Katherine warned, but Mersiha had already slipped into the inner office.

Dr Brown was sitting behind his huge oak desk as usual, almost dwarfed by his big leather chair. Mersiha reckoned he used the oversized furniture to compensate for his lack of stature, but in fact it had the opposite effect – it served only to emphasise what a small man he was. 'Hiya, Dr Brown,' she said. 'How are you today?' It hadn't taken Mersiha long to realise that the quickest way out of the psychiatrist's office was to be pleasant. The more she smiled, the more she seemed anxious to answer his questions, the sooner he'd tell her that the session was over and that he'd see her the same time next week.

'I'm fine, Mersiha. Sit down, why don't you?' Mersiha flopped down on to one of the two grey sofas by the window. Dr Brown waited until she was sitting before he got up from his own seat and walked around the desk. 'How's school?' he asked.

'Mainly Bs,' she said. 'I got an A in chemistry, though.'

'It's still your best subject?'

Mersiha nodded. 'Chemistry and art. Pretty eclectic, huh?'

Dr Brown nodded. 'How are you sleeping?'

Mersiha shrugged laconically. 'Okay, I guess.'

'Dreams?'

'Sure. Everybody dreams.'

Dr Brown smiled. Mersiha smiled back. She'd grown to

enjoy the verbal jousting with her therapist, though she knew it was important not to antagonise him too much.

'I meant bad dreams. Nightmares.'

'Some,' she admitted. 'But not as much as before.'

'What about sleepwalking?'

Mersiha smiled sweetly. 'If I walk when I sleep, I wouldn't know about it, would I?'

Dr Brown smiled back with equal sweetness, but his eyes glittered like wet pebbles. He walked over to a floor-to-ceiling bookcase and picked up a wooden figure and took it over to the sofas. He handed it to her as he sat down. 'Have you seen one of these before? It's a Russian doll. They call it a *matrioshka*.'

Mersiha held the smooth wooden figurine and studied it. It was a peasant woman with a green and red shawl around her shoulders, big black eyes and scarlet lips. It was in two pieces that seemed to be screwed together. It felt heavy, as if it was solid. 'Sure. I had one of these when I was a kid. It's pretty.'

'How long have you been coming to see me, Mersiha?' Dr Brown asked, holding out his hand for the doll.

Mersiha shrugged and passed it back to him. 'Two years, I guess.'

'It's more like three,' Dr Brown said as he set the doll down on the table. 'Imagine that's you,' he said.

Mersiha sighed theatrically, but Dr Brown flashed her a warning look. He was serious. 'Okay,' she said.

Dr Brown tapped the doll with the flat of his hand. 'It's hard outside, it looks solid. When you first came to see me three years ago, that's what you were like. Hard. But the hardness doesn't go right through. As you know, it comes apart. Try it.'

Mersiha twisted the two halves. They separated easily. Inside was another figure, slightly smaller but in a different paint-scheme. It was also in two halves. She moved to pull them apart, but Dr Brown held up his hand to stop her.

'That's the stage we've got to, you and I. During the conversations we've had, I've come to know a little bit about what goes on inside your head, your thought processes. But you've only told me so much.'

He nodded at her, encouraging her to pull the second doll apart. She did as he wanted. Now there were three dolls on the table. 'But as you can see, there's more to be discovered inside the second shell. And it goes further than that. Keep on going.'

Mersiha unscrewed the third doll. There was a fourth inside. And a fifth inside that. By the time she'd finished there were seven dolls standing on the coffee table in front of her. Only the smallest was solid. Dr Brown picked it up and held it between a finger and thumb. 'This is you too. This is the real you, at the heart of all the shells.' Mersiha stared at the wooden doll. The face seemed to be staring back at her with wide eyes. 'You've surrounded yourself with shells, Mersiha. You've protected yourself by putting layers and layers on top of your real feelings.'

Mersiha pulled her eyes away from the doll. Dr Brown was giving her his earnest smile, trying to put her at ease. It looked artificial and his eyes were as cold as the painted eyes of the Russian doll. 'I'm not doing it deliberately,' she said.

'No, I know that,' the psychiatrist said. 'It's a defence mechanism. You're frightened of being hurt again because of what happened to you when you were younger. That's why you find it difficult to make friends. You've told me that yourself, haven't you? You've lots of acquaintances, but no real friends. Perhaps you're worried about letting people get close to you.'

'I love my dad,' she said. 'And Katherine.'

Dr Brown smiled, and this time there was more warmth in it. 'I know you do. And they love you. And you know they'll always love you. No matter what you do.'

'I guess,' Mersiha said. She knew that the psychiatrist was trying to get some show of emotion from her. She concentrated on the blinds on the window behind him and counted the slats. Once, soon after she'd started the Wednesday afternoon sessions, Dr Brown had almost made her cry until she'd seen something in his eyes, a look that made her realise that he had wanted her to break down. She'd only been thirteen at the time but she'd vowed that she'd never give him the satisfaction of seeing her cry. Her tears would be his trophies.

'Why do you think you don't have many friends?'

'I don't meet many people I want to be friends with.'

'Even at school?'

Mersiha snorted. 'Especially at school.'

'What do you mean?' Dr Brown asked.

'They're just kids,' she said.

He smiled. 'They're your age,' he said quietly.

Mersiha thought for a while before answering. 'They haven't been through what I've been through.'

The psychiatrist studied her for a few seconds. 'Would you like to tell me about it?'

Mersiha stared at the blinds, still counting. Twenty-six. Twenty-seven. 'No,' she whispered. 'No, I don't think so.'

THE BIRTHDAY GIRL

* * *

Mersiha sat in the front passenger seat of Katherine's Toyota Corolla. It was an automatic and still had its new-car smell, despite the half-filled ashtray. The car had been a birthday present from her father, but Katherine seemed to treat it with contempt. It hadn't been washed since the day it had arrived outside their house, wrapped in a huge red bow. There was a paint scrape on the rear left side and the back seat was covered with old magazines.

She sighed and leant back, pushing her hands against the roof of the car. The time she spent alone in the car while Dr Brown briefed Katherine was often worse than the counselling sessions themselves. It didn't seem fair. Mersiha wished that psychiatrists had the same sort of client confidentiality code that priests and private detectives had. Katherine insisted on the post-session chats with Dr Brown, despite Mersiha's protests and pleadings. In a way Mersiha was glad, because it gave her an added incentive to keep her secrets locked deep inside. There was no way she would open up to Dr Brown if he intended to tell all to Katherine.

Mersiha yawned and stretched. When she opened her eyes Katherine was walking towards the car, brushing her blonde hair behind her ears. 'Okay, kiddo, let's go,' Katherine said as she slid into the driver's seat. 'Do you still want ice-cream?'

'Do birds sing in the woods?'

Katherine looked across at Mersiha and raised an

eyebrow. 'I hope that's the only version of that saying you use.'

Mersiha widened her eyes innocently. 'What do you mean?' she asked.

Katherine grinned. 'You know exactly what I mean.' She started the car and eased it forward. 'Chocolate chip?'

Katherine waited until later, as they sat either side of a chocolate sundae and attacked it with long-handled spoons, before raising the subject of Dr Brown with Mersiha. 'How do you think the session went today?' she asked.

Mersiha shrugged and spooned up a maraschino cherry. 'Okay,' she said.

'He said he thinks you're making terrific progress.'

'He does?' Mersiha said, surprised.

'Uh-huh. But he'd like you to open up to him more.'

They ate in silence for a while, each waiting for the other to speak. Eventually it was Katherine who broke the silence. 'He only wants to help you. If you were to open up to him, the nightmares might stop.'

'They have stopped,' Mersiha said. Katherine raised an eyebrow. 'Almost,' Mersiha added.

'He's right, you know. If you suppress things, they have a way of coming out in other ways.'

'I know, I know. There's no need to go on about it. I'm okay. It's not like I'm crazy or anything.'

Katherine smiled. 'No, that's for sure. You're a very clever, very pretty, very lovely girl. And I love you with all my heart.'

Mersiha smiled. She offered her spoon to Katherine, giving her the maraschino cherry. Katherine put her lips to it, carefully, like a cat feeding.

'One day, maybe I'll be able to talk about it. But not

just now.' Mersiha was suddenly serious. 'It's as if I've locked all the bad stuff away and if I open the door it'll all come pouring out. I don't think I'll be able to handle it. Sometimes I realise how much bad stuff there is behind the door, and it scares me.'

Katherine nodded. 'Okay, kiddo. That's okay. Just so long as you remember that we're here for you.'

Mersiha smiled. 'Do bears . . .'

Katherine raised her spoon. 'Watch it, young lady!'

Sal Sabatino surveyed the menu and beamed at the grey-haired waitress as she hovered expectantly. 'So what's good tonight, huh?' he asked.

The waitress scratched her ear with the end of her pencil. 'The calamari's going well, Mr Sabatino.'

'Yeah? What, fried?'

'Baked is better. In a white wine and lemon sauce.'

Sabatino nodded thoughtfully and scratched one of his several chins. 'Yeah, but I really feel like fettuccini carbonara, you know? I love the big pieces of bacon. None of that chopped ham they use in some places.'

'Only the best for you, Mr Sabatino.' The waitress stood patiently by the side of his table. She knew better than to rush Sal Sabatino. One of the customers at another table tried to catch her eye but she pretended not to notice.

'And the sauce. Oh, that sauce. My cholesterol level is going up just thinking about it.' He patted his ample waistline which was only half hidden by the tablecloth. 'You know what my blood pressure was at my last medical? One hundred and fifty over a hundred.' The waitress frowned, not sure if that was good or bad. 'I got it. I got it. I'll have the calamari, like you said, and a half-portion of the fettuccini, as an appetiser.'

'Excellent choice, Mr Sabatino.'

Sabatino handed her the menu with a flourish. 'And bring me a bottle of my usual. Well chilled.'

'Of course, Mr Sabatino.' The customer who'd been trying to get the waitress's attention waved frantically as she headed towards the kitchen, but she didn't stop. She knew that Sabatino wouldn't take kindly to his order being delayed for even a few seconds. He wasn't a man who liked to be kept waiting.

Sabatino sat alone in his corner, close to the stairs which led down to an emergency exit and with his back to the wall. Two of his bodyguards, big men in dark suits, sat at a table by the entrance to the dining room, sharing a bottle of mineral water and trying to look as if they had nothing more sinister than deodorant under their arms. One of the men was chewing on a small unlit cigar. He saw Sabatino looking his way and raised an eyebrow, the only indication that he'd noticed. Sal Sabatino loved his food, but he preferred to eat alone. He toyed with his knife as the waitress returned and opened a bottle of white wine with a flourish. She poured a splash into his glass and he tasted it, rolling it around his mouth before swallowing. He nodded his approval. Sal Sabatino loved everything Italian. He loved the food, he loved the wine, he loved the music, he loved the dark-haired fiery women. He loved it all. Sal Sabatino's one regret in life was that he hadn't been born Italian.

He was refilling his glass for the second time when

THE BIRTHDAY GIRL

Maury Anderson appeared in the doorway, mopping his forehead with a large red handkerchief. The bigger of the two bodyguards reached inside his jacket and got to his feet, but Sabatino waved his hand, a large gold ring flashing under the overhead lights, and the man sat down again.

Anderson walked over to Sabatino's table, shoving the handkerchief back into his trouser pocket. He made no move to shake hands and he waited until Sabatino nodded at the vacant chair before sitting down. The waitress scurried over with a menu but Sabatino shooed her away. 'My guest won't be staying,' he said. Sabatino picked up his glass and scrutinised Anderson as he drank. The man was clearly nervous, though the sweat was probably the result of the night's high humidity. 'So, Maury, how did the meeting go?'

Anderson's eyes darted from side to side as if he were frightened of being overheard. 'Not good,' he said.

'What do you mean?' Sabatino's voice dropped an octave and about twenty degrees.

Anderson shivered. 'The bank's putting its own representative on the board. A guy called Nelson.'

'So?'

'So he's going to be going through the books.'

Sabatino screwed up his face as if he had a bad taste in his mouth. 'Where's this guy based?' he asked.

Anderson slipped a business card across the table. 'This is his card.'

Sabatino picked up the pristine white card and studied it like an entomologist examining an unusual specimen. 'What's he like?' he asked.

'Late twenties. Aggressive. Ambitious. African American.'

Sabatino smiled to himself. Political correctness was so pervasive in modern-day America that it had even become part of a clandestine conversation. 'Yeah? I bet he's only ever seen Africa in an atlas,' he said. 'If he's black, why not just say he's black?'

Anderson sniffed and wiped his nose with the back of his hand. 'Yeah. He's black. Sorry.'

'You wanna know what's wrong with this fucking country?' Sabatino asked, though the question was clearly rhetorical. 'People are scared to say what they really think. They self-censor, that's what they do. You know those three guys that've been doing those robberies in Guilford? You know the ones? Picking on old folks, raping the women, beating the husbands and stealing everything that's not nailed down? You know they're black, I know they're black, but what does it say in the papers? Three assailants, that's what they say. And why do they say that? Because it's politically incorrect to say that they're black, that's why. What's the world coming to, Maury? Tell me, what's the world coming to?'

'I've no idea, Mr Sabatino.'

'It's a hell of a world, Maury. A hell of a world. So this Nelson, he's gonna be sniffing around, is he?'

Anderson nodded. The waitress appeared with Sabatino's fettuccini carbonara. Sabatino unfurled his napkin and placed it on his lap. 'Okay, Maury, I'll give you a call if I need anything else. You keep an eye on this Nelson for me, okay?'

Anderson hesitated. He scratched the end of his nose with the first finger and thumb of his right hand. 'There is one thing, Mr Sabatino.'

Sabatino tore his eyes off the pasta. 'Not here, Maury. Vincenti will take care of you outside.'

Anderson grinned. 'Thanks, Mr Sabatino. Thanks a lot.'

Anderson stood up and held out his hand, but Sabatino was already twirling his fettuccini around his fork. The financial director shrugged and walked away. The smaller of the two bodyguards, the one chewing the cigar, handed him a rolled-up copy of the *Baltimore Sun* on his way out. Inside was a polythene package containing an ounce of cocaine. Maury Anderson had a major habit, and it was a habit that, for the moment at least, Sabatino was prepared to feed. At some point in the future Anderson would outlive his usefulness, literally, and it would be time to take him on a picnic. Sabatino was looking forward to the prospect.

Mersiha tip-toed down the darkened stairs and into the study in her nightgown, closing the door behind her. She sat down in her father's chair and switched on the computer and its monitor. The screen flickered for a few seconds, then it asked for the password. She typed in her own name. It had been the password for as long as she could remember; her father never changed it.

A menu flashed on to the screen. Towards the bottom of the menu was the program that kept track of the company's finances. She called it up and brought up the most recent profit and loss account. She ran her finger down the screen, silently mouthing the figures. Total income was well down on the previous year, but expenses were several hundred thousand dollars higher. The payroll and the company's Medicare payments made up the bulk of the outgoings. She closed the file and called up the report her father used for forecasting cash flows. She chewed the inside of her lip as she studied the figures. If the Middle Eastern order came through for the MIDAS system, the cash flow would keep the company going for at least three months. But that was purely a forecast; the money, and indeed the order, had yet to be received.

Mersiha called up the balance sheet. Over the months she'd been following her father's financial problems, it had been the balance sheet which had caused her the most headaches. At first she hadn't been able to make sense of the lists of assets and liabilities, but she'd spent hours in the school library reading every economics and business book she could get her hands on. It had been hard going, but gradually she'd worked out how to read the company's records and now she could tell almost at a glance how the company was doing. Its current account showed a substantial drop on the previous month, and accounts receivable had also dropped. Only capital equipment had stayed the same, and Mersiha knew that was pretty much a hypothetical figure anyway. Who would want to buy second-hand manufacturing equipment if CRW couldn't sell its own products?

While the assets were considerably down, the company's liabilities continued to rise, and it clearly wouldn't be long before they crossed over and the firm had a negative worth. Mersiha felt a sick feeling in the pit of her stomach. She checked the financial projections every week or so, and the picture was getting steadily worse. She wished that there was something she could do to help her father, but she knew she was powerless. She was just a kid. She'd give anything to be rich, to be able to write her father a cheque big enough to solve all his problems. She hated to see her father unhappy, hated it with a vengeance.

She called up QUICKEN, the program her father used to follow his personal finances. He had three bank accounts, and she checked the balances in all of them, then she went through his credit card billings and household expenses. As usual the biggest purchases had been made by Katherine. Several pairs of shoes, a gold bracelet, lots of clothes. The company's financial problems hadn't persuaded her to cut back at all; she was still spending as if there were no tomorrow. Even so, there was plenty of money in the bank accounts, and the house was almost paid for. It was only the company that was in trouble. That, at least, was something.

Mersiha switched off the computer and the monitor and crept back upstairs to her bedroom. She lay in the dark, staring at the ceiling with unseeing eyes, trying to work out what she could do to help.

Mersiha was in the kitchen when the telephone rang. 'I'll get it!' she yelled, and picked up the receiver. It was Dr Brown. 'Oh, hiya, Dr Brown. What's up?' she said, opening the refrigerator and pulling out a carton of orange juice with her free hand.

'Hello, Mersiha? No school today?'

'Study period,' she said. 'The school doesn't mind if we do it at home. It's an honour system.'

'Well, make sure you study hard. Is your mother there?'

'Sure,' Mersiha said. She pressed the 'hold' button and put the receiver back on the wall. She filled a glass with orange juice and put the carton back in the refrigerator before walking through to the hall. 'Katherine! It's Dr Brown,' she called upstairs. Katherine was in the bedroom, reorganising one of her many dress-filled closets.

'Okay, honey, I'll take it up here.'

Mersiha took a sip of orange juice and went back into the kitchen. Buffy scratched at the back door and Mersiha opened it for her. The dog sat there, her tongue lolling out of the side of her mouth, a chewed frisbee at her feet.

Mersiha bent down to pick up the plastic disc, and as she did she heard Katherine's voice over the phone's intercom. 'Hello?' Katherine said. Mersiha let the frisbee fall to the ground and went over to the phone to switch off the intercom.

'Katherine? It's me.'

'Hello, Art.'

'Can we talk?'

Mersiha froze, her finger just inches away from the button. Behind her, Buffy whined. Mersiha felt her stomach grow cold. They were going to talk about her, she was sure of it. She closed her eyes, fearing the embarrassment to come.

'I think so. Tony's still at the office.'

'Good. Katherine, I have to see you.'

'Now?'

Mersiha tensed. Whatever Dr Brown was concerned about, it must be serious.

'Can you get away?'

'Tony'll be here in an hour.'

'Please.'

'Tomorrow. What about tomorrow?'

'It's important. I need to see you now.' Mersiha opened her eyes. She'd never heard the psychiatrist talk this way before. He sounded like a small boy, pleading for attention. Her stomach grew colder and she clasped her arms around her chest as if trying to warm herself.

'Okay. I'll try.'

Mersiha heard the line go dead. She stared at the telephone. Buffy whined and pushed the frisbee with her nose. Mersiha wondered what Dr Brown was going to say to Katherine, and she had a sudden feeling of dread. Whatever it was, it couldn't have been good news. Bad news, she knew, always travelled fast. The telephone speaker began to make a buzzing sound. Mersiha switched it off. She heard Katherine's high heels on the stairs and she rushed out of the back door.

Freeman turned his Chevrolet Lumina into the driveway and sounded his horn as he saw Mersiha at the far end of the garden. She waved half-heartedly and carried on playing with the dog. Freeman frowned. Usually Mersiha came running up to greet him and more often than not she'd carry his briefcase for him. He parked the car in front of the house and walked over to where she was sitting under a large willow. 'Hi, pumpkin, what's up?'

Mersiha shrugged. 'Nothing much.'

Buffy wandered over to Freeman and put her head up,

asking to be stroked. Freeman patted her on the head, his eyes on Mersiha. 'Trouble at school?' he asked.

Mersiha shook her head. 'No, school's fine.' She kept her eyes averted as if unwilling to look him in the face. Freeman squatted down so that his head was almost level with hers.

'Anything I can do?' he asked. She looked up and Freeman could see tears in her eyes. 'What is it?' he said. He was suddenly seized with a feeling of panic. Mersiha never cried. Never. 'Is Katherine okay?'

Mersiha threw her arms around Freeman and hugged him tight. He could feel her hot breath against his neck. 'Don't ever leave me, please. Please don't leave me.'

Freeman squeezed her. 'I won't leave you, pumpkin.'

'No matter what?'

'Of course.' He untangled her arms from around his neck. 'Has something happened?'

She shook her head and wiped her cheeks with the back of her hands. Freeman held out a handkerchief but she refused to take it. 'I'm okay,' she said. 'I just got a bit sad, that's all.'

Freeman put his hands on the girl's shoulders. She looked small and vulnerable and his heart went out to her. He wanted to wrap his arms around her and protect her, to banish all her fears for ever. 'There's no need to be sad. Everything's all right now,' he said.

She nodded but Freeman could see that she wasn't convinced. 'Come on, let's go inside. Katherine's probably got dinner ready.'

Mersiha looked as if there was something else she wanted to say; there was a pleading in her eyes. Freeman realised with a jolt when he'd last seen the imploring look. It was when he'd found her in the camp, her head shaved, wearing rags. 'I don't want to go in yet. I'll come in soon. Okay?'

Freeman pinched her chin gently. 'Okay, pumpkin. I understand.' He stood up and went inside on his own. Katherine was chopping tomatoes. He put his briefcase on the kitchen table, went up behind her and hugged her. 'What's wrong with Mersiha?' he said.

'What do you mean?' Katherine asked, as she sliced the last tomato.

'She looked down in the dumps. Wouldn't tell me what was wrong.'

Katherine shrugged. 'She seemed happy enough an hour ago.' She picked up a large onion and began peeling it.

'No problems at school?' he asked.

'Not that I know of,' she said. 'Maybe she's having her period.'

Freeman grinned. 'That's a sexist remark, if ever I heard one,' he said.

'I wouldn't make fun of me while I've a knife in my hand,' Katherine said. 'Remember *Fatal Attraction*.'

'Okay, okay,' Freeman said, slipping his arms from around her waist and planting a kiss on the back of her neck. 'What's for dinner?'

'Pasta, with tomato and basil sauce.'

'Sounds great,' he said. 'Can you go easy with the garlic? I've got a meeting with our union officials tomorrow and it's going to be hard enough to get them to look me in the eyes as it is.'

'Sure.' She chopped the onions into tiny cubes and scraped them off the cutting board into a large pan on the stove. 'Can you look after the pasta? I'm going out for a while. Nordstrom's is having a sale in Towson. I'm meeting a few of the girls there.'

'Why don't you take Mersiha? Do a little mother-daughter bonding?'

Katherine shook her head. 'She's got homework to do.' She looked at her watch. 'I have to go.' She sniffed at the red sauce as it bubbled in the pan. 'Let this simmer for about fifteen minutes. The pasta's in the fridge, the instructions are on the packet.'

'We'll be fine,' Freeman said. 'You go, you don't want to keep the girls waiting.'

Katherine went upstairs to change. Freeman walked over to the kitchen window. Mersiha was still sitting under the willow tree. She appeared to be looking in his direction but when he waved there was no reaction. He checked the heat under the saucepan, noted the time on the stove timer, and went upstairs. Katherine was in the bathroom in bra and pants, stepping into a light blue dress. Freeman grabbed for her as she straightened up, slipping his hands around her full breasts and pushing himself against her. He nuzzled her neck. 'You smell good,' he said.

She tried to button up the front of the dress, but Freeman kept a hold of her. 'Come on, how about a quickie?' he asked, only half joking.

'Three reasons. I'm late, Mersiha's going to walk in at any moment, and you're sweaty.' She reached behind with both hands and rubbed them against his groin. He felt himself grow hard. 'Maybe later,' she said.

'How about a kiss?' he said. 'A consolation prize?'

Katherine twisted around and put her arms around his neck, the full length of her body pressing against him as she kissed him. He moaned as she slipped her tongue between his teeth and he tried to push her back, on to the bed.

She pulled her head back and tapped him on the nose with her index finger. 'Later,' she said. She stepped back and buttoned up her dress. 'You'd better keep an eye on that sauce.'

'Yeah, a man's place is in the kitchen,' he said.

He went back downstairs. The sauce was simmering nicely so he took his briefcase through into the study. He sat down at his desk and turned on his computer and monitor. He knew the figures in the financial spreadsheet by heart but he wanted to look at them again nonetheless, as if by going over them one last time he'd uncover a hidden cash reserve or profit centre. He slumped back in his chair and ran a hand through his hair. Prepared phrases kept popping into his mind. Well placed for the economic upturn. A temporary profits reversal. Negative cash flow resulting in a cessation of dividend payments. The fancy language meant only one thing. The company was haemorrhaging money and would continue to do so for the foreseeable future. 'Shit,' he said, out loud.

Katherine appeared at the door. 'What's wrong?' she asked.

Freeman looked up. She was wearing full make-up and she'd brushed her hair until it shone. He knew how important it was for her to look good in front of her peers. Her friends were the bitchiest group of women he'd ever come across outside of a prime-time television show. They seemed to take a delight in ripping each other apart, like sharks turning on their own at the scent of blood. Freeman reckoned the reason they were always going out together was because they feared that if they weren't there they'd be the target of the scorn and derision. Better to turn up and be a part of the bitching than to be absent and be the butt of it. 'You look fabulous,' he said. He didn't want to get dragged into a discussion about the company's worsening financial situation.

'Why, thank you. Don't forget the sauce.'

'I won't. Have a good time.'

She blew him a kiss and left. A few moments later he heard her car start up. He switched off the computer and went into the kitchen. He rapped on the window with his knuckles but Mersiha didn't get up. He opened the back door. 'Hey, pumpkin, supper's ready!' he called.

Mersiha got to her feet and walked over, her hands thrust deep into the pockets of her jeans. He ruffled her hair as she walked by him. 'Katherine's out so it's just you and me.'

'Where did she go?' she asked, her voice a flat monotone.

'Shopping,' he said, sniffing at the sauce. There was a strong smell of garlic which almost masked the basil. 'Can you get the pasta? It's in the fridge.'

Mersiha frowned. 'Shopping? Are you sure?'

'That's what she said, pumpkin. Come on, pass the pasta.'

'I'm not hungry,' Mersiha said, and rushed out of the room. Buffy sat in front of the stove and watched her go. The dog looked up at the food on the stove, at the door, and then back at the stove. She sat down and woofed quietly.

'Yours is in the tin,' Freeman told the dog as he went out of the kitchen after Mersiha. 'Get it yourself.'

He found Mersiha in her bedroom, face down and hugging her pillow. He sat down next to her and reached out to stroke her long black hair. 'Hey, whatever it is, it can't be that bad,' he said softly. 'Can't you tell me about it?'

She shook her head, still buried in the pillow.

'Is it school?' Another shake. 'A boy?' That produced a short, harsh laugh, muffled by the pillow. 'Girl stuff?'

She moved quickly, rolling over and grabbing him around the waist, her head in his lap. There were damp patches on her cheeks. Freeman felt totally helpless. She was his little girl and he was supposed to take care of her, to keep all the bad and hurtful things at bay, but until he knew what the problem was there was nothing he could do. 'It's all right, pumpkin,' he said. 'I'm here.' He smoothed her hair with the flat of his hand. It was jet black with the exception of a small group of pure white hairs to the left of her parting. The few white hairs seemed to emphasise how black the rest were.

Freeman ate supper alone in front of the television. He ate mechanically, his thoughts divided between Mersiha and his forthcoming meeting with the union officials. When he'd finished he carried the plate and fork through into the kitchen and put them in the dishwasher. He'd put pasta and sauce in a bowl for Mersiha but as she hadn't come when he'd called he'd put it in the oven to keep warm. He took it out of the oven, picked up a clean fork, and took them upstairs to her bedroom. He knocked on the door but there was no answer. 'Feeding time,' he called, but she still didn't reply.

He opened the door and peered around it. Mersiha was asleep, her arms still hugging the pillow. Freeman put the pasta on her bedside table and covered her with the quilt. Her hair had fallen across her face like a black curtain and Freeman brushed it away, taking care not to wake her.

She was fifteen, going on sixteen, and she was already becoming a woman, but she slept like a little girl. He stroked her cheek with the back of his hand. It was as soft as a baby's skin. Freeman leant over and planted a kiss on her forehead. 'Sleep well, pumpkin,' he whispered.

Her eyelids flickered and opened, but she was still asleep. 'Don't leave me, Daddy,' she murmured. 'Don't ever leave me.' Before Freeman could reply her eyes had closed and she was snoring softly.

Freeman was in the study going over his financial spreadsheet for the thousandth time when he heard Katherine's key in the front door-lock. He looked at his watch. Nine thirty. He switched the computer off and went through into the hall where she was removing her coat. He looked around for the collection of shopping bags that usually followed a trip to the mall with the girls. 'So, what did you get?' he said. 'Or shall I wait for the credit card bills?'

'You got off lightly,' she laughed, putting the coat in a closet.

'You didn't buy anything?'

'I put a couple of things on hold. I'll sleep on it,' she said, and kissed him lightly on the cheek.

He caught a whiff of a fragrance he hadn't noticed before. It smelled more like aftershave than perfume, but that wasn't unusual. Katherine often preferred masculine fragrances and was for ever borrowing his aftershave. 'What's the scent?' he asked.

Katherine shrugged. 'We were trying samples in the

perfume section,' she said. 'Don't ask me to name names, though.' She walked into the kitchen. 'How was supper?' she asked.

'Yeah, it was okay.'

'Just okay?'

'It was terrific. A gastronomic delight.'

'Hmmmm. Good old Scottish understatement.' She peered into the saucepan. It was still half full. 'I could make you something else.'

'It was fine.' He went up behind her and held her around the waist. 'Mersiha still seems unhappy.'

'Did she say what was wrong?'

Freeman slipped his hands up to her breasts and kissed her on the neck. 'No. Do you think we should increase her sessions with Art? Maybe have her see him twice a week?'

'I'll ask him next time I see him,' she said.

'Bed?' asked Freeman, kissing her neck.

'I want to read a little first,' said Katherine, pulling away. 'You go up first. I'll join you later.'

'Are you sure?' asked Freeman, unable to keep the disappointment out of his voice.

Katherine gave him a sisterly peck on the cheek. 'I'm sorry. You know how shopping with the girls always gives me a headache.' She patted his groin with her hand. 'I'll take a rain check. Okay?'

'Okay. I've got work to do anyway.' Freeman watched her walk into the sitting room before heading for the study and the unchanging spreadsheet.

* * *

Mersiha woke up with a jolt, covered in sweat, her whole body shaking. The nightmare had been so real, so vivid, that it was several seconds before she realised she was safe in bed and not back in Bosnia. She lay on her back and stared up at the ceiling. The dreams always came when she was insecure; she didn't have to be a psychiatrist to realise that. It was the one thing she dreaded most – losing her family and being sent back to the camp.

Her mind was a whirl, filled with images of her past. Her father, dead in the street. The pain her mother had endured until it became too much for her. The school. Always her thoughts went back to the school. She rolled over and hugged her pillow. It was Art Brown who was to blame. Art Brown and his questions, always probing, always trying to get inside her head. Now the psychiatrist had discovered something, something so important that he'd had to see Katherine at short notice, something that was so secret that Katherine hadn't even told her husband where she was going. Tears welled up in Mersiha's eyes. 'I won't cry,' she promised herself, blinking them away. 'I won't cry.'

Anthony Freeman was helping himself to a coffee from the office machine when Maury Anderson came up behind him and tapped him on the shoulder with a rolled-up copy of *USA Today*. 'I don't know how you can drink that stuff,' he said.

'If I don't get a caffeine injection I get headaches,' Freeman said. He poured a second cup and carried it through to his secretary's office. Anderson followed in his wake. 'Here's yours, Jo,' Freeman said, putting the cup on his secretary's desk.

Freeman and Anderson went into the inner office. Anderson back-kicked the door closed behind them and sat down on Tony's couch. He swung his feet up on the coffee table, knocking aside a pile of defence magazines. 'When are you gonna do something about this furniture, Tony?'

Freeman shrugged. 'If it was good enough for Katherine's father, it's good enough for me.' The cheap factory-made desk and filing cabinets were chipped teak veneer and the carpet was threadbare. The sofa on which Anderson was sprawling sagged from years of use and one of the legs of the coffee table had been replaced with wood that didn't quite match. The furniture, and the office with its view of the car park, had once belonged to Freeman's father-in-law and he'd inherited it along with the chairman's job. 'Besides, I figure that if we meet Nelson here, he's going to realise that we're not wasting our money on office furnishings. The same can't be said if we take him up to your place, right?'

Anderson smirked. 'Guess you're right. Did you see CNN?'

Freeman frowned. 'No, what's up?'

'There's been a new wave of arrests in Seoul. Six military officials. The government's serious about this clampdown on kickbacks for weapons procurement. Everyone's getting real jittery.'

'Yeah, but it's not as if we've done any business with the South Koreans,' Freeman said.

'Not because we didn't try,' Anderson said, stretching out. 'It just makes it harder everywhere else. Sort of makes you wish for the good old days when Iran was buying a billion dollars of military hardware every year from the United States, doesn't it?'

The intercom buzzed. It was Freeman's secretary, announcing that Lennie Nelson was in the outer office. Freeman sighed and asked her to shown him in.

'High noon,' Anderson said as he got to his feet. 'Say, what do you call a blind elk with no legs?'

'What?'

'Still no eye-deer,' Anderson said.

Freeman tried not to laugh as the door opened and Nelson strode in, his right arm outstretched, a predatory smile on his lips. 'Tony, good to see you again,' he said, shaking hands. His grip was firm but once again Freeman couldn't help but notice how moist the man's hands were. Nelson shook hands with Anderson, then looked around the office. Freeman could tell from the look on the man's face that he wasn't impressed by the cheap furnishings, and when he sat down he pulled at the knees of his trousers as if trying to minimise the contact between the expensively cut material of his suit and the worn fabric of the sofa. Anderson was fighting to stop himself from grinning.

Freeman raised his coffee cup. 'Can I get you anything, Lennie? Tea? Coffee?' he asked.

'Dry martini with a twist?' Anderson added.

Freeman glared at Anderson the way he looked at his dog when she misbehaved. Anderson pretended not to notice, which was pretty much the way Freeman's dog usually reacted.

'Coffee will be just fine,' Nelson said. Jo was standing at the door and she nodded. She looked expectantly at Anderson but he shook his head.

'So, I don't suppose the board meeting's here, is it?' Nelson asked.

'We've got a boardroom upstairs,' Freeman said.

'Any news on the orders front?' Nelson asked.

'Nothing yet,' Freeman replied.

'The way I hear it, the US is pumping billions into Israel to maintain its security,' Nelson said. 'You can figure all the Arab countries are gonna have to do the same. That's gotta be good news, right?'

'Unfortunately, those billions are going on big defence systems, aircraft and missiles,' Anderson said. 'At the moment there aren't too many crumbs falling off the cake. Bigger doesn't necessarily mean better, not so far as we're concerned, anyway.'

'Because you're not getting a share?' Nelson asked.

'And it isn't going to get any better,' Freeman said. 'The best example is the fighter aircraft business. Back in the 1950s the US military would buy two thousand fighters a year, keeping lots of firms and tens of thousands of people working. In the sixties that had dropped to six hundred fighters a year, and that number had halved a decade later. Even in the Reagan years, with the defence budget doubled, they still only bought three hundred a year. The total expenditure keeps going up, but it doesn't keep pace with the unit cost. And who profits? The big manufacturers, that's who. All the smaller firms can't compete.'

'You know where it'll end?' Anderson asked. 'If things continue the way they're going, by the year 2050 the military will be buying one plane a year. It'll be the best plane ever made, and it'll certainly be the most expensive, but it'll still only be one plane. And there'll only be one manufacturer.'

'You don't really believe that,' Nelson said. Jo popped into the office with Nelson's coffee and copies of the minutes of the previous board meeting.

Anderson grinned. 'It's maybe an exaggeration, but the principle holds good. All the money is going to the big boys, which means there's less to go around for firms like us. I just thought you'd like to know where we stand.'

'I appreciate the briefing,' Nelson said coldly. 'Are we almost ready?'

Anderson looked over his shoulder as a car drove by the building. 'Katherine's here,' he said to Freeman.

Nelson flicked through the minutes of the last meeting. 'That's Mrs Freeman, right?'

'Uh-huh. She's on the board. It was her father who founded the business.'

'Okay, I didn't realise she was the founder's daughter. I see she's listed in the minutes as K. Williamson. That's her maiden name, right?'

Freeman nodded. 'She has forty per cent of the voting stock, and has done since she was eighteen. She never bothered to re-register them under her married name.'

'Josh Bowers,' Nelson read. He looked up from the minutes. 'He's your Development Director, right? I'm looking forward to meeting him. We're still waiting for Bill Hannah?'

'That's usually the way it goes,' Anderson said. 'Bill lives in a retirement home out in Hunt Valley and he insists on driving himself. He's almost ninety so it takes him a while.'

'Bill was one of my father-in-law's original backers,' Freeman explained. 'He has a ten per cent stake in the company. He's been gradually selling off shares over the years to pay medical bills and such. He's not well.'

'He's been not well for the last fifteen years,' Anderson laughed. 'The old man will outlast us all.'

Freeman grimaced. He remembered how Anderson used to say the same about Katherine's father. They had all expected him to live for ever. Freeman still felt ill at ease in the chairman's office as if he expected him to walk back in to reclaim his desk. The great Charlie Williamson. Freeman never thought of the man by name. He was always Katherine's father, or his father-in-law. Freeman wasn't sure why that was, but it might have had something to do with the fact that the two men were never close. The old man had always resented Freeman marrying his daughter, and Freeman in turn had always been overawed by him. Nothing had surprised Freeman more than discovering after Charlie Williamson's death that he'd named his son-in-law as his successor.

Nelson stood up and straightened the creases of his trousers. He picked up his briefcase and looked at Freeman expectantly. 'We could wait for him in the boardroom,' he said.

They took the stairs. It was only one floor up to the executive offices and the elevator was notoriously slow. Katherine's father always said that he preferred to be closer to the workforce than to the accountants, and after Freeman took over as chairman he saw no good reason for moving upstairs. Anderson excused himself and popped into the bathroom. Nelson seemed more impressed by the offices on the executive floor and he nodded his approval as Freeman showed him into the wood-panelled room. The oak table was big enough to seat twenty and was more than fifty years old. On the wall behind the head of the table was a gilt-framed oil painting of Charlie Williamson, a Bible in his right hand and an evangelical gleam in his eyes.

'That's your father-in-law?' Nelson asked, nodding at the painting.

'Uh-huh,' Freeman said. 'The man himself.'

'He looks like a guy who was used to getting his own way.'

'He was strong-willed, all right,' Anderson agreed as he walked into the room. 'Charlie Williamson wasn't a man you'd want to cross.'

They were interrupted by the arrival of Katherine and Josh. Freeman introduced them to Nelson and then they took their places, Freeman sitting at the head of the table, the dour visage of CRW's founder staring over his shoulder. A few minutes later, Bill Hannah arrived, apologising profusely for being late. He was followed by Freeman's secretary who quickly handed out copies of the minutes of the previous meeting to those who hadn't already received them.

With a dearth of new orders, most of the meeting was taken up by Josh describing the progress his research department was making with new products. He tried to be as upbeat as possible, but it was clear that it was going to be a year at best before he had anything close to a saleable system. Throughout Josh's presentation, Nelson leant back in his chair and played with his gold pen, a look of barely concealed disdain on his face.

There were only two items of Any Other Business: one raised by Anderson, the other a request by Nelson to say a few words. Anderson's was short and to the point. He'd been looking around for additional investment resources and one of the company's backers, a New York-based venture capital outfit, Ventura Investments, had agreed to put an extra half a million dollars into the business in exchange for shares. Anderson was enthusiastic about the deal, but Nelson frowned and tapped his pen on the oak desk. 'What's their holding just now?' he asked.

'Seventeen per cent,' Anderson said. 'It'll go up to twenty-one if this deal goes ahead.'

'It'll mean the existing shareholders will see their stakes diluted,' Nelson said. 'Will they be happy with that?'

Katherine nodded. 'If it means extra money coming into the company, I don't see how we can refuse,' she said.

Hannah nodded in agreement, but he seemed less happy with the prospect.

'Who are these people?' Nelson asked.

'They're a group of local businessmen who've pooled their funds to back various speculative investments,' Anderson said. 'Total worth is about twenty million.'

'How long have they been investors in CRW?' Nelson asked.

Anderson folded his arms defensively and thrust his chin up. 'Why? What's the problem?'

'No problem,' Nelson said. 'I was just wondering how long they'd been shareholders.'

'It's in the accounts.'

'The accounts only show shareholders with more than five per cent of the company. They could have had a small stake for years.'

Anderson nodded, conceding the point. 'About three years,' he said. 'They came straight in with their seventeen per cent holding.'

'How did they hear about the company?'

Anderson looked across at Freeman as if pleading for support. There was nothing Freeman could say. It had been Anderson who'd brought them in as investors. At the time Freeman had been chained to a boiler in a cellar in Sarajevo. 'I can't remember,' Anderson said. 'I'll go back through the file. I still don't see what the problem is.'

'To be honest, Maury, CRW doesn't strike me as a speculative investment. Venture capital is like seed corn, it's not fertiliser. You don't use venture capital to shore up a loss-making company.'

'They thought our problems were temporary, that we're due for a turnaround,' Anderson said.

Nelson scribbled a note on his leather-bound writing pad. He nodded without looking up. 'Where would they get that impression from?' he asked.

Anderson was lost for words. He looked at Freeman, then at Katherine, then back to Freeman. Freeman shrugged. 'I don't get this,' Anderson said. 'The banks won't lend any more to us, this guy's waiting like a vulture for the first signs of weakness, but when I come up with people who are willing to invest in us, he sits there asking why. Look, Lonnie, have you ever heard the expression "don't look a gift horse in the mouth"? Like, maybe we should just thank them and take their money?'

Nelson studied Anderson for a few seconds. He seemed totally relaxed, except for the slow tapping of his pen, whereas Anderson had wound himself into a state of considerable agitation. 'First of all, it's Lennie, not Lonnie. Second of all, if we're throwing proverbs around, what about "beware of Greeks bearing gifts"? There's a very good reason why the banks won't increase your credit lines just now. There's no good reason why a group of venture capitalists would want to put more money into the firm. That's all I'm saying.'

Anderson's cheeks had reddened and he was clenching and unclenching his hands like a weightlifter preparing to go for his personal best. 'So, what do you suggest, Lennie?' he said.

Nelson smiled and shook his head. 'I'd just like to know more about them, that's all. You're CRW's financial director. It goes without saying that I trust your judgment.'

'Well, that's something,' Anderson said, though he didn't look any happier.

'We're still going to have to vote on whether or not to issue the new shares,' Freeman said.

'And it'll have to go before a full shareholders' meeting,' Nelson said. 'The annual meeting is next month, right?'

Freeman nodded. 'That'll be soon enough, right, Maury?'

Anderson said nothing, but he nodded. At least he'd stopped clenching his fists. Freeman called for a vote, and it was unanimous. The board's decisions usually were. Jo minuted the decision and Freeman turned to Nelson. 'There was something you wanted to say to the board, Lennie?' he said.

Nelson pushed his chair back and stood up, surveying the room for a moment or two before speaking. 'I wanted to say a few words about the business, and where I see it going, so that we can all give some serious thought to the future of CRW.' He looked at the portrait of the firm's founder. 'The defence industry has changed a lot since Mr Williamson began manufacturing armoured vehicles in his barns near Annapolis. He was astute enough to see in the early years the importance of electronics, and to redirect the company to its current activities – missile guidance systems and video circuits. But I think it fair to say that if he were alive today, he'd realise that the company must undergo another change if it is to survive into the next century.'

Katherine looked over at Freeman, and he knew exactly what she was thinking. What right did this man have to say that he knew what her father would think? He'd never met the man. And if they had met, Freeman doubted that Katherine's father would have been impressed by the thrusting young banker.

'The whole defence industry is labouring under heavy debt with shrinking profits and low margins, and it seems to me that the larger contractors have sought various solutions: some have gone after more international orders, others have diversified into other businesses, down-sized or gone into joint ventures. What I have in mind for CRW is a combination of these solutions, tailored to meet our needs.'

Freeman exchanged worried looks with Anderson and Katherine. He didn't like the way the conversation was going, but Nelson was effectively holding a loaded gun to their heads. Without the bank's backing they were dead in the water.

'Joint ventures, coupled with aggressive down-sizing,' Nelson continued, oblivious to their looks. 'That's the way to go.'

Freeman frowned. 'Aggressive down-sizing?' he said.

'Many developing nations are lining up to get involved in licensed production of weapons systems. It gives them an opportunity to build up an indigenous defence industry, while at the same time earning foreign currency. There are lots of examples, especially out in Asia. Countries such as Singapore and South Korea, Indonesia and Taiwan. Of the countries I've looked at, Taiwan and Singapore have the most appeal.'

Anderson leant forward, his chin in his hands. 'The most appeal for what?' he said.

'For the sub-contracting of the company's manufacturing interests.' Nelson waited for them to react.

Katherine's mouth dropped. Even the portrait of her father seemed to express disbelief. 'You mean close down the factory?' she said.

'Only the manufacturing facilities,' Nelson said. 'Sales and administration would continue to be based here, but obviously a smaller workforce would require fewer support services. Personnel, accounting, clerical – there would be savings in all departments.'

Freeman held up a hand like a policeman stopping traffic. 'Wait just one minute,' he said. 'Are you saying that we stop manufacturing here in Maryland? That we lay off our employees and move to Taiwan?'

'I estimate that we would save approximately six million dollars in operating costs in the first twelve months, though admittedly that doesn't include the one-time closure costs. But there would also be one-time profits from the sale of the company's properties.'

Freeman shook his head emphatically. 'Let's get something straight,' he said. 'We're a manufacturing company. We make things. We make things and we sell them. That's the way it's always been. That's the way it'll stay.'

'It doesn't make sense,' Nelson said patiently. 'You can halve your manufacturing costs by switching production to the Far East. You can put the company back on a firm financial footing.'

'This is a business,' Katherine protested. 'It's made up of people. Human beings. We owe them our loyalty. Some of those men have been on the payroll for more than thirty years.'

Nelson sighed patiently. 'It's those men who are dragging this company down,' he said. 'Think of CRW as a tree, a tree that's starting to die. You can either stand by and let it wither away or you can prune the dying branches.' He looked at the board members one at a time as he spoke, like a defence attorney giving his closing speech to a jury. 'And I can tell you here and now, if you don't do something, the bank will. In my opinion, you have something like six months to act. After that there'll be nothing left to save. Even Chapter 11 won't be an option.'

'That sounds like a threat,' Katherine said.

'Mrs Freeman, we're a bank, not the Mafia. We don't make threats, we make loans. But we have the right to foreclose on those loans.'

'But we're talking about people here. Men with families. Men who depend on us for their livelihoods.' Katherine took a cigarette from her handbag. Her hand shook as she lit it and inhaled. Her eyes narrowed as she studied Nelson through the smoke. 'You know nothing about this company, Mr Nelson. You don't have the right to tell us to throw our workforce on the scrapheap.'

'I know numbers, Mrs Freeman. That's what I do. You can be as sentimental as you like, but when all's said and done it all comes down to money. I admire your loyalty to the employees, but I'm afraid it's misplaced. Do you seriously believe that the employees are going to stand by you if this company goes under? Do you think they'll have any sympathy for you while you're standing in the unemployment line?' He shook his head, answering his own rhetorical question. 'They'll be taking care of themselves. They won't give you a second thought.' He paused for a moment. 'I'm sorry if you're upset by what you're hearing, but you have to realise that the bank has your best interests at heart. We're the only friends you have.'

Anderson sniggered. 'With friends like you . . .' he said, leaving the sentence unfinished.

Nelson pretended not to have heard him. 'You have to look at the benefits of this,' he said. 'The company will be profitable in a way it's never been before. You'll have more money for research and development of new products – something that I'm sure Josh would appreciate. And during the development phase, you won't be saddled with a cash-draining workforce. You go to the Taiwanese with the product, and they'll manufacture it to order. I'll tell you something else – the quality of their work will probably be better than you get here in the US. And once you've filled the orders, you stop production. The Taiwanese don't have the same labour laws or unions that we do.'

Anderson massaged the bridge of his nose. 'This is just your way of getting the bank's money back, isn't it?' he asked.

Nelson rested his hands on the back of his chair. 'Absolutely not,' he said. 'You know as well as I do, Maury, that if the bank was to foreclose on its loans tomorrow, we'd recover our money in full. But if CRW aggressively down-sizes, transfers its production overseas and gets new products in development, I think you'll see the bank taking a much more relaxed view of your operations.'

Anderson sat back in his chair heavily. Freeman could see that the finance director wasn't convinced by Nelson's scenario, and Katherine had a look of dismay on her face. Josh seemed unimpressed, but he usually expressed little interest in anything that took place outside his laboratories and test rigs. Bill Hannah raised a hand, like a child wanting to ask a question of his teacher.

Freeman nodded at him. 'Yes, Bill?'

'What about the technology transfer?' Bill asked. 'I'm sure the Defense Department would have something to say about us giving our military technology to the Taiwanese.'

Nelson smiled. 'Good point,' he said. 'That might have been the case with the missile guidance systems, but the bottom has dropped out of that market. Products such as the MIDAS minefield system are actually quite low-grade in terms of technology. It's not as if we're talking about ballistic missiles.'

'That means you expect our new products to be along similar lines, then?' Hannah asked.

'I certainly think that Josh and his team should be looking at products less focused on military use, that's true,' Nelson said. 'Video security systems, video telephones, products which would have far wider applications than defence.'

Katherine looked up at the painting of her father as if wishing that the old man would step out of the gilded frame and take over the meeting. Then she looked at Freeman, and he knew that she was comparing his performance with the way her father would have handled the situation. He could see from the look in her eyes that the comparison wasn't favourable, and he decided that he'd have to say something.

'I don't think you quite appreciate the extent of the market for mine clearance systems,' he said. Nelson folded his arms across his chest as he listened to Freeman. 'Do you know how many uncleared landmines there are in the world?' Freeman asked. He waited until Nelson shook his head before answering his own question. 'More than one hundred million,' he said, uttering each word slowly for full effect. Nelson didn't appear impressed, so Freeman continued. 'There were some seven million alone planted in Kuwait by the Iraqis and the Kuwaitis have already spent more than 750 million dollars clearing them. Let me run some other figures by you. Kurdistan, five million mines. Angola, nine million. Vietnam, three million. Cambodia, four million. Despite a concerted international effort to clear Afghanistan of its ten million or so unexploded mines, the experts have only managed to clear about twenty-five square kilometres – with dozens of mine clearance experts killed or wounded. Even the British had to deal with fifteen thousand mines in the Falklands. According to the State Department, mines kill 150 people a day around the world. And countries like China and Italy are still producing up to ten million anti-personnel mines a year. Locating and neutralising those mines is big business, Lennie.'

Freeman put his chin up defiantly, as if daring Nelson to argue with his statistics. The banker smiled condescendingly. 'Look, you don't have to make a decision on this right now,' he said. 'I realise it's a big step, and I know you're all going to have to give it some thought. I'll put out some feelers, see if I can come up with some manufacturers who CRW might be able to use. Hopefully I'll have something by the next meeting.' He looked at Jo, making sure that she was minuting everything he said. She smiled at him, her pen still scratching across her pad in careful shorthand. Lennie adjusted his tie. 'That's all I have to say,' he said, sitting down and placing his hands flat on the desk. The nails were immaculately manicured, Freeman noticed.

Katherine looked at Freeman as if she expected him to say something else, but he was unwilling to be drawn into an argument with the banker. He ignored her and simply announced that if there was no further business the meeting was over.

Nelson shook them all by the hand, one by one, then picked up his briefcase and left without a backward look.

Katherine waited until Bill Hannah and Josh had left before she rounded on Freeman. 'I can't believe you let him ride roughshod over you like that,' she said.

'What do you mean?' Freeman asked.

'Oh, come on. You know exactly what I mean.' She stabbed out her cigarette in a crystal ashtray as if she were gouging it into his eye. 'You sat there and let him tell you how to run the company. Our company.'

Anderson pushed his chair back and stood up. 'I'll catch you both later,' he said, sensing an argument.

'No, you should stay, Maury,' Katherine said, her eyes still on Freeman. 'You're as much a part of this company as Tony and me.' He looked as if he'd prefer to go, but he did as Katherine asked, standing with his back to the wall as if he were facing a firing squad. 'My father must be turning in his grave,' Katherine continued. 'That man is suggesting we throw away everything he built. I won't stand for it.'

Freeman couldn't help smiling. She was every inch her father's daughter, her confidence at times bordering on arrogance. 'He's only looking after the bank's interests, honey,' he said. 'It's only a suggestion. It's going to have to go before a full shareholders' meeting, and the bank doesn't have any votes, remember. Between you and Bill you have more than enough votes to block any motion you don't like.' Katherine didn't seem mollified. She took out another cigarette and lit it with her gold lighter, a present from her father. She tapped the lighter on the packet of cigarettes. Her mouth was a tight line and her eyes were cold.

Mr Kahn sipped his glass of water and looked at Mersiha through narrowed eyes. He put the glass down on the table and ran his index finger around its rim. 'You seem to be taking a very hostile attitude today,' he said levelly.

'It's something I feel very strongly about,' Mersiha said. She had been arguing with him for more than half of their session, about par for the course. Mr Kahn came to the Freeman house once a week to tutor Mersiha in Muslim theology, but the older she got, the more Mersiha resented the time she had to spend with the teacher. She'd protested to both her mother and her father, but both were insistent. As part of the deal to get her out of Bosnia, they'd agreed that she be taught about her Muslim heritage, and even though they were now thousands of miles away from Sarajevo they were determined to abide by that agreement.

'The views presented in the Koran might well be unfashionable in the more liberal atmosphere here in the United States, but nevertheless they are God's teachings, passed to Muhammad by the angel Gabriel.' Mr Kahn smiled at Mersiha, and it was a friendly gesture. He had a good heart, Mersiha knew. In all their hours together he had never once raised his voice or expressed any annoyance. He actually seemed to enjoy her spirited rebuttals and arguments, as if by testing his faith she only served to strengthen it.

'But this is the twentieth century,' she complained. 'I mean, it's soon going to be the twenty-first.'

'And throughout all those centuries, the word of the Koran has been listened to and obeyed. Why do you think that is?'

Mersiha shrugged. 'Because it's easier to obey a book than it is to think for yourself.'

Mr Kahn shook his head. 'But that's simply not true, Mersiha. It would be much easier to live your life as you wanted, without worrying about rules or laws. Choosing to live by the Koran means closing a lot of doors.'

'Especially for women. The Koran says that women are not equal.'

'That's true, the Koran does say that men and women are to be treated differently. But isn't that also the case in this country?'

'Yeah, but the Koran isn't talking about women as the gentle sex. It describes them as being inferior. They have to cover their faces in public.'

Kahn shook his head. 'The Koran says only that women should cover their breasts, Mersiha. It does not mention faces. It's true that many women choose to cover their faces, but not because it says so in the Koran.'

'Because their husbands insist.'

'Perhaps.'

'And what about adultery? The Koran says the woman has to be stoned, right?'

Kahn smiled and shook his head. 'You've not been doing your homework,' he chided. 'The Koran says the punishment for adultery is public flogging. For both parties.'

'That's barbaric.'

'Adultery is barbaric, Mersiha.'

'And the Koran says it's okay to beat women if they do wrong. That a man can have many wives.'

'Not many,' Kahn corrected. 'Two, three or four. No more.'

'Whatever,' Mersiha said. 'But a woman can't have more than one husband.'

'Very few Muslims in this country take more than one wife. They adapt to the customs here.'

'So you're saying that the Koran isn't always right?'

Kahn smiled. 'The Koran is the word of God. And God is always right.'

Mersiha pulled a face. 'There's no God.'

Kahn raised an eyebrow. 'Why do you say that?'

'Because it's true. Because if there was a God the world wouldn't be such a terrible place.'

'What do you mean?'

'Wars. Murderers. Serial killers.'

'You can't blame God for that. It's men who are responsible. And if all men heeded the Koran, there wouldn't be so much evil in the world.'

Mersiha sighed and leaned back in her chair. Arguing with Mr Kahn was as futile as trying to grab mist.

'What about accidents? Natural disasters? Disease? You think God would allow AIDS?'

'Only He knows what His plans are. We can only live in the world as it is.'

'But if He knows the way things are, why doesn't He do something to change it? Why doesn't He make the world a better place?'

Mr Kahn smiled smoothly. 'I cannot speak for God. I can only interpret the Koran. But I can say that often out of great suffering there comes great good.'

Katherine came into the dining room and put a reassuring hand on Mersiha's shoulder. 'Is everything okay?' she asked. 'You seemed to be having a spirited argument.'

Mr Kahn stood and gathered up his books. 'A discussion, Mrs Freeman, nothing more than that. I consider myself lucky to have such an articulate student.' Katherine smiled down at Mersiha, pleased at the compliment. 'I wish that more of the youngsters I teach would take such an interest in the subject. But I'm not sure if your daughter accepts all my arguments.' He put his books into his black leather briefcase and shook Katherine's hand.

'I'll see you out, Mr Kahn.'

As she opened the front door, the teacher put his hand on Mersiha's shoulder. 'I meant what I said, Mersiha. I am glad that you put such thought into your beliefs. To accept blindly is not faith. Faith comes from belief, and I want you to believe in Islam. All I ask is that you keep an open mind.'

'I will, Mr Kahn,' she lied. She watched him walk to his car. Mersiha's mind was already closed to the subject of religion. She went through the charade of listening to Mr Kahn only because her father insisted. She even enjoyed arguing with him, but for her there was no question of her ever believing in the existence of a supreme being. She had seen too much in her short life, too much killing, too much pain, too much cruelty. She knew without a shadow of a doubt that there was no God. At least not any more. Mr Kahn was fooling himself.

Sal Sabatino sat back in his chair and studied the bank of video monitors on the wall. The Firehouse was jumping. The nightclub had been doing most of its business on Friday and Saturday nights, and in an attempt to boost trade early in the week he'd organised a wet t-shirt contest. It had paid off, pulling in a younger crowd than usual, but they seemed to have plenty of money and so far there'd been little in the way of trouble.

One of the video cameras downstairs was trained on the small stage where girls were lining up to dance around in a see-through shower cubicle. Sabatino leaned forward to look at one of the girls, a brunette with shoulder-length hair and a great body. She was just the way Sabatino liked them: long legs, tight backside, trim waist and small breasts. And young. That was the most important thing. It had been a long time since Sabatino had had sex with a girl over eighteen years old. The girl on the screen was perfect. She had the innocent look that he craved, as if she was just a little out of her depth. She kept looking around, seeking reassurance that she was doing the right thing, standing on the stage in a t-shirt and bikini bottom, about to show them all what she was made of.

'See that one, Vincenti? What do you think?'

Vincenti leaned across Sabatino's desk and scrutinised the girl on the screen. He licked his fleshy lips and screwed up his eyes before nodding. 'Sweet.'

'Sweet,' repeated Sabatino. 'Yeah. Sweet. A perfect description. Almost ripe, huh? Another fruit analogy, huh? You'd appreciate that, huh, Vincenti?'

Vincenti scowled but didn't reply. Sabatino raised his eyebrows and wiggled them suggestively. He loved goading Vincenti. He was his best man, totally dependable with a cruel streak that appealed to Sabatino, but he did have one weak point – his homosexuality. Vincenti had the rugged good looks of a sporting-goods model and he was used to turning female heads as he walked through The Firehouse, but his tastes ran to moustached body builders, ideally dressed in leather. Sabatino reckoned that much of the man's inherent viciousness sprang from his suppressed sexual nature. Only Sabatino knew of his true sexual orientation, and he teased him about it only in private. Sabatino's view was that so long as Vincenti did his job, he could screw whoever or whatever he liked.

The blonde in the shower cubicle scampered out, soaking wet, and her place was taken by an overweight black girl with breasts the size of melons. The crowd was howling and she jiggled up and down for maximum effect. Sabatino shuddered. She was repulsive. Vincenti went back to sit on a couch by the window. There was nothing on the video monitors to hold his attention.

The brunette didn't look as if she was more than sixteen years old. They were supposed to be at least eighteen to get in, but the guys on the door had been told to use their discretion. They knew that nothing pulled in the big spenders more than wall-to-wall pussy. And the brunette looked like she'd have a pussy as tight and hot as any Sabatino had ever experienced. She was laughing at the big black girl bouncing around under the stream of water, and her hand flew up to cover her mouth. It was a child-like gesture and one that aroused Sabatino even more.

Someone knocked on the door to his office. 'Yeah?' he called. It opened and Jacko, one of his security men, stepped into the room. His tuxedo was straining at his shoulders. Sabatino had never seen the jacket buttoned.

'Sorry 'bout this, Mr Sabatino,' he said.

'No sweat, Jacko. What's up?'

Jacko stepped aside to reveal a young black girl, her hair piled up on top of her head in a beehive. She was wearing a white silk shirt and tight white pants with cheap gold jewellery around her neck and on her fingers. Her chin was up defiantly, but Sabatino could see from her eyes that she was worried. Behind her stood another black security guy with a tuxedo and shoulders that matched Jacko's. Both men were wearing Ray Ban sunglasses. 'This bitch was dealing,' Jacko said, his face impassive.

'Crack?'

'Coke.' Jacko walked over to Sabatino's desk and dropped three small plastic packets next to his Rolodex. There was maybe a gramme in each bag, no doubt diluted by brick dust or talcum powder.

'I wasn't dealing. I was buying,' the girl protested.

Sabatino crooked his finger at the girl. 'Come here,' he said.

She was wearing high-heeled white boots and they clicked along the floor as she walked into the centre of the office. Jacko stood guard by the door but Sabatino waved him away. 'I can handle this,' he said. Vincenti left the room without being asked. He knew what was going to happen and that his presence wasn't necessary. He closed the door behind him.

Sabatino looked across at the television monitors. The brunette was third in line, tugging at the bottom of her t-shirt as if trying to cover her thighs. Sabatino licked his lips. 'No one deals drugs in my place,' he said.

The girl raised her eyebrows. 'I wasn't . . .'

Sabatino held up a hand. 'Don't fuck with me, okay? Just don't fuck with me.' He picked up one of the small bags and threw it in her face. 'You wanna do some blow in the john, that's fine. You wanna shoot up, that's fine. But you don't deal. If you get caught dealing, my place gets closed down. Am I getting through to you?'

She looked as if she was going to argue again, but Sabatino glared at her. 'Yeah. I hear you.' She started towards the door.

'Hey! Where do you think you're going?' Sabatino barked.

'I was gonna go.'

Sabatino smiled. 'You were gonna go? You're not going anywhere until I say so.'

'Yeah?'

Sabatino leisurely reached over to his intercom and pressed a button. 'Come back in here, Vincenti,' he said, his eyes on the girl.

The office door opened and Vincenti reappeared. Sabatino nodded towards the girl. 'This bitch is giving me a hard time,' he said.

Vincenti said nothing. He simply walked up to the girl and punched her in the stomach. The breath exploded from her lips and she doubled over, her hands clutched to her midriff. Her chest was heaving as she gasped for air and she slowly dropped to her knees. Sabatino watched the brunette on the video monitor. So young. Sabatino loved the texture of young flesh. The tautness of it. The smell of it.

Vincenti stood over the black girl as she slowly recovered. He leant down and with one huge hand pulled her to her feet. 'You do as Mr Sabatino, says, you hear?' he said.

The girl nodded, then coughed. She massaged her stomach with her gold-ringed fingers. Vincenti held on to her long enough to make sure that she could stand unaided, then he went outside again.

Sabatino tore his gaze away from the screen. 'Anyone who wants to buy anything in The Firehouse, they come to me, okay?'

The girl nodded. 'Okay,' she said.

'Usually if we catch someone dealing, Vincenti takes care of it. He takes care of people for me. He especially likes taking care of young girls. Am I getting through to you?'

'Yeah,' she gasped.

'The only reason he's not taking care of you right now is because he thinks I might have a good time with you. Do you know what I mean by that? I'd hate there to be any misunderstanding.'

'A good time? Yeah, I know what you mean.'

'So are you gonna give me a good time? Or do I get Vincenti back to take care of you?'

The girl swallowed. She nodded slowly.

'I can't hear you,' Sabatino said.

'Yeah. I'll give you a good time,' she said.

Sabatino smiled. 'Good,' he said. 'Now, take your shirt off.'

The girl undid the buttons of her shirt and slipped it off her shoulders. She wasn't wearing a bra but she made no move to cover her breasts, as if she knew instinctively that to do so would only annoy Sabatino. She looked around for somewhere to put the shirt.

'Drop it on the floor,' Sabatino ordered. She obeyed instantly. 'Now the boots. And the pants.'

Sabatino leaned back on his chair and watched the girl strip. Her skin was a glorious brown, the colour of milk chocolate, and it was totally unmarked. In Sabatino's experience, black skins tended to scar easily and heal badly and the contrast emphasised any imperfections, but this girl's skin was perfectly smooth and even. She was wearing red panties, cut high up the legs and low at the front. Through the flimsy material he could see her pubic hair, trimmed into a neat triangle.

'Take them off,' Sabatino ordered. He stared as she slipped her thumbs either side of the panties and eased them down her long, smooth legs. They fell to the floor and she stepped out of them, naked except for the jewellery. The gold only served to emphasise her nakedness. Sabatino rubbed the palms of his hands on his trousers. It wasn't just her looks that turned him on, it was the power. The fact that he could compel her to stand naked in front of him. He wondered how many men she'd taunted with her beauty, how many men she'd refused to go out with. He could imagine her leading on would-be suitors, then turning them down with a snide remark and a sneer. Not Sabatino, though. She'd do anything for him, anything he wanted. Sex wasn't about looks or personality or even money. It was about power and fear.

'How old are you?' he asked.

'Eighteen,' she said.

Sabatino kept looking at her, up and down, and eventually she averted her eyes, staring down at the floor.

'Get your black ass over here.'

She looked up sharply and for a second it seemed that she was going to reply, but she could see from Sabatino's face that it wouldn't be a smart thing to do. She walked slowly over to his desk. Sabatino looked at the bank of screens. The brunette was next to go into the cubicle.

Sabatino pushed his chair back so that there was space between himself and the desk. He pointed between his legs. 'Kneel down.' The girl hesitated. Sabatino sneered at her. 'Hey, if you don't want to do this, we can get the guys back here and they can take you for a ride. It's up to you.'

The girl knelt down. Sabatino grabbed her right breast and squeezed it savagely. Her mouth tightened, she grunted but refused to scream. 'Smile like you're fucking enjoying it or I'll really hurt you.'

Tears welled up in her brown eyes and she nodded. 'Okay, Mr Sabatino. Okay, whatever you say.' She smiled. Her lower lip was trembling. Sabatino stroked her cheek with his right hand and ran a finger along her soft lips.

'That's better,' he said. 'Unzip my pants.'

She pulled down his zip in one smooth movement. 'You've done this before,' he said. She looked up and nodded. She looked scared. Sabatino felt himself grow harder. 'Do it,' he said.

She opened her mouth and licked her lips, but he wasn't

looking at her; his eyes were on the video screen. A tall, thin redhead was climbing out of the shower cubicle, her enormous breasts barely confined by her wet t-shirt. The brunette stood by the empty cubicle, staring at the stream of water pouring from the shower head. Sabatino wondered if she was going to change her mind. He felt the smooth wetness of the black girl's mouth envelop him. She moved her head up and down but there was little sensation. She wasn't trying.

Sabatino grabbed her hair and pulled up her head. 'Don't tell me that's the best you can do,' he hissed. 'Mouth like yours, you can give better blow-jobs than that. I know you can. Don't try to cheat me. Okay?'

'Okay,' she said quietly.

Sabatino sat up and she flinched. He smiled at her reaction, then reached for one of the small cocaine-filled packets. He ripped it open with his teeth. 'Maybe this'll give you an incentive,' he said. He sprinkled the white powder over his genitals and tossed the empty bag on to the floor. He didn't have to tell her what to do. She opened her mouth and began to suck him again, this time with much more enthusiasm.

Sabatino moaned and ran his hands around the back of her neck. He felt her tongue run up and down his shaft, searching for the drug she craved and intensifying his pleasure at the same time. The telephone rang. It was his private line. He picked it up with his right hand, leaving his left on the girl's neck. Her head bobbed up and down and he could feel the inside of her mouth all the way along his length. 'Yeah?' Sabatino said.

'Mr Sabatino? Mr Sabatino, it's me. Maury.'

'This is not a good time, Maury,' Sabatino said. The

black girl lifted her head but he clamped his hand on her neck and pushed her back down.

'It's important,' Anderson said.

'It's gonna have to wait.' Sabatino could feel himself building to a climax. He opened his legs wider and the girl moved her head faster. She grunted in time with her movements, small animal-like sounds that excited Sabatino even more.

On the screen, the brunette turned around and began to play self-consciously with her small breasts. He could see her nipples harden under the white cotton material. Sabatino moaned. She looked so young with her hair soaked. Fifteen maybe. He began to push himself further into the black girl's mouth, trying to go in as far as he could. He felt her gag but he pressed her neck down and pounded into her.

'Are you okay, Mr Sabatino?' Anderson asked.

Sabatino ignored him. He grunted as he came, his last few strokes lifting his backside off the chair. The brunette stepped out of the shower, waved to the audience, and skipped off the stage. Sabatino settled back in his chair and pushed the black girl away. She fell on the floor, her legs sprawled wide and her hair in disarray.

'Mr Sabatino, what's going on?'

'Nothing,' Sabatino snapped, holding the phone against his ear with his left shoulder as he zipped up his trousers. 'Just give me a minute, will ya?' The black girl lay on the floor where she'd fallen. Sabatino glared at her and waved her away. The feelings of lust had evaporated and now he felt only disgust for the teenager. He watched her as she picked up her clothes and dressed. She seemed to realise how his feelings had changed and she kept her back to him.

'Mr Sabatino? We've got a problem.'

'We? What do you mean, we?' Sabatino's voice was ice cold.

'This guy I told you about, the bank's representative on the board. Nelson.'

'Yeah, what about him?'

'He wants to shut down the company and transfer production overseas. Says it'll save us millions.'

'He's probably right,' Sabatino agreed. The girl squeezed into her tight pants, bouncing from foot to foot. Sabatino had a sudden urge to hurt the girl, to tie her down and whip her until she bled. He wanted to mark the perfect skin, to scar her for ever, a permanent reminder of the power he had over her. He'd seen fear and pain in the girl's eyes, but Sabatino wanted more. Much more. She fastened her shirt and grabbed her boots, running out of the office barefoot as if she knew what he had on his mind. He wondered if she realised how lucky she was that he was on the phone.

'Yeah, but that's not all,' Anderson continued. 'He wasn't happy at Ventura increasing its stake in the company. He said he didn't understand why you'd want to put more money into the company, what with the problems we're having and all.'

'By "you", I hope you mean the partnership and not me personally.'

'Oh, sure, yeah, he doesn't know who's involved, though he did say that he wanted to make some enquiries. And, Mr Sabatino, he's really going to give our books a going over. I'm not sure how well they'll stand up to close inspection, if you know what I mean. Some of the amounts you've been putting through our accounts are pretty big, you know?'

'Yeah, I know exactly what you mean,' Sabatino said. 'Well, thanks for bringing this to my attention, Maury. I'll take it from here.' He replaced the receiver, sat back in his chair and stared at the bank of video monitors. The girl in the shower cubicle was in her twenties and carrying several pounds more than was good for her. Loose rolls of fat vibrated around her hips and her thighs jiggled more than her breasts. Sabatino shuddered.

Mersiha ran her hands through her hair and tried not to look at Dr Brown. They were nearing the end of the session and his soft, insistent voice was beginning to annoy her. She wanted to walk out of the office, to tell him to leave her alone, but Katherine was waiting outside and leaving would cause more problems than it would solve.

They were covering the same old ground. How was she sleeping? Not good. Was she having nightmares? Yes. How was she getting on at school? Fine. What did she think the problem was? She didn't know. She had expected the psychiatrist to mention the fact that he'd asked to see Katherine, but he hadn't raised it. The fact that he hadn't, worried Mersiha. She felt that they were going behind her back for some ulterior motive, but she had no idea what that motive might be. Katherine hadn't mentioned it either.

'Mersiha, why don't you regard Katherine as your mother?'

The question caught Mersiha by surprise and she turned to look at Dr Brown, her mouth open. 'Excuse me?' she said.

'You call your father "Dad" but you don't call Katherine "Mom".'

Mersiha raised her eyebrows. 'She isn't my mother.'

Dr Brown nodded. 'But Tony isn't your father, either. Strictly speaking.'

Mersiha's brow furrowed. 'They're my parents now. I know that. I mean, I know they're not my real parents, but they are my parents. If you see what I mean.'

The psychiatrist smiled as if he understood everything. 'Do you feel closer to your dad than Katherine, is that it?'

Mersiha shrugged. 'Maybe.'

'Because you knew him first?'

'Because he saved my life,' she said flatly. 'Because if it wasn't for him, I'd be dead.'

'And when did you first call him "Dad"? Can you remember?'

'After I came to America, I guess. I don't think I ever called him anything else.'

Dr Brown wrote something down on the notepad on his desk. 'And you've never felt like calling Katherine "Mom"? It's always Katherine?'

'I guess so.'

'Why do you think that is?'

'I don't know. Has she mentioned it to you?'

'I've discussed it with her, but only in the context of how you relate to your new family.'

'My only family,' she corrected him.

Dr Brown inclined his head, conceding the point. 'You still miss your real mother, don't you?'

'Of course. I miss all my family.'

'And you think of them often?'

Mersiha could feel tears welling up in her eyes and she blinked. She stared at the blinds on the window. It wasn't fair of him to try to manipulate her like this. He only wanted to see her cry.

'Perhaps you should try calling her "Mom". I think she'd like that.'

'It doesn't feel right. Not yet. When the time's right, I will.' She wanted to rub her eyes but she kept her hands down by her sides.

'Would you like to tell me what happened to your real mother?' His voice was soft and coaxing, like a child molester's.

'No,' Mersiha said firmly. She looked at her wristwatch.

Dr Brown sat in silence, waiting to see if she would say anything else, but Mersiha continued to stare at the blinds. 'Okay, Mersiha, let's call it a day,' he said eventually. 'You go and wait in the car while I have a word with your mother.' He smiled without warmth. 'With Katherine,' he added.

Mersiha let herself out of the office and walked over to Katherine's car. It was a warm day and she didn't feel like sitting, so she paced up and down, replaying the session in her mind. She hated the way Dr Brown tried to second-guess her all the time. It was as if he were playing mind games with her.

She looked over at the window of Dr Brown's office, wondering what he was telling Katherine, what they were saying about her. She frowned as she noticed that the blinds were closed. She was sure they had been open before. She put her head on one side and stared at the blinds, a growing feeling of dread in her heart. She began walking towards the window as if her legs had a life of their own.

There was a narrow gap at the bottom of the blinds and she bent down and pressed her face to the window. Dr Brown's desk obscured most of the view but she could just make out two figures, standing in front of the bookcase. Dr Brown and Katherine, holding each other, kissing so hard it was as if they were trying to devour each other. Mersiha watched, horrified.

Mersiha lay on her back, staring at the ceiling and wishing that time would pass more quickly. She looked across at the Mickey Mouse alarm clock on her bedside table. Mickey's right arm had to move through another twenty minutes before she'd go downstairs. From the bed she could see the full moon glaring balefully down. She had no alternative, she knew that. She'd considered telling her father, but she had no wish to see him hurt. Besides, what if he divorced Katherine, what then? More than half the kids in her class had divorced parents and they seemed to split into two camps: those who spent all their time shuttling between two homes and those who saw their fathers only every second Saturday. No. She couldn't face that. Whatever she did, her paramount concern was to keep her father happy.

One of Mersiha's first thoughts had been to confront Katherine, to tell her that she knew what she'd been up to and that she was to stop the affair immediately. But if she did that the relationship between them would sour for ever. And Mersiha was also scared that if she did try to put pressure on Katherine, she'd walk out. Mersiha knew that her adoptive parents had a rocky relationship. She'd heard them arguing late at night when they thought she was asleep, usually about money and occasionally about Luke. If Katherine knew that Mersiha had discovered the affair, it might be the last straw. Despite the arguments, she knew that her father loved Katherine, and it would break his heart if she left. That left only one course of action.

Mersiha looked across at the alarm clock. Fifteen more minutes. She wasn't worried about her parents hearing her moving about the house, but if they were awake they'd be sure to hear the car starting up. If there were any other way she'd have preferred not to have used the car, but Dr Brown lived more than twenty miles away in Parkton, to the north of Baltimore, and she could hardly call a taxi. She looked at the clock again. The minute-hand had barely moved. Mersiha decided not to wait any longer. It was agony lying and waiting. She had to do something or she'd go crazy.

She sat up and reached for the small flashlight she'd put in the top drawer of her bedside cabinet. She'd bought new batteries at a Rite-Aid store on the way to school the previous day. She switched the flashlight on and placed it on the bed so that it illuminated the closet. She took off her nightgown and slipped it under her pillow. The clothes she'd decided to wear – black Levi jeans and a black turtleneck pullover – were under her bed. She put them on, then slipped black boating shoes on to her feet. Her Baltimore Orioles baseball cap was on the chair by the window and she put it on, tucking her hair inside it. Her collection of stuffed animals sat together under the window. She put two of the biggest, a green hippo and a honey-coloured teddy bear, under the quilt and patted it down so that it gave the impression of a sleeping body. She picked up the flashlight and listened at the bedroom door. Once she was sure that the house was completely silent she pulled it slowly open and tiptoed into the hall and down the stairs, holding her breath all the way.

The door to her father's study was open and she crept inside. The cabinet where her father kept his guns was to the left of his desk, so she sat in his chair while she spun the combination lock. She'd seen him open it on several occasions, though she doubted that he realised that she'd memorised the combination. Fifteen to the left, eight to the right, nineteen to the left. Click. She pulled the door open and knelt down by the side of the cabinet. She sat back on her heels and looked at the wooden stocks and metal barrels as they gleamed in the moonlight. There were two pump-action shotguns which Tony and Katherine used when they went clay pigeon shooting at Loch Raven. Alongside them were several hunting rifles which used to belong to Katherine's father. He had died the year before Mersiha had come to America. Tony Freeman never hunted, but Katherine had refused to get rid of the guns and Tony respected her wishes to the extent that once a month he took them out and thoroughly cleaned and oiled them. Mersiha had sat and watched as he worked on the weapons, but he'd never allowed her to help.

On racks at the top of the metal-lined cabinet was a collection of pistols, all of which had been owned by Katherine's father. Several were collector's items, almost antiques, and until Mersiha had arrived they'd been on display on the wall. There were several turn-of-the-century Colts, an 1891 pearl-handled single-shot Smith and Wesson, a British Webley-Mars which had been used in the First World War, and others that Mersiha wasn't able to identify. There were several modern handguns, too, because Katherine's father had been a devout believer in self-defence. Some of the handguns were extremely powerful – a .357 Magnum-calibre Colt Python and a .44 Ruger Super Blackhawk – but Mersiha knew exactly which gun she wanted. It was in a case at the bottom of the cabinet, a Heckler & Koch HK-4. It was similar to a gun her brother had used in Bosnia. What made it different from most other guns was that it came with four separate barrels, springs and magazines so that it could be assembled in four different configurations, allowing it to make use of different-calibre bullets: .22 LR, .25 ACP, .32 ACP, and .380 ACP. Mersiha's brother had always said that they never knew what ammunition they'd pick up, so the HK-4 gave him a flexibility that might one day save their lives. Mersiha smiled grimly. How wrong he'd been.

She took the case down and opened it. The gun lay in a thick piece of foam rubber, all its various extra components laid out in their own pre-cut slots. The gun was in its .380 ACP configuration which wasn't what Mersiha wanted, so she broke it down and reassembled it using the .22 LR components. At first she couldn't lift off the slide and barrel, then she remembered that she had to depress the latch in the trigger guard first. She felt as if her brother were chuckling over her shoulder as she moved the slide and barrel forward and then up.

When she was finished she put the case back on its shelf and closed the cabinet. From the bottom drawer of her father's desk she took a small steel key. The safe where her father kept the ammunition was set into the floor under a wooden panel behind the door. There was a box of .22

cartridges there and she took out half a dozen and one by one slotted them into the gun's magazine. She closed her eyes and held the gun against her cheek, the metal cold to the touch. The memories flooded back. Her brother, shooting a Serb soldier in the back as he was running away, then laughing and shooting him again in the head as he lay on the floor. Her brother holding the gun to the groin of a Serb sniper, taunting him before blowing his manhood off. It seemed as if all her recollections of Stjepan involved the gun. She opened her eyes and tried to imagine her brother without a gun in his hand. It was hard. She sifted through the mental images that were all that remained of him. There was always a gun or a rifle there somewhere. She tried going back, to the time before the Serbian invasion of her homeland, to the time when their mother had taught them English on the kitchen table after they'd cleared the supper plates away. She could hold that picture in her head, the way their mother had tutted whenever they made a mistake, the way she'd smiled when they'd done well, but her memory played tricks with her. Instead of a pencil in Stjepan's hand, there was a gun. The gun. The HK-4. They'd taken everything from her, the Serbs. They'd taken her parents. Her brother. And her memories. She realised with a jolt that her finger was tensing on the trigger and that the safety wasn't on. She looked at her wristwatch. It was time to go.

Buffy was asleep in her basket but her ears pricked up and her eyes opened as soon as Mersiha stepped into the kitchen. 'Shhhh!' Mersiha whispered. The keys to Katherine's car were hanging on a hook by the kitchen door. Buffy whined, asking to go out, but Mersiha glared at her and pointed to the dog's basket. 'Bed,' she hissed. Buffy did as she was told, her tail between her legs.

Mersiha slipped out of the kitchen and carefully closed the door behind her. It was a cool night and she breathed in the night air like a drowning man. Her heart was racing so fast that she thought it would explode. She put a hand to her chest and took deep breaths. It wasn't what she was about to do that made her so nervous, it was the fear of getting caught. Of what her father would say. Of the hurt she'd see in his eyes.

She switched the flashlight on and walked across the grass to the garage. Both cars were parked there. She pushed Katherine's car out on to the road before starting the engine. It had been a long time since she had been behind the wheel of a vehicle. Her new parents had steadfastly refused to allow her to drive their cars, insisting that she wait until her sixteenth birthday. She'd never told them she'd learnt to drive when she was twelve years old, that her brother had fixed wooden blocks to the pedals of an old Russian truck so that her feet could reach and so that she could change gear without the sound of crunching metal. She used to drive while her brother and his friends rode in the back, guns at the ready, and compared with the war-torn roads of Bosnia, Route 83 North from Baltimore was a breeze. She kept the car at just under the speed limit all the way to Parkton. She knew there would be few police around at that time of night, but there was no point in tempting fate. The further away from her house she drove, the calmer she felt. By the time she arrived in Parkton she was completely calm, totally focused on what lay ahead.

*   *   *

Art Brown always slept face down, had done ever since he'd been at college and a friend of his had died after an all-night drinking session, choked on his own vomit. After a few years it had become a habit, and now, a quarter of a century after the death of his friend, he couldn't sleep in any other position. The right side of his face was pressed into the pillow, his eye squashed shut, but he could open his left eye to see the blue luminous figures of his bedside clock. It was a quarter past two. Something had woken him from a deep sleep, a noise from somewhere downstairs. Normally he never woke up in the middle of the night so he listened intently, trying to pin down whatever it was that had startled him awake. Maybe he'd left a door open, or it could have been a car backfiring. Parkton wasn't a hotbed of crime – burglaries were relatively rare because most of the homeowners were armed or had big dogs, and the crime of choice among the well-heeled suburban residents tended to be tax evasion rather than breaking and entering. Somewhere off in the distance a dog barked. Maybe that was it, he thought. Maybe it had been the dog.

He closed his eyes and relaxed, trying to get back to sleep. The warmth of the bed turned his mind to thoughts of Katherine Freeman. God, the woman was incredible; there wasn't anything she wouldn't do in bed. He sighed as he remembered the last time she'd come to his house. She'd walked straight by him as soon as he'd opened the door and headed up the stairs unbuttoning her dress and calling over her shoulder that she could only spare an hour.

By the time he'd run up the stairs she was lying naked on the bed, a sly smile on her lips. She hadn't even given him time to take off his shoes, let alone his trousers. She'd motioned with her finger for him to lie on the bed, then she'd expertly unzipped his trousers and slipped him inside her, fastening her legs around his waist so that he couldn't have withdrawn even if he'd wanted to. He'd exploded inside her in a matter of seconds, but she'd carried on moving, pounding against him until he'd grown hard again. She knew just what to say and do to get a man aroused and to keep him that way until she'd been satisfied. And God, the woman took some satisfying.

Brown could feel himself growing hard. Even when she wasn't with him, she could turn him on. He knew it was unethical, sleeping with a patient's mother, but he'd known that the first day she'd stepped into his office. She was so obviously available, it had stood out a mile, and within a week of their meeting she'd been in his bed. He knew that he was taking advantage of the resentment she felt towards her husband following the death of their son, and he doubted that he was the only extra-marital lover she had, but he couldn't stop himself. Their relationship was purely sexual. They had almost nothing in common except for bed and her daughter, and he knew there was no question of her ever leaving her husband to live with him, but for the moment that was enough for him. He sighed as he remembered how she'd taken him in her mouth, straddling his chest as she went down on him, brushing his thighs with her hair. Brown slid his hand down the bed, between his legs. If he couldn't have her there and then, at least he could have her in his mind. He gripped himself tightly, and pictured her soft, wet mouth.

'Dr Brown?' At first he thought he'd imagined the whisper, that he was hearing Katherine in his mind, but when the voice spoke again he realised that there was someone else in the room. His eyes shot open and he whipped his head around, so fast that he heard his neck crack. He was still lying on his right arm, still holding himself, and he couldn't raise his chest off the bed.

'Who is it?' he mumbled, his throat so dry that the words sounded strangled. It was a girl's voice. What the hell was a girl doing in his bedroom? He felt something hard press against the back of his neck. Something hard and circular. His stomach churned as he realised what it was. The barrel of a gun.

'Don't move,' the girl said. It wasn't a ghetto voice, that much he was sure. There was none of the sing-song bravado that he heard in the voices of the inner-city kids whom he treated at his surgery whenever the city's welfare services came up with the money. The girl was young, the accent suburban, the voice vaguely familiar. The pressure of the gun increased as she leant across and switched on the brass lamp on his bedside cabinet. He could see her out of the corner of his left eye, but not clearly enough to recognise her. He heard a clunking sound and then three musical tones. She'd picked up the phone and dialled a three-figure number. He realised with a feeling of dread that she'd called 911. Emergency services.

'Yes,' she said, quietly. 'Send an ambulance to 113 Lauriann Court, Parkton. Gunshot wound.' She replaced the receiver, then Brown felt the gun barrel pull away. 'Turn over,' she said.

Brown rolled on to his back. His right arm tingled as

the blood began to flow again. 'Mersiha?' he said as he recognised his visitor. 'What's going on?'

Mersiha Freeman was standing at the left side of the bed, a gun in her right hand and two towels draped over her left arm. Her black hair was hidden in a baseball cap and her face seemed unnaturally white in the light from the lamp. He tried to sit up, but Mersiha pointed the gun at his head. 'Stay where you are,' she said, her voice cold and flat.

'What are you doing?' he asked. His mind was racing. Mersiha had never shown any violent tendencies in all the time she'd been undergoing therapy, and she'd seemed perfectly rational during their last session. She was generally a bright, well-balanced girl, and while she had problems, they weren't the sort that would be expected to lead to her standing in her therapist's bedroom brandishing a pistol.

She threw a towel at him and it fell across his chest. He'd last seen it hanging on a rail by the shower in the guest bedroom. 'We can talk about this, Mersiha,' he said. It was important to get her talking, he knew. He was a trained psychiatrist, she was just a troubled teenager; once they began communicating he'd be able to calm her down. He'd dealt with manic depressive teens before. They were relatively easy to defuse, once you got them talking. 'I want you to tell me what's upset you. We've always gotten along so well in the past. I'm not just your doctor, I'm your friend.'

Mersiha wrapped the other towel around her right hand, enveloping the gun so that all that could be seen was the last half-inch of the barrel. 'There isn't any problem that can't be solved by talking it through,' Brown said. He flashed his professional smile, but his legs were shaking under the quilt.

'Hold the towel,' she said, waving the gun at his chest. He gripped the towel with his right hand. She took hold of the quilt and pulled it off the bed. He was naked and he could feel his penis shrivel and his scrotum contract.

'Mersiha, come on, this is getting out of hand,' he said, unable to stop his voice from quivering.

'You will not see Katherine. Ever again.'

'What are you talking about?' Brown said.

'You know what I'm talking about. If you even so much as talk to her, I'll kill you. Do you understand?'

'Mersiha, listen to me. What happened between your mother and me, it didn't mean anything. It doesn't mean that she doesn't love you.' Brown could see that she wasn't listening, he wasn't getting through to her. He looked across at the telephone. If she really had spoken to 911, it wouldn't take more than fifteen minutes for the ambulance to arrive, and the police would be sure to come, too. Gunshot, she'd said. Brown tried to calculate how long they'd been talking. Two minutes. Three, maybe.

'This isn't about Katherine,' Mersiha said. 'It's about my father. I don't want him hurt. If he ever found out . . .'

'He won't!' Brown interrupted. 'I swear. I swear on my own mother's life. But please, don't shoot.'

'I have to,' she said quietly. 'Don't you see, Dr Brown? I have to demonstrate to you that I'm serious, otherwise you'll think I'm just acting like a child.'

'I don't think you're acting like a child, Mersiha. But if you really want to behave like an adult, you should put the gun down and talk this over with me. Will you do that?' His voice was shaking and he could feel that his whole body was bathed in sweat.

Mersiha shook her head. 'Listen to me, and listen good.

If you ever see Katherine again, I'll kill you. If you call our house again, I'll kill you. If my father ever finds out that you slept with her, I'll kill you. Do you understand?'

Brown nodded, unable to speak.

'No one will believe that a fifteen-year-old girl did this to you. But if you tell anyone what I did, I'll come back and kill you. Do you understand?'

Brown nodded again. He stared at the gun barrel protruding from the towel, praying that she'd left the safety on, that she didn't know how a gun worked, that she was only trying to scare him. How long? Four minutes? Five? Oh God, they wouldn't get here in time.

Mersiha wound a flap of towel over the front of the gun barrel so that the whole weapon was now hidden from his view. Brown suddenly realised why she was covering the gun: to deaden the sound when she fired. 'Mersiha . . . please . . .' he whispered. He felt his bowels relax and a warm glow spread between his legs. He'd soiled himself.

Mersiha aimed the gun at his left leg and fired. Brown's leg jerked and he felt as if he'd been whacked with a baseball bat. A hole the size of a quarter spouted blood a couple of inches below his left knee. He was surprised at the pain. It felt more like a dull throb than what he thought a gunshot wound should feel like, but gradually the ache was replaced by a bolt of searing heat, like a red-hot poker being twisted in the wound. The rest of his body felt as if it had been chilled in comparison, and he began to shake violently. He could smell his own mess and he felt sick.

'Use the towel,' Mersiha said.

Brown looked up as if he'd forgotten that she was there.

'The towel,' she repeated. 'Use it to stop the bleeding.'

Mersiha turned and walked out of the room. She didn't look back.

She walked to the car, resisting the urge to run. If she were unlucky enough to be seen leaving the house any witnesses would be more likely to remember someone running. She kept her head down so that the peak of the cap hid her face. She'd tucked the gun into the waistband of her trousers and pulled the sweater down over it. The towel she carried, swinging it as if she didn't have a care in the world. The expended cartridge had caught in the cotton material and she'd been careful not to drop it. Now it nestled in her back pocket.

The car engine was still cooling, clicking like an insect, and it roared into life as soon as she turned the key. She kept the lights off until she'd got to the end of the road, then switched them on. She headed towards 83 South, the gun pressing against her stomach like an erection.

She heard the ambulance before she saw its flashing lights, then it rushed by her, heading for Dr Brown's house. She didn't see any police cars but she was sure that one would be sent to investigate the shooting. She smiled as she wondered what Dr Brown would tell them. She knew she was taking a risk: if the psychiatrist told them that she'd shot him, they'd be able to get to her house long before she got home. They'd be waiting for her, standing at her doorway with the handcuffs ready, her adoptive parents wringing their hands and wondering where they'd gone wrong. She snorted quietly. It would never happen, not in a million years. Dr Brown had too much to lose. It would all come out, the fact that he'd been sleeping with the mother of a patient, and the tabloids would love that. But it wasn't just the fear of being exposed that would keep the psychiatrist's lips sealed. He'd looked into her eyes as she'd pulled the trigger, and she knew what he'd seen there. He'd seen the eyes of a killer, someone who'd killed before and who would have no compunction about killing again. She was just as capable of putting a bullet into his brain as she was of shooting him in the leg. It was ironic. He'd tried for almost three years to get some understanding of what went on in her mind, yet he'd learned more about her in the few minutes she'd spent in his bedroom, too late for him to use the knowledge.

Mersiha wound down the window, checked in the mirror to see that there was no traffic behind her, and tossed the towel out. It whirled through the air, flapping like a clumsy bird, and then she lost sight of it. She looked at the dashboard clock. She'd been away from the house for less than an hour. Just as she'd planned.

She switched the headlights off as she got within a half-mile of her house, put the car in neutral and switched the engine off as she approached the driveway, coasting the last hundred yards into the garage.

Buffy was out of her basket as soon as she heard the kitchen door creak open. She wagged her tail furiously and barked with delight, but Mersiha clamped her hands around her muzzle. 'Hush!' she hissed. Buffy struggled, trying to get free, but Mersiha tightened her grip. 'Be quiet,' she whispered. Buffy put her tail between her legs, not sure why she was being punished, but Mersiha didn't release her until the dog had calmed down. She pointed to the basket and Buffy obeyed, looking at her mistress with sad eyes, hoping for a sign that her anger was only temporary. Once the dog had curled up and put her nose on her tail, Mersiha stroked her behind the ears. 'Good girl,' she whispered. 'That's a good girl.' Buffy's tail flickered but she kept low in the basket and made no sound.

Mersiha put the car keys back on the hook by the door and tiptoed through the hall to her father's study. She closed the door quietly and then opened the gun cabinet and took out the HK-4's case. Working quickly and quietly, she reassembled the gun in its original configuration and put the barrel, spring and magazine she'd used back in their compartments. She stared at the case, checked that nothing was missing, then closed it and put it back in the cabinet, resetting the combination lock. Then she opened the safe in the floor and put back the unused ammunition. She put the key back in the bottom drawer and crept back upstairs to her bedroom. Ten minutes later she was fast asleep.

Freeman was buttering toast when Mersiha came downstairs, still in her nightdress. 'Hiya, pumpkin,' he said. 'You're up early.'

'So are you,' she said, taking one of the slices of toast.

'Hey, that's mine,' he laughed. She raised her eyebrows and took a big bite, then handed it back to him. 'That's okay, keep it,' he said. He patted his stomach. 'I guess one piece is enough for me. Katherine says I could stand to lose some weight.'

'You look fine,' she said, 'for a dad.'

'What do you mean, for a dad?'

'You know,' she said, sitting down and pouring herself a mug of coffee.

'I'm not sure that I do. Do you want jelly?' Freeman still had difficulty referring to strawberry jam as jelly. To Freeman, jelly conjured up images of the green wobbly stuff with whipped cream on top, served at birthday parties to screaming children. To Americans, jelly meant jam, and to make it worse they often insisted on eating it with peanut butter.

Mersiha shook her head. 'I mean, you're in great shape – for someone your age. You know what I mean.'

'Thanks, pumpkin.'

'Now you're mad at me. That's what I get for being honest.'

Freeman scraped some of the butter off and put the dirty knife in the sink. That should save at least twenty calories, he thought. 'I'm not mad,' he said.

Mersiha giggled. 'If it makes you feel any better, Allison Dooley said she thought you were kinda cute.'

'Yeah? Which one's she?'

Mersiha popped the last morsel of toast into her mouth. 'The girl I have riding lessons with. Short mousy hair, braces. Acne like you wouldn't believe.'

Freeman grinned. 'Enough. And don't talk with your mouth full,' he said, wagging a finger at her.

'I've finished,' she said, wiping her hands on a piece of kitchen roll. 'So why are you up so early?'

Freeman sat down at the table and stirred a spoonful of sugar into his coffee. 'We've organised a demonstration for a group of overseas buyers over at the Aberdeen Proving

Grounds. I've got to get there early to help set things up. What's your excuse?'

'English test. I need some last-minute cramming.'

'Yeah? What's the subject?'

'Thomas Wolfe. We've been reading *You Can't Go Home Again*.'

Freeman nodded. 'It's a good book. One of the great American novels.'

'I've never understood why Americans keep calling their language English.'

'They're probably too lazy to change it,' Freeman said, as Katherine walked into the kitchen.

'Too lazy for what?' she asked, patting Mersiha on the head.

'Nothing,' Mersiha said. She stood up and went back upstairs.

Freeman picked up his briefcase and kissed Katherine on the cheek. 'Today's the big day. Keep your fingers crossed.'

'Sure, honey.' She opened the door for him and patted him on the shoulder as he went out, the way a mother might say goodbye to a child. There was something vaguely condescending about the gesture and Freeman wondered if she was annoyed with him. He wished that he had time to talk to her, but he was already behind schedule.

He drove north to the Aberdeen military base, calling Anderson on the car phone to confirm that he'd be there by eight o'clock. Anderson was in one of the company vans and was just driving on to the base. Aberdeen had once been a thriving military town, with tens of thousands of soldiers and support services, everything from softball leagues to amateur dramatics, but it had shrunk to little more than a token presence. Another victim of the peace dividend.

By the time Freeman arrived, Anderson was supervising the setting-up of the observation area, little more than a temporary stage on which seats would be placed, and a backdrop illustrating the MIDAS equipment under large letters spelling out: Minefield Immediate De-activation System.

Two of the firm's technicians were planting smoke grenades on a prepared area of turf several thousand metres square. Freeman went over and nodded his approval. 'Hiya, Tony,' said one of the technicians, a portly, balding man called Alex Reynolds who had been with the company for twenty-six years. 'This is the big one, right?'

'It'll be great if it comes off, so don't spare the grenades,' Freeman said. 'Lots of smoke, lots of bangs.'

Anderson walked over and slapped Freeman on the back. 'Hiya, Tony. You ready?'

'Sure,' Freeman said. 'Are the VIPs all taken care of?'

Anderson nodded. 'I wined and dined them and dropped them at their hotel at one o'clock in the morning. I thought Arabs didn't drink, but these guys were really putting it away.'

'I hope they don't arrive with hangovers,' Freeman said.

'Don't worry. It'll be just fine. One of their generals was telling me that the sale's a foregone conclusion, they're only over here because they wanted to visit New York so that their wives could do some serious shopping.'

'So we're an excuse, is that it? Great. Just great.'

Anderson grinned. 'Listen to what I'm saying, will you? They're going to buy the system no matter what happens today. They'd have bought it sight unseen. I can handle these guys, they were eating out of my hands last night.'

'Not the left one, I hope.'

'Come on, guys, I've got to concentrate on these,' Reynolds said. 'They're only blanks but I could still lose a hand.'

Freeman nodded and he and Anderson walked back to the observation platforms. 'They're going to be picked up in limousines?'

'Stretch limos. Stop worrying.'

'And you've got back-up systems, just in case?'

'I've got a dozen in reserve. Come on, relax. Hey, what do you call a castrated blind elk with no legs?' Freeman shrugged. 'Still no fucking eye-deer,' Anderson said.

Freeman smiled at the bad joke and wiped his hands on his trousers. 'Look at this, the sweat's pouring off me. Do you think we should get fans or something?'

'Tony, they're fucking Arabs. They're not gonna be worried about the heat.' He stood in front of Freeman, his hands on his hips. 'Do you want me to handle this? You're not looking well.'

'No, it's okay. I'm just a bit under the weather, that's all.' He looked up at Anderson and forced a smile. 'Really, I'll be fine.'

Anderson didn't look convinced. 'I'm gonna give the systems a final once-over, just to be on the safe side. I think worry's contagious.'

Freeman sat back in the chair, his hands clasped behind his neck as he surveyed the testing area. Anderson was right. The equipment wouldn't fail, and the buyers would be impressed. It was as safe as money in the bank. He was worrying about nothing.

THE BIRTHDAY GIRL

*   *   *

The delegation arrived promptly, ferried from the Peabody Court Hotel in two black stretch limousines. Anderson had even arranged for their country's flag to be flying from the car aerials. Freeman looked over at Anderson and nodded his approval. It was a nice touch.

There were six men in the party, two of them in flowing white robes, three in green military uniforms with golden epaulets, rows of medals and matching black moustaches, and the youngest wore a sharp Italian suit and carried a black leather briefcase. Anderson had seen the man open the briefcase at the hotel and he'd gleefully told Freeman that it contained cash – bundles of hundred-dollar bills. They greeted Anderson like a long-lost brother and shook hands with Freeman. Freeman introduced them to Josh Bowers. The Arabs greeted him with curt nods. It was clear that they regarded him as a hired hand.

Anderson ushered them to their seats and handed them leather-bound folders containing the company's latest promotional literature and photographs of the MIDAS equipment being used by Thai troops on the Cambodian border.

'Gentlemen, thank you for coming,' Freeman said. 'Over the next half-hour we hope to persuade you that MIDAS is the system of choice when it comes to quick, efficient breaching of minefields.'

From a table to his left, Freeman picked up a dummy landmine, a plastic disc the size of a side plate. He held it up. 'The modern landmine,' he said. 'Plastic container,

133

filled with explosive, no metal parts to be detected by traditional means. Cost to the buyer, a little over three dollars. Cost to the infantry crossing the minefield – at best a wounded man who needs immediate evacuation, at worst a dead soldier or disabled equipment. Dropped from helicopters, scattered from planes or missiles, huge areas can be blanketed with mines which then remain deadly for decades. Anti-personnel mines can slow down advancing troops, or can be used by terrorists for maximum disruption at minimum cost.'

Freeman threw the mine on to the ground in front of him. It was a dummy, but he had to suppress a smile when he saw one of the generals flinch. 'What is needed is a cost-effective system that can neutralise such fields without the need for specialised units,' he continued. 'The beauty of the MIDAS system is that it can be carried and utilised by standard ground troops with a minimum of training.'

Two of Freeman's employees, men who worked on the MIDAS production line, stepped out of one of the trailers, dressed in desert camouflage fatigues and black combat boots. They were carrying M16s and on their backs were MIDAS haversacks in matching camouflage material.

'Picture the scenario. A platoon, isolated from its main force, finds itself cut off by a minefield. Enemy troops are close behind, time is running out. In the normal course of events, it would take more than five hours to clear a path just a hundred metres long. The platoon would be lost. But with MIDAS, it's a different story.'

The two men jogged to the edge of the prepared area. 'The clock is ticking,' Freeman said. The men knelt down, put their rifles on the ground and slipped off their haversacks. They opened the haversacks and each lifted out a plastic tray. From the tray they each took out a grey bulbous projectile, about the size of a bottle of washing-up liquid. There was a fitting on the bottom which screwed into the barrel of their rifle, and they installed them with quick twists. 'Thirty seconds,' Freeman said.

The men lay on the ground, pointed their rifles over the field and turned to look at Freeman. He nodded, and a second later both men fired. The projectiles soared into the air in a puff of smoke accompanied by a dull, thudding explosion. They arced through the air, pulling a line behind them which whistled as it unwound from the bottom of the haversacks.

'The rocket-assisted projectile pulls two hundred metres of explosive line behind it,' Freeman explained as the projectile fell to the ground. 'Because of the rocket's on-board gyroscopic guidance system, the line shows a deviation of less than one degree from its intended trajectory. Forty-five seconds have passed.'

The men took small metallic pistol grips from the haversacks and looked across at Freeman again. He nodded, and they pressed small rubber switches on the sides of the grips. The explosive lines detonated, kicking up earth and grass and creating plumes of black smoke. The detonation was accompanied by a series of explosions and puffs of white smoke as the grenades went off. The wind was coming from the east and it blew the smoke to the side, away from the observation platform. Freeman had insisted that Anderson check the wind direction in advance.

'The explosive line clears a path over a metre wide through the minefield, simultaneously detonating all mines close to the line and those that are tripwire-activated. In less than one minute our platoon has two metre-wide paths through the minefield.'

The two men picked up the haversacks and their M16s and jogged along the cleared paths to the other side of the prepared field. At the far end they turned and waved their weapons above their heads.

Freeman turned back to the observers. 'And that, gentlemen, is the MIDAS touch.' He smiled to show that he knew it was a bad joke. The Arabs looked at him blankly so Freeman quickly continued. 'Several of the systems can be used together to provide a path for vehicles, or to clear airfields that have been immobilised. The MIDAS system comes complete with markers to define the cleared path, and a dozen lightsticks so that it can be followed at night.'

He looked across at Anderson to see if there was anything he hadn't covered. Anderson nodded his approval. Freeman clasped his hands together at waist level as he addressed the visitors. 'I can confidently say that our mine clearance system is more effective, more economical and more portable than any produced by our competitors. In addition, we can guarantee immediate delivery on any order up to five hundred units and our production line is capable of assembling new units at the rate of one hundred a week.' One of the military officials put up a black gloved hand to stifle a yawn and Freeman realised that it was time to draw the presentation to a close. 'If there are any questions, we'd be more than happy to answer them.'

The Arabs looked at each other, but no one had anything to say. Five minutes later they were in their limousines, heading for the airport.

'What do you think?' Freeman asked Anderson as they watched them go.

'Piece of cake,' his partner said.

'The military guys seemed bored.'

'That's just their way. They don't want to appear too keen, that's all. Their order will be on my desk before the week's out.' He sniffed and pinched his nose.

'Are you okay?' Freeman asked. Anderson's eyes looked red, as if he'd been rubbing them.

'Head cold,' Anderson said. 'I've got some medicine back at the office.'

'Hell, you should take the rest of the day off. You've earned it. Go to bed with a couple of whiskies, sweat it out.'

'Yeah, maybe I will,' Anderson said. 'You can hold the fort?'

Freeman pulled a face. 'What's to hold?'

Anderson held up an admonishing finger. 'I won't listen to this. You're turning into Mr Gloomy again.'

'Go home, Maury.'

Anderson slapped him on the back and went over to the car park where he'd left his white Corvette.

Freeman went over to the field where Alex Reynolds was patiently disarming and digging up the smoke grenades that hadn't been detonated during the demonstration. 'You did a good job, Alex,' he said.

'It's a great system. They'd be crazy not to buy it,' Reynolds said. 'What do you think?'

Freeman looked across to the car park, where Anderson

was over-revving his Corvette. 'I don't know. Just keep your fingers crossed.'

He spent the rest of the afternoon in his office deciding whether or not to book exhibition space for an arms show that was being organised in Berlin later in the year. It was important to keep the product on display – advertisements were all well and good, but they produced little in the way of hard orders. The arms shows were where the buyers went with their cheque books and shopping lists, and there was even an element of impulse buying among some of the Third World countries, especially once they realised that Freeman's company wasn't averse to paying 'commissions' to middle-men. But the shows were getting increasingly expensive, and there was no shortage of exhibitors. Following the break-up of the Soviet Union, dozens of new suppliers were flooding the market with products, some of them military surplus but much of them new equipment at prices well below those of Western manufacturers.

Far Eastern manufacturers were also trying to capture a bigger share of the market, and as most of them were subsidised they happily paid the extortionate charges the organisers were asking. Freeman's company didn't have the luxury of a government hand-out, and every penny counted. The smallest exhibition area at the Berlin show cost more than three thousand dollars a day, and that was before travelling and hotel expenses, plus the cost of shipping their equipment across the Atlantic. He read through the glossy brochure and studied the layout of the exhibition hall. On the back was a list of exhibitors who had already signed. The big boys were all there – multi-billion-dollar corporations from the United States and Europe such as McDonnell Douglas, General Dynamics, British Aerospace, Plessey, Thompson-CSF, and Deutsche Aerospace – and dozens of firms from all over the Far East were represented. Mitsubishi Heavy Industries had taken out a huge stand close to the refreshments area, a shrewd move. Chinese firms had already pre-booked five per cent of the space, and Freeman recognised one of them as being a rival manufacturer of mine clearance systems.

He knew that he had no choice, so he pulled out a company cheque book, made a cheque out for the deposit, and filled out the application form, requesting a small stand close to the main entrance. He dropped the envelope in his out tray and picked up his briefcase.

He drove home, his brow furrowed. His mind wasn't on the road and he almost clipped a car as he switched lanes on the highway. He waved an apology to the driver, a blue-rinsed old woman who was eating a hamburger as she drove with one hand, and forced himself to concentrate. It wasn't easy. The firm's financial problems kept creeping back into his thoughts, insidiously at first, a nagging worry at the back of his mind that wouldn't go away, but kept on growing until all he could think about was the negative cash flow, the salary bill and the lack of orders. He began to have imaginary conversations with possible buyers, his bankers, and with Anderson, and before long he was talking to himself out loud. He caught a truck driver looking at him and realised how it must look, a mumbling middle-aged man with a face like thunder. He turned the radio to a station playing classical music, hoping that would calm him down, and hummed quietly as he drove the rest of the way home.

Katherine's Toyota wasn't in the garage but the back door was open so he guessed that Mersiha was home. He dropped his briefcase on his desk, then called up the stairs, asking if she was there. She came running down the stairs and hugged him, then grabbed his hand and pulled him into the kitchen. 'Do you want a beer, or a soda?' she asked.

Freeman said he'd have a Coke and she took a can from the refrigerator, poured it into a glass for him and then sat down with him at the kitchen table. 'How did it go?' she asked.

Freeman reached over and ruffled her hair. It always amused him how much interest she showed in his business. 'No way of telling,' he said. 'We pulled out all the stops and they made appreciative noises, but the only thing that counts is if they come through with an order.'

'When will you know?'

'When the order arrives. Until then we just have to wait.'

'They're being inscrutable, huh?'

'It's the Chinese who are inscrutable. The Arabs are just impossible to read. Speaking of reading, how did the English test go?'

'It was a breeze.' She switched into a halting mid-European accent. 'Now I speak English good, yes?'

'Mersiha, you never spoke English like that, not even when I first met you.'

She switched back to her normal voice. 'Yeah, now I'm the all-American girl. Do you think I have an accent?'

Freeman shook his head. 'Only when you lose your temper,' he said.

'I do not!' she laughed.

He drained his glass. 'I'm going to shower,' he said. On his way out of the door he noticed that the red light was flashing on the bottom of the phone. He pressed the playback button. The message was from Nancy in Dr Brown's office. She asked if Katherine would call back as soon as possible. Freeman thought she sounded close to tears. He turned to look at Mersiha. 'Any idea what that's about?'

Mersiha shrugged. 'My appointment isn't until the day after tomorrow. Do you want me to call her?'

'No, that's okay. Tell Katherine when she gets back.' As he headed up the stairs he heard Katherine's car growling down the drive. 'There she is now,' he called down to Mersiha.

Five minutes later, as he was soaping himself in the shower, Katherine came into the bathroom. He saw her through the rippled glass screen as she leaned against the sink. 'Do you wanna join me, Kat?' he called. When she didn't reply, he slid the glass partition open. Katherine was deathly pale, her hands either side of her face, her steepled fingers covering her nose as if stifling a sneeze. 'What's wrong?' he said. A sudden fear gripped his heart. 'Is Mersiha all right?'

'It's Art Brown. He's been shot.'

'Shot? Is he okay?'

'He's in Johns Hopkins.'

Freeman got out of the shower and grabbed a towel. Water pooled around his feet as he went over to his wife. 'What happened?'

'Nancy said it was a prowler. Yesterday morning. He must have been in the house looking for something to steal and Art disturbed him. I can't believe it. What is this country coming to?'

Freeman wrapped the towel around his waist and held Katherine, trying to find a compromise position where he could comfort her without soaking her clothing. 'He's going to be all right, isn't he?' he asked.

Katherine nodded. 'He was shot in the leg. But the bullet just missed an artery, Nancy said. He could have died. In Parkton, of all places. The suburbs are supposed to be safe, for God's sake. It's not as if it happened in East Baltimore.'

Freeman stroked her hair. 'I know, I know,' was all he could think of saying.

'You're not even safe in your own home these days. Car-jackings, robberies, shootings, even in the suburbs.' She pulled away from him. There were damp patches on her shirt from his wet chest and he could see the outline of her breasts through the material. 'I'm going to lie down,' she said. 'Maybe I'll take a pill.'

Katherine often had trouble sleeping and she had a bottle of Sominex in her bedside cabinet. He watched her walk down the hallway to the bedroom, a little surprised at her reaction because it wasn't like her to show so much emotion, not since her father had died, anyway. An aunt, admittedly one with whom she'd had little contact in recent years, had died after a short illness a few months earlier and she hadn't shown a tenth of the grief she was showing over a bullet in Art Brown's leg. Freeman scratched his wet hair. Maybe it was because Dr Brown was closer to home. Katherine took Mersiha to all her sessions with the psychiatrist and they'd met socially at various charity functions, but even so her reaction seemed a little extreme. He wondered if there was something else worrying her.

He towelled himself dry, put on a bathrobe and went into their bedroom. She was already under the covers, a red satin sleep-mask over her eyes. The bottle of sleeping tablets was by the bed and she was snoring softly, but Freeman had the feeling that she was only pretending. He stood for a while, watching the slow rise and fall of the quilt, then he dressed in jeans and an old sweatshirt and went downstairs. Mersiha was still in the kitchen, sitting at the table and reading the *Baltimore Sun*.

She looked up and tapped an inside page of the newspaper. 'It's here,' she said. 'It happened yesterday morning. Isn't it amazing?'

Freeman sat down next to her and she slid the paper across to him. There were only half a dozen paragraphs on the page. The shooting in the leg of a Parkton psychiatrist wasn't considered a major news story on a day when two young girls had been killed in a drive-by shooting and a police officer had been shot in the chest during a city drugs bust. According to the article, an intruder had entered through an unlocked door and had surprised Dr Brown in his bedroom. The psychiatrist had told police that a young black male had threatened to shoot him unless he'd told him where he kept his money. When Dr Brown had insisted that there was no money in the house, the intruder had shot him once and fled. The description Dr Brown gave to the police fitted about half of the city's young black males. The gun had been a .22-calibre, the weapon of choice among inner-city drug dealers.

'Amazing, isn't it?' Mersiha said. 'I was supposed to see

him tomorrow evening. That's why Nancy called. I guess that means no more sessions for a while.'

Freeman folded the paper and gently rapped his daughter on the head. 'I'm sure it'll take more than a bullet in the leg to stop Dr Brown from seeing you. Katherine said he'll be out of hospital in a day or two.'

Mersiha shook her head. 'She said Nancy gave her the names of some other shrinks. She said Dr Brown wouldn't be working for a while.'

'We'll see,' Freeman said. 'And don't call them shrinks. At sixty dollars an hour they're highly trained professional psychiatrists, okay?'

Mersiha laughed. 'Sure, Dad. Whatever you say. Where's Katherine?'

Freeman nodded upstairs. 'In bed. She isn't feeling very well.'

'Shall I take her up something?'

'No, let her sleep. She's tired.' Freeman looked at his watch. 'Do you want to catch a movie?'

Mersiha's eyes widened. 'Yeah, sure!' she said. 'That'd be great.'

Katherine took the blue and white striped laundry bag out of the wicker basket and carried it over her shoulder to the bathroom opposite Mersiha's bedroom. She pulled out the laundry bag full of Mersiha's dirty clothes and dragged both bags down the stairs to the laundry room. After she'd emptied both bags on to the table, she quickly sorted through the pile, putting the whites on one side and everything else into the washing machine. She reached for a pair of Mersiha's black Levis and turned them inside out. There was something hard inside one of the back pockets. Katherine slid her fingers into the pocket and pulled out the object. It was a brass shell case, and it glittered under the fluorescent lights.

She frowned, tossed the cartridge into the air and caught it. She made a fist and put it to her lips, blowing into her clenched hand like a magician preparing to make it disappear, but when she opened her fingers it was still there. She put it into the pocket of her dress and carried on throwing the dirty laundry into the washing machine.

Later, with the machine started on its washing cycle, she poured coffee into two mugs and carried them through into the sitting room where her husband was sitting with his feet on the coffee table, a stack of papers on his lap.

'Thanks, honey,' he said.

Katherine put the mugs on the table and tossed him the brass cartridge. Freeman caught it one-handed. 'What's this?' he said, frowning.

'What does it look like?' she asked.

'I know what it is, honey. Why are you giving it to me?'

'I found it in Mersiha's jeans?'

'You what?'

'I found it in the back pocket of her jeans. I just want to know what we're going to do about it. Or to be more accurate, what you're going to do about it.'

'Me?'

Katherine raised one eyebrow archly. 'Tony, I don't want to keep repeating myself. That's a cartridge case, isn't it?'

Freeman nodded. 'Yeah, a .22 by the look of it. What on earth would she be doing with it?' He looked up. 'Do you think she got it at school?'

'I've no idea,' Katherine said.

'Have you found anything else?'

'I haven't searched her room, if that's what you mean. You know how closely she guards her privacy. I think you're going to have to talk to her. She's being funny with me at the moment.'

'Funny?'

'She doesn't seem to want even to be in the same room with me.'

'What sparked that off?'

'God knows. But I don't think she's in the mood for a heart-to-heart, not with me anyway. Besides, she's always been a daddy's girl.'

Freeman couldn't help but smile. 'We're both her parents. Maybe we should tackle her together.'

Katherine shook her head. 'She's sure to feel threatened if we both confront her.'

'Toss you for it?' Freeman joked.

Katherine pointed her finger at her husband. 'It's your turn.'

'What do you mean, my turn? I tell you what, you take this one, and I'll give her the sex talk. Deal?'

Katherine smiled. 'You know full well that I gave her the sex talk two years ago. And the menstruation talk. And the drugs talk.'

'I did the drugs talk,' Freeman reminded her.

'You gave her the first drugs talk – I had to redo it a couple of weeks later. Your jokes about not remembering much about the sixties garbled the message somewhat.'

'Okay, okay,' Freeman said, holding up his hands in surrender. 'I'll give her the gun talk.'

'We just have to know where she got it from, that's all.'

'She might have found it.' Freeman slipped the cartridge case into his shirt pocket. 'So, what's happening with Art?'

Katherine lit a cigarette, took a deep drag and then exhaled before replying. 'I don't know. I just don't know. I can't even get through to him on the phone. All Nancy will say is that he's reducing his workload and that we should get someone else. She's nice about it and all, but it's like talking to a brick wall.'

'It doesn't make sense,' Freeman said. 'He said she was making progress. I can't see how he can drop her and call himself a professional. Do you think I should have a word with him?'

Katherine shuddered as if something cold had trickled down her back. 'Maybe. I don't know. Whatever you like.'

'Are you okay?' He reached out and put his hand on her wrist. She smiled nervously and slowly withdrew her hand from his touch, using it to brush her hair needlessly behind her ear.

They sat in silence for a while. Freeman didn't know why she was being so cold. He couldn't imagine what he'd done to upset her. He ran the conversation back in his mind, searching in vain for a clue to her annoyance.

'I'll speak to her, don't worry,' he said. 'But I'm sure it's nothing. Is she asleep now?'

'It's after eleven. What do you think?'

Freeman realised that whatever he said would only make

matters worse. He decided to say nothing. He picked up his papers and pretended to study them. Katherine glared at him for a few seconds before she realised he wasn't going to answer. 'I'm going to bed,' she said frostily, extinguishing her cigarette. 'Don't wake me when you come up.' Her high heels tapped across the floor, echoing like pistol shots.

It was the same dream as always, but that didn't make it any easier to bear. Mersiha knew that she was dreaming, and part of her even knew that she was actually lying safe in her bedroom, but the terror and shame she felt were every bit as intense as if it were actually happening to her in the real world.

Her mother was there, but then she always was in the dream: screaming and pleading, held down by the men with guns. Mersiha was pleading, too, not for herself but for her mother, begging the men to leave her alone. The room was dark, but she could see the faces of the men, sweating skin and wide eyes, mouths distorted with hatred and lust, and she could see the blood on her mother's mouth, like badly applied lipstick. Hands grabbed for Mersiha, hands that ripped at her clothes and pinched and slapped, not because she was resisting but because they wanted to hurt her. They wanted her to cry, but she refused to give them the satisfaction. No matter what they did to her they would see only contempt in her eyes.

She was lifted bodily off the ground by unseen hands and rotated like lamb on a spit as her clothes were torn from her, and then they threw her down on to one of the many mattresses that were lying on the floor. She began to scream, knowing what was going to happen and that there was nothing she could do to prevent it. She began to scream, in pain, in sorrow, and, more than anything, in anger.

Freeman sat by the side of Mersiha's bed, rubbing the palms of his hands together. He hated to see the way his daughter was suffering, but Art Brown's advice had been unequivocal – waking her in the middle of a nightmare would do her more harm than good. The dreams had to run their course – it was her mind's way of dealing with the trauma. It was a healing process, like the gradual closing of a wound.

Mersiha tossed, her face bathed in sweat, her arms trying to fend off unseen assailants. Freeman could only imagine what she was going through. He reached over and stroked her forehead, hoping that in some way she'd know he was there, with her, even though she was still asleep. Her mouth opened and closed as if she were forming words, but no sounds came. He tried to read her lips, but whatever she was saying in her dream, it wasn't English. At least she wasn't screaming any more. She began shaking her head from side to side, her arms outstretched. Despite the torment she was going through, she wasn't crying. She looked angry, and for some reason he couldn't understand on a conscious level, Freeman was suddenly immensely proud of her.

*　　*　　*

Lennie Nelson unscrewed the cap from his plastic bottle of Evian water and put it next to his salad. He stabbed a piece of cucumber with his white plastic fork, dipped it in the Dijon mustard dressing and ate it as he studied his notes on Ventura Investments. He had gone as far as he could in discovering who was behind the investment vehicle, and his workload didn't allow him the luxury of the extended investigation he knew would be necessary if he was to make any further progress.

He'd called the Securities and Exchange Commission. They had no record of Ventura, but that was hardly surprising because it wasn't a public company and didn't appear to have raised money by issuing shares. The Corporations Bureau in Annapolis also drew a blank. The nature of the investment suggested a limited partnership, but he'd scoured state records to no avail. This surprised him, because he was sure that Maury Anderson had said that Ventura was composed of local investors. That had sparked the thought that maybe the investors had something to hide, and that thought had led swiftly to Delaware. Companies operating all over the United States were incorporated in Delaware to take advantage of the state's favourable regulations and low tax rates.

He contacted a company search operation in Wilmington, and in less than a day they'd struck gold – Ventura Investments was indeed a limited partnership. But the only name on file was that of a New York lawyer and the only address was the lawyer's Seventh Avenue office.

There was no way of telling who the actual principals were, and Nelson knew that it would take more than a phone call to the lawyer to find out. He speared a chunk of tomato and chewed it thoughtfully. New York was closer to home, and he had good contacts in the Big Apple, but whichever way he played it he was going to come up against an impenetrable wall of silence. Impenetrable by legal means, anyway. What Nelson had to decide was how far he wanted to push it. He remembered how nervous CRW's financial director had been during the board meeting. The man was definitely hiding something.

Nelson made up his mind. He reached for his Rolodex. The card containing Ernie Derbyshire's address and phone number was well thumbed. As usual the private detective wasn't in his office, but Nelson left a message on his answering machine.

Nancy looked up, startled, as Tony Freeman entered the waiting room. She positively beamed when she recognised him. 'Mr Freeman,' she said. 'We're not expecting you, are we?'

'No, Nancy, I just dropped by to see Dr Brown. Is he in with a patient?' Freeman could tell from her face that he wasn't, but she quickly recovered and held up a hand like a policeman attempting to stop traffic. There were small scratches on her hand, as if she'd been gripped by strong fingers with unclipped nails, and as he got closer to the reception desk Freeman could see a faded yellow bruise under her left eye. She put a hand up to the old injury as if trying to conceal it from his gaze. Freeman smiled to ease her embarrassment. 'I just wanted a few words with him, Nancy.'

'I'll have to ring through first . . .' she began to say, reaching for the intercom, but Freeman was already on his way to Art's office.

The psychiatrist was sitting on one of his couches, his left leg sticking out to the side. The left trouser leg had been cut up to the thigh, presumably to allow for the bandage underneath, and was held together with safety clips. Brown jumped as if he'd been given an electric shock. 'Tony? What's wrong?' he asked.

'Just wanted a few words, Art,' Freeman said, closing the door behind him. 'How's the leg?'

'Healing,' Brown said. 'I was lucky. An inch either way and the bullet would've shattered the kneecap or gone through the artery.'

Freeman sat on the edge of the psychiatrist's desk, crossing his arms, as if it were his office and Brown the visitor. 'I see it hasn't stopped you from working.'

Brown's eyes narrowed, and for several beats the two men stared at each other like poker players trying to get the measure of their opponent. 'I'm cutting back on my workload, Tony,' the psychiatrist said eventually. 'I have to. The assault was a real shock to my system. It's not just the physical damage.'

Freeman nodded sympathetically. 'That sounds like the sensible thing to do,' he agreed. 'But I don't understand why you have to stop seeing Mersiha. I'd have thought that a teenager with her sort of background would have been one of your priorities.'

Brown licked his lips nervously. 'I've given Katherine

a list of alternative therapists,' he said. 'They'll be more than happy to take her on.'

'Nancy gave her two names, Art. Two.'

'I'll give you more. There's no shortage of good people in Baltimore.' Brown's cheeks were beginning to redden and he bit down on his lower lip.

'Art, what the hell's wrong with you? You know how important it is that Mersiha feels secure. She can't switch therapists like this. She has to have stability in her life, she has to feel safe. You yourself told me that, right at the start, remember? After what she's been through, she has to know she's safe.'

For a brief second Brown's lip curled up in the semblance of a sneer, but just as quickly it disappeared and was replaced by his professional smile. 'I'll pass on her file, Tony. And you know as well as I do that she's much better than she was.'

'She's still sleepwalking. She's still having nightmares. We still don't know what happened to her in Bosnia. She hasn't spoken about it. Not once.'

Brown looked away, unwilling to meet Freeman's accusatory gaze. 'You don't know the pressure I'm under,' he muttered.

'No, I don't,' Freeman said. 'You're turning your back on a teenage girl who needs your help.' There was no reaction from the psychiatrist. Freeman sighed, at a loss for words.

The door opened and Nancy popped her head round. 'Everything all right, Dr Brown?' she asked, in the same tone with which she probably addressed her husband after he'd had a few drinks. Brown nodded, not looking at her. 'It's just that your five o'clock appointment is here.'

'I won't be long, Nancy,' Freeman said quietly.

Nancy hesitated for a moment, as if there were something else she wanted to say, then she closed the door.

'What's wrong?' Freeman asked.

'Nothing's wrong.' Still the psychiatrist avoided looking at him.

Freeman snorted softly, a mixture of annoyance and amusement. It had suddenly occurred to him that Brown was now in the same position as his patients normally were – sitting on the sofa, avoiding eye contact and putting up barriers. But he didn't have the time, or the inclination, to continue probing the man's psyche. 'Okay, Art. This isn't getting us anywhere. Just give me Mersiha's file and I'll be on my way.'

'Impossible,' the psychiatrist said, shaking his head. 'Out of the question. I'll send it on to whichever psychiatrist you decide on, but you can't have it. Medical records are confidential.'

'She's my daughter,' Freeman insisted.

'That doesn't make any difference,' Brown said. 'Children have rights, too. I could be sued.'

'Who's going to sue you, Art? I'm not. I'm sure Mersiha won't. I think you're being a little paranoid.'

'Medical records are confidential,' Brown repeated.

Freeman pushed himself away from the desk and walked over to a bookcase crammed with textbooks, most of them on child psychology. 'I'm going to take over her case,' he said. 'I'll need the file.'

'You're not a psychiatrist.'

Freeman turned to look at Brown. 'I can get her to talk to me. I'll get to the bottom of whatever it is that's troubling her.'

'You could do more harm than good.'

'You think dropping her mid-treatment is good for her, do you?' Freeman asked, raising his voice. 'You don't think that'll harm her?'

'You need a qualified psychiatrist, Tony. A specialist.'

'No. She needs someone to talk to. Someone she can trust.'

Brown sighed and rested his head on the back of the sofa. He closed his eyes as if fighting off a migraine. 'It's not as simple as that. Mersiha has highly developed defence mechanisms. You don't get through them by just talking to her. You have to know what you're doing.'

'So, I'll read the file. That'll be my map.'

Brown shook his head violently, his eyes still tightly closed. 'The file isn't a map. It's a diary. It only records where I've been, not where I'm going.'

Freeman stood looking down at the psychiatrist. He had a sudden urge to kick Brown's wounded leg. 'Give me the file, Art.'

'You're not qualified.'

'I'm more than qualified. I love her.'

'That's the worst possible qualification.' Brown licked his lips, staring at Freeman's anxious face. He slowly shook his head. 'No,' he said. 'It wouldn't work.'

Freeman struggled to stay composed. 'I'll make a deal with you, Art,' he said.

'A deal?'

'Something's bothering you, and to be honest I don't give a shit what it is. All I care about is my daughter. Let me read her file, here and now. Once I've read it, I'll be out of your hair for good. I'll never tell anyone you showed it to me, and I'll never mention it again.'

155

'And the stick?'

'The stick?' queried Freeman.

'I see the carrot. What's the stick?'

Freeman smiled without warmth. 'I'll make your life miserable. I'll hound you day and night. Something's worrying you and I'll keep digging until I find out what it is. I'll hire detectives, I'll ask questions, I'll keep on at you until I get some answers. I'll speak to whatever professional organisations you're a member of, I'll talk to the hospitals where you're employed as a consultant, I'll pester your patients and I'll speak to the press.'

'I'm not hiding anything,' Brown said defensively.

'I don't care,' Freeman said.

Brown looked at him for several seconds, then inclined his head towards a filing cabinet by the side of the desk. 'Under F. Top drawer,' he said. 'You'll excuse me if I don't get up, won't you?'

Lennie Nelson paced up and down. For the hundredth time he looked up at the announcements board. The train from New York was running ten minutes late and he had to be back in the office within the hour. The slats on the board flickered and whirred and when they stopped moving the delay had increased by another ten minutes. He cursed under his breath. Damn Amtrak and damn Ernie Derbyshire.

The private detective had sounded nervous over the telephone and had insisted on a meeting. He'd wanted to see Nelson in New York but the banker had explained that it was totally out of the question. Derbyshire had reluctantly agreed to come to Baltimore, but had insisted that Nelson pay all expenses. And he'd said that he wanted an extra two thousand dollars. Nelson had protested but the detective had said that the information he had was more than worth it. He wouldn't say any more on the phone.

Nelson decided to have his shoes shined while he waited for the New York train to arrive. It was just after eleven o'clock in the morning so the station was quiet and all three shoe-shine chairs were free. Nelson sat in a high chair and opened the *Washington Post* as the balding middle-aged man worked on his shoes. His mind wasn't on the newspaper. Whatever Derbyshire had discovered, it had to be good for the detective to ask for a face-to-face meeting. They'd only ever met once before, several years earlier. Since then all their business had been done by phone or mail. Nelson could feel his hands sweating. Maybe Derbyshire had uncovered the evidence the bank needed to pull the plug on CRW.

Time dragged interminably, but eventually the board whirred again and announced that the train from New York had arrived. The man gave the black Ballys a final polish and Nelson handed him a ten-dollar bill, telling him to keep the change. He climbed out of the chair as the train passengers began to walk through the station concourse. He spotted Derbyshire immediately: a tall, thin man with uncombed greying hair and a stoop. He was wearing a fawn raincoat that had seen better days, and scuffed brown loafers that had clearly never made the acquaintance of shoe polish. He nodded as he got closer to Nelson, but made no move to shake hands. 'How's it going, Lennie?' he said. He looked furtively to the left and right, as if fearing that he was being watched.

'What's wrong?' Nelson asked. 'Is someone after you?'

'Nah,' Derbyshire said. 'I need to visit the men's room. Where is it?'

'Can't it wait?' Nelson asked impatiently. 'I've got to get back to the office, pronto.'

'Jeez, just let me take a leak, will ya? My prostate ain't what it used to be.'

Derbyshire spotted the men's room and headed for it, leaving Nelson standing by the information desk. He looked at his watch and pulled a face. Whatever Derbyshire had, it had better be good. A pretty black girl in a charcoal-grey suit walked by swinging a briefcase. She smiled at Nelson and he grinned back. As she walked outside she looked over her shoulder and gave him another smile. Nelson cursed Derbyshire again.

The private detective came out of the men's room. His hands were still wet and he wiped them on his coat. 'Is there somewhere we can go?' he asked. There were wooden seats all around the waiting area but Nelson realised that the man wanted somewhere private. He took Derbyshire out of the station and down Charles Street to a small coffee bar. Nelson ordered coffee, Derbyshire a glass of milk. 'Coffee goes right through me,' the detective said apologetically.

Nelson looked at his watch pointedly. 'What's this all about, Ernie?'

'Have you got my money?' Derbyshire asked. Nelson sat back and folded his arms. He didn't say anything. Eventually Derbyshire got the message. He reached inside his coat and took out a grubby envelope. He put it on the table in front of Nelson, but when the banker reached for it,

Derbyshire grabbed his hand and squeezed. 'I'm not happy with you, Lennie. Not happy at all.'

Nelson frowned. 'What the hell is up with you?'

Derbyshire nodded at the envelope. 'That's trouble. Big trouble. I should be asking you for more money. Two thousand dollars isn't gonna cover my hospital bills if anyone finds out what I've done.'

Nelson leaned forward. Their waitress returned with a mug of coffee and a glass of milk. Nelson said nothing until she was on her way back to the kitchen. 'Okay, Ernie. Stop playing games. Spill the beans.'

Derbyshire grimaced. He took a sip from his glass. When he put it back down on the table he had a white foamy moustache on his upper lip. He wiped it away with the back of his hand. 'The agent you gave me, the lawyer, wasn't one I'd worked on before so I didn't have any contacts. Nice office, though. Really prestigious, all the trimmings. It's a small firm. I tried approaching one of the secretaries but she wouldn't have anything to do with me and I couldn't risk trying anything else. That meant I had to do a little breaking and entering . . .'

Nelson held up a hand. 'I don't want to hear what you did, Ernie. That's nothing to do with me.' Nelson knew that the private detective had spent two years in prison after a security guard discovered him standing over a lawyer's desk with a flashlight in one hand and a miniature camera in the other. The banker didn't want to hear about any illegal activities. He just wanted the facts.

'Yeah, yeah, I understand,' Derbyshire said. 'Okay, so I got the Ventura file, no problem.' He tapped the envelope. 'There's copies in there. There are two investors in the partnership. Russians.'

'Russians?' Nelson repeated. It was the last thing he'd expected to hear.

'Yeah, but not just any old Russians,' Derbyshire said. He took a pack of Marlboro cigarettes from the pocket of his raincoat, tapped one out and stuck it between his lips. 'Russian gangsters. Mafioski, the newspapers call them. I've included a few of the choicer cuttings in the envelope.' He patted his pockets, looking for matches. 'They're brothers. Gilani and Bzuchar Utsyev. Bzuchar lives in Brighton Beach. He owns a couple of restaurants, a trucking company and a taxi firm. He's just opened a marina up in New York State. But the bulk of his income comes from drugs, extortion and prostitution. Have you got a light?' Nelson shook his head. Derbyshire waved at the waitress and mimed lighting his cigarette. She came over with a book of matches. Derbyshire winked and lit up, exhaling through clenched teeth as if reluctant to allow the smoke to escape.

Nelson toyed with his mug of coffee. 'Gangsters?' he repeated. 'You're telling me they're gangsters?'

'Uh-huh. Damn right. The younger brother – Gilani – changed his name – to Sabatino, of all things.'

'Sabatino?'

'Yeah, don't ask me why. Sal Sabatino. He lives here in Baltimore. Runs a nightclub, but I couldn't find too much on him. He keeps a lower profile than his brother. Everything I could get is in the envelope.' Derbyshire leant forward as if he was frightened of being overheard. 'They're worse than gangsters, Lennie. Bzuchar's a psychopath, by all accounts. Worse than Al Capone, worse than Dillinger, worse than any Mafia don you've ever heard of. They left Russia in the late eighties. God knows why, because they'd already made a fortune out of the black markets. They come from a place called Chechenya – it's close to the southern borders of the old Russia, between the Black Sea and the Caspian Sea. It declared itself a republic when Gorbachev split the country up. The whole country is run by mobsters – it's the Russian equivalent of Sicily.'

Nelson picked up the envelope and slowly turned it in his hands. 'The evidence is all in here?' he asked.

'What you've got there is what I got from the lawyer's files, and from the *New York Times* cuttings library. But if you want the real dirt, it's gonna cost more.'

'How come?'

'Because all the good stuff, the stuff about their illegal operations, came from a friend of mine in the FBI. If you want paperwork to back it up, he's gonna want a pay-off.'

Nelson tapped a corner of the envelope on the table. 'How much will your friend want?'

'It's gonna cost five.'

'Five hundred?'

Derbyshire sneered at the banker. 'We're not talking about running a licence plate through the MVA computer, Lennie. We're talking about FBI files.' He drained his glass noisily, then banged it down with a dull thud. 'Five thousand. And you're not gonna be dealing with me – I'll put him in touch with you.'

Nelson considered the detective's proposal. Five thousand dollars was a lot of money, but if it proved beyond a doubt that Ventura Investments was a money-laundering vehicle run by gangsters, it would be a major coup for him, and the death knell for Walter Carey's career. Put like that, it was an attractive proposition. 'Let me read this first,' he said. 'If I need more, I'll get back to you.'

'Fine,' Derbyshire said, holding out his hand.

Nelson took a cheque from his inside pocket and slipped it over the table to the private detective. Derbyshire took the cheque, scrutinised the figures and the signature, and pocketed it. He pointed a warning finger at the banker, and narrowed his eyes. 'Whatever you do, don't tell anyone that I was involved in this. These guys are killers. My life is on the line here.'

'What do you think I am?' Nelson replied. 'You think I'm going to admit that I know what you've been doing? You're a professional consultant, nothing more. That's what you're shown as in our accounts, and that's all I know.'

Derbyshire shook his head. 'No. That's not good enough. I don't want my name connected with this at all. I don't wanna be on any file, I don't wanna be on any computer.' The detective's face was flushed and he was sweating. 'You know what banks are like. They leak information like sieves. If I'd known that the Utsyev brothers were involved I wouldn't have touched this case. For any amount of money. They're fucking animals, Lennie. They make the Mafia look like Mormons.'

Nelson flicked the edge of the envelope with his thumbnail. Derbyshire wasn't faking, trying to drive up the price. He was genuinely scared, and he didn't look like the sort of man who'd scare easily. 'Okay, Ernie. I'll be in touch.'

'Yeah, well, when you do, don't mention their names, either on the phone or in writing. If you want the FBI guy to get the stuff for you, tell me you want the football statistics. I'll then get him to contact you direct. Remember, it'll be five grand.' Derbyshire stood up and leaned over the banker. His face was so close to Nelson's that Nelson could smell his milky breath. 'Watch your back, Lennie. That envelope could be the death of you.' He raised his eyebrows and nodded, then turned on his heels and walked quickly out of the coffee bar, his coat flapping behind him like a loose sail in the wind.

Freeman knew it was bad news even before he picked the fax up off his desk. He'd been in one of the development labs with Josh Bowers, discussing a potential modification to the MIDAS deployment system over chicken salad sandwiches and cans of 7-Up, and when he arrived back in his own office his secretary was missing and the fax was face down next to his in-tray. If it had been routine it would have been in the tray with the rest of his correspondence. If it had been good news then Jo would have rushed up to him, waving it like a victory flag, her cheeks flushed with excitement. No, it was bad news, and before he read the first words his stomach was churning with the realisation that CRW hadn't got the Middle East order.

He read the brief letter with a heavy heart, though he was enough of a realist to know that it wasn't unexpected. Despite Anderson's unflagging confidence, Freeman had suspected that the Arabs wouldn't come through, that their trip to the States was nothing more than a holiday for the wives and that CRW's demonstration had been just a window-dressing sideshow. 'Shit, shit, shit,' he said, screwing the fax up into a tight ball and tossing it into a wastepaper bin. He flopped down into his chair and beat a tattoo on the desk with the palms of his hands. The day hadn't been a total loss. The Thai Army had just reordered another fifty of the MIDAS systems for use on their border with Laos, and a dealer in Hong Kong had been on the phone first thing that morning about a possible deal with Vietnam. The Vietnamese border with China was heavily mined, and they were still discovering minefields left by the Americans. Freeman tried to look on the bright side, but there was still a hard ache in the pit of his stomach, a feeling that no matter how hard he tried, no matter how hard he worked, the company was continuing its inexorable slide into oblivion. It was starting to look more and more as if Lennie Nelson was right. Drastic down-sizing at home with manufacturing sub-contracted overseas might be CRW's only salvation. But he knew that Katherine would never stand for it. To her CRW was more than a business. It was a monument to her father.

Jo appeared in the doorway, a nervous smile on her lips as she looked to see how he was taking it. 'I'm sorry,' she said.

Freeman held his hands up, palms showing, and grimaced. 'Gotta roll with the punches,' he said.

'There'll be other orders,' she said, leaning against the door-jamb.

'Sure,' he said.

'Really. I can feel it. And my psychic said there was going to be a lot of activity at work.'

'Your psychic?'

'Sure. I see her every two weeks. She's never wrong. Well, hardly ever.'

'Yeah? Next time you see her ask her where I left my gold pen, will you? It was a present from Katherine and she'll kill me if I've lost it.' Freeman grinned to show that he really wasn't upset about not getting the order.

Jo laughed, relieved, and went back to her desk. Freeman swivelled in his chair and stared out of the window, a faraway look in his eyes. Anderson drove into the parking lot and into his reserved space. Freeman watched him sit for a while before he opened the door of the Corvette. He wondered if Anderson had already heard the news. The financial director was sitting with both hands on the steering wheel, his head slightly forward as if at any moment he'd rest his forehead between them. When he finally got out of the car and pulled his briefcase off the back seat he'd regained his composure. He seemed light on his feet, as if a puppeteer's strings were attached to his shoulders, lifting him with subtle jerks as he walked.

Ernie Derbyshire sucked on his cigarette as the escalator whisked him up from the platform and into the bedlam that was Penn Station. Rush hour was in full swing and the waiting area was packed with commuters scanning the overhead monitors for their trains home, briefcases tightly gripped, hands hovering over hidden wallets, feet ready for the dash down to the train so that they could be sure of a seat. Penn Station at rush hour. Hell on earth.

Short-skirted hookers prowled through the crowds, cruising for after-work action like sharks looking for food, hips swaying, lips parted and breasts pointing like anti-aircraft guns at any likely target willing to pay fifty bucks for half an hour of illicit sexual contact. Pimps in jeans and bomber jackets watched from the sidelines like trainers waiting for their horses to perform, one eye looking for possible johns, the other on the lookout for the transport police. Pickpockets were out in force, singly and in groups, watching for the tourists and out-of-towners who lacked the street smarts of native New Yorkers. The less subtle practitioners of theft, the muggers and handbag snatchers, loitered by the toilets with the patience of spiders.

No one gave Derbyshire a second look. Not the hookers, not the pickpockets, not the muggers. He blended into the crowd like a chameleon: too tired to want sex, too down-at-heel to have a wallet full of cash, too nondescript to be remembered. He passed through the main concourse like a shadow, his hands deep in his pockets, his eyes shifting from right to left, his cigarette held tightly between his lips.

Commuters burst into action as the announcer gave details of the next Metroliner to Washington, DC. They poured down the stairs to the platform, eager to get home. Derbyshire hunched his shoulders in anticipation of the chill wind that he knew would be waiting to greet him outside the station. Unlike the fleeing commuters, he had no wish to escape the city. It was his home, and despite the daily murders, rapes and muggings, he felt safer in New York than he did anywhere else in the world. He turned to look at a station clock and licked his lips. Time for a drink, he thought, and then maybe a cheeseburger and a night in front of the TV. He remembered the cheque that Nelson had given him. It was Friday. He mentally cursed himself for not asking for cash. He wouldn't be able to deposit it until Monday, and until he did, it was nothing more than a piece of paper. It wasn't that he was short of money – he had several bank accounts, both in the US and in Switzerland – it was more that he hated loose ends, and an uncashed cheque was the worst sort of loose end. He was so busy thinking about the piece of paper in his inside pocket that he didn't see the two men until they were upon him, one on either side, gripping his arms with hands as strong as pincers, smiling as if they were long-lost friends.

'Smile, you piece of fucking shit,' said the one on his left, a bruising linebacker of a man with a dark wool overcoat and a thick red scarf around his neck. The man's left hand was thrust deep into his pocket.

The man on Derbyshire's right was a slightly smaller man with an unkempt moustache and orange-peel skin. His hair was slicked back and he had a shaving burn where his neck met his chin. His right hand was also hidden in the pocket of his raincoat. He stepped closer to Derbyshire and pressed whatever it was he was hiding against Derbyshire's groin. 'You're not smiling, shit-for-brains,' he whispered, an insane grin on his face, his voice a nasal New Jersey whine. 'Smile or I'll blow your nuts off.'

Derbyshire smiled weakly. Orange Peel nodded. 'Good,' he said. 'Now, let's go for a ride.'

Derbyshire started to protest but the gun was pressed against his groin once more and he did as they wanted. He knew there was nothing he could say: they were just messengers, come to bring the bad news. He knew too that there was no point in struggling. They were professionals, bigger, stronger and faster than he was. He shuddered and the two pincers tightened as if the movement was a prelude to an escape attempt. 'Okay, okay,' he muttered.

The two heavyweights gently frogmarched him out of

the station and towards a taxi rank where the drivers of yellow cabs waited with ill humour. A black Towncar pulled up with a squeal of brakes and Derbyshire was hustled into the back seat. Four hands patted him down as the Towncar accelerated away from the kerb. 'I'm not carrying,' he said.

'We'll check for ourselves, if you don't mind,' Orange Peel said.

The driver, a bull-necked giant wearing Ray Bans, gave a quick look over his shoulder as he powered through an amber light. 'Got him, then?' he asked redundantly.

The two heavyweights ignored the driver. Red Scarf thrust his left hand into the pockets of Derbyshire's pants and pulled out his wallet. Derbyshire said nothing. This wasn't a mugging. Red Scarf flicked through the credit cards and driving licence, and sneered at the few banknotes the wallet contained. 'Times tough, are they?' he said, slipping the wallet inside his overcoat. He checked the pockets of Derbyshire's jacket and pulled out the envelope containing Nelson's cheque. Derbyshire's face remained impassive. He was in deep shit, no doubt about it, but he didn't want to give the messengers any idea of how worried he was.

Red Scarf flipped the envelope open with one hand and slid the cheque out with his thumb. He whistled theatrically and showed it to Orange Peel. 'Business must be looking up,' he said.

The body-search over, the two men sat in silence, their guns still hidden in their coats. Derbyshire put his head back and stared at the roof of the car, wondering if he'd be able to put together any sort of workable cover story, and if he'd get the chance to tell it.

The car headed for the Lincoln Tunnel, joining the converging ranks of cars and trucks fleeing Manhattan. Derbyshire looked surreptitiously out of the side windows, half hoping that he'd see a police car, but knowing that even if he did there'd be nothing he could do. Before he'd have time to react, he'd have a fist in his groin at best, a bullet at worst, and the Towncar was as soundproofed as a brass coffin. The homebound commuters were all on automatic pilot, their eyes staring blankly ahead, listening to their car stereos or talking on their cellular phones or picking at their various orifices. A normal Friday rush hour.

Freeman knocked on his daughter's door. 'Mersiha?' he called. There was no answer, but Freeman didn't open the door. Ever since she'd first arrived in his home he'd known how important it was that she have her own space, a sanctuary where she could hide from the world, if that was what she wanted. He never entered her bedroom without her permission. He knocked again.

'Come in,' she said, her voice slurred with sleep.

He pushed open the door. 'Are you decent?' he said, knowing that she would be. He'd never seen her naked. Even before she began to develop the physical signs of womanhood she was shy, and he had always respected her desire for privacy. She had the quilt pulled up to her chin when he looked in. She was squinting at her bedside clock. 'What time is it?' she asked.

'It's late,' he said. 'Almost eight o'clock.'

Mersiha groaned. 'I'm sorry,' she said. 'I forgot to set the alarm.'

'That's okay – I haven't had breakfast yet. You get ready, I'll put the coffee on. Do you want anything to eat?'

'A high-cholesterol, low-fibre Scottish fry-up?' she said.

'Your request is my command, Oh mistress,' he said. 'Get a move on.' She giggled but kept the quilt under her chin as he closed the door.

Freeman was frying eggs, using a spatula to splash hot fat on the yolks, when she appeared in the kitchen. She was dressed for sailing – black Levis, Reeboks, a baggy white pullover and her hair tied back with a red bow.

'Get the orange juice, pumpkin,' Freeman said, sliding the eggs on to their plates. From the grill he added bacon, sausage and halved tomatoes and put the plates on to the table with hot toast and butter. Mersiha filled glasses with fresh orange juice from the automatic juicer and sat down opposite him.

She picked up her knife and fork and set to with a vengeance. Freeman watched her, amazed at the speed with which she tackled food. She always finished everything on her plate as if she never knew where her next meal was coming from. It didn't take a psychiatrist to understand why she ate the way she did. It wasn't too many years ago when she'd been close to starvation.

'What?' she said.

'What do you mean?' he asked.

'You're staring at me,' she said, her eyes shining.

'You're so pretty. I can't believe I have such a pretty daughter.'

Mersiha tutted and raised her eyebrows, but she was

clearly pleased by the compliment. 'I bet you say that to all your daughters,' she said.

'Only the pretty ones.' Freeman started eating his breakfast, but he was only halfway through by the time Mersiha had finished. 'Get the sandwiches – they're in the fridge,' he said. 'Grab some cans of Coke too.'

'You made sandwiches?' she said, impressed. 'You'll make someone a great wife.'

'Watch it,' Freeman laughed. Mersiha picked up his duffel bag and put it in the boot of the Lumina while he finished eating. She was in the passenger seat when he came out, her seat belt already in place.

'Did you say goodbye to Katherine?' Freeman asked.

'She was asleep,' Mersiha said quickly. Freeman looked at her. There was something in her tone which suggested that she hadn't tried to say goodbye. She turned away and looked out of the window. 'This is going to be a great day for sailing,' she said. 'Look at the tops of those trees.'

Freeman smiled despite himself. Mersiha had Katherine's knack of changing the subject. He started the car and headed down the driveway. In his driving mirror he caught sight of Katherine watching from the bedroom window. He waved his arm out of the window but he didn't see her wave back.

The drive to Annapolis took less than an hour. Mersiha chatted happily, about school, about sailing, about her fast-approaching birthday. Freeman had suggested that they arrange a party for all her friends, but Mersiha kept insisting that she'd rather have a quiet dinner. 'Just you and me,' she said.

'And Katherine,' Freeman said.

'Yeah. Of course.' Her voice had gone suddenly cold at

the mention of Katherine. Freeman didn't ask her what the problem was, and within seconds she'd changed the subject again, asking him when the boat was due to be lifted out of the water for its anti-fouling treatment. Art Brown's file on Mersiha had emphasised how pointless it was to confront her directly. She would react by dodging the line of argument, and if pressed she'd withdraw into herself and simply stop talking. Freeman had noticed that himself, of course, but seeing it written down on medical reports made it appear to be a genuine mental problem and not just shyness.

The file had also spelled out Mersiha's reluctance to make friends, something else which Freeman and his wife had noticed. Brown had hypothesised that the early death of her real parents and brother had left her incapable of making emotional commitments, that she was frightened of letting anyone get close in case they were also taken from her. That made sense to Freeman, but once again it had seemed that all Brown had done was to state the obvious. And a reluctance to hang out at the mall with the local cheerleaders didn't explain her sudden coldness towards Katherine. Getting to the bottom of that was going to take some gentle probing.

Brown had been right about Mersiha's file being little more than a diary. He'd been very efficient in recording the sessions, all with dates and times, presumably to help with his billing, but Freeman had discovered no insights into the workings of his daughter's mind. If he'd seen the file sooner, he would probably have suggested to Katherine that they put an end to the treatment. Brown himself admitted several times in the file that he was making little progress in persuading Mersiha to open up. The key to her problems, Brown said, lay in what happened to her as a child, but she had built an impenetrable wall around that part of her life.

Freeman could barely imagine what it would be like to lose both parents at such an early age. It was no wonder that she always seemed so interested in what he was doing and where he was going. Having lost her real parents, she must have lived in fear that her adopted family would also be taken away from her, no matter how many times Freeman reassured her that she was in America to stay. The violent death of her brother, the attempt to kill her in the basement, her time in the Serbian internment camp, any one of those events would be enough to scar a child mentally for life. It was a constant source of wonder that Mersiha hadn't turned out to be a bed-wetting sociopath rather than the bright, beautiful girl she was. Sleepwalking, insecurity and a little secretiveness were a small price to pay for what she'd been through.

She looked across at him and smiled. Her teeth were perfect, her smile that of a cover girl, and it was all natural – she'd never needed retainers or any dental work beyond a couple of small fillings which the dentist blamed on too many sweet things when she'd first moved to the States. Freeman wished that her real parents could still be around to see how their girl had grown. They'd have been very proud.

'What?' she asked.

'What do you mean?'

'You're grinning at me.'

'So? I'm happy.'

Her smile widened. 'Yeah? Me too.'

He drove in silence for a while. 'Have you and Katherine

had an argument?' Freeman asked eventually. He kept his eyes on the road.

Mersiha sat without replying for a while. Her hand reached for the radio controls but she pulled it back at the last moment as if she realised that it would be impolite to disturb the silence with music. 'No, we haven't argued,' she said.

'It seems to me that you're not talking like you used to. You used to enjoy hanging around with each other. You used to behave like sisters.'

'Maybe I'm just getting older.' Mersiha sounded suddenly sad as if a melancholy memory had just intruded into her thoughts.

'You don't think she resents you, do you?' he asked.

'You sound like Dr Brown,' she said.

'Sorry,' Freeman said, 'I didn't mean to. It's just that you're becoming a young woman, and Katherine has always taken a real pride in the way she looks.'

'I remind her that she's getting older, you mean?'

Freeman smiled. 'Pumpkin, we're all getting older.'

Mersiha ran a hand through her thick black hair. She could be a model, Freeman realised. She had the look, and the confidence. 'I don't know what's wrong,' she said. 'I've just been a bit low lately, that's all.'

'Thinking about home, you mean?'

She shook her head. 'This is my home,' she said.

'Good,' Freeman said. 'I'm glad you feel that way. Really.' He saw the marina in the distance, the masts of countless yachts standing to attention like soldiers on parade. 'Can you do me a favour?'

'Sure.' She replied without hesitation.

'Make an effort to reassure Katherine, will you? She

loves you, she really does. She takes any sign of coolness personally. She might not say so, but inside I know it really hurts her. She needs reassurance, too.'

Mersiha sighed. 'Yeah, okay.' Freeman held out his right hand, his little finger crooked. Mersiha interlinked the little finger on her left hand with his and they shook. That made it an unbreakable promise. Mersiha took her hand away first. She looked out of the window and sighed again.

Ernie Derbyshire's head felt as if it was going to explode. He tried lifting it, to ease the pressure, but the strain was too much and he flopped back. Breathing hurt, swallowing hurt, everything hurt, but the anticipation of what was to come was worse than any physical discomfort. He closed his eyes and thought back to the days when he was a child, hiding under his bed from a father who drank too much and who took a perverse pleasure in beating his offspring with a studded leather belt. At five years old his backside was as scarred and marked as a deep-sea fisherman's hands.

Derbyshire had hated his father, hated him with a vengeance, and he'd have run away from home if only there had been somewhere for him to go. He'd tried closing his eyes tight and wishing that he was somewhere else. The young Derbyshire had convinced himself that if only he could imagine a place in perfect detail it would become real, and he could escape there, away from the damp basement flat and the abusive father. It was a field with a grass that was greener than he'd ever seen in the Bronx, with buttercups and dandelions and big spreading trees and a cloudless blue sky. Small songbirds sat in the trees, singing and calling, and through the middle of the field bubbled a stream of icy-cold water. Derbyshire could picture himself paddling in the stream, his socks and shoes off, smooth hard pebbles pushing up between his toes.

A railway track skirted one end of the field, wooden sleepers and gleaming steel rails lying on a bed of gravel. Derbyshire had walked along the rails, jumping from sleeper to sleeper, promising himself that if he avoided treading on the gravel he'd be able to stay in the safe place for ever. He'd never seen a train, though occasionally he thought he'd heard its shrill whistle in the distance. The young Derbyshire thought it was the train which was the problem. Until he could picture the train, the place would never be real, but no matter how hard he tried it remained elusive, just around the corner, out of sight, and whenever he opened his eyes he was still underneath the bed, his face down in the dust, hiding from the belt and the beating.

He heard the rattle of the bolt that kept the cold-room door locked and he opened his ice-crusted eyes. His breath plumed around his face and through the misty vapour he saw two pairs of legs step through the door. He'd been hanging upside down for so long that his brain automatically rerouted the signals from his eyes and he had no problem identifying Red Scarf and Orange Peel. They were wearing thick coats with wool scarves around their necks and leather gloves. They were carrying baseball bats. Derbyshire began to tremble.

The two heavies circled Derbyshire, scraping the bats along the concrete floor. It was a game they played, a game they'd been playing for almost six hours. They'd left him alone all Friday night, letting his imagination run riot, then they'd questioned him for an hour or so, smiling and offering him cigarettes and telling him that if he played ball with them then they wouldn't play ball with him. Red Scarf had laughed loudly at that, but his eyes had remained flint hard and Derbyshire knew that he'd been lying. For most of the time he'd been hanging by his chained feet from a hook in the ceiling, surrounded by sides of prime beef. They'd got physical for the first time just after eleven o'clock. He remembered the time because Orange Peel had made a point of looking at his watch and asking his partner when they were going to have lunch. Red Scarf had said something about not being hungry just then, and as he finished speaking he'd whacked the back of Derbyshire's legs with his baseball bat like Babe Ruth going for a home run. Derbyshire never knew where the next blow was going to come from. They took a perverse delight in catching him unawares, varying the rhythm and the target areas, extending the torture way beyond what he'd have believed was possible. His legs were a mass of screaming nerves, and he was sure his left knee had splintered. Red Scarf had aimed most of his blows at Derbyshire's stomach and groin, and the detective had almost choked on his own blood and vomit.

The routine was always the same. They taunted him. They beat him until he passed out. They left him alone. Derbyshire had no idea how many times the routine had been repeated. He had no recollection of individual beatings, just the cycle of pain.

'How's it going, shit-for-brains?' Red Scarf asked.

'Just hanging around,' Derbyshire mumbled. He had a sudden feeling of déjà vu, as if he'd made the same quip before.

'He's a funny man,' Orange Peel said from somewhere behind him.

'A very funny man,' Red Scarf agreed.

Orange Peel slammed his bat into Derbyshire's left kidney and the detective grunted, biting his teeth together. He was almost too tired to scream any more. He closed his eyes again and tried to escape to the safe place. Another blow, this time between his shoulders, hard enough to start his body swinging.

They'd left the cold-room door open so Derbyshire didn't hear the third man come in, but when he opened his eyes again he saw a pair of professionally shined shoes and above them dark blue trousers with a crease as keen as a surgeon's scalpel. Derbyshire's gaze travelled up to a black cashmere coat, to a white silk scarf, and above it, a gaunt face, the eyes as cold and lifeless as the slabs of beef. The cheeks were hollow, the lips fleshy and pale, and the hooked nose belonged more to a predatory bird than to a man. It was a cruel face, a face that didn't smile very often. The hair was steel grey and closely cropped, a convict's haircut. Derbyshire recognised the face from the newspaper cuttings he'd given Lennie Nelson. It was Bzuchar Utsyev.

Utsyev smiled malevolently down at Derbyshire, the way a vulture might greet a prospective meal, then turned to Red Scarf. 'He's told you everything?' he asked.

Red Scarf grinned and whacked the baseball bat against the palm of his own left hand, making Derbyshire wince. 'Couldn't think of anything else to ask him, boss.'

Utsyev ran his hand across his chin as if feeling for stubble. 'His contact?'

'A guy called Lennie Nelson. A high-flier with the First

Bank of Baltimore.' He grinned. 'A nigger,' he added, as if the fact would appeal to Utsyev.

Utsyev held out his hand. Without being asked, Red Scarf handed over the cheque. Utsyev studied it as if it were a search warrant. 'For services rendered?' he asked Derbyshire. When the detective didn't answer, Utsyev tore the cheque into small pieces and threw them into his face like confetti. Some of them stuck to the blood and sweat and Derbyshire looked like a man who'd tried to heal his own shaving cuts and had done a particularly bad job of it.

'You want us to keep hurting him?' Orange Peel asked, weighing his bat in his hands.

'What do you think? Do you think he's suffered enough?' Utsyev seemed genuinely interested in how the men felt. They looked at each other, wondering what he really wanted to hear.

Red Scarf shrugged. 'He doesn't scream as much as he did at first,' he said, looking at Orange Peel for support.

Orange Peel nodded enthusiastically. 'We've been working on him since this morning. He's hurting, all right.' He looked at Utsyev and seemed to detect the beginnings of a frown. 'Of course, we could keep going for a while. No problem.'

'No problem at all,' Red Scarf agreed. He smacked the bat against his palm again as if to emphasise his enthusiasm.

Utsyev nodded his approval. 'What about you, Derbyshire? What do you think?'

Derbyshire glared at his tormentor through puffy eyes. 'Just don't kill me. Please. I've got a wife. A kid.'

Utsyev looked across at Red Scarf. 'He had a photo in his wallet,' Red Scarf confirmed. 'Ugly bitches, both of 'em.'

'He should have thought of them before he stuck his nose in our business,' Utsyev said. 'Give him another beating. Break his fucking hands as well. Then we'll take him for a picnic.'

The two heavies began hitting the detective straight away, keen to impress Utsyev. He watched them go about their work for a minute or so, then left them to it.

Derbyshire closed his eyes tight and tried to picture his safe place – the green field, the trees, and the train track. In the distance he could hear the whistle of a steam engine and he went to stand on the track. As unseen blows rained down on his legs and chest, he clung to the image of the train, roaring down on him, wheels clicking, pistons hissing, whistle screeching. Derbyshire smiled through the pain. The train was coming. It really was.

Katherine Freeman sat with her legs curled underneath her on the sofa as she smoked a cigarette and stared at the framed photograph of Luke and Tony. She missed her son fiercely. She no longer felt the agonising pain of the loss – that had mercifully faded some eighteen months or so after the accident – and she now rarely dreamed of him, but there was still an ever-present sense that something was missing from her life. She exhaled deeply and studied her husband's smiling face through the smoke. Grinning as if he didn't have a care in the world, bursting with pride for his beautiful, smart, bubbly, healthy son.

Once the sharp pain had faded, Katherine would play a game in her imagination, replaying the accident in her mind and giving herself the power to change its outcome, to have Luke survive and to have Tony go crashing through the windscreen and die in the road. At first she played the game despite herself. Images would creep up on her, almost against her will, as she carried out the housework or sat trying to read a magazine. She'd find herself picturing Luke, alive and well and loving her, and she'd shut him out, knowing that it was only wishful thinking. But later, after the doctors had told her that she'd be unable to have any more children, she would lie in bed and summon up the images of Luke, standing by his father's grave, holding back the tears, squeezing her hand bravely and telling her that it was all right because he'd take care of her, no matter what. She would have married again, of course, but only after a respectable period, and it would have to be someone who got on with Luke. A father figure, but not a replacement for Tony. There would never be anyone to replace him. She'd explain that to Luke, and he'd nod and say that he understood, but that he was pleased that Mommy had found someone to make her happy. Maybe in time he'd even call him Daddy. Katherine could play the game for hours, picturing her life with Luke, wiping his tears and sharing his triumphs, even though she knew that the longer she played, the worse the hurt when she came back to earth. Back to the real world, a world of Tony and no Luke.

Katherine realised with a jolt that the cigarette had burned down to its filter tip. She tossed it into the ashtray. A tear ran down her cheek and she wiped it away. The doorbell startled her out of her reverie. She looked at the gold carriage clock on the bookcase. Tony and Mersiha wouldn't be back for hours. She dabbed her eyes with a handkerchief and then walked through the hallway and opened the front door. Maury Anderson stood there, smiling like an eager-to-please puppy. 'Hello, Maury,' she said, wondering if he could tell that she'd been crying. 'Tony's not here.'

'I know,' he said, his grin widening. 'Can I come in?' Katherine stepped aside and Anderson walked into the house as if he owned it. Katherine closed the door and followed him into the sitting room. 'Tony said he was taking Mersiha sailing,' Anderson said, as if an explanation was called for.

'Do you want a drink?' Katherine asked, going over to the drinks cabinet.

'It's a bit early for me, but you go ahead,' Anderson said, dropping down on to the sofa by the fireplace.

Katherine put her head on one side like an inquisitive bird as she weighed Anderson up, wondering if he'd meant it nastily or if it was just because he knew her so well. She decided it was the latter and turned her back on him to pour herself a generous measure of brandy and Coke. She felt rather than heard him ease himself up off the sofa and come up behind her. His hands slipped around her waist, then slid upwards until he was holding her breasts. He squeezed gently, rubbing her nipples with his thumbs through the material of her dress. She gasped. 'Damn you, Maury,' she whispered. 'You know how that turns me on.'

Anderson brushed his lips against her hair and then kissed her shoulder. He nipped her with his teeth, not hard enough to hurt but enough to make her gasp again. 'No,' she said, but even she could tell from her voice that her heart wasn't in the denial. Anderson's hands roamed up and down her body, always returning to her breasts, and she felt him press himself against her.

'I want you,' he whispered.

'I can tell,' she said.

'I want you now,' he said, his voice thick with desire. Katherine sipped at her drink. Anderson tightened his grip on her breasts as if to punish her for her nonchalance. 'Now,' he repeated.

'No,' she said, putting the half-empty glass down. She twisted around so that she was facing him. Anderson's hands moved as she did so, sliding back over her breasts as if held there by magnets. 'Not here.'

'He won't be back for hours,' he insisted. 'You know what he's like when he's on that boat.'

His head jerked forward and he fastened his mouth to her lips, slipping his tongue between her teeth like a lizard. Katherine almost gagged. She pushed him away. 'Maury, no,' she pleaded.

'Come on,' he said. He tried to kiss her again but Katherine twisted her head to the side and his lips landed on her cheek.

'What part of no don't you understand, Maury?' she said.

'The part where your mouth says no but your body says yes,' he said.

Katherine couldn't argue with that. She could feel how hard her nipples had become under his caresses and she was breathing like a train. Anderson could play her body like a violin, and he knew it. 'Bastard,' she whispered. Her insides had turned to liquid. Anderson's eyes burned into her as if he knew how wet she was between her legs, how ready she was for him. 'This isn't fair,' she said. Anderson moved his face towards her, more slowly this time, and she let him kiss her, softly at first, and then with passion. His hands moved confidently to the top button of her dress, his lips never leaving hers. The button popped and he moved down to the next one.

Katherine put her hands on his shoulders and pushed him back. 'No,' she said, more firmly this time.

'No?' Anderson seemed genuinely stunned by her refusal.

'I told you right at the start, never in this house.'

'But they won't be back for ages,' he whined, like a small boy being refused the last chocolate biscuit.

'It's one of the rules,' Katherine said. 'If you want to play the game, you have to obey the rules.'

'Rules are made to be broken,' he said, trying to kiss her again.

'Not this rule,' she said.

'You're crazy,' Anderson said. 'We've made love in motel rooms all over Maryland. What's the difference? You have a weird sense of morality.'

'First of all, we've never made love,' she said, putting her fingers on his lips to shut him up. 'We've had sex, and I'm not saying it's not great sex . . .' Anderson grinned and she glared at him. The grin vanished. '. . . but it's not love, Maury. Don't ever confuse what we have with love. Okay?' He nodded. Katherine kept her fingers pressed against his lips. 'Second of all, it's not morality. It's etiquette. This is Tony's home. I'm not going to desecrate it by having sex with you, or any other man, in his bed. Do you understand?'

She slowly took her fingers away from Anderson's lips.

His eyes sparkled. 'How about we do it on the floor, then?' he said.

Katherine laughed, and pulled him towards her, kissing him hard on the lips, keeping her eyes open so she could watch him. She moved her right hand down his chest, tracing circles around his stomach, feeling the muscles there tense and hearing him groan with pleasure. She pressed her lips harder against his, biting and nibbling as she slid her hand between his legs. He was panting as they kissed, though his eyes were still tightly closed. She stroked him through his trousers, then, like a farmer grabbing a wayward chicken, she seized his balls and squeezed. He jerked away as if he'd been given an electric shock, but Katherine maintained her grip.

'Ow, ow, ow,' Anderson said, his eyes wide open.

'Maury, believe me, this is hurting me more than it's hurting you,' Katherine said sweetly.

He shook his head. 'No, no, no,' he said, shifting his weight from foot to foot. 'Let go. Let go. Let go.'

Katherine released some of the pressure, but gave his testes a little squeeze to let him know it could be reapplied at any time. 'Now listen to me, Maury, stop thinking with your dick and go arrange us a motel room. Just nod if you agree.'

He nodded enthusiastically. His eyes had begun to water and Katherine couldn't help but smile. 'There's a good boy,' she said, and patted the front of his trousers.

*   *   *

Freeman sat staring at the horizon, only half aware of Mersiha's slight corrections to the wheel as she kept the red telltales horizontal and flat against the sail.

'What are you thinking about, Dad?' Mersiha's voice jolted him out of his reverie.

'Sorry, what?' he replied, though he'd heard the question. He was playing for time, thinking of an answer so that he wouldn't have to tell her what was really on his mind.

'You looked really sad,' Mersiha said.

Freeman could see himself reflected in the lenses of her sunglasses. He was about to say that he was thinking about work, but he held himself back. If he ever hoped to get Mersiha to open up to him, he had to be equally honest with her. Lies, even white ones, would only dilute their relationship. 'I was thinking about Luke,' he said quietly.

Mersiha swallowed and looked up at the mainsail, avoiding his gaze.

'I miss him,' Freeman said.

'I'm sorry,' she said.

'No, there's nothing for you to be sorry about. I think about him a lot. I was just thinking how great it would be if he was here, enjoying this.'

'Did you ever take him sailing?' Mersiha said.

Freeman shook his head. 'No, we didn't have a boat then.'

'He was seven when he died, wasn't he?'

He nodded. It was the first time Mersiha had asked questions about Luke's death, and Freeman wondered if in the past he'd been giving off signals that it wasn't a subject to be broached. 'Three weeks after his birthday.'

The wind changed suddenly and Mersiha made quick, expert corrections to the wheel. The boat's speed remained constant. Freeman nodded his approval at her skill. 'What happened, Dad?' she asked. 'I know it was an accident, but I never . . .' Her voice tailed off as if she were worried about going any further.

'I was driving my car. Not the Lumina. The car we used to have. Luke used to love riding in the car. That's why I was thinking about how much he'd enjoy the boat.' A forty-foot twin-masted ketch passed them on their port side and Freeman waved at the helmsman, an elderly man in a bright blue windcheater. 'What he really liked to do was to sit on my lap while I drove.' He licked his lips. His mouth had gone suddenly dry. 'Katherine always told me it was stupid, and she'd never let me do it when she was in the car. I'd taken him with me to the mall, to pick up something. Food. Bread, I think, and some other things that Katherine wanted. Luke kept asking me if he could drive. I said no, but he wouldn't stop. He didn't cry, he knew that if he cried he'd never get his way, he just kept on asking politely. Eventually, when we were only half a mile away from home, I let him have his way. He took his seat belt off and sat on my lap, playing with the wheel, hitting the horn.'

Mersiha had stopped looking up at the sail and its red telltales. Freeman's reflection appeared to fill the lenses of her glasses. 'I didn't see the truck. Not then. When I think back now I can see it, I can remember everything. The small teddy bear tied to the front bumper, the garland of flowers hanging from the driver's rear-view mirror, the look on his face. His mouth was wide open. I think he was screaming. Or maybe he had the radio on and was singing along with it. That's all in my memory, but I know that at the time I wasn't aware of seeing it. The police told me later that he'd taken the corner too wide. He was only a few feet over the middle, but it was enough.'

'Was the driver drunk?'

'No. In a way it might have been better if he had been, then at least I could have blamed him. The road was narrow, the bend just a bit tighter than he'd expected. He wasn't speeding, he just drifted over the middle. We slammed into him.' Freeman took a deep breath, filling his lungs with salty air. 'It took less than a second. One moment Luke was sitting on my lap, giggling and holding the wheel. Then the car started to spin and Luke was thrown forward. The windshield shattered at the same time – I don't know if it was the crash or Luke hitting it. I tried to grab him. I caught hold of his left leg but he was moving too fast. Inertia, you know? He was only seven years old but the acceleration was just too much. It was like trying to hold on to a racehorse. If I hadn't been wearing my seat belt, I would have been thrown out too. Sometimes I wish I had been.'

'No,' Mersiha said firmly. 'You mustn't say that.'

'All I had left was his sneaker. He went under the rear wheel of the truck as the car spun away. The car went off the road and hit a tree. When I came round I was still holding the sneaker. They had to cut me out of the car, but other than a few cuts and bruises I was fine. I didn't even have to stay in the hospital. I was fine and Luke was dead.' Freeman was glad that he was wearing sunglasses because he didn't want Mersiha to see the tears in his eyes. He blinked behind the dark lenses.

'It wasn't your fault, Dad,' she said. She was gripping the wheel so tightly that her knuckles had whitened.

'Oh yes it was, pumpkin. There's no one else I can blame.

The guy driving the truck was just doing his job. The car's safety system protected me just like it was supposed to. If Luke had been wearing his seat belt he wouldn't have died. That's all there is to it.'

'You think about it a lot, don't you?'

Freeman nodded. 'Every day.'

'I dream about Stjepan all the time,' Mersiha said. 'I miss him.'

'I guess when someone dies you miss them for ever. It doesn't hurt so much after a while, but you always miss them.'

Mersiha smiled. 'Yeah. I guess.' She concentrated on the telltales for a while, keeping the boat slicing through the waves with deft touches to the wheel. 'It isn't your fault, Dad,' she said eventually. 'Sometimes bad things happen. You just wanted to make Luke happy. It's not your fault the truck was there.'

Freeman sighed. Deep down inside he knew that Mersiha was right, but he'd blamed himself for so long it would take more than sympathetic words to take the hurt away. Katherine had blamed him too, initially with razor-sharp words that had cut deeper than any knife and later with ice-cold looks and turned cheeks that had wounded more than the words. They'd eventually reached an uneasy truce, continuing to talk about Luke without Katherine apportioning blame, but to Freeman it seemed that the reproach was always there, lurking in the background.

He stood up and lumbered along the deck to stand behind Mersiha. He put his arms around her slight body and hugged her tight as he rested his chin on the top of her head.

Ahead of them was a smaller yacht, and Mersiha steered

away from it, giving it plenty of room. The mainsail started to flap and Freeman released his daughter to pull on the main sheet until the sail was properly trimmed. 'Dad?' she said.

'What's up?'

'Nothing.' She stared at the yacht as it passed on their port side but didn't acknowledge the young couple who were sailing it. Freeman gave them a half-hearted wave. He could tell from her silence that it wasn't nothing.

'Come on, pumpkin. What is it?'

She seemed to struggle with herself for a few seconds before answering. 'Well,' she said hesitantly, 'I was wondering . . .'

'Yes?'

'Well, was I a replacement for Luke?'

Freeman frowned. 'A replacement?'

'You know what I mean. Luke died, so you wanted another child.'

He took off his sunglasses and shook his head. 'Oh no, don't think that,' he said. 'I wanted you to live with us because of who you were, not because I wanted to replace Luke. I'll always love Luke, and I'll always miss him, but Katherine and I weren't looking for another child.'

'Katherine can't have more kids, right?'

'That's right.' Freeman was surprised that she knew that.

'I heard her telling one of her friends once,' she explained. 'It made me wonder if that's why you adopted me.'

'We adopted you because we love you. You, Mersiha. Not a replacement for Luke. In the same way that

Katherine and I are now your parents, but we'll never take the place of your real parents.'

'I guess,' Mersiha said.

The boat was well over on its side as it carved through the water, so Freeman had to hold on to the guard rails to make his way back to the wheel. He stood by Mersiha's side and put an arm around her shoulder.

'I hope I don't die,' she said. Freeman felt a rush of sadness at the matter-of-fact way she said it, and for a moment he was lost for words. After he'd read Brown's file and realised how little hard information it contained, he had gone to a large bookshop in Towson and bought a handful of psychiatric books. One had been on child suicides. He had selected it only because it had a long section on teenage depression, but what he'd read about suicide had scared him. According to the book there were one thousand teenage suicide attempts every day in the United States – and eighteen were successful. Eighteen children killing themselves every day of the year. The most common trigger for suicide was the loss of a parent, either through death, divorce or separation. Admittedly five times as many boys attempted suicide as girls, but for both boys and girls firearms were the method of choice. He put his hand into the pocket of his jeans and his fingers touched the brass cartridge case. He'd been meaning to ask Mersiha where it had come from, but realised that it wasn't a subject that he could raise now. It would suggest a lack of trust, that he and Katherine had been spying on her. All the books had been adamant on one point – there was no point in confronting children directly. Their thoughts had to be explored circumspectly so that they didn't think they were being quizzed. He had to get through to her by communicating rather than confronting. Mersiha had made a start – for the first time she'd lifted the veil that hid her innermost thoughts. Freeman had learned more about her during the few hours they'd spent on the boat than Brown had gleaned from months of questioning, and he wasn't prepared to spoil it by asking her about an empty cartridge which in all probability she'd picked up while out walking her dog. As she looked up at the telltales on the mainsail, Freeman hooked the cartridge out of his pocket and flipped it over the side, into the white-foamed water.

Katherine Freeman lay on her back and stared at the ceiling, her head in the crook of Anderson's arm. She felt empty inside, as if the forty-five minutes she'd spent in bed with him had been nothing more than a step aerobics session. She smiled as she wondered how the two activities compared in terms of burning up calories. She didn't get quite the same burn in the gym, but she definitely felt better about herself afterwards.

Anderson's left hand lay on her stomach as if laying claim to the territory. He was like that, Katherine knew – he'd like nothing more than to have her in Tony's bed, like a dog urinating on a gatepost. Been there, done that. Ever since she'd hit puberty, men had always seemed to want to possess her sexuality, starting with her father's stifling over-protectiveness and his refusal to allow her to go out with boys until she was past her teens. When she'd finally escaped to college it was only to find that almost every man who ever asked her out was proposing marriage within days and throwing jealous fits when she expressed her desire for independence. Space was what they called it now, and that was what Katherine was always striving for. Her own space. That was why she'd agreed to marry Tony. Not just because she loved him, but because he gave her all the space she wanted. Katherine smiled. Maybe he gave her too much space, but that had always been his way. They'd met when she was twenty and he was three years older, studying for his MBA. It was his Scottish accent and strong thighs which had first attracted her, but she'd soon realised that the attraction she felt owed more to his quiet maturity than to his physical attributes. It wasn't that she was looking for a father figure, that was certain, because the two men were totally different, both in looks and in personality. Tony was never possessive, he never gave her the wounded smile when she said she wanted to stay in on her own or go out with the girls, and if she didn't phone there were no late-night acrimonious calls demanding to know where she'd been. Tony had been the first boyfriend who hadn't asked her to tell him that she loved him. He'd declared his affections early on in their relationship, but hadn't pressed her, in the same way that he hadn't tried to force her into his bed. He'd waited, and his patience had eventually paid off. She did love him, deeply, and she couldn't imagine ever being married to anyone else.

The best analogy she could think of to describe their relationship was that of a falconer she'd seen in Scotland, on a trip to see his few remaining relatives, shortly after they'd married. They'd stayed in a crumbling old Scottish castle that had been converted into a guest house, and one morning, as they'd been walking arm in arm over the mist-shrouded hills, they'd seen an old man with a hooded hawk on his arm. They'd stood entranced as the man removed a small leather hood from the bird's head and held his arm out. The hawk had cocked its head on one side, then flapped up and away, powering up into the sky until it was just a black dot among the clouds. It had hunted for almost twenty minutes, eventually bringing down a small bird and feasting on it among the purple heather. The man had waited patiently. At no time did he whistle or call the bird, not even when it had finished eating. He just stood with his arm to one side, waiting until the hawk decided it wanted to return. It came eventually, slapping its claws against the man's forearm and flapping its wings to maintain its balance. It held its head still while the man put the hood back on, and then they walked off into the mist, man and bird. That was how Katherine felt about her husband. He offered her stability and sanctuary, and she knew that his arm would always be there when she returned. He didn't have to call or whistle, because he knew she'd always be back.

'What are you thinking about?' Anderson asked, his words ramming into her consciousness like a piledriver.

'I was wondering what time it was,' Katherine lied. She might be prepared to offer Anderson her body, but she was damned if she'd allow him inside her head. He was physical recreation, nothing more. 'I've got to go,' she said.

'They'll be out for hours yet.'

'Give you an inch and you take a mile,' Katherine complained.

'An inch!' Anderson protested.

'You know what I mean.'

'You can stay for another half an hour, can't you?' he whined.

Katherine felt her hackles rise. She reached over and patted his groin. 'Doesn't feel to me like you're up to it, darling,' she said.

'Bitch,' he laughed, rolling out of bed. He padded over to the bathroom. 'I'll be back.'

Katherine stared at the light-fitting in the middle of the ceiling. She could just about make out her reflection in the polished brass. Tony and Mersiha probably wouldn't get back until dark, but she still had to get the evening meal ready. Something quick. She ran through the contents of the freezer, mentally rejecting anything that would take more than an hour to cook. She eventually selected a beef stew she'd frozen the previous month which would only need microwaving. There were plenty of carrots and some nice courgettes, and there was a chocolate mousse in the refrigerator. She relaxed, knowing that she could have food on the table by the time Tony and Mersiha arrived home.

She realised that she needed to go to the bathroom. Better to go right away than to risk offending Anderson's sensitivities by stopping him mid-thrust. He took his sexual prowess very seriously. There wasn't a robe handy, but it didn't matter because he had seen all there was to see of her body, and it had been a good many years since Katherine had felt anything like shyness. She pushed open the door.

Anderson was bent over the wash basin holding a small metal spoon under his nose. He sniffed deeply, then pushed the spoon into a small glass vial filled with white powder and repeated the procedure with his other nostril.

'What the hell are you doing, Maury?' Katherine said, leaning against the door.

He sniggered, widened his eyes and grinned. 'What's it look like I'm doing?' he asked.

'It looks like you're taking drugs,' she said contemptuously.

'For Christ's sake, I'm doing a little coke, that's all.' He held out the vial. 'Want some?'

Katherine looked at him, her eyes cold. 'No, Maury, I don't want some. And I don't think I want to be in the same room as someone with that amount of cocaine in their possession.'

Anderson shook his head. He was more animated than he had been before and there was a wildness about his eyes. 'Nobody cares these days, Kat. It's crack they're after, not coke . . .'

'Don't call me Kat,' she said, interrupting.

'What?'

'I've told you before. Don't call me Kat. That's Tony's name for me. Not yours.'

'Okay, okay,' he said. 'I'm sorry.' He screwed a stopper into the top of the vial and put it by the wash basin. He reached for her but she stepped back, putting her hands up to fend him off. 'What the hell is wrong with you?' he asked.

'I didn't know you took drugs,' she said.

'I don't take drugs. I use cocaine – sometimes.' He held his hands in front of her, palms up in surrender. They were shaking, Katherine noticed. 'It's not like I'm an addict or anything.'

'Does Tony know?'

Anderson sneered. 'Of course not.' He reached for her again but she knocked his hands to the side. 'He doesn't know about anything,' he added pointedly.

Katherine narrowed her eyes. 'Watch it, Maury. You're married too, remember.'

'In name only.'

'Don't play that game with me,' Katherine said. 'She's your wife. And she's as much in the dark as Tony. Let's just keep it that way, shall we? I don't think either of us wants a divorce, do we?'

Anderson sighed and put his hands on his hips. He was as naked as Katherine, but he too was totally unashamed. Katherine couldn't stop her gaze from dropping to his groin. He saw the look and smiled. 'Let's go to bed, Katherine,' he said.

'I don't think so. Going to bed with someone on drugs is like sleeping with a drunk. I have more self-respect than that.'

'There's no comparison,' he said. 'Drink dulls your senses, cocaine intensifies them. You've never had an orgasm unless you've had one on coke.' He rubbed his nose with the back of his hand.

'You need help,' she said, but once again her gaze had dropped. Anderson stepped towards her, slowly this time, and put his hands on her hips.

'I don't need help. I need you.'

Katherine shook her head, but she knew that her heart wasn't in the denial. Anderson saw the weakness in her eyes, and he slowly knelt down in front of her, planting soft kisses on her stomach. 'No, Maury,' she whispered, closing her eyes and stroking the back of his head. His hands reached around her backside and pulled her towards him, his tongue probing between her legs. 'No,' she repeated, but this time he knew that the 'no' was a 'yes'.

His tongue licked the inside of her thighs and she moved,

opening her legs wider so that he could go further inside her. She opened her eyes and saw herself reflected in the mirror above the wash basin. The depth of passion in her eyes almost startled her. The hips that were pushing against his face seemed to have a life of their own. It was as if she were watching someone else, a stranger. She tightened her grip on his hair, pulling it hard, trying to hurt him. Anderson groaned in pain, but his licking intensified as his hands roamed over the back of her legs. The Katherine in the mirror smiled. She was back in control.

Lennie Nelson increased the pace, feeling his thigh muscles start to ache as his legs worked. He kept one eye on the speedometer that told him how fast he'd be going if the exercise cycle wasn't bolted to the floor and the other eye on the running track on the lower level. Two jocks were running hard, taking turns to pace each other, and a grey-haired grandmother type was walking briskly in brilliant white Reeboks and breathing like she was seconds away from a heart attack. The running track was one of the least-used areas in the Downtown Athletic Club. The patrons of the club were mainly a yuppie crowd who preferred the gleaming hi-tech exercise equipment or the aerobics classes where they could show off their designer sneakers and leotards. It wasn't a clientele that liked to sweat.

Nelson liked the club because it was fairly close to the bank's offices. There was always plenty of space to park his car, and it was a terrific pick-up joint. He had no problem picking up girls in the city's clubs and bars, but he preferred girls who worked out and his hour-long fitness regimen gave him plenty of opportunity to see what was on offer. He took a quick look at his watch. He had another five minutes to go before he switched over to the bench press.

He wiped his forehead with the arm of his Johns Hopkins sweatshirt, a relic of his undergraduate days. Down on the running track the two jocks were standing, hands on hips, watching a tall blonde girl, her hair tied back in a ponytail that reached almost to her waist. She had a fluid, easy run, and the ponytail bounced against her purple running vest as she loped along. She checked a stopwatch as she ran. She had good legs, long and lean and not too muscled, and a trim waist. The jocks were obviously talking about her. Nelson wondered what the front view looked like. As she followed the track around to the left, she moved out of his field of vision. The two jocks began jogging after her. The next time she came around she was running on the outside of the track and Nelson was able to see her figure as she ran by. She had firm breasts, bigger than he normally saw on girls who liked to run, and she was strikingly pretty with high cheekbones and flawless skin. Unlike most of the female clientele of the club, she didn't appear to be wearing make-up.

The two jocks tried to catch up with her, but she picked up speed as she passed out of his vision again. The next time she came around she had put even more distance between the two guys, and they were bathed in sweat. Nelson smiled. The girl could run all right. He realised he was overdue for the bench press so he reluctantly slid off the saddle.

There were only 140 pounds of weights on the bar so he added another ten to either side before lying back on the bench. He grabbed the bar and began to lift, concentrating on his breathing as he worked. His breathing became more laboured and the muscles in his arms began to burn. He welcomed the pain. It proved that he was pushing himself, and Nelson was always trying to extend his limits, physically and mentally. He could feel his pulse pounding in his neck and the pores on his face opened, bathing him in sweat. He blinked his eyes and pushed harder.

As he looked up past the bar he saw black shorts and a purple shirt. It was the blonde. 'Need someone to spot you?' she asked. She wasn't from Baltimore, he realised. The mid-west, maybe. She looked like a girl who spent a lot of time on the beach.

'Great,' he said.

She moved to stand at the end of the bench, her hands at either end of the bar, ready to grab hold in case he faltered. Nelson strained, determined to keep the weights moving for as long as possible. A beautiful girl was the best incentive, especially one who was leaning forward so that her breasts swung just feet from his face and who was smiling encouragement with a mouth that filled his mind with erotic thoughts.

'Come on, you can do it,' she coaxed. 'Another five.'

Nelson gritted his teeth. If she expected five, he'd give her ten. He counted them off. 'Yes. Yes. Yes,' she said in time with his lifts. Nelson imagined that she'd do the same thing in bed, urging him on in time with his rhythm. She seemed genuinely pleased when he finished his set and helped him put the bar back on its rest. He sat up and grinned. 'Thanks,' he said.

'Sure,' she said, shaking her head so that the ponytail flicked from side to side. 'Do you wanna do me?'

He smiled at the double entendre. 'I'd love to,' he said.

She managed fifteen lifts before she started to strain and she did another five after that. After he'd helped her put the bar on its rest she lay on the bench, gasping for breath. He wafted her with his towel and she giggled. 'Thanks,' she said. 'I'm Jenny, by the way.'

'I'm Lennie,' he said. 'What do you wanna do next?'

'What I want is a decent drink, but what I've got to do is another thirty minutes of weight training.' She stood up. Her legs looked even better close up, smooth and silky all the way up to where they disappeared into her shorts. She was only a couple of inches shorter than he was, and Nelson was six feet tall. He liked that. Tall girls always turned him on. Especially tall white girls.

'How about we work out together, then I'll buy you that drink?'

She nodded. 'Deal,' she said. 'Choose your weapon.'

Nelson looked around the exercise room. 'Stairmasters,' he said.

'Good choice. I need to work on my legs.'

Nelson watched her as she walked over to the machines. He shook his head as he admired her long legs. They definitely did not need working on. They were just perfect. She looked over her shoulder, caught him staring at her, and smiled. He stepped on to the machine next to her and they matched each other step for step.

Later, after they'd showered and changed, he met her in the club's bar and bought her a vodka and tonic while he drank a beer. She'd undone the ponytail and her hair hung straight down her back where it rippled each time she moved her head. He had to keep fighting the urge to reach

201

out and touch it. He could only imagine what it would feel like to have it draped over his naked body. Jenny told him that she was in public relations, working for an independent company that represented several manufacturing concerns. Nelson was genuinely surprised to discover that she was quick-witted and intelligent and had a highly paid job: the first time he saw her he'd assumed she was a photographic model or at least had a career that would make use of her stunning looks.

Several times Nelson saw guys turn to look at her as they headed for the bar, and he felt a surge of pride that she was sitting with him, hanging on his every word and touching him occasionally on the knee. He told her about the house he'd recently bought, a four-bedroomed colonial in a predominantly white neighbourhood to the north of the city, and she said she'd love to see it. It was an opening he couldn't fail to follow up and he asked her if she'd like to go back for a drink. She studied him with steady green eyes over the top of her glass as if weighing up her options, then she nodded and said she'd love to. Five minutes later they were in his Jaguar, heading north up Charles Street, Dire Straits on the CD and the smell of her perfume almost overpowering him.

He pushed his foot down hard to give her an idea of the car's power, and the engine growled.

'I love a stick shift, don't you?' she said as he changed up from second to third. She slipped her hand over his and squeezed. 'You get so much more control.'

He looked across and saw that she was smiling. She held his gaze and he knew that she was available. More than available, she was ready, willing and able. He doubted that he'd be taking her home that night. When he turned away from her he saw the bus, looming ahead of him, and he hit the brakes, hard. The Jaguar's braking power was every bit as impressive as its engine performance and it stopped with yards to spare. A white Cadillac almost rear-ended him in turn. 'Sorry,' he said to Jenny.

She shook her head, showing that it didn't matter. She moved her legs together as she stretched them out and he heard the whisper of silk. It was a sound filled with promise, and he felt the stirrings of another erection. Down, boy, he thought. There'd be plenty of time for that later.

Mersiha guided the yacht into its berth with confident turns of the wheel. Freeman stood at the bow, but it was clear that she didn't need his input. He'd suggested that they come in using the engine, but Mersiha had insisted on showing that she could do it under sail. The wind was onshore so she'd rounded up into the breeze and allowed the boat to drift back against the dock. She timed it to perfection, bringing the boat perfectly parallel to the wooden jetty as Freeman dropped fenders over the side to protect the topside. They quickly stowed the sails and made the boat fast.

'Nice job, First Mate,' he said appreciatively.

'Thanks, Captain,' Mersiha said, saluting.

'I'm serious,' Freeman said, checking the tension of the stern line. 'That was as good a bit of seamanship as I've ever seen.'

'Thanks, Dad. You're a good teacher.'

Freeman smiled and ruffled her hair. 'I think we should stop this mutual appreciation society, don't you?'

He gave the boat a quick going over and, satisfied that everything was tied down, they headed for the car.

Freeman rolled his shoulders as he drove home. He could feel his neck muscles begin to stiffen. Sailing was hard work. He never realised just how tiring it was until afterwards, and he knew that he'd sleep well that night. He always did after a day on the bay, even though Mersiha had done more than her fair share. He looked over at his daughter as she snored quietly, like a sleeping cat. He was proud of her. He was glad that he'd told her about Luke. At least now she knew that he and Katherine loved her in her own right. He was glad, too, that she'd started to open up to him. Being alone on the water had helped. She was generally more talkative on a one-to-one basis. Freeman had a sudden thought, that he'd take Mersiha on a holiday, just the two of them. The end of her school term was fast approaching, and Maury was more than capable of looking after the business. Freeman would find a place that resembled Bosnia, a place with rolling countryside, fields and forests, a place that would remind her of home. A log cabin somewhere in the mid-west, maybe. He'd have to speak to a travel agent, to find a place that would be suitable, somewhere out of the way, isolated, where he could nourish the relationship, forge the bond that would allow her to trust him completely. The idea appealed to him so much that he had an urge to wake her up and tell her there and then. He resisted and let her sleep on, but the more he considered the idea, the better it felt. He'd have to clear it with Katherine, of course, but he was sure she'd agree.

Mersiha slept all the way home, only waking as Freeman turned into the driveway and parked behind Katherine's car. She rubbed her eyes with the back of her hands. 'Sorry,' she murmured.

'Don't be silly. You were tired.'

'I wanted to talk.'

'You wanted to sleep.' They climbed out of the car and walked together around the back of the house and into the kitchen. Katherine was there, taking warm plates out of the stove.

She looked over her shoulder and smiled at Freeman. 'How was it?'

'Perfect. What's cooking?'

'Beef stew. Is that okay?'

'Sounds great.'

'Stew okay for you, Mersiha?' Katherine asked.

Freeman noticed that Mersiha looked at him before answering, as if acknowledging her earlier promise. 'Lovely. Do you want any help?'

'It's almost ready,' Katherine said, clearly pleased by the offer. 'You could drain the carrots for me.'

Mersiha put a lid on a saucepan of sliced carrots and poured the water off as Freeman laid the table. He winked at his daughter and she winked back.

Later, after Mersiha had gone to her room to get on with some homework, Freeman and Katherine settled down in front of the fire. Katherine was reading an old copy of *Vogue*, her mind clearly not on the magazine. She ran her index finger around her tumbler of brandy and Coke. A lit cigarette lay in the ashtray, untouched.

'Penny for them?' Freeman asked.

Katherine's head jerked up. 'What?' she snapped. Then

she saw his look of concern and her face softened. 'Sorry, Tony. I was miles away.'

'Anything I can help with?'

She shook her head. 'I was actually thinking about Lennie Nelson, believe it or not. I was wondering what my father would have made of him.'

'He'd probably have given him very short shrift. Your father didn't appreciate outsiders sticking their noses in his business. I know he thought long and hard before allowing me in.'

'That's true,' she said, smiling at the memory. 'He had you pegged as a fortune hunter, remember?'

Freeman doubted that he'd ever forget. Katherine's father had either scared away or bought off all her previous suitors, and he'd attempted the same with Freeman. He had never told Katherine about the old man's last attempt to drive him away. It had been in the study of the Williamson mansion in Annapolis, a book-lined room with a roaring fire and a Chinese rug on the floor. It seemed to Freeman that he'd spent a long time staring at the blue hand-woven silk rug and its images of dragons and snakes as the old man had outlined his terms: a cheque for fifteen thousand dollars and a one-way ticket back to Scotland, in exchange for agreeing never to see Katherine again. The old man hadn't been quite that direct – there had been a long preamble about the family, their desire to see Katherine married to someone of her own class, someone of her own intellectual standing, someone who could keep her in the lifestyle to which she'd become accustomed – and there was a lot of ego-massaging, about how Freeman was a nice guy, salt of the earth, hard-working and no doubt totally trustworthy, but that really he wasn't right for the only child of one of Maryland's most powerful industrialists. Not to say richest. Freeman could still picture the rug in his mind.

'Still, you won him over, didn't you?' Katherine's words jogged him out of his reverie.

Freeman smiled and nodded. He couldn't remember exactly what he'd said to the old man, not the precise words. He knew that he couldn't show anger, or hatred, that any show of emotion would prove only that Katherine's father was right, that he was unworthy of her hand. He explained that he had been put in an impossible position, that he had no wish to take her away from her family, and that he knew her well enough to understand that it would be an impossible task anyway. Katherine's love for her family, and her father in particular, went far beyond anything she could ever feel for a lover. So if her family rejected him, he had no alternative but to walk away. The old man had smiled and reached for his cheque book, but Freeman had shaken his head. The money wasn't important, he'd said. The money was nothing. Freeman's family owned several farms in the north of Scotland, and while he'd never be as rich as Katherine's father, he'd certainly never be short of money. It was the first and only time he'd spoken about family money with the old man. He had turned on his heels and walked out of the study, sure that it was the last time he'd ever set foot in the mansion. He was wrong. The following day Katherine phoned, inviting him to dinner. With her father.

The old man never mentioned the discussion in the study, and Freeman could never work out whether the offer to pay him off had been a genuine one, or if it was just the final test to see whether he really loved Katherine. Whatever, the old man had given his blessing and six months later they'd married.

'Yeah, eventually I did,' he said. 'I doubt if Nelson would have been able to. Your father would have run him out of town.'

'Lynched him, more like,' Katherine said. She was joking, but her father had views that wouldn't have gone down well in present-day politically correct America.

'I think we should give Nelson the benefit of the doubt,' Freeman said.

'We'll see,' she mused, picking up her tumbler and looking at him over the top. 'Did you speak to Mersiha?'

'About what?'

'Don't give me that wide-eyed innocent look, Freeman. You know what about. Whatever you said, she was as nice as pie tonight.'

'Nah, it's your cooking.'

Katherine sniffed pointedly. 'I hope that's not a crack about my culinary abilities. Wasn't the stew thawed enough?'

'The stew was thawed just fine. My compliments to the chef.' He ducked as the magazine sailed through the air, missing his head by inches.

'By the way,' Katherine said. 'Did you ever ask her about that cartridge I found?'

Freeman shrugged. 'The opportunity didn't come up,' he said. 'But I had an idea.'

'Uh-oh.' She sipped her drink and waited for him to continue.

'I'd like to take her away for a few days. A sort of vacation.'

'Father–daughter bonding?'

'It went really well today, Kat. She spoke about her brother for the first time. I think she's starting to open up.'

'And you want to go alone? Just the two of you?'

'If that's okay with you. It would just be for a few days. We could all take a vacation together later on in the year if you like, but yeah, I'd like to do this on my own. I really think it'll help.'

'Where would you go?'

Freeman leant forward. 'That's my brainwave,' he said eagerly. 'I'm going to find somewhere like Bosnia. Somewhere that'll remind her of her home. Mountains. Forests. Farmland. If I can get her in that environment, but also an environment where she feels safe, I think it might set her thinking. And talking.'

Katherine frowned. 'I don't know, Tony. It might be a bit much for her.'

'I don't think so. Besides, I'll be careful. I'm not planning to put her through the third degree. I'll take her hiking. Fishing maybe. And we'll talk. If she wants to. Hell, I can't do any worse than Art Brown. His files were devoid of any insight into her psyche. Plenty of observations, but he hasn't a clue as to why she's the way she is. I'm sure I can do better than that.'

'You're sure? You're sure it won't do more harm than good?'

'No, I'm not sure. But she'll be sixteen in a few days. She'll soon be an adult. I don't want her to have these nightmares for the rest of her life. And what about college? How do you think she'll get on if she's still sleepwalking in her twenties?'

Katherine nodded. 'Where would you take her?'

'I don't know. Colorado maybe. I'll speak to a travel agent.'

'When?'

'She's due a week off soon, right? That thing they do in Maryland to save money in winter.'

'You mean Energy Conservation Week? I think the idea is to save the world's natural resources.'

'Yeah, whatever. It's the perfect opportunity. I could make it a birthday present. Just a few days, a week at most.'

'You're sure you're not just trying to get away from me?' she said, pouting.

Freeman walked over and knelt down before her. 'Don't be silly, Kat. I love you.' He kissed her on the lips. He could taste the brandy and Coke. She kissed him back, sliding her hand around the back of his neck and running her fingers through his hair. He broke away first. 'I'll always love you,' he said, his eyes shining with desire.

'I know,' she said. She kissed him again, harder this time.

The drive from the city centre to his house in Tuscany Road was always a major ego boost for Nelson. On the way up Charles Street he crossed North Avenue and its crack-houses, hookers and street beggars which typified Baltimore's urban decay, the image the city fathers tried so hard to gloss over by promoting its convention centres, Inner Harbour shopping malls and baseball stadium. Though he'd never admit it to anyone, North Avenue was where Nelson came from. He'd been brought up in a two-bedroomed cockroach-infested row house close to the corner of North Avenue and Greenmount, one of five children, with a father who left when he was three months old and a mother who sold heroin to make ends meet. She was long dead, his mother, and so were two of his brothers, one of a drugs overdose, the other shot by a burglar high on cocaine. That was par for the course in Baltimore. What wasn't typical was the fact that Nelson had escaped from his background, had worked his way through college and graduate school and had started on a career path that was going to take him all the way to the top. There wasn't anything a young, good-looking, ambitious black male couldn't do with a Democrat in the White House and affirmative action the order of the day.

Further up Charles Street, between 29th and University Parkway, was Johns Hopkins University, where he'd studied with a vengeance, studied harder than anyone had ever studied before because he had something to prove and something to escape from. He'd spent more hours in the library than he had in bed, and when he wasn't studying he was flipping burgers at Burger King, washing dishes at countless restaurants and bagging groceries for overweight white suburban housewives. After four years he left Hopkins with a BA, dishpan hands and student loans that kept him on a diet of beans and rice for a long time. It had also given him an appetite for work that stood him in good stead in the world of banking. He was always first at his desk and he made it a point not to leave if there was anyone else on the floor.

Nelson could see that Jenny was impressed by the large colonial houses shaded by leafy trees with two-car garages and lawns that needed ride-on mowers. He slowed down and drove the Jaguar up to his house. 'I love it,' she said as she walked up to the front door. 'How long have you lived here?'

'A couple of years,' he lied. He'd actually bought it just six months earlier and it was mortgaged to the hilt.

He unlocked the front door and ushered her in, switching the lights on as she walked into the hallway. She looked around appreciatively, put her bag by the door, and went into the sitting room. As always the room was immaculate – he spent so little time there it rarely got untidy. There were two leather chesterfields either side of a fireplace with a gas fire that looked like it was filled with real coal, a steel and chrome shelving system which contained his stereo and CD collection, and a big-screen television. Nelson had seen the furniture in the window of a downtown store and had bought it as a job lot. He'd even gone to the trouble of matching the thick-pile carpet to the colour used in the window display. 'Can I get you a drink?' he asked.

'Sure. What have you got?'

'I've got vodka in the icebox.'

'Great.'

Nelson went into the kitchen and opened his refrigerator. He had a bottle of Absolut next to his ice cubes, but in the vegetable chiller he saw something he thought Jenny might appreciate even more. He took the bottle of Tattinger champagne out and carried it into the sitting room with two long-stemmed glasses. She was standing by the window, toying with a vase of freshly cut flowers. His cleaning lady replaced them every three or four days. 'How about this instead?' he asked.

'Terrific,' she said. 'Are we celebrating?'

Nelson popped the cork and deftly poured the champagne into the two glasses. 'Meeting you,' he said. 'It's the best thing that's happened to me for some time.'

'Sweet-talker,' she said, taking her glass. She raised it in salute, then sipped. 'Mmmmm, good,' she said. She looked at the fireplace. 'Does it work?' she asked.

'It's gas, but it looks like the real thing,' he said. He put his glass on the mantelpiece and knelt down on the sheepskin rug in front of the fire, turning the gas on and pressing the igniter button. Yellow and red flames flickered among the fake coals. As he straightened up he felt Jenny's hand touch the back of his head and then stroke his neck. He rested his cheek against her thighs and closed his eyes. She knelt down beside him and put her glass on the hearth and before he knew what was happening she was kissing him, her lips pressed tightly against his, her soft tongue probing between his teeth. He kissed her back, passionately, and his hands reached for her breasts, stroking them, teasing the nipples until they hardened. She broke away, gasping for breath. 'Do you have any pillows?' she asked.

'Pillows?' he repeated, confused.

She stroked the sheepskin rug, her scarlet nails highlighted by the white fur. 'I've never done it on a sheepskin rug,' she said.

Nelson grinned, unable to believe his luck. 'I'll be right back,' he said.

He rushed upstairs, took off his jacket and grabbed two pillows from his bed. He had a sudden thought and went through to his bathroom. He gave himself a couple of squirts of a minty breath freshener and from the top shelf of his medicine cabinet he took two Trojan condoms. He didn't like wearing them, but more and more girls insisted on it, until they got to know him anyway. He was halfway out of the bathroom door when he had another thought and returned for a third. He didn't want to have to break off for replacements if things went as well as he expected them to. He slipped the condoms into his back pocket.

When he got back downstairs, Jenny was standing naked by the fireplace, holding the two champagne-filled glasses. Her clothes were in a tidy pile on one of the sofas. 'What took you so long?' she asked, handing him a glass.

Nelson dropped the pillows on to the rug and loosened his tie with one hand as he took the champagne. Jenny clinked glasses with him. 'This is going to be the best,' she promised. She'd arranged her long blonde hair so that it hung over her breasts and almost to her crotch. It was the most erotic sight Nelson had ever seen – she was naked and yet at the same time hidden. His throat felt as dry as sand and he gulped the champagne down in one go. Jenny picked the bottle of champagne off the mantelpiece and refilled his glass. As she moved, Nelson could see the triangle of soft blonde curls where her thighs joined.

He took his tie off and threw it on top of her clothes and began unbuttoning his shirt. He couldn't take his eyes off her body. For the first time he saw a scar across her stomach, a slightly raised line that wound from her navel across to her left thigh. It wasn't a clean surgeon's cut but jagged and rough as if it had been a long time healing. He found the scar suddenly thrilling. He could picture her in a knife fight, eyes narrowed, crouched like a tigress.

'Let me do that,' she said, stepping forward. She undid his buttons, taking her time and scratching his chest with her nails as she worked, her eyes fixed on his. He lifted the glass to his lips and drained it. She took it from his hand and put it on the coffee table. Nelson stood behind her, and as she straightened up he cupped his hands around her breasts. She groaned throatily and leant against him, slipping her hands behind her back and between his thighs. He nuzzled his face in her hair. Her perfume was intoxicating and he breathed it in. Her hands moved expertly, touching and teasing him until he felt he was going to burst.

She turned, panting as she slipped the shirt off his shoulders. As it dropped to the ground he grabbed her and kissed her. He pressed his lips against hers as if trying to devour her, and as she sucked on his tongue she reached for his trousers and he felt her undo his belt and pull down his zipper. She did it tantalisingly slowly, kissing him all the while and moaning with passion.

Nelson ran his hands through her hair and down the small of her back. His hands felt rough against her skin as he caressed her firm buttocks. He felt his trousers fall around his ankles and then her hands moved inside his boxer shorts, holding his flesh for the first time. 'Lie down on the rug,' he gasped.

She laughed and did as she was told while he ripped off his socks and shorts. He stood over her, drinking her in with his eyes, as she moved her legs apart and smiled up at him. 'Like what you see?' she asked.

'Oh, sweet Jesus, yes,' he said, trembling. He dropped down on his knees, his arms trembling. He was surprised at the way he was reacting to her. He'd been with beautiful girls before, black and white, and it certainly wasn't the first time he'd had sex on the sheepskin rug, but she was turning him into a trembling jelly. He was finding it hard to breathe and was sweating profusely. He lay down next to her, licking and kissing her neck as his hands roamed over her body. His right hand moved over the scar. He could feel the raised line and he traced it across her stomach and over her thigh, then he moved his hand between her legs, trying to probe inside her, but she resisted, clamping her thighs together and denying him access. He tried to force her thighs apart but she resisted more; her leg muscles were like steel. Then she moved quickly, pushing him on to his back and kissing him again. She reached between his legs and held him, moving her hand faster and faster, until all he could think about was what she was doing and how good it felt. 'How does that feel?' she said, her voice shaking a little in time with her movements.

'It feels . . . unbelievable,' he said.

She moved slowly down his body, tickling the inside of his thighs with her fingertips as she allowed her hair to play over his skin. He closed his eyes and rubbed them with the back of his hands. When he opened them again he had trouble focusing. There seemed to be two ceiling fans even though he knew there was only one.

Jenny planted soft kisses around his stomach as she ran her hands up and down his legs, scratching with her nails and driving him mad with desire. He wanted to be inside her more than he'd ever wanted anything in his life, but he was finding it harder to stay awake. It couldn't have been the champagne – he'd only had two glasses. His eyelids felt heavy and he forced them apart. There were four ceiling fans, then the four split into eight, then there were more than he could count. The room was spinning and he tried to sit up, but Jenny slid a hand up his chest and pushed him back on to the rug. She felt so strong, or maybe it was just that he was losing his strength. He tried to talk, to tell her that something was wrong, but his mouth wouldn't work. She must have realised that he was having problems because she stopped playing with him and he felt her move up so that she was lying next to him, her hair across his chest like a silky blanket. She was smiling. 'How do you feel now?' she asked, though it sounded as if she was talking through water.

His mouth tried to form the words but he couldn't speak. His eyes wouldn't stay open. The last thing he saw was the smile on her luscious lips and the sparkle in her eyes. The last thing he heard was her voice. 'Good,' she whispered.

Jenny waited until Nelson's eyes had closed and he was snoring quietly before she rolled off the rug and got to her feet. She looked down at the sleeping man with contempt. She didn't like blacks – in fact she'd asked for an extra fifty per cent when she saw his photograph. They'd paid – it wasn't as if they were able to bring a racial discrimination lawsuit against her and they knew that Nelson liked blondes. She tied her hair back into a ponytail with an elastic band and dressed quickly. Nelson snored, loudly this time, but there was no need for her to hurry. The drug was good for thirty minutes. Plenty of time. She could taste him and she wanted to spit but knew that wasn't a good idea. He'd almost made her gag when he'd stuck his tongue into her mouth, but she had to keep him turned on so that he wouldn't notice that the champagne had been drugged. She shivered as she realised how close he'd actually come to making love to her. Another couple of minutes and she wouldn't have been able to keep him off her. She shuddered at the thought.

She walked over to the light-switch by the door and turned the main light on and off, then went over to the window and looked out on to the street. The doors of a white Cadillac opened and two heavy-set men got out carrying black nylon holdalls. Jenny opened the door for them. They didn't even acknowledge her presence.

From her bag she took a pair of medical gloves and snapped them on, then she went to get the champagne bottle and glasses from the sitting room. One of the men had taken a battery-operated vacuum cleaner from his bag and was hoovering Nelson from head to toe as the other man slowly turned him over.

Jenny washed and dried the glasses in the kitchen and put them back in the cupboard. The empty bottle, the cork, and the foil wrapping went into her bag. Then she took a piece of kitchen roll and wiped everything in the house she'd touched, including the light-switch. By the time she'd finished, the two men were carrying Nelson's naked body upstairs.

Sal Sabatino poured himself a glass of wine as he checked the rows of figures in the accounts book. Through his feet he could feel the pulsing beat of a rock group whose name he couldn't even pronounce. He smiled as he totalled up the numbers on his calculator. The Firehouse was a money machine, one of the most popular nightclubs in Baltimore. It was a cash business, perfect for laundering the money his brother made from their New York activities. But it had another advantage – it provided Sabatino with a steady supply of young girls, the sort who'd do practically anything for a noseful of cocaine or a chance to get close to the bands who played at The Firehouse. Sabatino couldn't have been happier. He sipped his wine, enjoying the flavour and the bouquet.

Like the nightclub, Sabatino wasn't what he appeared to be. He had taken an Italian name, he looked more Italian than most Italians and he spoke with a pronounced Italian accent, but in his heart of hearts he could never forget that he was Russian, no matter how hard he tried. He wasn't even Catholic. The small gold crucifix he wore around his neck was as much an affectation as his accent – he'd been brought up as a Muslim, though it had been many, many years since he'd been inside a mosque.

Sabatino loved to be mistaken for an Italian. A Russian mobster was a joke, a thick clod with lots of muscle and no brains, but an Italian gangster, that was something else. The Italian dons commanded respect. Sabatino craved respect, more than money, more than power, more than sex. It wasn't as if he didn't have an Italian heritage. His father was an Italian soldier who was taken prisoner by the Russians towards the end of the Second World War and shipped to Chechenya, a landlocked province close to the southern border of the old Soviet Union. His mother was a young widowed farmworker who had struck up a conversation with a good-looking prisoner-of-war who was digging ditches under the not-very-watchful eye of a bored guard. Somehow the Italian soldier and the Russian peasant had managed to steal a few minutes together, a hurried, frantic coupling with the minimum of undressing, and nine months later Gilani Utsyev had entered the world, kicking, screaming and unwanted. Sabatino's mother told her parents that she'd been raped, and it was only years later that she tearfully confessed that his father wasn't a masked rapist but an Italian soldier who had died of malnutrition in the prisoner-of-war camp.

Sabatino's childhood was the stuff nightmares are made of. He received little or no attention from his mother's family, who considered him an unwanted embarrassment, and he was just two years old when Stalin exiled the whole population of the mini-state to Siberia and Central Asia for allegedly co-operating with the Germans. It wasn't until he was fourteen years old that he and Bzuchar returned to their homeland, their mother dead and buried in the frozen Siberian soil. The lack of a father and the years in exile killed any loyalty the brothers might have had for their family or country. They fled the country shortly after the dissolution of the Soviet Union, and were already settled in the United States when Chechenya declared its independence in November 1991.

It was only when he arrived in America that Gilani felt able to change his name and to adopt the heritage of his unknown father. His mother hadn't asked the prisoner-of-war for his name: Sabatino was above the first Italian restaurant he'd seen in New York. Now the only person to use his old name was his brother. No one else dared to.

A knock at the door disturbed his day-dreaming. The door opened and one of his bodyguards showed in the blonde. He didn't know her real name, and he didn't need to know. She was a looker. Tall, blonde and statuesque, but about five or six years older than he liked his girls.

He preferred them younger and darker, and smaller, but he wouldn't have minded finding out how she'd be in the sack. She looked like she'd be able to crack walnuts with her thighs. His gaze travelled up her body, lingered over her breasts. 'How did it go?' he asked, his eyes finally finishing their journey and reaching her face. Such a pretty mouth, he thought. He would have been tempted to forgo his preference for brunettes, temporarily at least, if it hadn't been for his brother's warning. This one wasn't to be touched.

'Without a hitch,' she said. 'It might be a day or two before they find him.'

'That's not a problem,' Sabatino said. He opened a desk drawer and took out a padded envelope. He handed it to her and she slipped it into her bag.

'Is there anything else I can do for you, Mr Sabatino?' she asked, holding his stare.

The bodyguard had closed the door. They were alone in the office. Sabatino picked up his glass and swirled the wine around. She was coming on to him, there was no doubt about it, but he knew that it wouldn't be free. The girl was a professional, but then again Sabatino wasn't averse to paying for his pleasures. She stood straighter, pulling her shoulders back to emphasise her breasts. Erotic thoughts filled his head and she smiled as if to say that she knew what he was thinking and would be quite happy to do whatever he wanted – for the right price. 'Anything?' she added.

Sabatino grinned. His brother had said don't touch the hired help, and crossing Bzuchar wasn't something a sane man would do, not if he wanted to keep the use of his legs. They might be brothers, but when his temper flared Bzuchar was like a wild animal and lashed out without

221

thinking. Sabatino had once seen him stick a fruit knife in a man's throat because he'd interrupted him while he was telling a joke. Sabatino raised his glass to the girl. 'Some other time, maybe,' he said.

She nodded. 'Are you sure?'

Sabatino's face hardened. Flirting was one thing, but now she seemed to be playing with him. He wondered if his brother had asked her to test him, to see whether or not he'd disobey him. 'Get out,' he hissed. 'Get the fuck outta my office.'

He turned his back on her and didn't see her leave. His hand was clenched around the stem of the wine glass and as the door closed it snapped. The broken glass fell to the floor, leaving a small cut on his hand. Blood oozed from the wound and Sabatino sucked it, like a baby feeding from its mother's breast.

Mersiha woke to the sound of blackbirds singing in the trees behind the house. She lay for a while listening to them. It brought back memories of when she was a child, back when she shared a bedroom with Stjepan. He could mimic their song, and he'd often lie in his bed whistling to them and laughing as they called back. Mersiha had tried to copy him, but she could never get the birds to reply to her.

Later, after her parents had been killed, the blackbirds were still around, still singing. Whenever the rattle of gunfire or the whistle and roar of mortars died away, the birdsong would always return. By the time she was twelve, Mersiha had seen hundreds of dead bodies, but she'd never seen a dead bird. She thought that the birds had some mystic power that enabled them to escape the death and devastation that ravaged her homeland, until Stjepan explained that the dead birds were swiftly carried off by predators and eaten.

Mersiha closed her eyes and concentrated on the birds, declaring their territorial ambitions with songs so beautiful it made her want to cry. If only humans would fight wars by singing, she thought. Then her parents wouldn't be dead and Stjepan would still be around to sing to the birds for her. She felt tears prick her eyes and she fought to contain them.

'Mersiha!' She heard her name being called and for a wild moment she imagined that it was her brother. 'Mersiha!' It was her father, calling her to breakfast.

He was sitting at the kitchen table munching on one of Katherine's low-fat, high-fibre rabbit-food breakfast cereals when she arrived. Katherine put a plate of wholemeal toast and a mug of hot tea in front of Mersiha. 'When you've finished this I've got a surprise for you,' she said.

'Yeah?' Mersiha said, buttering her toast and smearing her father's precious Silver Shred over it. The lemon marmalade was hard to find in the States and he had friends in Scotland regularly send him over supplies, along with PG Tips tea bags, Heinz baked beans and salad cream. She deliberately spread the marmalade thickly because she loved the look of anguish in his eyes, like a child threatened with losing his favourite toy. He raised a warning eyebrow and Mersiha giggled. 'Is it a pony?' she asked in a little-girl's voice. She winked at her father.

'No, it's not a pony,' Katherine said, flicking a tea towel at her.

'So what's the surprise?'

Katherine tutted. 'If I told you, it wouldn't be a surprise, would it?'

'I guess not.' She munched on her toast and sipped her tea. 'How's the diet, Dad?' she asked, nodding at the bowl of cereal.

Freeman curled his lip and growled like a dog. Buffy sat up in the corner, her ears up. 'It's delicious,' he said.

'It's good for you,' Katherine said, pouring herself a cup of black coffee.

'Hmmm. This advice is brought to you from a heavy smoker,' Freeman said.

'I'm quitting,' she retorted.

'When?' Freeman asked.

'Soon. Don't press me.' She sat down next to him, ruffling his hair.

'You could always smoke the cereal,' Mersiha suggested. Katherine pointed her index finger at her and she pretended to duck an imaginary blow. 'Uh-oh, the waggly finger.'

Freeman smiled and Mersiha could see that he was pleased with the banter, that he was happy again now that she and Katherine appeared to be friends. She felt the smile harden on her own lips as she realised how false it all was. She could make jokes, she could laugh with Katherine, but at the back of her mind was the image of Katherine in bed with Dr Brown, sweating and moaning and betraying her father. She realised she was frowning and she forced herself to relax. The important thing, the only thing that mattered, was that her father was happy. She'd do anything to make sure he stayed that way.

'Try hiding it under your spoon, Dad,' she joked. 'It always works for me.'

Freeman smiled ruefully. 'It's fine,' he said. 'Honest.'

When Mersiha had finished her breakfast and loaded up the dishwasher, Katherine kissed Freeman goodbye and picked up her handbag.

'Isn't Dad coming?' Mersiha asked.

'Girls only,' Katherine said briskly. 'Come on.'

Mersiha hesitated, but Freeman made a small shooing motion with his hand. 'Go,' he said. 'Enjoy yourself.'

Mersiha wanted to protest, to say that she had no wish to spend time alone with Katherine, but remembered what she'd promised her father. 'See you later,' she said. He winked and she winked back.

She followed Katherine to the car. They both climbed in and fastened their seat belts. 'So what's the surprise?' she asked.

'We're going shopping.'

'That's my surprise?'

Katherine smiled. 'Sort of. You're going to have a make-over. And a new dress. And we're getting your hair done. Then you're having your photograph taken. Then we're going to show your dad the new you.'

Mersiha beamed. 'Really?'

'Yup. Even your dad doesn't know. I want to see his face when he sees you all made up. And the dress is for your birthday dinner on Monday.'

Katherine made small-talk as she drove to the White Marsh shopping mall, and Mersiha did her best to sound interested. She knew that Katherine was making an effort to be nice, so she did her best to respond, but no matter how she tried she couldn't get Art Brown out of her head. What she wanted more than anything was a promise from Katherine that it wouldn't happen again, but that wish would have to remain unfulfilled. There was no way Mersiha could tell her that she knew about the affair. Or that it was she who had ended it.

The holiday her father had suggested might be just what she needed. A week away from the house, alone with her father, might push the memory of Katherine's infidelity away and allow her to start again. She hoped so.

They were so different, the brothers Utsyev. Anyone seeing them together wouldn't have known they were from the same country, never mind the same womb. Sabatino was corpulent with the olive skin that betrayed his Italian genes, with black hair that always appeared greasy no matter how often he washed it. His face was wrinkle-free and baby smooth with soft fleshy lips, and he could go several days without shaving.

Bzuchar Utsyev was two years older but the age difference appeared much greater; he was lean and wiry and looked as if he'd spent a lifetime outdoors. His skin was dry and leathery, his hair close-cropped and grey, and his eyes had the lifeless stare of day-old fish. But when the brothers were together, it was as if they were twins. There was a tangible bond between them which excluded everyone else, and each seemed to know what the other was thinking before a word was uttered. It was a bond that had been formed in the days of Stalin's purges, when the brothers Utsyev were orphans in a strange land, when they could depend only on each other and no other.

The two men embraced in the office above The Firehouse, Sabatino sighing like a virgin on her first date, Bzuchar gripping his brother like a drowning man holding a lifebelt. 'Everything is okay?' Bzuchar asked.

'Everything's just fine,' his brother said.

Bzuchar put his hands on Sabatino's shoulders and looked into his eyes. 'My little brother, the Italian,' he said, grinning.

'My big brother,' Sabatino replied. 'The New Yorker.'

Bzuchar patted Sabatino's expanding waistline. 'Too much pasta,' he chided.

Sabatino shrugged. 'Gives the girls something to hold on to. What can I say?'

Bzuchar faked a punch to his brother's stomach, then hugged him again.

'Do you want a drink?' Sabatino asked.

'Yeah,' Bzuchar said, 'but none of that Italian fizzy wine. I'll take a bourbon.'

Sabatino went over to his drinks cabinet and poured three fingers of Jack Daniels into a crystal tumbler. There was a bottle of Frascati already open and he splashed a good-sized measure into a glass. They toasted each other in Russian and drank deeply. 'So, what do you think of Jenny Welch?' Bzuchar asked.

Sabatino shrugged noncommittally. 'She seemed efficient.'

'Yeah. Great figure, huh? Amazing legs.'

Sabatino shrugged again. 'Didn't notice,' he said.

Bzuchar grinned. 'Bullshit. You wanted her, didn't you?'

Sabatino wondered what the bitch had said to his brother. 'Don't be stupid,' he said. 'She was way too old for me.'

'Still go for the young stuff, huh? You've gotta watch out for that jailbait, Gilani.' He looked around the office for somewhere to sit. He decided on Sabatino's chair behind the desk. Sabatino knew better than to object.

'Nelson won't be troubling us any more,' Bzuchar said. He grinned. 'Did she tell you how she did it?' Sabatino shook his head and took a long sip of wine. Bzuchar raised his glass to his brother. Down below, in the disco section of the nightclub, one of the disc jockeys began a sound check. Sabatino could feel the vibrations through the soles of his feet. 'She made it look like a gay suicide. Great, huh? Kills the guy and his reputation at the same time. Talk about two birds with one stone.'

'Do you think that'll be the end of it?' Sabatino asked.

'What, you think the bank will be too busy covering up the scandal to bother with his investigation?' He pulled a face as if the bourbon was leaving a sour taste in his mouth. 'I don't think so, Gilani. That's why I'm here in this godforsaken city.'

Sabatino sat down on a leather sofa and waited for Bzuchar to explain the reason for his visit. Nelson had been the instigator of the investigation, but Bzuchar was right. There'd be files and notes and eventually Nelson would be replaced. Down below, rap music began to pound. Sabatino hated the music but it brought in the crowds and their money. Given the choice he preferred opera, but there was little call for culture in Baltimore. Rap music, drugs, cable television and baseball were the main entertainments for the city's inhabitants, and the brothers made a good living from the first two.

'It won't take long for Nelson's replacement to realise what's been going on,' Bzuchar said. 'It won't take too much digging to discover the money your man's been washing for us. He ain't gonna have time to cover his tracks, so I've decided on a pre-emptive strike. We're going to take the company over, lock, stock and barrel. We pay off the shareholders and the banks, then it's our company and to hell with them.'

'That's going to cost us,' Sabatino said.

Bzuchar drained his glass, then stood up and went over to the drinks cabinet. 'I've had some number-crunchers go through the figures Anderson gave us,' he said as he refilled his tumbler. 'We can sell off the profitable parts of the business and use that to pay off some of the loans. We take the land we want and sell the rest and we'll be getting a few tax breaks as well. The total shortfall after we've paid off all the bank loans will be about three million dollars. That's chickenfeed compared with what we'll be making on the development.'

'And how do we persuade the shareholders to sell?' Sabatino asked.

Bzuchar's eyes sparkled like diamonds. 'Easy,' he said. 'You make them an offer they can't refuse. Just like *The Godfather*.'

Katherine parked the car and took Mersiha to a boutique on the second floor of the huge shopping mall. She helped her go through the racks, suggesting dresses she thought would be suitable but letting Mersiha have the final say. Mersiha went into the changing rooms with half a dozen dresses on hangers and tried them on, parading in front of Katherine for her approval, even though she already knew which one she wanted: a short black sleeveless dress, cut low at the back, which showed lots of thigh and a respectable amount of cleavage. She kept it until the last, standing in front of the changing-room mirror before going out to show Katherine.

'It's a little . . . revealing,' Katherine said hesitantly.

'It's the style,' Mersiha said, pulling the hem down an extra centimetre.

'Hmmm. You've certainly got the legs for it. Turn around.'

Mersiha turned on the spot. She knew Katherine was right – she did have good legs, long and tanned and with small, neat ankles. Men had been turning to look at her legs since she was fourteen, especially in the summer when she wore shorts to school. Recently their gazes had been drifting higher too. When it had first happened she'd been a little frightened and had tried to hide the signs of approaching womanhood under baggy pullovers and jeans. It had brought back memories of what had happened in Bosnia, how women had been raped and killed by men with guns, used and abused and then killed. She blocked the memories and admired the dress in the mirror. It made her look older, eighteen maybe. It was elegant, but it was fun, too. She had a white linen jacket that would look just great over it, and it would be a terrific dress to dance in.

The young assistant hovered nearby and Katherine handed over her gold American Express card.

'Thanks, Katherine,' Mersiha said.

'Happy birthday,' Katherine responded. Mersiha kissed her lightly on the cheek. A baby's kiss.

Their next trip was to a shoe shop where Katherine bought her a pair of black high heels, then they had cappuccinos in a small coffee bar. 'Your father is going to love that dress,' Katherine said.

'He can wear it if he wants,' Mersiha replied, giggling. They laughed together, and for a moment Mersiha felt that things were back the way they used to be. Before Mersiha knew Katherine's secret.

'You can wear that when we have your photograph taken,' Katherine said. They walked arm in arm to the photographer's studio, a franchise operation at the far end of the mall between a pet store and an 'Everything For $1' outlet.

Several seats were occupied by women having their hair done and make-up applied. On the walls was a series of poster-size glamour photographs – lots of big hair, shining eyes and soft skin. 'They're going to do that to me?' Mersiha said. 'I don't believe it.'

Katherine had made an appointment for eleven o'clock. A willowy blonde dressed all in black came out of a back room and began gushing over Mersiha, running her fingers through her hair and turning her chin from side to side. She introduced herself as Tanya, organised a cup of coffee for Katherine as she waited, and then whisked Mersiha off to a leather and chrome chair in front of a wash basin.

Tanya lifted Mersiha's hair to see what it would look like shorter, then piled it up high on her head. 'It would look really great like this,' she said enthusiastically.

Mersiha shook her head. 'No. My dad likes it long.'

'It's your hair,' Tanya insisted.

'No,' Mersiha repeated.

If Tanya was offended by Mersiha's terseness, she didn't show it. 'Okay, okay, but what about these white hairs here?' She separated the small group of white hairs close to her parting. 'They really are white, aren't they? They're not grey. I could cut them. Or dye them so they're not so obvious.'

'No,' Mersiha snapped, so vehemently that Tanya took a step back. Mersiha realised that she'd overreacted so she smiled as sweetly as she could. 'I like them just the way they are.'

Tanya was quick and efficient. She was only a few years older than Mersiha and she talked non-stop about the latest Hollywood gossip. She seemed to read nothing but the showbiz tabloids. Mersiha let her chatter wash over her. She watched Katherine sit and read a copy of *The New Yorker*, taking a cigarette out and then seeing a 'no smoking' sign and replacing it.

'Your mom said you had a black dress you want to wear for the photographs,' Tanya said.

'Yeah, is that okay?'

'Sure, whatever you want. You can change in the back, then we'll do your make-up.'

Mersiha took the dress from Katherine and put it on in a changing room at the back of the store. She admired it again in a full-length mirror, sliding her hands down her hips where it clung like a second skin. 'This is one hot dress,' she murmured to herself, then felt her cheeks redden as she realised what she was doing. She'd never had a boyfriend, she'd never even been kissed by anyone other than relatives, and here she was flirting and pouting with her own reflection. It wasn't that she didn't like boys. Like the rest of the girls at school she spent hours talking about them, watching them, rating them, but unlike most of her contemporaries she'd never actually been out with one. She'd been asked, several times, but something had always held her back. It didn't need a psychiatrist to explain why. She shuddered as the memories of what had happened to her in Bosnia flooded back. The hatred, the violence, the pain. All of it caused by men, men with lust in their eyes. It was the lust which Mersiha feared more than anything. She was about to remove the dress and put it back in the bag when Tanya stuck her head into the changing room.

'Wow! That's lovely,' Tanya said. 'It looks amazing on you.' The two girls went back into the salon and Mersiha sat down in front of the mirror.

Tanya dabbed moisturiser on Mersiha's face, then picked up a pair of tweezers. Mersiha moved her head back instinctively and Tanya smiled. 'I'm going to tidy your eyebrows. I promise not to touch the white hairs.'

Tanya plucked a few stray hairs from Mersiha's eyebrows. 'You've got terrific skin,' she said. She paused. 'How old are you?'

'Fifteen,' Mersiha answered. 'Well, almost sixteen.'

'Have you got a boyfriend?'

'No. Not yet.'

Tanya made a whistling sound through pursed lips. 'Well, you're not going to have any trouble getting one, I can tell you. They'll be around you like flies.'

'Thanks,' Mersiha said, unconvinced.

Tanya applied foundation and Mersiha felt it tighten her skin, as if a mask were being stretched across her face. Then she applied blusher with a thick brush. Katherine came up behind Mersiha and touched her lightly on the shoulder. 'I need a cigarette, kiddo, I'll be outside,' she said.

'Okay.' Mersiha studied her face in the mirror. The blusher had emphasised her cheekbones, giving her a severe appearance. She looked older already. Tanya picked up a sky-blue pencil and Mersiha watched as she worked on her eyes, opening them one at a time to follow what was going on.

'And now, ta-da, mascara. Every girl thinks she knows how to put this on, but there's a right way and a wrong way.' Tanya pulled a mascara brush out of its tube. 'Brush from the roots to the tips, upper lashes first on both eyes, then lower. Your lashes are really long, so you should hold a rolled tissue underneath so that you don't get it on your skin. Then do the upper lashes again.' Tanya held a piece of tissue under each eye as she worked on them.

Then she selected a tube of pink lipstick and showed it to Mersiha. 'This shade will look really good.' Mersiha watched carefully in the mirror. When Tanya had finished, she unpinned Mersiha's hair, brushed it out, and stood back. 'What do you think?' she asked.

Mersiha sat staring at her reflection, stunned. The face that looked back was almost that of a stranger. She'd never seen herself looking so pretty. 'Wow,' she said softly.

'Pretty neat, huh?'

'Wow,' Mersiha repeated. She pursed her lips a little. The way Tanya had painted them made them seem fuller. Sexier. She turned her head to the side. Her eyes seemed bigger and brighter and the blusher on her cheekbones made her face seem narrower. The foundation looked, and felt, strange, like a mask. Without thinking, she lifted a hand to touch it, but she drew it back, not wanting to spoil the effect. 'It's almost too much,' she said.

Tanya nodded. 'Oh, yeah, of course it is. What I've done is full photographic make-up. You'd use a bit less if you were going out at night, and a lot less for daytime. Experiment a bit. You'll soon get the hang of it.'

The stylist turned the chair away from the mirror. Katherine came back into the store as Mersiha stood up. 'Kiddo, you look fantastic,' she gushed. She smiled at Tanya. 'You've done a terrific job.' Katherine ran the back of her hand against Mersiha's hair. 'It's strange – you need make-up to look older, I have to use even more to try to look younger.'

'Oh no, you look fabulous too,' Tanya said. 'You can tell that you're mother and daughter.' For an instant Mersiha's smile froze.

Katherine sat down and watched Mersiha over the top of her magazine as the photographer, a young bearded guy in his early thirties, came out of his studio and introduced himself. His name was Ted and he had a nasal New York accent, though his vocabulary was often that of a West Coast surf bum. He had a goofy grin and Mersiha thought that under all his facial hair was probably a good-looking guy. He took her into the studio, and sat her down on a green leather armchair, fussing over her until he was satisfied that she was sitting in the right position – back straight, head tilted slightly up and to the left, one hand poised under her chin. To Mersiha it felt too posed, too artificial, but Ted said she looked 'really cool, totally', and she thought that once he might actually have said 'groovy'.

He had a large camera mounted on a tripod, but he took an instant shot with a Polaroid camera first to show her what it was going to look like. She had to admit that the effect was stunning. 'Awesome, huh?' Ted asked.

'I can't believe I look like that,' she said, handing the Polaroid picture back to him.

'The camera doesn't lie,' he said, 'much.'

He stood behind his camera and used a remote switch to operate it so that he could stand up straight and give her instructions. 'A bit more to the left, curl your fingers a bit, think beautiful thoughts, open your lips just a shade more.'

Mersiha did as he asked. Her fingers had gone numb and her arm ached, but if the finished effect was going to be anything like the Polaroid, she was quite happy to put up with a little discomfort.

'Have you ever thought of doing any modelling work?' Ted asked.

'No,' Mersiha laughed. 'Of course not. I'm only fifteen.'

'You'd be surprised how young most models are,' he said. 'In fact these days, the younger the better. You've got the face – and the figure.'

Mersiha tensed instinctively at the mention of her figure. She'd forgotten that she was wearing a revealing dress and that it had ridden almost up to her thighs as she sat in the chair. She squirmed and tried to pull the hem down, but Ted told her not to move. 'Trust me, it looks perfect,' he said.

She forced herself to relax, but Ted had already decided that he wanted to set up a different shot. He photographed her in a multitude of poses – sitting, standing, looking over her shoulder, face on, her face tilted up, down, sideways – until it seemed to Mersiha that there were no other options left. 'Do you always take as many pictures as this?' she asked.

Ted shrugged: 'You should see some of the girls I have to photograph. Their mothers bring them in here and expect me to work miracles on them. I tell you, you'd have to smear Vaseline on the lens and shoot them through a blanket to make them look halfway decent. But you, you've got a look.'

'A look?' Mersiha repeated, unable to keep the amusement out of her voice.

'I meant what I said about you being a model. You could do it. I'll give you my card on the way out. You should speak to your mom.'

'What sort of modelling are you talking about?'

'Nothing sleazy. Your looks are too good for that. High fashion, that's what you'd be good at. I don't mean runway modelling because you're not tall enough or thin enough for that. But you'd find plenty of work in the fashion magazines, the sort we've got on the tables out there.'

Mersiha pulled a face. 'We'll see,' she said.

Together they went back to the salon. Katherine stood up and put her magazine down on the table. 'How did it go?' she asked.

'Okay,' Mersiha said.

'Better than okay, she was terrific,' Ted enthused. He took a business card from his wallet and gave it to Mersiha.

'Think about it,' he said, then disappeared back into his studio.

'Think about what?' Katherine asked.

'Oh, nothing,' Mersiha said.

'Come on, young lady. Spill the beans.'

'He just asked if I wanted to be a model, that's all.'

Katherine raised an eyebrow. 'Really? And what did you say?'

Mersiha shrugged. 'Nothing. What could I say?' She went back into the changing room, took off the black dress and put on her shirt and jeans. The make-up was a stark contrast to the casual clothes but she had no idea how to get it off without smudging it.

Tanya was talking to Katherine when Mersiha left the changing room, the dress rolled up in its carrier bag with the shoes. 'I was just telling your mom, we'll have contact prints ready for you early next week. We'll call, then you can come and choose the prints you want. How did it go?'

'Great. He really made me feel at ease.'

'Yeah, Ted's a terrific photographer. He used to work for some of the big magazines in New York. He's got an amazing portfolio.'

'So what's he doing in Baltimore?' Katherine asked.

'His mother's sick. He's moved in with her to take care of her.'

Katherine smiled sympathetically. 'Nice boy. Come on, Mersiha. Let's hit the road.'

Mersiha gestured at her made-up face. 'I can't go out like this.' Tanya looked at her wristwatch. 'I don't have another client for twenty minutes. I'll take that off for you and show you how to apply daytime make-up.'

'Great,' Mersiha said.

Katherine sighed and reached for her packet of cigarettes. 'I'll be outside,' she said.

Freeman heard the dog barking with joy before he heard the car, and he was standing with the front door open before Katherine and Mersiha had climbed out. Buffy ran over and pawed at Mersiha, her tail wagging like a metronome.

'How did it go?' Freeman asked Mersiha. She looked different, but it was only as she got closer that he realised she was wearing eye make-up and lipstick. 'You look fabulous,' he said.

Mersiha blushed. 'You should have seen me before,' she said.

'What do you mean?'

'Full war paint,' Katherine explained, kissing him on the cheek. 'They gave her the works before they took the photographs.'

'So where are they?' Freeman asked.

'They take a few days to get the prints ready, then we choose the ones we want them to blow up,' Katherine replied.

Freeman ruffled Mersiha's hair. 'I can't wait to see them.'

Mersiha pulled a face. 'I bet they'll be terrible.'

He noticed the bag she was carrying. 'Is that the new dress?'

'And shoes,' Katherine said. 'She looks stunning in them.'

'You're wearing them tomorrow?'

Mersiha nodded. 'Sure.' Buffy continued to paw at her stomach, wanting to play. 'Katherine bought me some make-up, too. I'm going to try to do it myself tomorrow.'

Freeman raised his eyebrows. 'Now, that, I'm looking forward to.' He stepped aside to allow Katherine and Mersiha into the house. Katherine winked as she went by. Freeman patted her backside affectionately and closed the door as Buffy slipped through.

Mersiha took a can of Coke from the refrigerator and sat down at the kitchen table. 'So, do you feel like a vacation?' he asked.

'A vacation?'

'Yup. You and me. Some father–daughter bonding.'

Mersiha looked at him, then at Katherine, then back to Freeman. 'Are you serious?'

He grinned. 'Sure. I thought we'd go to the mountains. Hike. Ski, maybe. I'll show you how to light a fire, skin a moose, build an igloo, all that wilderness stuff.'

Mersiha laughed. 'When?'

'The travel agent says she can get us tickets for a Saturday flight.'

'Next Saturday?' Katherine said. 'That's a bit soon, isn't it?'

'Saturday'll be great, Dad. Just great.'

'I thought the sooner the better, Kat,' Freeman said. 'We've got a board meeting the week after next and I've got to be here for that, obviously.'

'I guess so,' Katherine said. 'You are the chairman after all.' There was a sarcastic edge to her voice, but she softened it with a smile. 'Yes, you're right. You should go.' .

'You're not coming?' Mersiha asked.

Katherine shook her head. 'No, kiddo, I've got lots to do here. Besides, you know how I hate the great outdoors. We'll all go away together later in the year.' She patted Mersiha on the shoulder. 'You can bring me back a moose.'

'What size?' she asked, then giggled.

'What do you call a blind moose?' Freeman asked.

'No eye-deer,' Mersiha said quickly.

'How come you know that one?' he asked.

'School,' she said. 'But the version I heard was an elk. I'm not sure if a moose is a deer, is it?'

'Dunno,' Freeman admitted. 'What do you call a blind elk with no legs?'

'Still no eye-deer,' Katherine said.

'Sheesh, does everyone in Maryland know these jokes?'

Freeman was reading an article on Singapore's defence industry in the *Far Eastern Economic Review* when Maury Anderson burst into his office. 'You're not going to believe this,' he said, doing a soft-shoe shuffle across to Freeman's window. 'What a beautiful day this is turning out to be.'

'What aren't I going to believe?' Freeman asked. Anderson's mood swings were starting to become a little tiring. The good news could be a fifty-million-dollar order or the fact that the photocopier was working, depending on how his partner was feeling that day.

'Lennie Nelson's dead.' Freeman's mouth dropped and the magazine fell from his fingers. 'I knew you'd be pleased,' Anderson said, stretching his hands out to the side like a man crucified. 'It couldn't have happened at a better time.'

'He's dead?' Freeman said. 'You mean dead dead?' He wondered if he'd misunderstood, if Anderson meant that the banker was dead career-wise, because he couldn't believe that his partner would express so much glee over a man's death.

'As a doornail. Isn't it great? Isn't it the best news you've heard all day?'

Freeman was horrified at Anderson's attitude. 'Maury, get a grip, will you? What happened?'

Anderson did another soft-shoe shuffle to Freeman's desk and leant over it, his hands either side of the blotter. There was a manic gleam in his eyes. 'That's the best part,' he said. 'You're not gonna believe it. It's so great.'

'Just tell me, Maury. You're starting to get on my nerves.'

'Okay, okay. Listen to this. They found him on his bed, stark naked, with several lines of coke, a stack of gay porn magazines and a plastic bag over his head.'

'You mean he killed himself? Suicide?'

Anderson began pacing up and down, waving animatedly. 'No, don't you get it? Don't you get it, Tony? He was a gasper! He was playing with himself while cutting down his air supply. Auto-erotic asphyxiation, they call it. He was as queer as a three-dollar bill. They found kiddie porn in a bedroom closet and all sorts of weird videos. My God, and he was trying to tell us how to run our business. I knew there was something wrong with him the first time I met him. Didn't you? Didn't you think there was something strange there?'

Freeman leant back in his chair and stared at Anderson. He'd never seen his partner as elated as this before. 'What the hell's wrong with you?' he asked.

Anderson stopped in his tracks as if he'd been poleaxed. 'What do you mean?'

'Look at you, grinning like the Cheshire cat because a man's dead. Lennie Nelson might have been a thorn in our side and I'll admit that he was a bit of a prick, but he was only doing what he thought was best for his bank.'

Anderson was stunned. 'Hey, come on now, don't tell me you're not glad that he's dead.'

'That's exactly right, Maury. I'm not glad. And his death doesn't change things for us. The bank will still be looking over our shoulder, they'll still want a man on our board. If it's not Nelson, it'll be somebody else.'

Anderson's eyes blazed. 'But that's just it, Tony. That's just it. It's going to be Walter.'

'Walter Carey? Are you sure?'

'I've got a friend in the bank. He just called me to give me the good news. The whole bank's talking about Nelson. I mean, nobody knew he was that way. Everyone thought he was a ladies' man.'

Freeman rubbed his chin thoughtfully. 'Have you heard officially?'

'No, not yet. I think Walter will probably want to tell you himself. I tell you, it's the end of our problems. Walter won't give us any shit about Ventura investing in us and he sure as hell won't have us chasing pie-in-the-sky joint ventures with the Chinese.'

'Taiwanese,' Freeman corrected. Anderson had a point. If Walter was going to be the bank's man on the board, it'd be tantamount to a return to the status quo. For a while anyway.

'Chinese, Taiwanese, who gives a shit? It means we can get on with running our business, our way.' Anderson punched the air. 'A queer. Who would have thought it, huh?'

The intercom bleeped on Freeman's desk. 'It's Walter Carey calling for you, Tony,' Jo said.

Anderson made a gun with his fingers and fired it at Freeman. He blew imaginary smoke from the tip of his finger and headed out as Freeman picked up the phone.

Freeman put down the menu as the waiter finished scribbling on his notepad. 'Anything to drink?' the waiter asked.

Freeman smiled at Katherine. 'Champagne?' he said.

'Definitely,' she agreed.

'Do you think champagne goes with Thai food?'

'I think champagne goes with everything,' Katherine said.

Freeman looked at Mersiha. 'Pumpkin?'

Mersiha's mouth dropped. 'You mean I can drink now that I'm sixteen?'

'No, what I mean is that you can have one glass of champagne now that you're sixteen.' Freeman nodded at the waiter. 'A bottle of champagne, the best you have,' he said. The waiter scribbled in his notepad again and scurried off. Freeman reached across and held Mersiha's hand. 'I can't get over how pretty you look,' he said.

244

'And the dress is fabulous,' Katherine agreed.

'Stop it,' Mersiha begged.

'I mean it,' Freeman went on. 'You should dress up more often.'

Mersiha shook her head. 'Once a year is enough,' she said.

Freeman had given Mersiha the choice of where she wanted to go for her birthday dinner and she'd chosen Thai Landing in Charles Street. He suspected that she'd chosen the Thai restaurant because she knew how much he liked it. He'd become a big fan of the fiery South-East Asian cuisine during a sales trip to Thailand, and the food at Thai Landing was every bit as delicious as any he'd had there.

'Sixteen years old,' he said. 'I can hardly believe it.'

'I know, I know. Soon it'll be college, then marriage, then children,' Mersiha sighed melodramatically. 'Then it's off to the old folks' home and I know the kids'll never visit.'

'You know what I mean,' Freeman said. 'It doesn't seem like three years since . . .' His voice tailed off as the memories flooded back. The basement. The killer with cold blue eyes. The bullets ripping into his legs. The concentration camp.

He looked down. Mersiha's hand was on top of his. It looked so small, like a child's. 'Thank you,' she said, quietly. 'Thank you for everything.'

Freeman's eyes began to sting and he blinked back the tears. He wasn't sure why he suddenly felt so sad. It was partly because he'd realised how close he'd come to losing Mersiha. If she'd been a little further away, if the gunman had fired a second earlier, if they hadn't found her in the camp . . . There were so many ifs. So many ways he could have lost her for ever. Fate had been on his side in Mersiha's case, but her presence also made him realise how unfair it was that he'd lost Luke. 'Tony?' Katherine said.

'I'm okay,' he said. He looked up and smiled. 'Just a bit emotional, that's all.'

Katherine reached over and took his other hand. She smiled at him sympathetically, as if she knew what he'd been thinking. The waiter returned carrying a bottle of champagne. He made a show of presenting the label to Freeman, then popped the cork professionally. When he'd filled their glasses he put the bottle in an ice bucket and went back into the kitchen.

Freeman picked up his glass and raised it in salute to his daughter. Katherine did the same.

'Happy birthday,' he said.

Katherine nodded. 'Happy birthday, Mersiha,' she echoed.

Mersiha blushed and picked up her glass. She waited expectantly, her eyes on her father. Freeman smiled at her. She knew what was coming and she was obviously relishing the anticipation. Katherine looked at him too, knowing that this was a special moment between father and daughter.

Freeman took a deep breath, then began to sing quietly, his voice only slightly more than a murmur because there were other people in the restaurant and he didn't want anyone else intruding into their celebration. 'Happy birthday to you,' he sang, his voice thick with emotion. 'Happy birthday to you. Happy birthday, dear Mersiha, happy birthday to you.'

Mersiha beamed. Freeman clinked glasses with her, then with Katherine. 'To my two favourite girls,' he said.

THE BIRTHDAY GIRL

*   *   *

Maury Anderson pounded his palms on his steering wheel as he powered the Corvette along the highway. He had the volume of the car stereo turned up as high as his ears could bear. He sniffed and rubbed the back of his hand across his nose, checking his driving mirror for the highway police.

His wife was down in Florida taking care of her sick mother and wasn't due back for another few days, so he'd picked up a large takeaway pizza which sat in a cardboard box on the passenger seat. In the glove compartment of his car was a small glass vial containing five grammes of cocaine. He was looking forward to a quiet night in. There was only one thing that would make the forthcoming evening perfect and that would be if Katherine Freeman were to pay him a visit, but he knew that was out of the question. He'd phoned her that morning and she'd explained that she was having dinner with Tony and Mersiha. There was no way she could get away.

Anderson ran a hand through his hair. A truck appeared to his right and for a second he almost lost control of the speeding Corvette. He gripped the wheel with both hands and accelerated away from the huge vehicle. Katherine Freeman was one hell of a woman, he thought. Tony was a lucky man. He snorted and shook his head. No, he wasn't lucky at all. Katherine might be Tony's wife, but she didn't belong to him. Anderson had been having an affair with Katherine for more than three years, meeting her in motels at regular intervals for just about the best sex he'd ever had. He smiled as he remembered that it wasn't only motels where they'd met. Twice they'd made love in the Corvette, and while it was cramped and uncomfortable it had given the act an excitement that brought back memories of his high-school days.

Anderson knew that he wasn't the only lover Katherine had taken, and she clearly saw nothing wrong in having affairs behind her husband's back. More often than not it was Katherine who initiated sex. She'd call him at the office and tell him which motel to go to, and she'd be waiting for him with a bottle of champagne on ice. In bed, there wasn't anything she wouldn't do for him, and she seemed to take as much pleasure from the act as he did. But she was always the first to go, often showering while he lay exhausted on the rumpled bed and leaving him to drop off the key. Once she was out of bed she wouldn't even kiss him. There was a coldness about her after they'd made love, a distance that he was never able to bridge. In a way that suited Anderson. His wife was the total opposite. After love-making she wanted to lie in his arms and talk, when all he wanted to do was to close his eyes and sleep. He liked the fact that he didn't have to sweet-talk Katherine, that she appreciated that their relationship would never go beyond recreational sex. But it worried his ego somewhat that she seemed so happy with the arrangement. At times he almost felt that it was him who was being taken advantage of.

He turned off the main highway and on to the road that led to his home, a comfortable ranch-house in Towson. The sky was starting to darken and several cars heading in the opposite direction had their headlights on. Anderson yawned and rubbed the back of his neck. It had been a long day in the office and his last hit of cocaine had worn off several hours earlier. He reached absent-mindedly towards the glove compartment and its vial of white powder, but pulled back when he realised what he was doing. Snorting at the wheel wasn't a smart move. Besides, he could wait. He wasn't an addict. A user, yes, but he could go for days without a hit if he wanted to. Well, hours, for sure. He didn't see the point of depriving himself of the high if he didn't have to. Cocaine helped him work, it made him more sociable, it lifted his thought processes to a higher level. The drug was a problem only if you let it get out of hand. Used sensibly it was safer than cigarettes or alcohol, and as far as Anderson was concerned, the sooner it was legalised the better.

He drummed on the steering wheel, nodding his head in time with the driving beat. He rubbed the bridge of his nose but found it hard to control the Corvette with one hand. He wondered if there was something wrong with the steering. Lately it had seemed that the car tended to drift at high speed, and he made a mental note to get it checked.

The light was on in the porch as Anderson stopped the car in front of the single-storey building. It came on automatically at dusk. His wife had insisted on having the light installed after a spate of burglaries in the area. The upmarket homes of Towson provided rich pickings for the intravenous drug users and sneak thieves of the inner city, and burglar alarm systems and bedside handguns were the norm rather than the exception. Anderson's wife kept a loaded Colt automatic in a cabinet by the bed; there was a shotgun in the closet and a very expensive alarm system.

He took the cocaine from the glove compartment and the pizza from the passenger seat and locked the car before stepping up on to the porch. A red light blinked on the Corvette's dashboard, another necessary security precaution. Car insurance costs were soaring in the suburbs as car thieves realised that the most expensive models were now to be found well outside the city centre. Middle-class professionals like Anderson had fled the city as it had fallen into decay, but by clustering together in suburban havens they'd only served to make themselves easier targets.

He unlocked the front door and walked quickly to the hall closet. Inside was the circuit panel into which he had to tap a four-digit code to deactivate the alarm system within twenty seconds. He fumbled with the pizza, trying not to tilt it as he opened the closet door, but he frowned as he realised that the system had already been switched off. He stood staring at the white-metal wall-mounted box, trying to recall if he'd left the house that morning without turning it on. It wasn't like him. His wife had drilled it into him how important it was always to have the security system on when they were out. She scoured the local papers for details of robberies and muggings in their area and pinned them to the refrigerator with small fruit-shaped magnets, and even though she was out of town her conditioning meant that Anderson would no more think of leaving the house without activating the system than he would of going out without his trousers. Still, the evidence was there before him. His frown deepened. Maybe there'd been a power failure. No, that wasn't possible because the porch light was on. He shrugged. Maybe it had just slipped his mind.

He closed the closet door with his shoulder and carried the pizza through to the kitchen. He dropped it down on the kitchen table and took the vial of cocaine out of his shirt pocket. Pizza or cocaine? It took less than a second to make up his mind. He could always reheat the pizza.

He headed for the guest bedroom. That was where he normally snorted the drug, away from his wife's prying eyes. Even though she wasn't around, he still felt safer taking the drug behind closed doors. As he walked by the sitting room, someone spoke his name. Anderson jumped backwards. The vial spun from his hand and shattered on the wooden floor. His eyes were wide and his whole body was shaking. Disparate thoughts ran through his mind: was he being robbed, were they armed, could he reach his shotgun, how had they got into the house, would he be able to get the spilled cocaine off the floor? He backed into the kitchen. He couldn't see the man who'd spoken; he must have been in the shadows. There were two doorways leading off the sitting room, the one he had gone through and another that opened into the hallway. All his senses seemed intensified. He could hear his feet scrape along the floor and he could smell an aftershave he didn't recognise, sweet and sickly. He realised with a jolt that he was standing with the kitchen light behind him and that anyone in the sitting room would see him in silhouette. He'd be a perfect target. He ducked involuntarily and scuttled towards the back door, scrabbling for the key which was already in the lock. As he turned it he remembered that the last time he'd seen the key it had been hanging on a hook by the refrigerator.

He yanked the door open. There were two men standing there. Big men with hard faces. Anderson turned, but before he could run a massive hand clamped down on his shoulder and gripped like a vice.

'Maury, what the fuck are you doing?' called the voice

from the sitting room. This time Anderson recognised the voice, but the recognition didn't make him any the less terrified.

The two heavies stepped into the kitchen. The one who was gripping his shoulder had bad acne, his skin pockmarked and rippled as if the flesh had been dragged along an asphalt road some time in the past. He grinned at Anderson, and it wasn't a pleasant expression. 'After you,' he said, and pushed Anderson forward.

Sabatino was sitting in a winged chair by the window. On the table next to him was a large framed photograph of Anderson and his wife, taken on their wedding day. When he'd left the house the photograph had been in its usual place, above the fireplace. His heart began to race like an over-exerted engine. Sabatino stood up and held out his hands like an old man welcoming a nephew. 'Maury, I'm sorry that we've come to your house uninvited.' He looked across at the wedding photograph. 'I suppose we should be grateful that at least we haven't had to disturb your wife, huh?'

'What do you want?' Anderson asked, all too well aware of how shaky his voice sounded.

'A chat. Just a chat.'

'Why here? Why now?'

The two heavyweights moved to stand either side of Anderson, like huge bookends. He hadn't seen them with Sabatino before. The man always had bodyguards close by, but never ones as big or as mean-looking as the two standing at his shoulders. 'We wanted a private chat, that's why.'

He became aware of another man in the room, standing in the opposite corner to Sabatino. He was taller than the Italian and thinner, with the gaunt look of a man who had trouble sleeping. As Anderson's eyes became used to the gloom he could make out a hooked, bird-like nose and hollow cheeks below dark spaces where he supposed the man's eyes were. He was standing like an undertaker overseeing a funeral, his back ramrod straight and his hands clasped behind him.

'My brother,' Sabatino explained. 'Bzuchar Utsyev.'

'Bzuchar?' Anderson repeated. The name didn't sound in the least bit Italian. Nor did the man's surname. And if they were brothers, how come they had different names? None of this made any sense.

'Don't worry about it,' said the man in the corner, obviously sensing his confusion. He stepped forward and switched on a table lamp. In its yellow glow Anderson could see that the man's hair was close-cropped and grey, emphasising the skull-like appearance of his head. 'I'm Gilani's brother, and his business partner.'

Anderson shook his head, confused. As far as he knew, Sabatino's first name was Sal, not Gilani. 'Pleased to meet you,' he said.

Utsyev smiled cruelly as if he knew exactly how pleased Anderson was to have him in his home. 'Why don't you sit down?' he said. 'This won't take long.'

'How did you get into my house?' Anderson asked.

'Sit down,' Utsyev ordered, pointing to a sofa.

The two heavies tensed and Anderson knew that Utsyev wouldn't ask again. He did as he was told, sitting as far away from Utsyev as he could get.

It was clear that Utsyev was running the show. Anderson looked over at Sabatino for guidance. The Italian had always played fair with him. They'd built up a good working relationship over the previous three years and had always been on the best of terms. Sabatino avoided his gaze. Anderson's stomach churned. What he needed was a cocaine hit and the confidence that the drug gave him. He sat with his hands in his lap, all too aware of how sweaty his palms were. He wiped them on his trousers. The two heavyweights moved to stand at either end of the sofa, their hands swinging freely at their sides. They were wearing black leather gloves. Anderson shuddered. Utsyev walked over to the side table next to Sabatino and picked up the wedding photograph. He looked at it, smiled thinly, then put it down again. 'Your wife is a very pretty woman,' he mused.

'Thank you,' Anderson said.

'No children?'

Anderson shook his head. 'No. No children.'

'I've never married,' Utsyev said. 'Never found a woman I wanted to marry.'

'Ah,' Anderson responded, as if that explained everything.

'So here we are,' Utsyev said.

'What do you want from me?' Anderson asked.

Utsyev sat down on a chair, smoothing the creases of his trousers. 'We are substantial investors in your company. But of course you know that, right?'

Anderson nodded. 'Right.'

'We have a sizeable stake in CRW. We'd like to increase that holding.'

Anderson looked across at Sabatino. 'I know that. Mr Sabatino's already told me what your plans are.' Still Sabatino wouldn't look him in the eye.

'No. Now we want complete ownership of the company.'

Anderson's mouth dropped. 'Say what?'

'We intend to take over CRW. Lock, stock and barrel.'

'Wait a minute,' Anderson said. He leaned forward, his whole upper body tense. 'This is a private firm. We have shareholders, sure, but we're not a listed company. You can't launch a takeover bid just like that.'

Utsyev smiled without warmth. 'We don't plan to launch a takeover bid,' he said. 'We will simply buy out the major shareholders.'

'You just don't get it,' Anderson said, shaking his head sadly. 'It's a family business. Katherine Freeman is the daughter of the founder. She'll never sell the company.'

'It's up to you to persuade her,' Utsyev said.

Anderson turned towards Sabatino. 'Will you explain to your brother that . . .?'

The slap was almost hard enough to knock Anderson off the sofa. He was so shocked by the blow that he didn't feel any pain. He looked up to see Utsyev standing over him. Utsyev backhanded him across the face again. Anderson fell back, his hands up to defend himself from further attacks. Utsyev glared at him, his forehead furrowed and his lips as thin as razors. 'You're talking to me, not my brother,' he hissed.

Anderson touched his face gingerly. He pressed his lips and his fingers came away covered in blood. 'I'm bleeding,' he said. Utsyev pulled a handkerchief from the breast pocket of his suit and handed it to him with a flourish. Anderson took it but didn't use it. He sat staring at the linen square, a look of amazement on his face. 'You hit me,' he said in disbelief.

Utsyev went back to his chair and sat down again, taking care to straighten the creases of his trousers. 'We are taking over the company, and you're going to help us. We're prepared to offer two million dollars in cash, and we'll take on the company's debts.'

'The company's worth more than that,' Anderson whispered.

'We're not talking about a fair market value,' Utsyev said. 'We're talking about what we're prepared to pay for it.'

'But . . .'

Utsyev held up a warning hand. 'I don't want to hear anything that starts with the word 'but', okay?'

Anderson nodded. 'Katherine won't sell. She and her husband know what the company's worth. They're on the board, they have access to the accounts. Besides, the bank won't allow it.'

Utsyev snorted quietly. 'We've already taken care of the nigger.'

'What?' Anderson said.

'The nigger. What was his name?'

'Nelson,' Sabatino said.

'Yeah, Nelson. We've already taken care of Nelson.'

Anderson was stunned. He looked at Sabatino, then back to Utsyev. 'You killed Nelson?'

Utsyev shrugged. 'I had it done. I can do that, Maury. As easy as breathing.'

Anderson was lost for words. He flopped back on the sofa, the handkerchief forgotten in his hand.

One of the heavyweights sighed as if blowing out a candle. Utsyev scowled at him and the heavy straightened his back like a soldier standing at attention. 'Nelson was getting too close to us. Did you know he'd hired a private eye?'

'No, I didn't,' Anderson said. He felt as if his world

was falling down around him. He needed cocaine and he needed it bad. The thought that there were several grammes sprinkled over the floor by the kitchen was driving him crazy.

'Yeah, he was digging around trying to find out who owned the company. Broke into our lawyer's office. Can you believe that?'

'No, no I can't believe that,' Anderson said. He rubbed his jaw. He could taste blood at the back of his mouth and one of his front teeth felt loose.

'Yeah, so we're gonna have to move quickly in case the bank puts someone else on our case. Once we own CRW and the bank's paid off, there'd be no point in anyone sniffing around. You've as much to lose as we have, you know. If they find out what you've been doing . . .' He left the threat unfinished.

'I hear you,' Anderson said. He wondered who this man was, this man who'd assaulted him, broken into his house, killed a banker and done God only knew what else. Sabatino had always been so pleasant, so helpful, ready with investment money when CRW needed it and with free cocaine on tap. This didn't make any sense.

'Okay, so you're gonna help us take over CRW. The Freeman woman and the rest of the shareholders can walk away with the cash, and everyone's happy. That okay with you, Maury?'

Anderson shook his head. 'Katherine won't sell,' he repeated.

'Then, like I said, it's up to you to persuade her.' Utsyev flashed a wolfish grin. 'Try pillow talk.'

Anderson sat bolt upright as if he'd been plugged into the mains. 'What?'

'You heard me,' Utsyev said. 'You've been screwing CRW's major shareholder. I'd have thought that might give you some leverage with the lady. What do you think, Gilani?'

Sabatino shifted uneasily in his chair. 'I guess so.'

'Yeah. I guess so,' Utsyev said, getting to his feet. He walked over to where Anderson was sitting and loomed over him. Anderson flinched. Utsyev pushed his face up close so that Anderson could smell the man's bitter breath. 'Look, Anderson, my brother has been supplying you with enough coke to keep half the city wired. We've got photographs of you entering and leaving several motels with Mrs Freeman, and we know where you and your lovely wife live. I'd say that gives us some leverage with you, huh?' Anderson said nothing. He dabbed the handkerchief to his mouth. Utsyev raised his hand and his lips tightened. 'Wouldn't you?'

Anderson nodded quickly. 'Yes,' he said.

Utsyev smiled and lowered his hand. 'Good. Then we understand each other.' He walked over to the fireplace and stood by it, rocking backwards and forwards on the balls of his feet. 'We'll give you a week. Do what you have to do.'

'I don't understand,' Anderson said.

Utsyev raised his eyes in exasperation. 'I suggest you persuade the Freemans by whatever means necessary that it's in their best interests to sell the company. It shouldn't be too hard bearing in mind the state it's in. Gilani tells me that you're gonna be losing money this year.'

'If it's in such a bad state, why do you want to buy it?' Anderson asked. 'I'll be able to get the books straight eventually, then you'll be in the clear.'

'That's for me to know,' Utsyev said. 'All you've got to worry about is getting control of the company. And look, there's an upside to this for you. We'll write off the coke Gilani's given you, throw in a few ounces more, and you can run the company for us until we've done with it.'

'What do you mean, done with it?'

'We only want some of the assets. We've no interest in the rest.'

'The land?'

'Like I said, that's for me to know. But if you haven't persuaded the Freemans and the other shareholders to sell, I'll take care of it. And I'll take care of you. Do we understand each other?'

Anderson nodded. He looked at the handkerchief. It was spotted with blood. 'Keep it,' Utsyev said. He nodded at the heavy with bad skin. 'Get the car, Ostrovetsky,' he said. The heavy disappeared into the hallway and a few seconds later Anderson heard the front door open and close.

Utsyev smiled, showing chipped and yellowing teeth. Anderson smiled back. He felt like a turkey being fattened up for Thanksgiving. 'I'll do my best,' he said.

Utsyev nodded like a priest taking confession. 'I hope that'll be good enough,' he said. 'Kiseleva, give our friend here a little something for his habit.'

The heavy with the red scarf walked nonchalantly over to Anderson and handed him a small polythene bag of white powder. Before he could take it, the heavy had dropped it into Anderson's lap and walked out, followed by Sabatino. Utsyev patted Anderson on the shoulder. 'You'll do just fine,' he said, like an undertaker addressing the recently bereaved.

The brothers climbed into the back of the limousine and

settled back into the plush leather seats. The car pulled away smoothly from the kerb and headed for the city.

'What an asshole,' Utsyev said.

'Yeah,' Sabatino agreed.

'I'm gonna enjoy taking him on a picnic,' Utsyev grinned.

'A picnic,' Sabatino agreed.

When the brothers Utsyev had been enduring their Siberian exile, a year before their mother died of malnutrition and a broken heart, they lived on a farm, working in the frozen fields in exchange for a bed in the barn and just enough food to keep them alive.

There was a cat on the farm, a big bruiser of an animal with a fight-scarred face and eyes full of hate. The cat hated the brothers Utsyev, and they hated him in return. It would sit and watch them as they toiled in the fields and tended the scrawny pigs and cattle as they collected the eggs from the few chickens that hadn't been slaughtered for the pot. Whenever they tried to get near it, it would stalk off with a bow-legged strut, its tail held high and its nose up in contempt. At first Bzuchar had tried to make friends with the cat. He'd cornered it once in the barn and had offered it his hand, a token of friendship. The cat had responded by hissing and striking out with a clawed paw, drawing blood and ripping a strip of flesh from his hand. From then on it was war.

The cat claimed dominion over the farm and all its buildings, and he regarded it as his right to go wherever he pleased. Whenever a window or door was left open, the cat would enter the farmhouse, steal whatever food had been left unattended, and squirt his ammonia-laced urine on as much furniture as he could.

Bzuchar threw rocks at the intruder, put down poisoned fish, set huge rat-traps baited with raw meat, but it was all to no avail. As the battle waged it seemed that the cat developed an almost human smile, as if it took pleasure in teasing the humans and urinating on their territory.

Bzuchar decided to try a different approach, satisfied that open conflict was getting nowhere. He ignored the cat, pretended not even to be aware of its existence as it stalked through the farmhouse and stole food from the kitchen table, and even put out a saucer of goat's milk for it in a back room. A room without windows. At first the cat ignored the offering, but as Bzuchar continued to feign indifference, the cat became bolder and the milk offerings more regular. Bzuchar had the patience of a saint. It was three weeks before he had the cat trapped in the windowless room, the door locked behind him and a wicker picnic basket in his hands. The cat spat and slashed, and ran around and around, looking for a way out. There was none, and again Bzuchar exercised his reptile-like patience, squatting on the floor, the basket in his hands and his eyes on the cat, occasionally licking his lips like a snake testing the air. For two hours he waited until the cat let down its guard. Bzuchar sprang forward and slammed the basket down, trapping the cat and transforming it into a hissing ball of matted fur and teeth. He slid a sheet of metal under the basket and then up-ended it and weighted it down with an old flat iron. He stood for a while with his hands on his hips, grinning at his trapped adversary, then he opened the door and called for his brother. Together they manhandled the picnic basket out into the cobbled courtyard, its occupant wailing and hissing like a grieving old woman.

Gilani had suggested that they take him to another farm, miles away, so that he could torment someone else, but Bzuchar had shaken his head and said that exile was too good for him. He wanted something more appropriate. Something more permanent. He disappeared into a barn and a few minutes later reappeared on a rusting, smoke-belching tractor which he parked next to the basket. The cat thrashed about uselessly, as if sensing what was to come.

Gilani had stood scratching his head, not wanting to appear stupid by asking his brother what he planned to do. His first thought was that Bzuchar was going to run over the picnic basket and crush the cat with the thick rubber tyres of the rattling old tractor, but it became clear that he had other plans. He took a coiled hosepipe and fitted it to the tractor's exhaust pipe, taking care not to burn himself on the hot metal. The other end of the hosepipe he slotted into the basket.

'Give me your coat,' Bzuchar had said, and reluctantly Gilani had handed it over. He'd started shivering, and had never known whether it was a reaction to the bone-numbing cold of the Siberian spring or anticipation of the killing. He'd watched, fascinated, as Bzuchar had dropped the coat over the wicker basket and jumped up into the tractor's seat. Bzuchar grinned wickedly, winked at Gilani, then stamped on the accelerator and gunned it, sending clouds of hot exhaust down the pipe and into the home-made gas chamber.

THE BIRTHDAY GIRL

Gilani would never forget the cries of the cat as it died. He'd seen and heard many men die since, almost too many to remember, but never again had he ever heard anything like the banshee screams of the cat. Not pain, not anguish, not fear. Anger. Pure, unadulterated anger. It echoed around the walls of the courtyard and up into the cold spring air, scaring the birds into silence and raising the hackles of a wolfhound five miles away on the other side of the hill. The screams had subsided eventually, followed by wheezing and spluttering, then coughs, then nothing.

Bzuchar had stuck the feline corpse on a pole and planted it in the middle of a field of beetroot, giving the birds a chance to exact their revenge on their tormentor.

It was the first killing by the brothers Utsyev, but not the last, and from that day on they never referred to a killing as a killing. Instead they took their victims on a picnic.

Utsyev rubbed his hands together. 'I've got a good feeling about this, Gilani. A really good feeling.'

'He picked up on the land pretty quick,' Sabatino said apprehensively.

'So what? We own the little shit, Gilani. We own him. The way he's been helping us launder money through the company, we own him.'

'Yeah, but what if the Freemans work out what we want the land for?'

Utsyev narrowed his eyes. 'First of all, they won't,' he said. 'As far as anyone else is concerned, it's a piece of useless industrial land which no one wants. Second of all, so what if they do? That land is worth millions to us because we can get planning permission for the marina. There's no way that they or anyone else could get the marina built. They don't carry the weight that we do.

263

They don't have the leverage that we do.' He laughed. It was a slow drawn-out sound, like the warning of a rattlesnake preparing to strike. The leverage was in the form of an incriminating videotape of a state official and photocopies of records pertaining to a Swiss bank account containing almost half a million dollars. 'And third of all, even if they find out that we're planning to build a marina on the site, they won't know what we're going to do with it. To anyone else it's just a hotel complex with berths for several hundred boats. But we don't give a fuck whether or not we make money from the marina or not because it's also the perfect way to get our drugs into the country. No more running them through the DEA patrols around the Florida keys, just straight into our very own marina then up I-95 to New York. That marina is going to be worth tens of millions of dollars in the first year it's in operation. From then on, the sky's the limit.'

He gripped his brother's leg just above the knee and squeezed tight. 'Oh yeah. And fourth of all, the company is tainted. No one's gonna believe that the Freemans weren't in on the money laundering. This way we cover our tracks, and we get our own marina. It's perfect. They can't do nothing, Gilani. They're caught between a rock and a hard place. We're gonna be richer than we ever hoped. And if I've gotta break a few heads along the way, well, who gives a shit, right?'

'Right,' Sabatino agreed. Bzuchar's hand gripped tighter, hard enough to hurt.

*   *   *

THE BIRTHDAY GIRL

Anthony Freeman walked back to his office, a cup of scalding coffee in each hand. Jo wasn't at her desk, so he put her coffee on her blotter and went to sit on his sofa to go through a stack of technical reports from the development department. Josh Bowers was pushing for more funding for a sniper spotting system he'd been working on for the best part of a year, but with CRW's precarious cash position Freeman knew that he had no alternative but to turn down his proposal. He wasn't happy about having to give Josh yet another thumbs-down because if the MIT-trained engineer wasn't given some encouragement soon he'd be looking for another job. And with his qualifications and experience, he wouldn't be looking for long.

Freeman sipped his coffee and studied Josh's figures. The market for the system was there, no doubt about it. It used a miniature video camera and a backpack-sized computer to track incoming bullets and calculate the source of the gunfire. The equipment could eventually be connected to a computer-controlled weapon that would be capable of returning fire on its own. Police forces and the military would be ready customers, but it would require at least a quarter of a million dollars to get a working model and as much again to put it into production. CRW didn't have five hundred dollars to spare, never mind five hundred thousand.

Jo blew into his office like a tornado, her hair flying behind her, a smile splitting her face almost in two. She was waving a fax in the air.

'Good news?' he said, getting to his feet.

'Oh, yes,' she said. 'Yes, yes, yes.' She thrust the document at him and waited while he scanned it, shifting her weight from foot to foot.

Freeman read it once quickly, and then read it again to make sure that he hadn't got it wrong. There was no mistake. 'My God,' he said.

'Isn't it great?' Jo gushed. 'Just when we needed it. It couldn't have come at a better time, could it?'

Freeman was stunned. He read through the fax for a third time. It was advance notice of an order from the Thai government for five hundred MIDAS systems. It would be worth just over seven million dollars, minus the usual 'commissions' to various Thai government officials and middle-men. The order would keep CRW's workforce going for several months and would solve the company's immediate cash-flow problems. The Thais were always prompt payers once a contract had been signed and the requisite bribes paid. 'This is unbelievable,' Freeman said. 'We didn't even tender for this. They've bought from us before, but never an order of this size. Our fairy godmother must be smiling down on us.'

Jo impulsively hugged him, hard enough to force the air from his body. 'Shall I draw up a memo to put on the noticeboards?' she said when she finally released him.

'Not yet,' Freeman said, shaking his head. 'Let's not count our chickens until they've signed on the dotted line.'

Jo tutted. 'You always look on the black side.' She flounced back to her desk. Freeman read the fax for a fourth time. He hoped that his secretary was right. He'd love to believe that they'd at least turned the corner, but there was still a nagging doubt at the back of his mind. He left his office, holding the fax. 'I'm going up to see Maury to give him the good news,' he said.

Jo nodded brightly and gave him a thumbs-up. Freeman

found Anderson sitting at his desk, his head buried in his hands. 'Are you okay?' he asked. It was unusual for Anderson to be tired in the middle of the day. He was normally a powerhouse, rushing around trying to get everything done as if his life depended on clearing his desk by dusk.

'Just had a bad night, that's all. What's up?'

Freeman handed over the fax and paced up and down as Anderson read it. He seemed to take for ever. 'Well?' Freeman said. 'What do you think?'

'Five hundred?' Anderson mused. 'They want to buy five hundred?'

'It's like a miracle,' Freeman said.

'But we didn't tender for this, did we?'

'No. It's come right out of the blue. It'll see us through till spring.'

Anderson gave him the fax. He ran a hand through his uncombed hair. He looked as if he hadn't shaved for a couple of days. 'That's great, Tony. Just great.'

'Are you okay?' Freeman said, concerned. He'd expected a bit more enthusiasm from his financial director.

'I'm fine. Just fine.'

Freeman tilted his head to one side, frowning. Anderson looked bone tired. There were bags under his eyes and his hands were trembling. He kept sniffing as if he was starting a cold. 'You should be at home, in bed,' Freeman said, sitting down on the edge of his desk. 'Take the rest of the day off. I'll follow up on this and I can look after anything else that crops up.'

Anderson shook his head. 'I'll be okay. Really.'

'Well, you look like shit.'

'Thanks. Thanks a million.'

Freeman waved the fax in his face. 'And you don't seem especially thrilled about this, either.'

Anderson sighed. 'It's only one order, Tony.'

'Come on, man. Get a grip on yourself. It's a lifeline and we're going to grab it with both hands.'

'Yeah, you're right.'

'I know I'm right. Now you go home and get rid of that cold.'

'Have you got time for a chat?'

'Sure. What's on your mind?' Freeman went over to one of the over-stuffed sofas and dropped down on to it. It enveloped him like a cloud.

Anderson picked up a pencil and tapped it on the desktop. 'The guys from Ventura Investments have been on to me about increasing the size of their investment.'

'Yeah, so you said.'

'No, they wanna put even more into the company.' The tapping intensified, like a woodpecker attacking a tree. 'They wanna make an outright bid.'

Freeman wasn't sure that he'd heard correctly, so he leaned forward. 'What?'

'They want to buy out the existing shareholders.'

Freeman sat stunned. What he was hearing didn't make any sense. 'Ventura Investments? The venture capital company?'

'That's the guys. They're prepared to offer two million dollars for the entire stock, plus they'll take on all CRW's bank loans. They'll run the company as a wholly owned subsidiary.'

'Maury, what the hell does a venture capital company know about running a defence contractor?'

Anderson gripped the ends of the pencil with both hands

as if preparing to snap it. 'They're businessmen. They'll knock the business into shape, sell off non-producing assets, they'll . . .'

'Whoa,' Freeman interrupted, holding up his hand. 'Stop right there. You mean they'll close us down. That's what you're saying.'

'They'll do what they have to do,' Anderson said, choosing his words carefully.

'If this company needs knocking into shape, we'll do it. You and I. We're the ones who are running CRW, not a bunch of bean-counters.'

'They're not bean-counters, they're professional managers.' Anderson's knuckles whitened as he gripped the pencil tighter. 'You were the one who said we should listen to Nelson and his plans for the company. What's wrong with letting the Ventura guys sort it out?'

Freeman stared at Anderson, shaking his head slowly. 'Listen to yourself, Maury. You're not suggesting we bring in outside advice, you're telling me that you want to sell the company to outsiders. This is my life, for God's sake. Yours too.'

'I'm not saying I want to do this. I'm saying that they're willing to buy, and it seems a fair price to me considering the state this company's in.'

'Do you think Katherine is going to sell her stake? Her father founded this company. He built it up from nothing.'

'Yeah? And between us we've just about run it into the ground.' The pencil snapped and Anderson looked at it as if wondering why it had broken.

'You're making it sound like we ruined the company, but you know full well that's not what happened. Things have changed. The world has changed. We're going to have to adapt to the new order and by God that's what we're going to do.'

Anderson shrugged and dropped the broken pencil into his wastepaper bin. 'It's not working out like we hoped. You're going to have to accept it. Better we sell out now and at least get something for our shares.'

'Our shares? The way I remember it, you don't have more than a few thousand shares. What do you get out of it if we sell out?'

'What do you mean?'

'You know what I mean,' Freeman snapped. 'The first thing the new management will do is to get rid of the present structure. We'll all be out of a job and the company isn't in a fit state to give us golden parachutes – unless you've already worked out a deal.'

'Oh, come on, Tony. I'm not doing this behind your back. I'm telling you exactly what I know. They've made an initial approach, that's all.'

'That's not what it sounds like to me,' Freeman said. 'What do they plan to do with the workforce?'

Anderson picked up another pencil and began toying with it. 'I don't know. Honestly I don't.'

'Do you at least know if they plan to keep production going?'

Anderson shook his head. 'I don't know what they intend to do.'

Freeman had the feeling that Anderson knew a lot more than he was letting on. Anderson looked up from the pencil and held Freeman's gaze. They sat looking at each other for several seconds without speaking. Anderson looked away first. Freeman wasn't prepared to let him off the hook that easily. 'What's going on, Maury?' he pressed.

Anderson shrugged. He squeezed the bridge of his nose and exhaled deeply. 'I'm just telling you what the Ventura people told me,' he said. 'They thought it would be more diplomatic if the approach came through me.' He tossed the pencil on to the desk and put his hands flat on the blotter. 'Look, Tony, it's a good offer and I think we should accept it. Things aren't going to get better, they're going to get worse, and the sooner you accept that the better. Let's sell out now while we still can. Next year we might not be able to get anything for CRW.'

Freeman stood up. 'You're wrong. If you want to pursue it further, I suggest you raise it at the next board meeting.' He headed for the door. 'But I can tell you here and now that Katherine will never sell out. Never.'

Anderson got to his feet. He held out one of his hands as if trying to grab Freeman and pull him back. 'Wait,' he said.

'What the hell is the matter with you?' Freeman asked.

'Don't go yet. Hear me out.' There was a pleading tone to Anderson's voice, like a beggar asking for spare change.

Freeman stood with his arms folded across his chest. 'I'm listening,' he said.

Anderson looked flustered. His hair was in disarray and there was a wild look in his eyes. 'You have to sell. And you have to tell Katherine to sell, too.'

'You're not making sense, Maury.'

Anderson's eyes flicked from side to side like a trapped rat looking for a way out. 'Wait. Just listen.' Freeman said nothing. He waited. Anderson seemed to be struggling to find the right words. 'These people . . .' He tailed off.

'What do you mean? What about them?'

Anderson's hands were shaking. 'Just listen to me. Listen to what I'm saying. These people, they want the company and I don't think there's anything you can do to stop them.'

Freeman went over to the desk. Anderson looked almost manic. His bloodshot eyes were wide and staring and his lower jaw was trembling like that of a child about to burst into tears. 'Maury, get a grip on yourself,' Freeman said.

Anderson took a deep breath. When he spoke it was slowly with a distinct pause between each word. 'You . . . have . . . to . . . sell,' he said, as if he could persuade Freeman to do what he wanted by the sheer force of his willpower.

'Go home,' Freeman said. 'You're sick or something. You're not yourself.' He shook his head sadly and walked out of the office. He heard Anderson call his name but he didn't look back.

Anderson controlled his Corvette with one hand as he called up Sal Sabatino on the car phone. He accelerated past a huge truck belching black smoke.

'Mr Sabatino? It's Maury. Freeman isn't going for it. There's no way he'll agree to sell.'

'Maury, this isn't my problem,' Sabatino said. 'It's yours.'

'Oh, come on, I've spoken to Freeman, what else can I do?' Anderson whined.

'You know what my brother told you,' Sabatino said. 'It's up to you.'

'Shit, it's not up to me any more. I've given it my best shot.'

'So your best isn't good enough. You want I should call my brother and tell him?'

'No!' Anderson exclaimed. 'Just give me a chance. Give me a fucking chance.'

'Maury, get off my back, will ya?' Sabatino sighed. 'You made your bed, you fucking lie in it.'

'Look, just listen to me, will you? I've told Freeman that I think he should sell out, I've run the figures by him, but he's not interested, he says . . .'

'You're starting to bore me, Maury,' Sabatino interrupted.

'He says it's a family business and the family is always going to be involved,' Anderson continued. 'So, I think you should talk with him. Explain the error of his ways. If he hears it from the horse's mouth . . . Not that I'm calling you a horse's mouth. You know what I mean.'

'Yeah, I know what you mean,' Sabatino said wearily.

'So what I was thinking was, maybe you should spell it out to Freeman. Tell him the way things stand.'

'That's what my brother is planning to do. Look, Maury, I don't see how my presence would change things.'

'Because I could introduce you as one of the investors. You could tell him that you're planning to keep the business running. Tell him anything he wants to hear, just so he'll persuade his wife to sell.'

'Have you spoken to the wife?'

'Not yet, no.'

'So take her to bed, screw her brains out, and tell her to sell.'

'You don't know Katherine Freeman.'

'Not as well as you do, no. But I know human nature.'

'I had another thought,' Anderson added.

'God help me,' Sabatino said.

'Yeah. When Lennie Nelson was on our backs, he kept saying that we should look for a buyer. What if we went direct to the bank and put the deal to them?'

'No,' Sabatino said sharply. 'The last thing we want is for the bank to go over the assets with a view to selling. Don't say a fucking word to the bank, okay?'

'Sure. Whatever you say.'

Sabatino went quiet and after a while Anderson wondered if he'd lost the connection. 'Mr Sabatino? Are you there?'

'Yeah, I'm still here. Okay, Maury. Let's give it a shot. You fix up a meeting.'

'Great. Fantastic.' Anderson ended the call. A young guy in a red Mazda was trying to overtake but he put his foot down hard and the Corvette accelerated away. He hated being overtaken almost as much as he hated talking to Sal Sabatino.

Mersiha was sitting at the kitchen table, her school books spread out in front of her, when Freeman walked in. 'Hiya, pumpkin,' he said, ruffling her hair. 'What's up?' Buffy looked up from the floor, gave a welcoming wag of her tail, then lay down again.

'The Civil War. Causes and effects. I'm trying to finish it before dinner.'

'Hmmm. You realise that some academics have devoted their whole lives to the subject?'

'Yeah, yeah, yeah. But all I'm prepared to give it is two hours, max.'

'My daughter the historian. And I thought I told you not to call me Max.'

'Ha, ha, ha, thump. Oh, sorry, that was the sound of my head falling off.'

The telephone rang and Freeman raised an eyebrow. 'Shall I get that?' he asked sarcastically.

'It won't be for me.'

'Where's Katherine?'

'Shopping.'

'With the girls?'

'Afraid so.'

Freeman picked up the phone. It was Anderson. 'Hiya, Maury,' Freeman said. 'Are you still in the office?'

'Just about to go. Are you around this evening?'

'Around? You mean at home?'

'Yeah. Are you gonna be there?'

'Sure. Why?'

'One of the Ventura people wants a word. We were wondering if we could come around and see you this evening.'

Freeman frowned and leaned against the kitchen wall. Mersiha was sucking the end of her pen as she read. 'Why can't we do this in the office, Maury?'

'He doesn't want it official, he just wants a chat.'

'I don't know. If he's got anything to say, I think he should say it to the whole board.'

'Hell, Tony, you, me and Katherine pretty much are the board.'

'Yeah, well there's a few notable exceptions who might take offence at not being consulted.'

'Walter won't mind. And I doubt if Bill or Josh care either way. Look, just a few minutes, that's all.'

'Katherine isn't here,' Freeman said.

'It's really you he wants to talk to.'

'I don't think it's a good idea.'

'Please, Tony.'

Freeman sighed deeply. There didn't seem to be any way to put the man off, short of a direct refusal. 'Okay,' he agreed. 'But keep it short.'

'Terrific, Tony. Thanks. We'll be there at seven, okay?'

'I suppose so,' Freeman said, still unhappy at the prospect of his evening being disturbed. He hung up the phone. 'What time's Katherine getting back?' he asked Mersiha.

She shrugged. 'Who knows? She went looking for shoes.'

'Ouch,' Freeman said. Shoes were one of his wife's biggest vices. She had several closets full of them but never passed up an opportunity to buy more.

'Someone coming round?' Mersiha asked.

'Business. Maury and a guy who wants to buy a piece of our company. Boring stuff.' He opened the refrigerator. 'Do you want a soda?'

'Diet Coke, decaf,' she said.

'No calories, no kick. Why don't you just drink water?' He tossed a can to her and she caught it one-handed.

Mersiha groaned and leaned back in her chair. 'Nag,

nag, nag,' she laughed, popping the tab and drinking from the can.

'Did she leave anything to eat?'

Mersiha shook her head. 'You know Katherine. Once she's on the trail of a hot pair of shoes . . .'

'Yeah, I guess.' Freeman looked inside the refrigerator again. There was half a cooked chicken and plastic containers of potato salad and coleslaw, and he found tomatoes, cucumber and an Iceberg lettuce still in brown paper bags. 'Ah, she came through,' he said. 'Chicken salad?'

Mersiha was loading their dirty plates into the dishwasher when the doorbell rang. 'We'll be in the study, pumpkin,' Freeman said as he went out into the hall, Buffy following at his heels.

He opened the front door to find Anderson about to ring the bell again. Standing next to him was an overweight man in a cashmere overcoat. 'This is Mr Sabatino, Tony,' Anderson said.

'Tony. Good to meet ya,' Sabatino said, stepping forward and gripping Freeman's hand. He pumped it vigorously, grinning with fake bonhomie. He was wearing a large gold ring which bit into Freeman's hand, and Freeman wondered if the man deliberately wore it to hurt. There was something about him that provoked instant dislike, though he couldn't quite work out what it was. It wasn't his looks – Freeman had more than his fair share of overweight friends with double chins – it was something to do with his attitude. He had the look of a man who was used to getting his own way, usually by what he thought passed for charm, and if that didn't work Freeman felt that he'd be prepared to use other, less civilised methods.

'Come in, Mr Sabatino,' he said, stepping to the side.

'It's Sal,' Sabatino said.

There were two cars on the road outside the house: Anderson's Corvette and a large sedan. There were two men in the sedan. Two large men. Mr Sabatino obviously wasn't a man who enjoyed travelling alone. One of the large men was chewing on a cigar. He studied Freeman the way an entomologist might look at an insect he already had in his collection. Freeman shuddered and closed the door. As soon as he showed his visitors into the study, Sabatino made himself comfortable on the leather sofa by the door. Buffy sniffed at his trousers and he scowled at her. She got the message and went off to find Mersiha. Sabatino looked at the gun cabinet and then at Freeman. 'You shoot, Tony?'

'Not really,' Freeman said. Anderson paced up and down, clearly nervous. 'Do you want a drink, Maury?' he asked.

'A drink? No. No, thanks.'

'What about you, Mr Sabatino? Sal, I mean.' Freeman had difficulty referring to the man by his first name. It implied a closeness and familiarity that he wasn't keen to encourage.

'Nothing for me, Tony.' Sabatino interlinked his fingers and cracked his knuckles. The noise reminded Freeman of twigs snapping underfoot. It wasn't a pleasant sound. 'Maury tells me that you're unhappy with our plan to increase our investment in your company.'

'The way Maury explained it, you're talking about a takeover.'

Sabatino made a shrugging gesture that suggested that it was all a matter of semantics. 'You've a cash-flow problem, we've got cash.'

'We?'

'Ventura Investments.'

'Which as far as we're concerned is a venture capital company. Why would a venture capital company want to own a manufacturing company?'

Sabatino pulled at the lobe of his left ear like an acupuncturist looking for a nerve centre. 'I didn't come here to justify myself.'

Freeman smiled thinly. 'So what did you come for?'

Sabatino leant forward, fingering his gold ring. 'We really want your company, and we're not going to take no for an answer.'

'What business are you in, actually?' Freeman asked.

'We're a group of investors, you know that.'

'Maury tells me that you own a nightclub in Baltimore. What was it called, Maury? The Firehouse?'

Sabatino turned to look at Anderson, a slow swivelling of the neck like a badly operated marionette. Anderson seemed to shrink against the wall. Freeman wondered what the hell was going on. Anderson was clearly scared to death of the man.

'It's true that I have entertainment interests, Tony. I run a multi-faceted organisation. Entertainment. Leisure. Property.'

'Manufacturing?'

'No. Not manufacturing.'

Freeman went to stand behind his desk. He wanted something substantial between the two of them, a barrier. 'What you're suggesting doesn't make sense, Mr Sabatino. CRW is a manufacturer. A manufacturer of specialist equipment. An outsider couldn't run the company.'

'I think you'd be surprised at what we can do, Tony.'

'That may be. But you're not going to get the opportunity.'

Sabatino's eyelids half closed and from his coat pocket he took out a sheaf of papers. He stood up and walked slowly over to the desk. 'I had my lawyer draw up the papers, Tony. It's a very generous offer.'

'It is,' parroted Anderson. 'It's very generous.'

'I couldn't sign that even if I wanted to,' Freeman said. 'It would need the agreement of the majority of the shareholders.'

'So call a shareholders' meeting.'

'There isn't time. I'm going on vacation this weekend.'

Sabatino dropped the papers on Freeman's blotter. 'Cancel it. Your health is a lot more important than a vacation.'

At first Freeman thought he'd misheard. 'What?' he said, stunned. 'What did you say?'

Sabatino smiled, like a tiger contemplating a meal. 'I mean that running a company like CRW must put a strain on you. On your marriage. On your family. I could take that strain off you. You're too close to the company. You're not able to do what's necessary to save it.'

'You sound just like Lennie Nelson,' Freeman said.

'Yeah? Never thought I'd have anything in common with a nigger.'

Freeman looked at Anderson in astonishment, unable to believe what Sabatino had said.

'I think you should leave, Mr Sabatino.'

'Not until you've signed the papers.' Sabatino stretched his arms along the back of the sofa as if he was settling in for a long wait.

Freeman stood up. 'No, I'd like you to go now.

I don't like your attitude, and I don't like you, Mr Sabatino.'

Sabatino's upper lip curled back in a sneer. 'Maybe I should wait for Mrs Freeman.'

'You keep away from my wife. If you've anything to say to the board, you can do it officially.'

Sabatino nodded slowly. 'You're going to regret this.'

'So you are here to threaten me?'

'I don't bother making threats, Mr Freeman.' Sabatino hauled himself to his feet. He glared at Freeman as he adjusted the sleeves of his jacket. He looked as if he was about to say something else, but then appeared to change his mind and walked out of the house without a word.

Anderson started after Sabatino, but stopped at the door to the study. He flinched as the front door slammed. 'That wasn't smart, Tony.'

'I think you should go too, Maury.'

Anderson paced up and down, rubbing the bridge of his nose. 'You've no idea what you've done,' he whined.

Mersiha peered through her bedroom curtains to watch Sabatino walk back to his car. The driver scurried to open the car door for him but Sabatino got to the handle first. Even from fifty yards away it was clear that he was furious. He was glaring at the house, and Mersiha backed away from the window, afraid that he'd seen her. She tiptoed back down the stairs. Earlier she'd had to press her ear to the closed door in order to hear Sabatino and her father, but now the door to the study was wide open and she didn't have to eavesdrop to hear her father and Maury Anderson arguing.

'What's going on with you two?' her father said.

'You shouldn't have spoken to him that way,' Anderson responded, his voice shaking.

'Why are you so scared of him? What is he, some sort of gangster?'

Anderson laughed harshly. Mersiha shivered and wrapped her arms around herself. It was the first time she'd ever heard her father argue with his partner. 'Sabatino has some very dangerous friends, Tony. He's connected.'

'Connected? You mean he's in the Mafia?'

'I don't know if he's in the Mafia, but he's got associates who are.'

'And you let this man invest in our company? What the hell were you playing at?'

For a while there was silence. Mersiha could hear someone pacing up and down on the carpet. 'I didn't have any choice, Tony. You weren't here. You were in Sarajevo, remember?'

'What are you saying?'

'I'm saying that when you were held hostage, I needed to raise money quickly. We had a ransom to pay, remember? And when that went wrong, we had to pay to send people in to get you out. The government didn't pay for that. CRW did. I had to keep the company running, and we had to raise money to get you out. Do you think the banks were queuing up to lend me the money? Even your beloved Walter wouldn't help. He'd have let you rot in that basement so long as we met our interest payments.'

'So you went to a gangster? Is that it?'

'No, that's not it. I was approached by an accountant,

on behalf of Ventura Investments. Everything seemed just hunky-dory. It was only afterwards that I met Sabatino. By then it was too late.'

Freeman sighed deeply. 'So you're saying it's my fault for being kidnapped?'

'I'm not saying it's your fault, no. But if you'd been here, things might have happened differently.'

'Yeah? Well whose idea was it to send me to Bosnia in the first place, Maury? Answer me that.'

Mersiha flinched as her father began to shout. She felt a sudden rush of guilt. If what Anderson was saying was true, she was partly to blame for her father's situation. She rocked backwards and forwards on the stairs nervously.

'Look, blaming each other isn't going to get us anywhere,' Anderson said. 'Sabatino wants to buy CRW. I think we should sell.'

'Fine. That's your opinion and you're entitled to it. But first the directors have to discuss it, then it goes to a full shareholders' meeting. And you know what Katherine and I are going to say.'

'Then you'll be making a big mistake, Tony. A big mistake.'

'That sounds like a threat. I'm starting to resent being threatened.'

'Take it any way you want. But I'll tell you now, if Sabatino wants the company, he'll get it. One way or another. He's a bully, a bully who's used to getting what he wants, and the more you try to deny him, the worse he gets.'

'What do you think he'll do?' Freeman asked, his voice quieter this time. Mersiha had to strain to hear.

'Best you don't wait to find out. Call him tomorrow and tell him you'll sell.'

'No.'

'At least sleep on it.'

'No. And I think you should consider your position with the company.'

'You mean you're sacking me?'

'I mean I don't think you can justify your place on the board any longer. If you wanted to leave, I wouldn't stand in your way.'

'You can't force me to resign.'

'Maybe you should sleep on it too.'

Mersiha heard Anderson walk towards the hallway and she scampered upstairs. She hid in the bathroom as Anderson left the house, then went back downstairs. Her father was sitting at his desk, his head in his hands.

'Dad?' she said, her voice trembling.

He looked up and smiled. 'Hiya, pumpkin. What's up?'

She walked into the middle of the room, rubbing her hands together as if washing them. 'Is everything okay?' she asked.

'Sure.' Realisation dawned. 'Oh, you heard us arguing?'

'Yeah. I guess.'

Freeman stood up and went over to her, putting his hands on her shoulders. 'It's just business, pumpkin. Nothing's wrong. Honest.'

Mersiha looked up at him, wanting to believe him with all her heart but knowing that he was lying. She'd heard Sabatino threaten him, and she knew enough about CRW's finances to know that the company was at risk of being taken over. She impulsively hugged her father, pressing her head against his chest. Freeman patted her on the back. 'Dad, be careful,' she whispered.

Freeman tried to laugh off her concern. 'Maury and I just lost our tempers, Mersiha. It'll all blow over by tomorrow.'

Mersiha wanted to ask him about Sabatino, but she knew that would mean telling him that she'd been eavesdropping. Besides, he wouldn't tell her the truth, he'd lie to protect her. She closed her eyes and hugged him, and silently promised herself that she'd help him out of his predicament.

Freeman was unloading the dishwasher when Katherine arrived home, laden down with shopping bags.

'God, I hate shopping,' she said, leaning against the door.

'I'd never have guessed,' he smiled. 'Shoes?'

'How did you . . . ah, Mersiha told you. Hmmm, I shall have to have a word with that young lady. Us shoppers should stick together. Where is she?'

'Upstairs, hitting the books.'

'Have you eaten?'

'Yup. Chicken salad.' He folded his arms and sat back in his chair. 'Maury was here earlier.'

'Oh really?' said Katherine. 'What did he want?'

'He brought Sabatino with him.'

'Sabatino?'

'The guy behind Ventura Investments. Kat, he's a gangster.'

'You mean he's . . .'

'I mean he's a gangster,' Freeman said. 'God knows what Maury's involved in.'

Katherine put her shopping bags on the floor. 'Let me get a drink,' she said. 'It sounds like I'm going to need one.' She went into the sitting room and Freeman followed her. He sat by the fireplace as Katherine poured herself a brandy and Coke and lit a cigarette. 'Now I'm ready,' she said.

Freeman explained how Anderson had broken the news that Ventura wanted to take over CRW, and how he'd brought Sabatino to the house. Katherine stared at Freeman through a plume of cigarette smoke as he told her how Sabatino had lost his temper and stormed out.

'And he threatened you?'

Freeman pulled a face. 'Sort of. I can't remember his exact words because I was seeing red at the time. But the gist was that I should watch my back.'

'Do you think we should call the police?'

'And tell them what? I don't think so, Kat. Maybe I overreacted. I'll talk to Maury tomorrow.'

'You're not thinking of selling the company, are you?'

'Of course not.'

'Good.' She stubbed her cigarette out. 'The company, is it in really bad shape?'

Freeman shrugged. 'It's critical, but not terminal. Walter's not going to pull the plug on us the way that Nelson threatened to, and we had an unexpected order today. God, yes, I forgot to tell you. The Thais have put in a seven-million-dollar order for MIDAS systems. That'll keep us going for a while.'

'So it's not all bad news?'

'No. But this Sabatino guy worries me.'

'I'm sure he's just a sore loser, that's all.' She took a long drink of her brandy and Coke. 'Did you mean what you said about him being a gangster?'

'Maury said he was connected to the Mafia.'

'Are you sure he wasn't exaggerating?'

'I don't know, Kat. It's hard to tell. He's been acting a little strangely lately. I'll have a word with him tomorrow, see if I can't straighten things out.'

Katherine drained her glass and waved it from side to side. 'You want one?'

'No, thanks. Maybe later.'

Katherine shrugged and poured herself another. 'It'll be all right, Tony,' she said. 'I'm sure it will.'

Mersiha sat on the stairs, listening to her parents talk. She was filled with anger at the man who had threatened her father. Freeman had made light of Sabatino's visit, but Mersiha knew that he was only doing that so that she wouldn't worry. Her father might be much older than she was, but he didn't understand how evil men could be. Sabatino was capable of great evil, she was certain. And it was up to her to protect her father. She owed it to him. She'd never appreciated before how much she was to blame for the company's financial problems. If Mersiha and her brother hadn't taken him hostage, maybe the company wouldn't be struggling now. It was her fault that he was in trouble, so it was only fair that she make it right. She'd solved the problem of Dr Brown. She'd do the same with the man called Sabatino.

*   *   *

Maury Anderson's Corvette was already in the car park when Freeman arrived at CRW's offices. Freeman wasn't looking forward to talking to his partner, though he knew he wouldn't be able to put it off indefinitely. He went straight to his own office, where Jo had his early-morning coffee ready for him.

'Maury's phoned for you, twice,' she said, handing him the mail.

Freeman walked up the stairs to Maury's office, figuring that he could probably do with the exercise. He took his coffee with him because he was certain he could do with the caffeine.

Anderson was at his desk, looking like death warmed up. His eyes had almost disappeared into black holes either side of his nose, he hadn't shaved, and his hair was greasy and unkempt as if he'd been running his hands through it. 'Tony. Hi.'

Freeman raised his mug in salute. 'You look like shit.'

Anderson grinned, and there was something manic about the gesture. 'Yeah, I didn't get much sleep last night. I'm sorry about what happened.'

'That Sabatino guy worries me.'

'He worries me too, Tony. Have you thought about what he said?'

'I haven't changed my mind. If he wants to make a formal approach to the board, that's his right, but I for one will vote against it. Guaranteed.'

Anderson continued to grin, but he shook his head. 'Big mistake.'

'Fine. But it'll be my mistake.'

'Okay. Okay. But I'll speak to him. I'll put him off. If you don't want Ventura taking us over, that's the end of it.'

Freeman sipped his coffee. Anderson seemed totally stressed out, as if he'd crack at any moment. And he didn't think for one moment that Anderson believed what he was saying. 'Maury, are you all right?' he asked.

'I'm fine,' he replied. His hands were trembling. Freeman noticed that Anderson's nose was running. He had an urge to offer the man his handkerchief, but before he could Anderson wiped his nose with his sleeve. 'I'm fine, really. Really, I'm fine.' He nodded rapidly, his eyebrows raised, trying to elicit agreement from Freeman, who shook his head sadly. 'What?' Anderson said. 'What?' He grinned again. 'I'm fine, honest. Look, I'll talk to Sabatino, I'll fix it. I got us into this, I'll sort it out. Okay?' Freeman shrugged. He didn't care either way.

'About what you said last night. About my job. Did you mean it?'

'I think we should both take time out, Maury. Consider our positions.'

Anderson nodded, a little too quickly to be natural. 'Okay. Okay. That's good.'

Freeman frowned at his financial director. 'You need help, Maury. Counselling. Something.'

Anderson rubbed his nose with the flat of his hand. 'Yeah. Whatever you say, Tony. Whatever you say.'

*   *   *

Mersiha climbed off the bus and waved goodbye to the driver. It was a bright, sunny afternoon but there was a chill in the air and she had the collar of her coat turned up against the wind. She hadn't been able to concentrate on her classes all day. Part of her was thrilled at the prospect of the vacation with her father, but she was also worried about Sabatino. She'd run countless scenarios through her mind as she sat at her desk, but none seemed even remotely realistic. Scaring a wimpish psychiatrist was one thing; it was quite another to threaten a gangster. Whatever she decided to do, she'd have to make sure it was foolproof. Buffy saw Mersiha walking towards the house and she came running over, all tongue and tail.

Freeman saw the black limousine when he was just a mile from his home. It was about a hundred yards behind his Lumina, matching his speed. The tinted windows prevented him from seeing into the back of the car but he knew exactly who was on his tail. Sabatino. His heart began to race. At first he couldn't understand why they were following him because Sabatino already knew where he lived, but then he realised that they were trying to intimidate him. The fear evaporated and was replaced by anger.

There was nothing he could do on the freeway so he kept

his driving at just below the speed limit, watching the limousine in his mirror. He had a phone in his car but Freeman knew that calling the police wouldn't solve anything. The limousine wasn't threatening him, he was in no apparent danger, and no matter how sympathetic the police might be, they wouldn't be able to take any action.

He slowed down and left the freeway. The limousine followed. It got closer to the Lumina. Sabatino clearly wanted Freeman to know that he was being followed. The closer Freeman got to his house, the closer the limousine got to the rear of his car, as if deliberately trying to provoke him. He considered stamping on his brake but realised that wouldn't solve anything. The Freeman house was at the bottom of a cul-de-sac, but the limousine wasn't deterred. It followed the Lumina right up to the driveway and sat at the entrance like a stalking leopard as Freeman drove into his garage. He climbed out of his car and stood staring at the limousine, his hands on his hips. He half expected it to drive away, but it sat there, immobile, though the engine was still running.

He walked towards the limousine. As he got closer he could see his reflection in the darkened glass, his hair dishevelled, his mouth open, and he slowed down and composed himself. This wasn't the time to be losing his temper. The rear window wound down with an electronic hum and expensive cologne and cigar smoke wafted out. Freeman could see that Sabatino was about to speak, but before he could get a word out Freeman grabbed the handle and pulled the door open. 'What's your problem, Sabatino?' he shouted.

Sabatino grinned back. He was holding a tumbler filled with red wine and he raised it in salute. 'Care for a drink, Tony?' he said.

'I want you away from my house,' Freeman said, his hands on the roof of the limousine.

'It's a public highway,' Sabatino countered. He looked at the driver. 'Hey, have we got our registration and insurance?'

'Sure have,' the driver said laconically.

Sabatino smiled at Freeman. 'Looks like we're legal, then.'

'You don't scare me, Sabatino.'

'Great. Because you don't scare me either, Tony. Now, how about we sign these papers before I don't scare your family.'

Freeman's eyes narrowed. He banged his hands down on the roof. Sabatino jumped, spilling red wine on his trousers. Freeman smiled with satisfaction. 'You leave my family out of this.'

'Sign the papers. Sell the company.'

'No.'

'You will, sooner or later.'

'I don't think so.'

'You should have a word with your partner. Ask him why he thinks you should sell.'

'I don't know what you've got on Maury, but it's not going to influence me one way or the other. The company's not for sale, and even if it was, I wouldn't sell it to you. At any price.'

Sabatino smiled, his eyes as hard as toughened glass. 'Looks like we'll be going on a picnic real soon, Tony. And I'm looking forward to it.'

'What?' Freeman said, his brow furrowed. 'What are you talking about?'

Sabatino leaned over and pulled the door shut. Freeman

stood glaring through the open window until Sabatino closed it. The car slowly drove away, leaving Freeman staring after it.

Mersiha stood at her bedroom window, her arms clasped around her chest. She'd seen the black limousine following her father's car and known immediately that it was Sabatino. Her heart had been in her mouth when she saw her father walk up and open the door. She'd half expected to hear a gunshot and see him fall to the ground. She wondered what her father had said to Sabatino. He'd obviously been angry because she'd seen him slap the roof of the limousine, and he stood glaring after the car when it drove away. Sabatino was tightening the screws. Mersiha realised that she was going to have to act, and to act soon. Next time the man confronted her father, there might well be a gunshot.

She sat on her bed, chewing on a pencil and studying the notebook on her lap. She tapped the pencil against her front teeth as she compiled a list of what she planned to do. Getting to a man like Sabatino was going to be a lot harder than dealing with Dr Brown. But she was prepared to try. She had no choice.

Freeman walked into the kitchen, still fuming. 'What's wrong?' Katherine asked.

'Sabatino followed me home. He's still trying to get me to sell the company.'

Katherine put down the carrots she was peeling and smiled. 'Persistent, isn't he?'

'This isn't funny, Kat. He sort of threatened me.'

'Sort of? What do you mean, sort of?'

Freeman shrugged. 'Well, he didn't actually put a gun to my head. But I got the drift.'

Katherine washed her hands under the cold tap. 'That's exactly what you said last time you two met. So I'll say again what I said then. Do you want to call the police?'

Freeman put his head on one side as he looked at her. 'He's very clever. He didn't really say anything that they could use against him, even if I had recorded it. But I know what he meant.'

'And Maury's no help?'

'Maury's on Sabatino's side, there's no question of that. Maybe I'll speak to our lawyers, see about getting an injunction or something.' He sat down at the kitchen table. 'Where's Mersiha?'

'Upstairs in her room. Tony, do you think you should go ahead with this holiday, considering what Sabatino's doing?'

Freeman sighed and rubbed his eyes with the back of his hands. 'I can't cancel now. She's really looking forward to it. Besides, what can he do? He can't get really heavy, can he? This isn't Chicago in the thirties.'

Mersiha reined her horse back as she watched Allison take the jumps. Allison was technically good, but she was always a little nervous and it showed. Her horse, Bonny, could tell that she wasn't one hundred per cent committed and took every opportunity to refuse a fence. Mersiha could see that Allison was also pulling the reins too hard while kicking with her heels, sending conflicting messages that only added to the horse's confusion. The result was a sloppy performance, one that Mersiha knew she could better. She might not be as technically proficient as Allison but she was much more confident and could exert far more control over her horse.

Allison approached a three-bar fence at a canter, but Bonny's ears went back and she snorted and made a dash to the left. Allison tried to pull her back on course but the damage was already done. Bonny bucked and slammed into the side of the fence, almost throwing Allison.

'Calm her down!' shouted Sandy McGregor, the instructor, waving his crop in the air for emphasis.

Allison regained control of her horse, her face red with embarrassment. 'Sorry,' she said.

'You were doing fine,' he said reassuringly. 'Next time ease off on the reins a bit, and make sure you take the fence head on. You came in at an angle and she wasn't sure where you were going. You've a good horse there, Allison, you've just got to tell her what you want.'

'Yes, Mr McGregor. Sorry.'

Allison walked Bonny back to the starting area and brought her to a halt next to Mersiha. Both girls were wearing white shirts and beige jodhpurs with black riding boots and hats. Mr McGregor insisted that all his pupils dressed that way. He was a kindly old man, grey-haired with ruddy cheeks from years spent outdoors, and was one of the best riding instructors in the state. He'd been teaching Mersiha since soon after she'd arrived in America, and though he was always sparing with his praise, Mersiha knew that she was one of his best pupils.

'Okay, Mersiha,' he called. 'Let's see what you can do.'

Mersiha gave a slight touch with her heels and her horse moved forward. She eased him into a rising trot and then went smoothly into a canter. 'Good boy,' she whispered, knowing that he liked to hear her voice. His name was Wilbur and she'd been riding him for almost two years. He was a brave jumper, eager to tackle any obstacle, though he sometimes had a tendency to rush.

They approached the first jump, a low wall, and Wilbur went crisply over, grunting as he landed. Mersiha turned him to the left and took a series of three jumps which got progressively higher.

'Good girl,' Mr McGregor said. 'Keep him going. Keep him going.'

Wilbur seemed to be spurred on by the instructor's shouts and Mersiha had no trouble getting him around the course without disturbing a single fence. Allison cheered her support as Mersiha joined her in the starting area. 'You were great,' she said.

'Wilbur's on form. He could have got around without me,' Mersiha said.

'I wish I could jump like you.'

'I've been riding longer, that's all. Anyway, you beat me hands down at dressage, you know you do.'

The two girls watched the next rider go around the jumping course under Mr McGregor's watchful eye. 'Allison, I need a favour,' Mersiha said.

'What?' she asked.

'I sort of need you to cover for me.'

'Oh my God, what are you up to?' Allison asked, intrigued.

Mersiha eased Wilbur closer to Allison's mount. The two horses stood together, nuzzling noses. 'I need to go out tomorrow night, but I don't want my parents to know.'

'Oh my God,' Allison repeated. 'Who is it?'

'You don't know him. He's not from school.'

'Oh my God,' Allison said, for the third time.

Mersiha tried to smile coyly. If Allison thought that she needed to slip away for a few hours with a boyfriend, she'd be happy to help, even if it meant telling a white lie or two. Allison had been able to get practically anything she wanted from her mother ever since her father had run off with a dental hygienist two years previously.

'Who is it? You just have to tell me who it is,' Allison gushed.

'I can't,' Mersiha said.

'Why not?'

'He's a bit older than me.'

'Oh my God! Oh my God! How much older?'

'You're embarrassing me, Allison. Look, will you help or not?'

Allison looked hurt. 'Of course. What do you want?'

'Can I say that I'll be at your house tomorrow night on a sleep-over? I'll tell my parents that we're studying together.'

'Cool. But what if they phone and you're not there?'

'I'll come to your house after school, then I'll slip away at about eight o'clock. I'll get the train into Baltimore, then I'll slip back later. If they call, you can say that I'm in the bathroom or something.'

'Yeah, but what happens when you don't phone them back?'

Mersiha shook her head. 'Look, I'm sure they won't call. They're going through this phase of trusting me, you know. Katherine will probably call in advance to check that's it's okay with your mom, but if they check up on me while I'm there, it's tantamount to saying they don't trust me. They won't call, I promise.'

'But what if my mom asks where you are?'

'Tell her I'm in the bathroom. Tell her I've gone home to get some books. Tell her I've been abducted by aliens. You know she won't notice whether I'm there or not.' Allison's mother had been hit hard by her husband's desertion and she'd begun drinking in a major way, putting away a couple of bottles of Californian wine each evening and often falling asleep on the sofa in front of videos of country and western singers. Half the time she didn't even know if Allison was in the house.

Allison chewed on her lower lip, then she smiled, showing glittering metal braces obscuring most of her teeth. 'Sure. But on one condition.'

'What?'

'Afterwards – you tell me everything. And I mean everything.'

Mersiha grinned. 'It's a deal.'

'Oh my God,' Allison sighed, flushed with excitement. 'Oh my God, oh my God.'

*   *   *

Sabatino sat back in his chair and fingered his telephone as he studied the closed-circuit cameras. It was still early so there wasn't much happening down in The Firehouse. He tapped the buttons on the telephone absent-mindedly, then picked up the receiver and rapidly dialled his brother's number in New York. It was his direct line and he answered on the third ring. 'Bzuchar?' Sabatino said.

'Who else would it be, younger brother?' Utsyev chuckled, like an old man. 'What's wrong?'

'How do you know something is wrong?' Sabatino asked, defensively.

'Why else would you be calling me this late? Aren't you normally in bed with one of your little conquests at this time of the evening?' Sabatino's brother chuckled again. Sabatino had the feeling that he wasn't alone.

'I went to see Freeman yesterday.'

'And?'

'And he doesn't want to sell.'

'What he wants isn't really relevant, is it?' He sounded impatient, as if he had better things to do than discuss the takeover of CRW. It wasn't like Bzuchar, thought Sabatino; he usually lived for business. There was obviously something else on his mind. 'We need the company. We need its land. We need its bank accounts and books to keep our little money-laundering secret safe. There's nothing more to it. Right?'

'I just wanted you to know what was happening,' Sabatino said. 'I'm going to have to increase the pressure.'

'That's not a problem, is it?'

'He's got a wife and a daughter and a big house. He's got a lot to lose. No, it won't be a problem.'

'So, do you need my help, or can you handle it?'

'I can handle it.'

'That's what I wanted to hear, little brother. Call me when it's done.' The line went dead. Sabatino sat fuming, glaring at the television monitor. It had been a bad idea to call his brother. He wouldn't call him again until he had CRW in the bag. But first he wanted some young flesh. Seventeen, maybe younger. Someone pretty, someone he could hurt.

Mersiha waited until an hour after her parents had gone to bed before slipping out of her room and downstairs to the study. She knelt down by the side of the gun cabinet and quickly twisted the combination dial and pulled open the door. Down in the basement the central heating boiler whooshed into life, startling her. She listened intently, but other than the clicking of the heating system there was no sound.

The Heckler & Koch HK-4 was in its case where she'd left it. She reassembled the gun into its .22 LR components and laid it down on the floor while she closed the case and relocked the cabinet.

She took the box of .22 cartridges and shook out a handful of shiny brass shells into the palm of her hand. One by one she loaded them into the HK-4's clip.

*　　*　　*

Freeman looked across at his wife, sleeping as she always did on her side with her knees drawn up against her stomach. The foetal position, he thought. He couldn't remember her sleeping like that before Luke had died. It was as if she were trying to protect herself against bad dreams. She looked so defenceless in sleep, like a child. Her breathing was soft and steady, her chest barely moving.

The digital clock on the bedside table clicked to 02.00. Freeman heard the stairs creak as Mersiha came upstairs. He'd heard her go down about half an hour earlier and he'd been lying awake to see what time she'd go back to bed. Only a minute or two and she was probably just paying a visit to the refrigerator, but half an hour suggested that she was sleepwalking again. He fought back the urge to get up and see if she was all right. The first few times it had happened, shortly after she'd arrived in America, he and Katherine had woken her up and she'd burst into tears, clearly shaken by the experience. Art Brown's advice had been just to let her walk around and go back to bed in her own time. The psychiatrist had described the sleepwalking as a physical symptom of her underlying mental turmoil, one that would gradually disappear as her therapy progressed. Letting her wake up in her own time seemed to work – it wasn't as if she tried to leave the house or did anything dangerous. Eventually she would return to her room and in the morning she remembered nothing about her nocturnal adventures. Dr Brown had been right. During her first few months in the house she'd sleepwalked almost every night, but now it happened only rarely.

Freeman heard her close her bedroom door. He relaxed and rolled over on to his side.

'What's wrong?' Katherine murmured, sleepily.

'Nothing,' he said. 'Go back to sleep.'

She snuggled closer to him and her hand stroked his chest. Her breathing deepened as her hand slowly made its way down to his groin. 'I'm not sleepy,' she said, though her eyes remained closed. She kissed his shoulder. Her lips were warm and moist. She kissed him again, harder this time, and he felt her tongue lick against his skin. Katherine was wearing one of his cotton shirts and as she rolled on top of him his hands pushed it up around her waist. She buried her face in his neck, her hair falling around him like a veil. Her lips fluttered around his neck and shoulder, small child-like kisses that were at odds with the hand that was groping between his legs. It had been several weeks since he'd made love to her, and he was already hard and ready for her. He gasped as she slid herself on to him and his hands moved inside the shirt and up to her breasts.

'I love you,' he said.

'I know you do,' she said, sleepily. She lay flat against him, only her hips moving.

He tried to kiss her on the lips but she kept her face pressed against his neck. He knew that her eyes were still closed, and he wondered if she was aware of what she was doing.

'Katherine?' he said.

'Hmmm?' she moaned, her hips moving faster and faster.

'Are you asleep?' he asked.

'Hmmm,' she murmured into his ear.

He reached up and stroked the back of her neck. She really was asleep, and he realised that in the morning she'd no more remember the love-making than Mersiha would recall her sleepwalking. He felt suddenly sad. He wanted Katherine to make love to him because she desired him, he

302

wanted it to be an expression of her love, but what she was doing to him was just a physical thing, a release. He wanted her attention. Her love. She pounded against him and he felt himself about to come. Part of him wanted her to stop but there was no denying how much he wanted her. 'I love you, Katherine,' he whispered into her hair, and then he came inside her.

Mersiha was devouring a low-fat yoghurt when Freeman walked into the kitchen. Buffy was sitting at her feet, her eyes glued to the yoghurt carton. The dog greeted Freeman with an enthusiastic wag of her tail but kept her attention focused on Mersiha's breakfast.

'Hiya, pumpkin,' he said, popping two slices of whole-meal bread into the toaster. The mail was lying on the kitchen table and he flicked through the envelopes: several bills, a handful of circulars, a once-in-a-lifetime opportunity to win ten million dollars addressed to 'The Occupier', and a bank statement. There was a brown envelope from the travel agency Freeman used, and he tossed it to Mersiha.

'The tickets!' she gasped. He nodded and she ripped it open. 'Denver,' she said.

'That's where we fly to, but our cabin is about seventy miles to the north-west. Near Estes Park, right next to the Rocky Mountain National Park.'

'Yeah, there's a map here,' Mersiha said, spreading it out on the table. 'It's off a highway called Devil's Gulch Road. Devil's Gulch Road! Isn't that great? Like something out of the Wild West.' She put the half-finished carton of yoghurt down and Buffy growled hopefully.

'I've hired a four-wheel-drive, the details should be there.'

'Yup,' Mersiha said, waving a typed letter. 'A Ford Bronco. There's a photograph of the cabin, too. Wow, it looks wild.'

Freeman smiled at her enthusiasm. The toaster popped as Katherine came in, wrapped in a white bathrobe, her hair still glistening wet. She kissed him on the cheek and Freeman wondered if she had any recollection of the previous night. She buttered his toast while he poured coffee for them both. 'Are those the tickets?' she asked.

'Yeah, the cabin looks great,' Mersiha said. 'It's miles from anywhere.' Katherine looked across at Freeman, her brow furrowed.

'It's not that isolated,' he said, before she could voice her concern. 'The nearest neighbour is about half a mile away.'

'What if you get snowed in?'

'We've got a four-wheel-drive,' Mersiha said.

'That'll be just what you need if you're stuck in the cabin for two weeks. You'll always be able to eat it.'

'There'll be stores within driving distance and it's close to a major road,' Freeman said. 'They rent it out right through the winter, Kat. It doesn't get snowed in. Besides, the travel agent said they're having a mild winter.'

'And you'll be back when?'

'Friday afternoon.'

'Do you want me to pick you up?'

'No need. I'll leave the car in the long-term lot.'

Katherine picked up the cabin brochure from the

table and looked through it. 'It's beautiful,' she agreed. 'You're going to have a terrific time. And look at this. Skiing, horse-riding, snowmobiling, sleigh rides, fishing, snowshoeing, mountain biking. Even hot-air ballooning.'

'Well, I don't know if all that'll be available,' Freeman said. 'It's the off season. A lot of the tourist places there are closed until May.'

Katherine frowned. 'A skiing resort closed for the winter?'

'It's not really a skiing resort, though it's close to lots of places where we can ski. But there will be plenty for us to do. We can get some practice in Western riding. None of that sissyish English style.' He winked at his daughter and she grinned up at him.

'Make sure you pack warm clothes,' Katherine said.

'Sure,' he agreed.

'I was talking to Mersiha,' Katherine laughed, 'but I suppose it goes for you too.' Mersiha held the yoghurt carton down for Buffy. The dog attacked it, her claws scrabbling on the tiled floor. 'What have I told you about feeding the dog at the table?' Katherine chided.

'Sorry,' Mersiha said, taking the prize away from the dog. Buffy glared at Katherine as if blaming her for the loss of the treat. 'Oh, I forgot to mention it. Allison is having a couple of girls over tonight for a study party. Is it all right if I go?'

Freeman looked over the top of his coffee mug. 'A study party? Two days before school breaks up?'

Mersiha shrugged. 'We've got a couple of projects that have to be done over the break. Allison wants to do all the preparatory work before I go on vacation. We'll go straight to school from Allison's house.'

'I suppose it's all right,' Katherine said. 'I'll speak to Allison's mother.'

'Great!' Mersiha exclaimed.

'So what's the project?' Freeman asked.

'Oh, some historical thing. Life during the Great Depression, something like that. Allison's our group organiser. I'll go and pack a few things for tonight.'

She skipped out of the room. Katherine looked through the travel details. 'Are you sure about this?' she asked.

'I am.' Freeman took the brochure and pointed at a colour photograph of a snow-covered mountainside. 'This is exactly like the hills around Sarajevo in the winter.'

'What – skiers, snowmobiles and hot-air balloons?' she asked archly.

'You know what I mean, honey. The trees, the rocky crags, the sky – it's just like it was in Bosnia. Only without the snipers.'

'Thank God.'

'Yeah, but it's the atmosphere that's important. I want to remind her of what it was like when I first met her.'

'So that she'll start to talk? Are you sure it's a good idea?'

Freeman drained his mug and put it by the sink. 'No, Kat, to be honest I'm not sure. But I want to give it a try. I can't go through life not knowing what happened to our little girl.'

Katherine walked over to him and put her hands on his shoulders. 'Okay, but make sure that you're doing it because it's best for her, not because it's something that you want to do. Deal?'

'Deal,' he agreed.

She looked into his eyes as if trying to read his mind, then suddenly leant forward and kissed him on the lips. Freeman was surprised at the gesture, but before he could respond Mersiha came back into the kitchen and she pulled away.

Mersiha was carrying a nylon bag over her shoulder. She kissed Katherine on the cheek and waved goodbye to Freeman. They watched as she went out of the back door, taking care to keep Buffy inside. 'She seems a lot better,' Katherine said.

'She was sleepwalking last night,' Freeman said, picking up his briefcase.

'God, no. I didn't hear her.' He smiled and shook his head.

'What?' she said. 'What are you smiling at?'

'Nothing.'

'What? Come on, you're grinning like the cat that got the cream.'

'Nothing,' he repeated. He kissed her on the forehead and went out to his car, smiling to himself.

The day seemed to drag interminably for Mersiha. The gun and ammunition were in her locker, wrapped in a hand towel. Twice during the day, Allison had sidled up to her and nudged her in the ribs, smiling with a glint of braces and winking conspiratorially.

Eventually the school day ended and Mersiha collected the weapon and her overnight bag. She was grateful for the fact that she went to school in the suburbs. In the Baltimore City schools, metal detectors were the norm because there had been so many drug-related killings.

'What's in the bag?' Allison asked as they walked towards the school bus.

'Clothes. Handbag. Make-up,' Mersiha replied. She wondered how Allison would react if she'd continued to list the contents. Gun. Ammunition. She smiled at the subversive thought.

Allison pounced. 'What are you grinning for?'

'Just thinking about tonight.'

'Oh, please tell me who it is.' They climbed on to the bus and sat together near the back. Allison leaned across. 'Is it Lester Middlehurst?'

Mersiha looked across at Allison and imagined shooting her in the head with the gun. It would probably be the only way to put an end to the torrent of questions. She smiled sweetly. 'No, it's not Lester Middlehurst. Now don't ask me anything else.'

'Okay. Okay.' Allison jiggled up and down on her seat excitedly.

Katherine Freeman closed her eyes and luxuriated in the hot water. She turned on the hot tap with her foot and swished the water around, enjoying the way the warmth gradually spread up her body. The feeling was decidedly sexual and her right hand slowly strayed between her legs as if it had a life of its own.

The telephone rang, jarring her out of her reverie. The nearest extension was in her bedroom and she was damned if she was going to get out of her bath. The answering machine picked up the call and she closed her eyes again. Her hand began to caress her soft, soapy skin.

She heard Maury Anderson's voice, urgently calling her name. 'Come on, Katherine, I know you're there. Pick up.'

She groaned. 'Now what?' she muttered to herself.

'Come on, Katherine. I'm not hanging up until you answer.'

She wondered if Anderson really did know she was in or if he was guessing. Either way, he'd already spoiled the moment for her. She climbed out of the bath and wrapped a towel around her shoulders before running into the bedroom and grabbing the phone. 'Damn you, Maury. I'm dripping water all over the carpet.'

'Katherine. I have to see you.'

'Is that all? You've dragged me out of the bath because you've got a hard-on? Isn't your wife back?'

'This is business. It's about the offer for CRW.'

'Fine. So why bother me at home? Can't you talk to Tony?'

'Tony's being totally unreasonable. Katherine, you have to get him to listen to reason.'

'Maury, love, I don't have to do anything.'

'We have to sell the company. You can't say no to a man like Sabatino.'

'Maury, go and screw your little wife. You can close your eyes and think of me if it makes it any better, but stop bothering me. You're becoming a nuisance.' She slammed the phone down and went back to her bath.

*   *   *

Mersiha toyed with her coffee cup. A thick beige scum had formed on the surface and she touched it gently with the tip of her index finger. It felt like human skin. She looked at her watch for the thousandth time. It was nine thirty. Too early to go to The Firehouse. A buxom, middle-aged waitress came over. 'You want me to freshen that, hon?' she asked. Mersiha smiled and nodded. The waitress splashed in more coffee. 'Can I get you anything to eat?'

'No. No, thanks.'

'Are you waiting for someone?'

Mersiha made a show of looking at her watch again. 'Yeah. But she's late.'

'Well, you just let me know if you need anything.' She moved down the counter, freshening coffee and trading quips with the diners. The Buttery in Charles Street was open twenty-four hours a day, catering to students and workers during the day and to insomniacs through the night. It was a comfortable eatery, never empty but never busy enough for a girl on her own nursing a coffee for more than an hour to be a problem. Mersiha had left Allison's house at eight o'clock. Allison's mother was already lying down on the sofa with a half-empty bottle of white wine by her side. Mersiha had caught the light-rail train into the city, her bag clasped close to her side all the way.

A biker with shoulder-length hair and old acne scars kept smiling at her and trying to make eye contact. Mersiha pointedly ignored him. Two overweight cops came in, their caps under their arms, and ordered coffee and doughnuts to go. Mersiha sipped her coffee, fighting back the feeling of panic that threatened to overwhelm her. The loaded handgun was in the bag at her feet, still wrapped in a hand towel. The cops scanned the diner professionally, comparing faces with mug-shots they'd been shown at roll-call. The elder of the two cops nudged his companion and nodded in Mersiha's direction. Out of the corner of her eye she saw them walk in her direction. She swallowed nervously. When they drew level with her, the younger of the two men put his hand on the butt of his pistol. Mersiha sighed and closed her eyes. It was all over. They'd find the gun and they'd give it to forensic experts who'd be able to show it was the same weapon that had injured Dr Brown, and that would be it. They'd take her away and lock her in a cell and she'd never see her father again. She cursed herself for her stupidity.

The cops walked by her and over to the biker. The younger cop hung back, leaning against the bar with his hand on his gun, as his partner approached the man. Mersiha couldn't hear what was said, but she could see the biker pull out his wallet and show his driving licence to the officer. They talked for a while and the cop pointed out of the window. All conversation in the diner had died away as its occupants strained to hear what was going on, but the cook had burgers and onions sizzling on a hot plate and the sound of frying food obscured what was being said. Eventually the biker and the cop laughed together and the atmosphere in the diner became more relaxed. The younger cop took his hand off his gun and took a sip from his paper cup. He looked over at Mersiha and smiled. She smiled back nervously.

The two cops left the diner, carrying their coffee and doughnuts, and a few seconds later the biker went out. Mersiha heard the angry growl of a motorcycle. The sound faded into the distance as the biker drove away. She slowly finished her coffee, and another refill, before paying her bill and picking up her bag. She carried it through to the women's lavatory and locked the door behind her.

There was a wooden chair in the corner of the room and she pulled it in front of the mirror. She sat down and unzipped her bag. From inside she took out her make-up supplies – lipstick, foundation, mascara, eye-liner and nail varnish – and lined them up on the shelf under the mirror. The black dress was rolled up in a protective bag and she hung it up on the back of the door. She looked at her watch. She had plenty of time. A club like The Firehouse wouldn't be busy until midnight.

Lori Fantoni wiped the counter surface clean and replaced the plastic-coated menus behind the bottle of ketchup. Her back ached and she pushed her knuckles against the base of her spine, leaning backwards and looking at the ceiling.

'Back giving you trouble again, Lori?' asked Curtis Baker, a retiree who always popped into The Buttery for a late-night mug of hot milk and a pastry before turning in.

'Tell me about it,' she wheezed, arching her back as far as it would go.

'I could give you a massage,' he offered.

Lori grinned and flicked her cloth at him. 'You can wipe that thought right out of your mind, Curtis.' He was a widower and Lori's husband had died three years earlier. Curtis asked her out every Friday as regular as clockwork, and just as regularly she turned him down. It wasn't the age difference – Curtis was in his seventies and she was only fifty-three – it was just that there wasn't a spark between them. No chemistry. And no money, either. Curtis had owned a small furniture business which had gone bust in the late eighties and he only had a small pension to live on. Lori had enough money troubles of her own not to want to tie up with a man like Curtis.

Two black teenagers slouched into the diner and slid on to stools at the far end of the counter. They were young, barely into their teens, but wore expensive leather jackets and were bedecked with gold chains and medallions. Lori shook her head sadly. There was only one way two young kids could earn enough money to dress like that, and it wasn't by flipping burgers in Mickey D's. She walked over to them and held out menus, but they shook their heads.

'Coffee and steak sandwiches,' said one. 'One heavy on the onions. One without.'

'Yeah, onions give me gas,' said the other.

'Sorry to hear that, hon,' Lori said. She poured two mugs of coffee, slid a bowl of whitener over and handed their orders to the cook. Close up the boys looked even younger than when she'd first seen them. One of them couldn't have been much older than thirteen. What was the city coming to? If she had a son, there was no way he would have been allowed out this late, and if she'd ever found that he was dealing drugs – well, she didn't like to think what she'd do. Children today, they just didn't get any moral guidance, not in the city anyway. Baltimore's slogan was 'The City that Reads', but like the rest of its one million or so inhabitants Lori knew that was a pipedream; the city had one of the lowest literacy rates in the country, and along with illiteracy went a lack of morals. It wasn't the fault of the children, she thought sadly. There was no such thing as a bad kid, just bad parents. And the city had more than enough of them.

She walked to the middle of the counter and began polishing it, her mind only half on the task. She didn't have any children. Hell, she didn't even have a husband any more. That was one of the reasons she liked working the night shift at The Buttery. She hadn't slept well for three years, not since she'd woken up to find her husband lying still beside her, killed stone dead by a massive coronary. Her days she could fill, with mind-numbing talk shows and movie re-runs, but time seemed almost to stop at night. That was when she missed her husband the most. And it was when she wished that they'd been able to have children. A son. Or a daughter. It wouldn't have mattered. One thing she was sure of, if they had had children, there was no way they would have been out on the streets late at night. Not like the two boys at the end of the counter. Or the girl, the young one who'd gone pale when Chuck and Ed had gone over to talk to the biker. She'd been in the washroom for almost twenty minutes, and if she didn't come out soon then Lori was going to knock on the door and ask if there was something wrong. She hoped that the girl wasn't on drugs or something.

The cook slid the sandwiches on to plates and garnished them with tomato and lettuce. Lori tucked her cloth into her waistband and put the food in front of the boys. They thanked her politely, as meek as choirboys. The door to the washroom opened and Lori looked up sharply, worried that she was going to see the young girl stagger out with blood pouring from her arm. What she actually saw took her even more by surprise. A beautiful black-haired girl in a tight dress walked out, high heels emphasising her long, shapely legs. The two teenagers turned and gawped at her, and Lori heard a long, low whistle from Curtis. The girl was carrying a sports bag over one shoulder. It was the same girl who'd been sitting hunched over her coffee, but now she looked stunning. Lori wondered what on earth was going on. The thought that the girl might be a hooker passed through her mind. Hookers regularly dropped into the diner for coffee or a meal after work, but this girl was nothing like them. She didn't have their hard eyes. She was young and fresh. Lori wondered where she was going so late at night. Wherever it was, she hoped that she'd be okay.

The girl stepped out of the diner and on to Charles Street without a backward look. Lori, the teenagers and Curtis all watched her go.

Mersiha walked carefully, watching where she placed her feet. She wasn't used to high heels. The temperature had dropped several degrees and she could feel goosebumps on her shoulders. She shivered. She'd have been better wearing a warm coat, but she knew she was going to have to leave The Firehouse in a hurry. A blue Toyota slowed down and a balding middle-aged man leered at her, licking his upper lip. He waved for her to come over to the car but she shook her head and moved away from the kerb. The car roared off. A young black man using a public telephone watched her walk by. He put his hand over the receiver and whistled at her. 'Hey, baby, do you wanna give me some of that?' he called. Mersiha ignored him. 'Come on, bitch.

You know you want it.' She shuddered. The man laughed harshly and went back to his phone call.

Mersiha hated the way men reacted to a short skirt and make-up, as if by dressing sexily she automatically became public property. Men seemed to assume that any girl out at night was fair game. They didn't seem to realise how intimidating it was for a girl on her own to be approached by strangers. Or maybe they did know and just didn't care. The man on the phone shouted something else at her. For a wild moment Mersiha felt like taking the gun out of her bag and pushing it under his nose so that he'd know what it felt like to be intimidated. That would wipe the smile off his face. She wondered what it would be like to pull the trigger and to see his head explode. The thought made her grin. The heel of her left shoe caught in a grating and she lurched forward, losing her balance and leaving the shoe behind. She hopped back and pulled it free, glaring at the errant footwear. Only a man could have designed something that served no other function than to make women's legs look longer. They pinched her toes, they made the backs of her legs ache, and they were a danger to walk in, but men were turned on by high heels so women had to wear them. She put the shoe back on her foot and walked on. She hadn't realised how far it was to the Greyhound bus terminal in West Fayette Street and it was much colder than she'd anticipated, so she stuck out her hand and flagged down a yellow cab. The driver was an Arab and he kept staring at her in the driver's mirror. She sidled along the seat to get out of his vision but he moved the mirror.

She reached into her sports bag. On top of her rolled-up sweater was a small black handbag on a gilt chain. She unzipped it and slipped her hand inside, feeling the comforting coldness of the loaded HK-4. She still wasn't sure exactly what she was going to say to Sabatino. He was a dangerous man, that went without saying, but Maury had told her father that he was a bully and bullies usually backed down if confronted. She remembered how Dr Brown had trembled at the sight of the weapon. Sabatino would probably react the same way. He'd realise that she was serious and he'd back off. Hopefully the threat alone would be enough. But what if he wasn't intimidated? What then? Would she shoot him? And would a bullet in the leg be enough? It had worked with Dr Brown, but he was a psychiatrist, not a gangster. What if Sabatino wasn't scared? What if he thought she was bluffing? How far would she be prepared to go?

The Arab was staring again. She could feel his eyes boring into her chest and she glared back at him. He averted his gaze. When he looked back she was still glaring at him, her face set tight. She felt nothing but contempt for the man, and she stared at him until he looked away again. This time he moved the mirror so that he couldn't see her face. Mersiha smiled. The driver had backed down. So would Sabatino. And if he didn't – well, then she'd do whatever she had to in order to protect her father.

The cab driver dropped her outside the bus terminal. She thought of asking him to wait but decided against it. He was more likely to remember her if she did, and anyway she didn't like the look of him.

A group of black teenagers were standing outside the entrance and they whistled as she walked by. One of them shouted something about her legs but she couldn't make out what it was. She found the left-luggage lockers and chose one in the middle to store her sports bag, slipping the key into her handbag after locking the door. The handbag was heavy but there was no indication from the outside that it contained a gun. She pulled the skirt down over her thighs and walked back outside. This time one of the teenagers blocked her way, his hands on his hips. 'Where you going, girl?' he asked. He was wearing baggy jeans with the crotch hanging down almost to his knees, a back-to-front football jersey under a leather jacket, and huge Reeboks. Despite the funny-looking clothes and his baby face, Mersiha was scared. His eyes were unfocused and he seemed to have trouble standing upright. She tried to walk around him but he moved in front of her again. 'You deaf, bitch? I said where are you going?'

His friends laughed. They circled around her, like hyenas around a wounded gazelle. Mersiha put her hand on her bag.

Someone laughed behind her. 'Bitch thinks we're gonna steal her purse.'

The teenager in front of her grinned. 'Bitch might be right.'

She moved to the side but a hand gripped her arm, the nails biting into her flesh. 'Don't,' she said. The teenagers laughed at her discomfort. They moved in closer, laughing and swearing. Mersiha undid the clasp of her bag and slid her hand inside. Her fingers tightened around the butt of the gun. 'Don't,' she repeated, her voice harder this time. One of the teenagers howled like a wolf, his head thrown back and his mouth wide open, showing several gold teeth. 'Don't touch me,' she said, her voice hardening. A hand touched her back and she whirled around, eyes blazing. 'No one touches me,' she hissed. 'No one.'

'Bitch has balls,' said one of the teenagers.

'Let's see, shall we?' said another, laughing.

'Touch me and you're dead,' Mersiha whispered.

The teenagers stood back, eyes wide in mock terror. One of them started trembling as if he were having an epileptic fit. 'Look, I'm shaking,' he said. The others burst into laughter. Another hand touched her, this time brushing her bare shoulder.

'I warned you,' she shouted, starting to draw the gun from the bag.

'Leave the girl be,' said a deep masculine voice from behind her. The teenagers stopped laughing. Mersiha turned to look at the newcomer. He was an elderly black man, a cleaner by the look at it, an old baseball cap on his greying hair and a dishevelled mop in his hand.

'This ain't your business, man,' said one of the teenagers, the youngest of the group but with the build of a basketball player, tall and lanky with huge hands which he flexed as he confronted the cleaner.

'This *is* my business, son,' the old man said. 'It's all our business. The girl has a right to walk undisturbed through the city. You can see that, can't you? You wouldn't want your sister interfered with, would you?'

'She ain't no sister,' said the guy in the leather jacket. His friends laughed and jeered, but the cleaner wasn't perturbed.

'She could be somebody's sister,' the old man said, pushing the baseball cap to the back of his head. Mersiha saw a thick black scar cutting across his forehead, an old, ugly wound that had healed badly. 'You gotta treat people the way you wanna be treated, the way you'd want your own family treated. Now leave her be.'

The teenagers looked at the old man, and at the mop he

was holding. They could have taken it from him easily, they were younger and stronger, but Mersiha could see that they were unwilling to confront him. There was something about his bearing that inspired respect.

'Go on now, girl,' he said quietly. 'Go on your way.'

Mersiha mouthed 'thank you' and walked away as quickly as the high heels would carry her. She took her hand off the gun and wiped her mouth nervously. Despite the cold night air, she was sweating.

There was a line waiting outside The Firehouse and she joined it. One of the doormen, an imposing black guy in a tuxedo, spotted her and motioned that she could go in. 'Pretty girls don't have to wait,' he said, opening the door for her. 'And you don't have to pay 'cos it's Ladies' Night.'

Mersiha smiled her thanks. She walked down a red-painted corridor, feeling like a morsel of food sliding down the gullet of some strange animal. Another doorman in an identical tuxedo opened a second door for her. Loud, pulsing music billowed out, along with warm, smoky air that smelled of sweat and cheap perfume.

The Firehouse was just that – a former fire station that had been turned into a nightclub. Red was the dominant theme, and many of the original fittings had been left in place, including a line of six poles stretching up to holes in the ceiling. Midway up the poles were man-size gilded cages in which young girls in bikinis writhed and gyrated in time to the music. The dance floor was packed and customers were standing three-deep at the bar. The crowd was mainly white, young, and stoned. Mersiha had never smoked marijuana but she'd been at several parties where it had been handed around, so she recognised the sickly-sweet smell. A man in his early twenties with slicked-back hair and a shiny suit came over to her. 'Hiya. I'm Simon,' he said, flashing her a film-star smile.

'Yeah. Hiya. I'm looking for someone.' At the far end of the building she saw stairs. Two men in tuxedos stood at the foot, their arms folded across their chests. Sentries.

'Well, look no further. You've found someone.'

Mersiha stepped to the side. 'Sorry. Not tonight,' she said.

'Pity,' Simon said as she walked away.

The two sentries looked down at Mersiha with hard faces. 'Ladies' room is down there,' said one, nodding towards the bar.

'Is Mr Sabatino upstairs?' she asked.

The smaller of the two men put his head on one side like a budgie studying its reflection in a mirror. 'Is he expecting you?'

'Sure,' Mersiha said, her heart racing.

'What's your name?'

'Allison,' she said, then cursed herself. She'd said the first name that had occurred to her. She hadn't meant to use the name of her friend. That was a mistake.

'Well, Allison, Mr Sabatino didn't tell us that he was expecting anyone.' He looked her up and down, taking in the short dress and the long legs. 'You're his type, though.'

'That's for sure,' his colleague said. 'I'll take her up.'

Mersiha followed him up the stairs to the offices. The man was huge, almost as wide as he was tall, and the tuxedo was stretched tight across his shoulders. 'Wait here,' he said over his shoulder, and knocked on one of the doors. It opened and he exchanged words with someone inside. The door opened further and the man in the tuxedo waved Mersiha over. 'You lied to me, girl. But he'll see you anyway.' His smile suggested that he knew something she didn't, and Mersiha shivered.

Sabatino was sitting behind a large desk next to a bank of television monitors that showed what was going on downstairs. His gaze wandered down her body, lingering over her breasts and thighs. Mersiha felt like a show dog being weighed up for first or second place. Another man stood slightly behind Sabatino, his back to a window, chewing on a cigar. He could have been one of the men she'd seen in Sabatino's car, good-looking but with mean eyes.

'So, what can I do you for . . . Allison?' Sabatino asked.

Mersiha tried to make herself look as vacant as possible, figuring that Sabatino wouldn't be attracted to anyone with more than a handful of brain cells. Vacant but sexy. It seemed to be working because Sabatino leaned forward to get a better look. 'It's sort of . . . er . . . personal, Mr Sabatino. Could I sort of see you in, you know, private?' To Mersiha's ears it sounded as if she was overdoing it, but Sabatino didn't seem to realise that it was only an act. Then again, he didn't look too bright himself. Mersiha pouted and thrust her breasts out. 'If that's, er, okay with you.'

Sabatino swivelled around in his chair and grinned at the man behind him. 'It's okay, Vincenti,' he said. 'I can handle this.'

The man nodded curtly and walked by Mersiha to the door. She heard him open and close it. The floor was vibrating through her feet, and even with the door closed Mersiha could hear the pounding music down below. If she did fire the gun, she doubted that anyone would hear it in the nightclub.

Sabatino stood up and sidled his large bulk around the desk. He walked up to Mersiha and stroked her hair. He seemed even bigger close up, dwarfing her with his presence. He was wearing a pungent aftershave that smelled of lemons. 'Pretty little thing, aren't you?' he mused.

His hand touched her cheek and she fought the urge to flinch. Instead she smiled as invitingly as possible. 'We won't be disturbed, will we?' she asked.

Sabatino frowned. Then his eyes widened. 'Did my brother send you?' he asked. Mersiha hadn't a clue what he was talking about but she nodded nonetheless. Sabatino giggled, and the sound was almost girlish. He went over to the door and locked it, then stood with his back to it, barely able to contain his excitement. 'Bzuchar knows just how I like them,' he said under his breath. He stood watching her for several seconds, like a butcher weighing up a piece of meat before making the first cut. 'Take off your dress,' he said eventually.

'What?' Mersiha said.

'You heard me. Take off your dress.'

Mersiha was so surprised that she took an involuntary step backwards. 'No,' she said.

'Just do as you're told. I wanna see what you've got.' He pushed himself away from the door and started to advance towards her, rubbing his sweating hands together. Mersiha reached into her handbag and pulled out the gun. Sabatino stopped dead at the sight of the weapon. 'What the fuck's going on?' he spat.

'Just stay where you are,' she ordered. She held the

gun in both hands, the barrel centred on Sabatino's groin.

'What is this? A fucking hit?'

'I want you to leave Tony Freeman alone,' she said.

'What?'

'Tony Freeman. CRW. I want you to leave his company alone. If you don't, I'll kill you.'

Deep lines creased Sabatino's forehead. He looked at the gun. Then he looked at Mersiha. 'You've got to be joking.'

'No, Mr Sabatino. I'm serious. If you don't promise to leave the company alone, I'll kill you.'

Sabatino squinted at her face as if he were looking into the sun. 'How old are you?' he asked.

'Old enough to pull the trigger. Now, will you do as I say? Or shall I put a bullet in your leg?'

Sabatino took a step forward. 'You're not going to shoot anything with the safety on,' he said.

Mersiha tightened her trigger finger without dropping her gaze. 'I'm not stupid, Mr Sabatino. I know the safety is off. If you want me to check, I'd be quite happy to test it on you.' She began to increase the pressure.

'No!' Sabatino said. 'Don't!'

Mersiha sneered at the man. He'd tried to fool her, and now he was frightened. He was a typical bully: vicious and overbearing when he thought he was in control, snivelling when faced with a stronger adversary.

'Who are you?' he asked, sweat visible on his forehead.

'I'm the person who's telling you to keep away from CRW. And I'll be the person who'll put a bullet in you if you don't do as I say.'

'You don't look like the sort of girl who's capable of killing.'

'Oh, I've killed before, Mr Sabatino. Believe me, I've killed.'

'I'm sure you have . . . what did you say your name was? Allison?' He put his hands in his pockets.

'My name's not important. And take your hands out of your pockets. Keep them where I can see them.'

Sabatino smiled agreeably. 'Whatever you want,' he said. His hands reappeared. 'Just keep calm, don't . . .' His right hand moved in a blur, upwards and out, and a handful of small change flew through the air. Mersiha reacted instinctively, ducking out of the way, trying to protect her face from the flying pennies and quarters. Sabatino moved quickly despite his size, and he reached her in three quick steps. He grabbed the gun and twisted it out of her grasp. Mersiha tried to back away but Sabatino slapped her, knocking her sideways. The blow spun her around and she fell against the desk.

Sabatino studied the gun in his hand. 'You were right,' he said. 'The safety was off.' He released the clip and held it in his left hand. 'Bullets, too. You weren't bluffing.'

He tossed the gun and clip on to the sofa and went over to her. She tried to wriggle away but Sabatino grabbed her by the throat. He laughed as she went for his eyes with clawed fingers and swayed back, easily avoiding her. He spun her around so that her back was towards him, then hit her between the shoulder-blades so that she slumped over the desk. 'Let's see what you look like without the dress,' he hissed, and pulled down the zip.

Mersiha tried to slip to the side but Sabatino rammed a knee between her legs, trapping her. 'No, you're not going anywhere,' he said, pulling her hair roughly. He kissed her on the neck and she felt his rough tongue rasp against her skin. She pushed back with her hips, trying to force him away, but the movement only made him even more excited. She felt him grow hard. 'That's it,' he whispered. 'Fight me. Fight me all the way. There's nothing you can do, little girl. I'm gonna fuck you like you've never been fucked before, then I'm gonna take you on a picnic.' He groped around her body and seized her breasts, squeezing them so hard that she yelped. Mersiha frantically looked around for something, anything, to use as a weapon. There was a diary on the desk, a lamp, a stapler, a wooden box containing correspondence, a brass letter-opener shaped like an aeroplane propeller.

She grabbed the letter-opener as Sabatino released her breasts and began to force her dress up over her hips. 'No!' she shouted.

He seized the back of her neck with one hand as he used the other to tear off her panties. The cotton ripped like paper and then she felt his hand on her flesh, roughly prising her legs apart. 'No!' she screamed again, and lashed out behind her with the letter-opener. She missed, her elbow banging into his thigh. She swung her arm lower, this time just missing his leg. Sabatino laughed at her clumsy attempts to attack him. He let go of her neck, using his knee to keep her pinned to the desk as he tried to take the letter-opener from her. He caught her wrist and twisted it savagely. She released the opener and he tossed it to one side. Mersiha heard it rattle against the wooden floor.

He pushed her skirt higher, up around her waist, and then she heard his zip being opened. The sound was virtually identical to the sound of her knickers tearing. She tried to push her upper body off the desk, but Sabatino forced her down with the flat of his hand. 'Struggle as much as you want,' he hissed. 'The more you struggle, the more I'll enjoy it.' He moved against her, forcing her legs apart. Something hard nudged against her inner thigh and she felt suddenly sick as she realised what it was. Memories flooded back. The men. The grasping hands. The sweaty faces. Her mother, begging.

Sabatino's knee pushed her right leg to the side. 'No,' she gasped. She lifted her foot up, then raked it down his leg, the heel scraping the flesh through his trousers. His leg jerked away and he howled. Mersiha kept driving down and impaled his foot with her heel. She put all her weight on it, pushing herself backwards and screwing her heel down. Sabatino screamed and let go of her, staggering backwards. As he pulled his foot away, the heel of her shoe snapped.

She whirled around, panting and shaking. She was in a half-crouch, her hands forming talons, her eyes wild, standing lop-sided because of the broken shoe. Sabatino was hopping on his good foot, muttering and cursing, his eyes filled with hate.

They both looked at the gun at the same time. Mersiha leapt for it. Sabatino tried to grab her but she slipped by him and dived on to the couch. She held the gun in her left hand and fumbled the clip with the right. Before she could ram it home, Sabatino hit her from behind, knocking her to the floor. As she fell she slammed the clip in place. Sabatino limped towards her as she rolled over and pulled back the hammer with her thumb. 'Don't,' she said, but he was beyond listening. He had a crazed look in his eyes, his mouth was bared into a sneer, and his trousers were wide open. He stumbled towards her, limping on his injured foot, his hands reaching for her. Mersiha fired twice. Both bullets hit him in the chest and he fell on top of her, still grabbing for the gun. He got his hands to the weapon and despite his injuries began to wrestle with her for possession of it.

He was strong, far stronger than she was. She felt the gun start to slip from her sweating fingers and she whimpered. She couldn't move her legs and the weight of his body made it difficult to breathe. One of his pudgy fingers squeezed into the trigger guard. She tried to pull the weapon away from him but he was too powerful. Blood trickled from between his teeth as if his gums had suddenly gone bad and dribbled down over her dress. She yanked at the gun and it went off, the noise deafening her. The bullet hit Sabatino in the throat. His hands jerked and the gun fired again. The bullet tore through the side of his jaw, blowing away bone, flesh and teeth. Mersiha screamed and from somewhere got the strength to roll out from under his dead weight.

She sat up, out of breath, her finger throbbing where it had been pressed against the trigger guard. There was blood on her dress. She wiped it with her hand and it smeared across the black material. It was all over her hands, wet and sticky.

Someone banged on the door, so hard that it rattled. 'Mr Sabatino? You okay in there?' Mersiha stood up. Sabatino had fallen on to the gun and she tried to roll him over. He was too heavy to move. She grunted and stood over him, holding his ankles and pulling his legs. Using all her strength, she could manage only to slide him a few inches. The gun remained trapped under his body. The door banged again and Mersiha dropped his legs. They hit the floor with a dull thud. 'Mr Sabatino! You all right?'

Mersiha backed away from the body. There were footsteps on the stairs outside, and the sound of someone kicking the door. She went over to the window, hobbling because of the broken heel. She kicked off her useless shoes and examined the window. Outside was a rusting fire escape which led down to the car park, two storeys below. There was no lock on the window. She slid it open. Two shoulders crashed against the door as she climbed outside, then she realised to her horror that she'd left her bag on the floor. She dashed back into the room, grabbed it and practically dived through the window and on to the fire escape, scraping her knees on the bare metal. She ran down the steps, taking them three at a time. She heard two gunshots and the sound of the door splintering as she reached the asphalt and ran barefoot into the darkness.

Allison Dooley lay back on her bed, watching the television with the sound turned right down. She was tense, dreading the phone call from Mersiha's parents which she was sure would come before her friend got back to the house. She looked at the alarm clock. It was after midnight. She kept telling herself that it was far too late for them to call, that they'd be asleep, but her imagination insisted on coming up with alternative scenarios: a fire, a break-in, a hundred and one reasons why they might get on the phone and wake her mother from her drunken slumber.

She'd thought about disconnecting the phones but decided against it in case Mersiha called. There was nothing to do but wait and worry.

A stone rattled against her window, startling her. She swung her legs off the bed, but before she could get to the window a second pebble hit the glass. Allison looked down on Mersiha, standing in the garden. She crept downstairs. Her mother was lying face down on the sofa, snoring, her left hand still holding the empty wine bottle.

She tiptoed to the kitchen and opened the back door. Mersiha rushed in and dashed upstairs. Allison relocked the door and followed her. She found Mersiha sitting at the dressing table, looking at herself in the mirror. 'So, how did it go?' she asked, closing the door and throwing herself on to the bed. Mersiha didn't answer. 'Come on, you promised,' Allison whined.

Mersiha shook her head, but said nothing.

'What was he like? Where's the dress?' Mersiha was still wearing her school clothes, though she'd put make-up on since she'd left the house. 'Put the dress on for me, please. Come on. You owe me, Mersiha.' She reached for the bag but Mersiha pulled it away and hugged it to her chest. Allison got off the bed and stood behind Mersiha and looked at her reflection in the dressing-table mirror. For the first time she could see that her friend's eye make-up and lipstick were smeared. 'What's wrong?' she asked.

Mersiha shrugged. 'It was nothing.'

'Did you have a fight? Is that it?'

Mersiha smiled wryly. 'Yeah. Sort of.'

'Did he hurt you?'

Mersiha stared at her reflection in the mirror. 'No,' she said quietly. 'He didn't hurt me.'

THE BIRTHDAY GIRL

*　　*　　*

Bzuchar Utsyev sat in the back of the stretch limo as it drove through the wintry streets of Baltimore, his face set in stone. His two bodyguards knew better than to disturb him so they too sat in silence. Utsyev hadn't said a word all the way from New York. The limo hit a pothole and lurched to the side as the driver fought to control the steering wheel, but Utsyev appeared not to notice. It was a cold morning and the few people on the streets were huddled in thick coats for warmth, their shoulders hunched against the bitter wind that blew in from the Inner Harbour.

'Here we are, boss,' the driver said, bringing the limo to a smooth stop in front of The Firehouse. Utsyev climbed out and stood staring up at the converted fire station. A man in a black overcoat was standing at the entrance, an unlit cigar in his mouth. He dropped the cigar on to the floor and stamped on it. 'Mr Utsyev,' he said, extending his hand.

Utsyev ignored the greeting. 'Who the fuck are you?' he growled. It was the first thing he'd said since the limo had pulled on to the New Jersey Turnpike.

'Vincenti,' the man said, letting his arm fall to his side. 'I worked for Mr Sabatino.'

'Not any fucking more you don't,' Utsyev said, barging past him and into the darkened nightclub. 'Show me where it happened.'

Vincenti followed on Utsyev's heels as he walked across the dance floor, their footsteps echoing off the brick walls. Several members of the nightclub staff stood around as if at a wedding party where the bride had failed to turn up. Utsyev's two heavies followed at a safe distance. They'd seen Utsyev's explosive temper before and didn't want to be too close if he erupted.

'Are the police still here?' Utsyev asked as he climbed the stairs.

'Been and gone,' Vincenti said behind him.

Utsyev didn't speak again until the two men were in the office, the door closed behind them. 'So tell me what the fuck happened,' he said, staring at a darkened patch on the wooden floor. There were no chalk marks on the boards, no sign other than the dried blood that a body had once lain there.

'It was a girl, a young girl. Seventeen, maybe eighteen, black hair. Pretty. Sabatino's type. I mean, Mr Sabatino's type.'

'And?'

'And she was with him alone. Then we heard a struggle. Then gunshots.'

'A struggle?'

'Yeah. We thought your brother was, you know . . . fucking her.'

'You can't tell the difference between sex and a struggle?'

Vincenti looked uncomfortable. 'Sometimes it was difficult to tell with Mr Sabatino. When he was with a girl there was often a lot of . . . noise.'

'Noise?'

'Yeah. Crying. You know. He was a bit . . .'

'Rough?' Utsyev supplied.

'Yeah, rough,' Vincenti agreed, clearly relieved that Utsyev understood.

'This girl, you'd seen her before?'

Vincenti shook his head. 'He didn't know who she was.'

Utsyev turned and studied the broken door. 'You kicked the door down?'

'Yeah. Me and Jacko.'

'And?'

'She was long gone. Down the fire escape. Your brother was already dead.'

Utsyev went over to the bloodstains and knelt down. He rubbed the dark brown patch with a gloved hand, then sniffed at it, like a tracker seeking a trail to follow. 'How many shots?'

'Four.'

'Professional?'

Vincenti frowned. 'Nah, I don't think so. It was . . . messy.'

'Messy? What the fuck d'ya mean, messy?'

'There were two shots in the chest, then one in the neck and one in the side of the head. Like she'd panicked. There was a gap between the first two shots and the second.'

'Which is what a pro would do. Whack him, then two shots up close to make sure.'

'Yeah, but you'd put two in the temple, or the forehead. She blew away half his face.' Vincenti spoke rapidly, less nervous now that he was being asked about technicalities.

'How long before the cops got here?'

'Ten minutes. Fifteen at the most.'

Utsyev stood up, rubbing his gloved hands together as if trying to get rid of the dried blood. 'What did you tell them?'

'That someone came up the fire escape and hit him

333

while we were outside. We saw nothing, just heard the shots.'

Utsyev nodded his approval. 'They buy it?'

'Seemed to.'

Utsyev walked over to the window. The frame and glass were covered in white fingerprint powder. There were dozens of prints – it was an old building. He opened the window and stuck his head out. The car park below was almost empty. 'Anyone see her go out?'

'No, Mr Utsyev. No one.'

Utsyev pulled back into the room. 'Okay,' he said, 'show me what you've got. What was your name again?'

'Vincenti.'

'Show me what you've got, Vincenti.'

Vincenti took Utsyev back into the corridor and along to another office. He stepped aside to allow Utsyev and his two bodyguards to enter and then closed the door behind them before opening a safe in the corner. From the safe he took a handgun, a pair of black shoes and a pair of torn panties. Vincenti held out the handgun. 'It's a Heckler & Koch, but an unusual model.'

'Serial number?'

'Yeah. Another reason why I don't think it's a professional hit.'

Utsyev nodded and picked up the panties. 'You got contacts in this godforsaken city that can trace it?'

'We've a coupla cops on the payroll can do it for us if the gun's legit.'

Utsyev absent-mindedly crumpled the white panties and wiped his nose with them, as if they were a handkerchief. 'Do it,' he said. 'And do it fast.'

'Understood,' Vincenti said.

Utsyev suddenly realised what he was doing with the panties and tossed them into the safe. He picked up the broken shoe and examined the heel. 'You're working for me now, Vincenti. Stick with me all the time, in case I need you.' He gestured at the two bodyguards. 'That's Kiseleva. The guy with the acne's Ostrovetsky.' The men nodded neutrally at each other. Utsyev tossed the shoe into the safe. 'I wanna find this fucking Cinderella, and soon.'

Mersiha spent her last day at school in a state of near-panic, certain that at any moment the police would walk into her classroom and take her off to jail. She was unable to concentrate on any of her classes. All she could think about was the gun she'd left at The Firehouse, trapped under Sabatino's body. The police would be sure to trace it to her father, and then it would all be over. And even if by some miracle they didn't find out that the gun was registered in her father's name, he'd discover it was missing the next time he opened the gun cabinet. It wasn't fair, she kept thinking, it just wasn't fair. All she'd been trying to do was help her father, and now it had gone horribly wrong.

She racked her brains for a way out of her predicament, but she kept going around in circles. There was no way she could get the gun back; her fingerprints were all over the weapon; the doormen would be able to identify her; she'd gone there with a loaded gun in her handbag. There wasn't a jury in the world who wouldn't think that she'd gone there with the intention of killing him. Premeditated murder, that's what they'd call it, even though she'd gone there only to scare him. The worst she'd intended was maybe to shoot him in the leg like she'd done with Dr Brown. It had been a huge mistake, she realised that now. The biggest mistake of her life.

At lunchtime she sat in the cafeteria with a tray of uneaten food in front of her. Allison walked up with her sandwiches and orange juice and was about to sit down, but then thought better of it and moved off to another table. Allison ate in silence, from time to time looking nervously across at Mersiha. She'd long stopped pestering her for details of the previous night's rendezvous.

Mersiha considered telling her parents what had happened, knowing that it would be better if they heard it from her rather than from the police, but at the back of her mind was the vague hope that something would happen to save her. It wasn't retribution that she feared because she'd already resigned herself to the fact that she would be punished. What she couldn't bear was the pain she'd see in her father's eyes when he discovered what she'd done. The pain and the disappointment. She looked down at the stainless-steel knife on her tray. She pictured herself taking the knife and drawing the blade across her wrist, imagining the blood drip, the way it had splattered down from Sabatino's wounds on to her black dress. Maybe that would be the best way out. At least she'd be spared the look in her father's eyes.

She reached for the knife and toyed with it. The blade was too blunt, she realised. She'd need something sharper. A razor blade, something that would cut cleanly and deeply. There were razor blades in the bathroom cabinet, she remembered. Katherine used them in her safety razor to shave her legs. Mersiha could lie in the bath, stretch out in the warm water, and do it. She held the image in her mind, lying naked in the warm water, one hand stretched out of the bath, blood running down her arm and on to the tiled floor, the razor blade clutched in the other hand. She imagined Katherine and her father bursting into the bathroom and finding her, crying over her body. Then the funeral, her coffin bedecked with flowers and wreaths, the priest talking about a young life cut short, her father crying, grieving the way he'd grieved for Luke. She shivered. No. She wouldn't kill herself, no matter how bad it got. She put the knife down on the tray. There had to be a way out, she thought. Allison was looking at her, a sandwich halfway to her mouth.

Mersiha forced a smile and Allison immediately looked relieved, taking the gesture as an indication that she should move tables. She picked up her tray and slid into the chair opposite Mersiha.

'Aren't you hungry?' she asked, nodding at Mersiha's untouched tray.

'Not really.'

Allison leaned over anxiously. 'Mersiha, I don't know what's wrong, but if there's anything I can do to help, all you have to do is ask, okay?'

Mersiha was touched by the girl's obvious sincerity, and she felt a sudden wave of guilt for the way she'd used her. 'Thanks,' she said. 'But there's nothing you can do. There's nothing anyone can do.'

Allison continued to eat her lunch, keeping a wary eye on her friend. Across the room, one of the teachers on cafeteria duty stood up to go, leaving a newspaper on the table. Mersiha jumped to her feet, knocking her tray and startling Allison. 'Sorry,' she said, dashing over to grab the discarded newspaper. It was an afternoon edition of the *Baltimore Sun*. She stared at the front page, taking in the stories as quickly as she could: a steel mill had announced redundancies, a little girl had fallen from her bedroom window, the President said he wanted to build closer diplomatic and trade links with China, and the police had discovered cocaine worth ten million dollars in a disused warehouse in the city.

Mersiha flicked anxiously through the paper. She found the story on page three. It was the biggest piece on the page, describing how the owner of The Firehouse had been shot to death. There was a black and white photograph of Sabatino standing in front of the nightclub, a bottle of champagne in one hand, a glass in the other. A police spokesman said it appeared to be a burglary that had gone wrong and that there were no suspects. Mersiha frowned. There was no mention of the gun, no description of the assailant. She re-read the story. It said that police were working on the theory that a man had climbed up the fire escape and had been surprised to find Sabatino there. There was definitely no mention of the gun. Or her shoes. And it said man, not woman. How could that be? Maybe it was a trick, maybe the police were deliberately withholding information like they did on television cop shows, hoping that she'd give herself away. But that didn't make any sense. At the very least they should have used an artist's impression of her – the doormen had seen her up close. There was something wrong. Something very wrong.

* * *

Freeman jabbed at his intercom button. 'Jo, any sign of Maury?'

'Sorry, no. He's not at home either.'

'Okay, can you get me Josh? Ask him if he'll pop in, will you?'

'Sure thing, Tony.'

Freeman looked over the new Thai contract as he waited for the Development Director to arrive. The Thais had already telexed twice requesting early delivery, so he was eager to get it couriered out to them. It was a pleasant change for customers to be pestering CRW for orders. Generally it was the other way around. But as Anderson had pointed out, it was just one contract. His intercom chirped. 'Josh is on his way up,' Jo said. Freeman signed the contract and took it out to her.

'Fed-Ex, please, Jo. I don't want this one getting lost in the mail.'

Josh arrived, a file under his arm and a pair of blue-framed spectacles pushed back into his red hair.

'Hiya, Josh. Go right in,' Freeman said. He followed him in and closed the door. 'How's production?' he asked.

'No problems – full steam ahead,' Josh replied. 'You can really feel a change in the optimism, you know? That Thai order has really boosted morale.'

'Yeah, that was the contract I just gave Jo.' Freeman sat down and steepled his hands under his chin. 'Look, Josh, I'm going to need your help. I'm taking my daughter to Colorado and I'll be away from the office all next week. I'd like you to hold the fort.'

Josh looked startled. 'Me? But what . . .?'

'Maury's having a few problems of his own right now,' Freeman said.

'I knew his mother-in-law was sick, but I didn't . . .'

'Yeah, it's a bit more complicated than that,' Freeman interrupted. 'He's been under a lot of pressure and I think it'd be better if he took some time off. I know you can handle it, Josh. You know this company inside out.'

Josh nodded, clearly flattered by the offer of extra responsibility. 'I'd be more than happy to, Tony. Anything I can do to help, you know that.'

Freeman sighed with relief. 'Jo can field most of the minor stuff, and there are no major contracts to be negotiated,' he said.

'What about the bank?'

'I'll have a word with Walter. This Thai deal has given us some breathing space, so he'll be cool about it.'

'Jo has your number in Colorado?'

'Ah. Unfortunately not. It's a cabin in the middle of nowhere and there's no phone. I'll try to arrange a portable or something and call you with the number. Failing that I'll check in with you from a payphone each day. But I'm sure you'll be able to handle everything.'

'I appreciate your faith in me, Tony. I really do. I won't disappoint you.'

Freeman watched Josh leave the office. He was still worried about leaving the company with Anderson going walkabout and Sabatino's threats still weighing on his mind, but his desire to spend time with Mersiha outweighed all other considerations. He shook his head, trying to clear his mind. Anderson would come to his senses after a few days' rest, and Sabatino was just a blustering fool who thought he could get his own way by playing the hard man. Everything would work out just fine.

* * *

Katherine was measuring kidney beans into a large pan when Mersiha walked in through the kitchen door, Buffy at her heels. 'Hiya, kiddo. How does my famous five-alarm Texan chilli sound for dinner?'

'Sounds great,' Mersiha said.

'How did it go last night?'

'Huh?'

'Last night. How did it go?'

'Oh. Great. Yeah, we got lots of work done.'

'Glad to hear it. I'd hate to think you were just watching MTV, painting your fingernails and gossiping about boys.' Mersiha headed for the hallway. 'What's the rush?' Katherine asked. 'Don't you want to help?'

'I've some stuff I want to put in my room, that's all. And I want to finish some work before tomorrow.'

'Not like you to be so tidy,' Katherine said.

'A new leaf,' Mersiha shouted, running up the stairs with her sports bag.

'Don't forget to pack!' Katherine called after her. She picked up a large onion and began to peel it. As she ripped off the outer skins she heard Mersiha switch on the television in her bedroom. So much for homework, she thought. Well, at least it was the news she was watching.

* * *

Mersiha lay awake, her eyes wide open as she stared up at the ceiling. She'd gone to bed early after supper, telling her parents that she wanted to get an early night before the following day's flight to Colorado. Buffy lay at her side, breathing heavily. The dog wasn't allowed in the bedrooms, but she'd seemed to sense how unhappy Mersiha was and when the house had fallen silent she'd crept upstairs and pushed open her door with her muzzle. Mersiha had welcomed the company and she gently stroked Buffy's head, taking comfort from the warm fur.

The shooting had merited only a brief mention on the Fox evening news and the main networks hadn't even carried the story. The Fox reporter had said that police were still working on the theory that a thief had shot the owner of The Firehouse. Something was definitely wrong, Mersiha thought, racking her brains for a reason why they hadn't mentioned the gun. There was no way she could possibly get away with what she'd done. Retribution was coming, but she didn't know how or when. It was like a big black storm cloud waiting to break.

Katherine poured coffee into Freeman's mug. 'They're calling for snow in Baltimore tomorrow,' she said. 'Why don't I drive you to the airport? You don't want the car sitting under six feet of snow when you get back.' She made to top up Mersiha's mug but Mersiha shook her head as she finished off her scrambled eggs.

'You don't mind?'

'There's a few things I want to pick up at the mall. It's

no trouble. Don't forget to leave a number where I can reach you.'

'There isn't a phone in the cabin,' Freeman said. 'Didn't I tell you?'

'You're joking.'

'No, I thought I told you, Kat. The cabin's often used for honeymooning couples, so they make a big thing about not being disturbed.'

'Tony – what if something were to happen? Say you had an accident. What if you get caught in a snowstorm?'

'The weather out in Colorado isn't bad. I took a look at the Weather Channel first thing,' he said. 'You'll get more snow here than we'll get at Estes Park.'

'But what if I need to get in touch with you in an emergency?'

Freeman handed her the rental agent's glossy colour brochure. 'There's the agent's number. They'll pass on a message. They're only a few miles away.'

'I'm not so sure about this,' Katherine said, lighting a cigarette from the gas stove.

'We'll be fine,' Freeman said. 'I think there's some sort of short-wave radio in the cabin, for emergencies. And I'm going to try to hire a portable phone.'

'Now that's a good idea,' she said.

'We'd better be going,' Mersiha pointed out, loading her plate and cutlery into the dishwasher. Buffy chuffed in agreement, assuming that she was going with them. 'Oh, Buffy, I'm sorry,' Mersiha said, kneeling down by the dog and hugging her. 'You can't come. But we'll only be away a week.'

Buffy barked happily, still assuming she was going to be taken for a walk. The dog licked Mersiha's cheek. Mersiha hugged her again, then picked up her blue nylon bag. 'I'm ready,' she said.

Freeman put on his waterproof skiing jacket and picked up his bag. 'Got everything?' Katherine asked. 'Tickets? Money? Credit cards? Snow plough?'

Freeman hugged her and kissed her on the lips. Mersiha went outside to the car, taking care that Buffy didn't escape. The dog began to whine, sensing that she was about to be left on her own. Mersiha climbed into the back seat. She was looking forward to the trip, but her enjoyment was tempered by the constant fear that the police would identify her as Sabatino's killer. She'd slept little the previous night. She'd gone over the killing again and again in her mind, but couldn't work out why the doormen hadn't described her and why the police hadn't tracked down the Heckler & Koch. It was a distinctive weapon and she doubted that there would be many in Maryland. It didn't make any sense. She should be in a cell being interrogated by Homicide detectives, not about to depart for a week's vacation in Colorado.

'Penny for them?' her father said as he got into the front passenger seat.

'Oh, I was just wondering if I'd packed everything, that's all.' Mersiha hated lying to her father, but she knew she had no alternative. What else could she say? 'Just thinking about the man I shot to death, Dad. Nothing much.'

Freeman reached over and pinched her cheek. 'Don't worry about it, pumpkin. Anything you've forgotten we can buy when we get there.'

'Ah, yes,' Mersiha sighed. 'America is truly a wonderful country.'

'You know what I could never work out?' he asked.

'What?'

'Where you got your sarcasm from. It's a total mystery to me.'

Katherine dropped her husband and Mersiha outside the United Airlines terminal, dispatching Freeman with a kiss on the lips and Mersiha with a big hug and exacting a promise to be careful if she went skiing. She still had misgivings about the two of them being holed up in a cabin in the wilds of Colorado, but she understood her husband's desire to get closer to Mersiha. She had been a part of their family for more than three years, but there was so much about her they didn't know: what had happened to her parents, what her life had been like in Bosnia, why she kept having nightmares. Art Brown hadn't managed to discover what made Mersiha tick; maybe Tony could.

Katherine realised that she hadn't fastened her seat belt and she immediately thought of Luke and the way he'd died. A small thing like a simple strap and buckle meant the difference between having a son and having a dark hole in your heart where a son used to be. She felt tears prick her eyes and blinked them away. She missed Luke, missed him the way she'd miss an arm or a leg – a constant awareness that something was absent and that life would never be the same without it. She turned to look at the passenger seat and pictured him there, his eyes sparkling, laughing and giggling and loving her. Her belief in God had died when she'd buried Luke. She knew that no omnipotent being would have taken away her boy and put her through the years of grief and misery and loss. There was no God, no Heaven, just the hell of life on earth with the memory of a dead son.

An old woman bent over the steering wheel of a Cadillac was dawdling down the middle of the road and Katherine accelerated and drove by, missing the car by inches. She almost didn't see the school bus turning in front of her and she jammed her brakes on, hard. Instinctively she reached over with her right arm as if holding back a child in the passenger seat. She realised what she'd done and closed her eyes, fighting back the tears. 'Damn you, Tony,' she said to herself. The Cadillac pulled up behind her and the old woman sounded her horn impatiently. Katherine took out a handkerchief and dabbed her eyes. She searched through the radio stations until among the mindless rap and rock music she found one playing classical music, and she kept to the speed limit all the way to the White Marsh shopping mall.

She had telephoned earlier to make sure that the photographs of Mersiha were ready to be collected. As soon as she walked into the store Tanya beamed and held up a large manila envelope. 'Mrs Freeman, these are just terrific,' she said. Katherine opened the envelope and slid out the glossy colour photographs. She looked at them one by one. Tanya was right, they were excellent. The face that looked back was Mersiha, but not the Mersiha that she'd just dropped off at the airport. The girl in the photographs was absolutely stunning. It was a face that could easily have graced the cover of *Vogue* or *Vanity Fair*, the face of a professional model. It wasn't just the make-up or the hair, or the way she'd been posed, it was the look in her eyes, the confident, measured stare of a woman who knew exactly what she wanted from life. 'She looks older, doesn't she?' Tanya said. 'She doesn't look like a fifteen-year-old.'

'Sixteen,' Katherine corrected. 'But you're right, she looks like she's nineteen. Twenty, maybe.'

'We're all talking about the pictures, about how good they are,' Tanya said. 'In fact, Ted wants to talk to you about them. I'll get him.'

Katherine put the photographs back in the envelope while Tanya went to fetch Ted. He came out of the studio, the same goofy grin on his bearded face that he'd been wearing the last time she'd seen him. Like Tanya, he was dressed all in black: jeans, t-shirt and linen jacket. The only touch of colour was the bright red wristband of his Mickey Mouse watch. 'Aren't they awesome?' he said.

'They're wonderful, yes. You've done a great job.'

Ted waved away the compliment. 'It's nothing to do with me, Mrs Freeman. Your daughter has a way with the camera. There's something in here that shines through the lens. Have you got time for a coffee?'

The change of subject caught Katherine by surprise. 'Excuse me?' she said.

'Coffee. I'd like a chat, and I thought . . .'

'Sure, coffee would be fine.' They walked together to the food court and Katherine found a table while the photographer ordered two coffees and carried them over.

'I wanted to ask if you and Mersiha had given any thought to what I said before?'

'About modelling? We haven't really discussed it.'

'You should.' He tapped the manila envelope in front of her. 'I could place those with any of the top magazines. Any of them. She's cover material.'

'She's a sixteen-year-old girl,' Katherine said.

'That's not unusual these days. There are lots of teenage girls making a good living from modelling. Do you know how much a girl like Mersiha could make in a year?' Katherine shook her head. It wasn't something she'd ever thought about, though she knew that runway models were highly over-paid for doing little other than wearing other people's clothes. 'A quarter of a million dollars, easily. And if she picks up a cosmetics contract you could triple that figure.'

Katherine sat back in her chair and ran her finger around the lip of her cup. 'Wow,' she said.

'Wow is right. A couple of years of modelling at that level and she'd be able to pay for her own college education. She'd be set up for life.'

'But what about the sort of people she'll come in contact with? She's only a child.'

'People like me, you mean?'

'No, of course not. But you hear stories. You know you do. Girls with stars in their eyes, ending up working the streets.'

'Not girls like Mersiha. She'll be with one of the best agencies in Manhattan. She'll be chaperoned everywhere, she'll work with only the best photographers, the best designers. She'll be protected, believe me.'

'I'll talk to her, see how she feels.'

'I wish you would. It's not often you come across a talent like hers. It's a gift.' He picked up his spoon and rubbed it with his fingers. 'I can see where she gets it from.'

Katherine tilted her head, wondering if he was about to make a pass at her. 'Gets what from?' she asked.

'Her looks.' He smiled, and Katherine noticed for the first time how white his teeth were.

'My looks?'

'Sure. She really takes after you. The same eyes. Great skin.'

'Ted, before you shove your foot any further into your mouth, I ought to tell you that Mersiha's adopted.'

Ted didn't appear to be fazed by the revelation. 'You're a very beautiful woman, you don't need me to tell you that,' he said.

'I hope you're not suggesting that I consider a modelling career, Ted. I'm a bit too old to fall for that line.'

'I'd love to photograph you.'

Katherine studied his face. He was good-looking under the beard, she decided. The facial hair wasn't there to disguise bad skin or a weak chin. And he had a ballet dancer's body, lean and tight, not an ounce of fat to be seen. 'You would, would you?'

'Uh-huh. I'd jump at the chance.'

'How's your mother? You live with her, don't you?'

Ted nodded and stirred his coffee. 'She's as well as can be expected. She's had heart problems for the last five years. She's too old for a transplant, she's just got to take it easy.'

'What about your father?'

Ted shrugged. 'He died when I was in my teens. She never remarried.'

'It was nice of you to move back to stay with her. I'd have thought New York was the best place for a photographer to be. It can't be much fun for you in Baltimore.'

'How did you know that? That I'd moved from New York?'

Katherine smiled and raised one eyebrow. 'Tanya told me.'

'Ah. The lovely Tanya.'

'She's your type, is she?'

Ted put his spoon down. 'No, she's not my type.' He held her look for several seconds.

'Am I your type?' Katherine asked, invitingly. Ted said nothing, but his smile answered her question. She leaned forward and put a hand on his wrist. 'I know a motel that's not far from here,' she said. Ted looked at his watch. Katherine raised her eyebrow again. 'This is a once-only offer, Ted. You just happen to have caught me on a bad day, so don't you dare tell me you're busy.'

Ted grinned. 'I'm not busy,' he said.

Katherine stood up. 'My car's outside,' she said. Ted walked half a pace behind her as she headed for the parking lot.

Freeman heard the answering machine kick in and his own voice tell him that he wasn't able to get to the phone. He winked at Mersiha before leaving his message. 'Hiya, Kat, just to let you know that we got to Denver okay. We're going to pick up the car and drive to Estes Park. I'm not sure how long it'll take. Take care, I love you.'

He handed the phone to Mersiha. 'Hi. Don't worry, I'm taking care of Dad. Hope you're okay. Bye.' Mersiha replaced the receiver. 'She's probably shopping,' she said.

'What's the betting that we go back to find another twenty pairs of shoes?'

'Even money,' Mersiha grinned. 'You should have taken the credit cards off her.'

Freeman laughed and gently punched her shoulder. 'Okay, let's go get our Bronco.'

'Can I get a newspaper?'

'Sure. There's a kiosk over there.'

He waited while Mersiha ran over and looked at the rack of papers. She came back, empty-handed. 'I wanted a Baltimore paper,' she explained.

'In Denver?'

'Yeah, I didn't think.'

'They might have the *Washington Post*.'

'No, I looked.'

'What is this? Are youu homesick already?'

'No, I just wanted something to read, that's all. Come on, I hear our Bronco calling.'

Ted put his hands behind his head and watched Katherine slip into her dress. 'I feel used,' he said, only half joking.

'You'll get over it,' she said. She sat down on the bed, her back to him. 'Can you zip me up?'

Ted did as she asked, then he lay down again. 'No, I mean it. I really feel like you've just used me.'

Katherine turned and kissed him on the forehead. 'I think we used each other,' she chided. 'Stop complaining.'

'Oh, I'm not complaining, I'm just stating a fact.' He stretched his hands up above his head and arched his back. 'Can we do this again?'

Katherine laughed. 'What, now?'

Ted laughed with her. 'No, not now. I think I'm going to be out of commission for a few hours at least. I meant some time in the future. Next week, maybe?'

Katherine sat in front of the dressing-table mirror and carefully applied lipstick. 'I don't think so, Ted.'

'God, what is it with you?' He sighed with exasperation. 'We just made love, and now you tell me you don't want to see me again.'

Katherine pointed her finger at him in the mirror. 'We didn't make love, we had sex. You shouldn't confuse the two.'

'But . . .'

'No buts,' she said. 'I wanted you, you wanted me, we had a great couple of hours . . .'

'Three,' Ted corrected.

Katherine laughed despite herself. 'Whatever.'

'Do you do this a lot?'

'Not a lot, no.'

'But you've been unfaithful before?'

'What is this, Ted? Twenty questions? Don't make me start to regret the time we spent together.' She stood up and smoothed down her dress. 'How do I look?'

'Good enough to eat,' he said.

'That's nice to hear.' She sat down on the bed again and stroked his chest. 'I don't consider what we did being unfaithful.'

'Semantics.'

'Maybe. But I do love my husband. And I'd never leave him.'

'But why . . .?' He was lost for words.

'Why would I go to bed with you, a complete stranger?'

Ted nodded. Katherine shrugged. 'I don't know.' Her hand strayed down his body and slipped under the covers.

'You do like me, don't you?'

Katherine frowned. 'That's a strange thing to ask.'

'But you do?'

She thought about it for a few seconds as her hand caressed the soft hair that grew on his stomach. 'I don't really know you, so I can't say if I like you or not.'

'You're brutally honest.'

'I suppose I am.'

Ted could feel himself growing hard as she toyed with him. 'You're a predator, Katherine Freeman.'

She smiled. 'What makes you say that?'

'You sought me out, brought me down, and now you're leaving my bones to bleach in the sun.'

She tightened her grip on him. 'This is the only bone I can feel,' she said slyly. Ted gasped. She slackened her grip but continued to hold him.

'So why? Why do you do it?' Katherine didn't answer, though she kept looking at him as she began to move her hand faster. 'Is it to get back at your husband?'

The hand stopped abruptly. 'What do you mean?'

'I don't know. I thought maybe he'd had an affair or something.'

'No. Tony's never been unfaithful.'

'How do you know?'

'I just know.'

'So what did he do to hurt you?' Katherine's eyes went suddenly cold and she slid her hand out from under the covers. 'Hey, don't stop,' he said plaintively.

'I have to go.' She stood up and picked up her handbag.

'Hey, I'm sorry if I said the wrong thing. Come back to bed.'

Katherine shook her head. 'You spoiled the moment,' she said.

'I'm sorry. Give me another chance.'

'I don't think so. I've got to go.' She opened the door but didn't look at him again, leaving him lying on the bed, his erection rapidly subsiding, wondering exactly what it was that he'd done wrong.

Utsyev and his men moved into Sabatino's house in west Baltimore to wait for Vincenti's police contact to identify the owner of the Heckler & Koch. Bzuchar Utsyev hated waiting. Hated it with a vengeance. He spent most of the day pacing up and down and making everybody's life a misery. The fridge-freezer was packed with food and Kiseleva had fried steak and eggs for them. There was a football game on television and Utsyev's men watched it while they waited. They opened a case of Budweiser but drank it sparingly, knowing that they might have to move out at any moment.

From time to time Kiseleva or Vincenti would ask Utsyev if there was anything he wanted, but he would just shake his head. There was only one thing he wanted and that was the name of the bitch who'd killed his brother. And for that he had to wait. Vincenti had called his contact and given him the gun's serial number, but there had been no indication of how long they'd have to wait for an answer. That was what made it worse, Utsyev realised, the fact that he didn't know how long he'd have to bide his time. Eventually Utsyev got tired of pacing and sat sprawled in an overstuffed armchair and drank his way through another bottle of bourbon as the sun set.

Early in the evening, Vincenti cooked pasta and seafood but Utsyev didn't feel like eating. He went upstairs to sleep in his brother's bedroom. The bed was huge and covered with what appeared to be a real fur bedspread that must have taken the lives of several rare and exotic animals. He threw his clothes on to a chair and fell on to the bed. The bourbon had helped dull the pain that had built up inside him, but the anger still burned deep. He wanted to hurt his brother's killer more than he'd ever wanted to hurt anything in his life. He'd pour drain cleaner down the bitch's throat, he'd shove forks into her eyes, he'd tear her limb from limb and eat her liver raw. She'd die like no one had ever died before. Utsyev's whole body tensed and his face contorted with hatred. He opened his eyes and found himself staring at his own reflection. The ceiling above the bed was mirrored. For a moment Utsyev was shocked at his own image, his skull-like face creased and haggard from two days without sleep, his hands clenched into fists, his mouth open in a grimace. Then he suddenly burst out laughing. It was just like Gilani to have a mirrored ceiling. He laughed louder, the sound becoming more ragged and disjointed, until he was cackling like an old crone and tears were streaming down his hollowed cheeks.

Katherine sat down at the dining-room table and looked through the photographs of Mersiha. Ted was right, there was something almost magical about them, something that set her apart from most of the girls her age. She wondered how Tony would react to the suggestion that Mersiha should take up modelling. He'd be proud of her, of that she was certain, but he'd want her to continue at school. His phone message hadn't said if he'd call back later that night, and he hadn't mentioned anything about a portable phone, so she guessed that he was still uncontactable. Anyway, there was no rush. Ted's offer didn't have a time limit. She could discuss it with Tony and Mersiha when they got back from Colorado.

She sat back in the chair and took another mouthful of her brandy and Coke as she reflected on her afternoon with the photographer. He'd been a good lover, considerate and enthusiastic, but she'd meant what she'd said about it being a one-off opportunity. She just hoped that he'd be able to keep business separate from pleasure. Men could be quite pathetic at times, once they started to think with their sexual equipment rather than their brains. Katherine smiled to herself. She could handle Ted.

Freeman followed Route 36 as it twisted and turned through the Roosevelt National Forest. The woods were starkly beautiful with towering pines and bleak rocks that stood bare against the powder-blue sky. On the higher peaks he could see snow, though it actually felt warmer than Baltimore. 'It's beautiful, isn't it?' he said to Mersiha.

His daughter hadn't spoken for the last ten miles. She'd

been staring out of the window at the hills. He had turned the radio off once they'd started driving through the forest – it had seemed somehow sacrilegious to defile it with man-made music. 'It's like home,' she said quietly, and Freeman knew that she didn't mean Maryland.

The scenery was strikingly similar to the area around Sarajevo. It made Freeman realise how thin the line was between war and peace. Yugoslavia must have been like this once – a quiet, peaceful place where tourists could drive around in rented cars without a care in the world. How quickly that had changed, from an Eastern bloc tourist resort to a country where neighbour murdered neighbour and where the hills echoed to the sound of heavy artillery and sniper fire. He reached across and patted Mersiha's leg. 'Do you miss it?' he asked.

Mersiha shrugged. 'I miss my family. I don't miss the place. There are too many bad memories. I don't ever want to go back there. It's tainted.'

It was a good word, Freeman thought. Tainted. Death could do that to a place. He could never drive along the road where Luke had died without reliving the horror of it, without seeing the truck wheels crush the life out of his son. He shuddered.

'Are you cold?' Mersiha asked, reaching for the heating controls.

'I'm okay.'

'You shivered.'

'I'm okay. We should be arriving at Estes Park any moment.'

Mersiha looked at the map on her lap. 'Yeah, you're right. Assuming we're heading north.' She grinned. 'We are heading north, right?'

'We could check the trees to make sure.'

'The trees?'

'Sure. Old Boy Scout trick. Moss only grows on the south side of trees. Or west. I can never remember which.'

'Don't bother. Look!' She pointed ahead. As the road curved the town came into view, nestled in a high mountain valley, surrounded by snowcapped peaks. Overlooking the town to the right was a large hotel with white walls and a red roof, set against a backdrop of towering cliffs.

'Pretty, isn't it?' Freeman said.

'It's the Stanley Hotel,' Mersiha said. 'Stephen King stayed there for a few nights when he was working on *The Shining*.'

'How do you know that?'

'Research,' she said, tapping the side of her nose. 'I thought it'd be covered in snow, like the hotel he described in the book. How high are we?'

'About seven and a half thousand feet above sea level. There's snow on the mountains.'

'Yeah, but none around the town.' Between the road and the hotel was a large lake, most of which was frozen over. Geese were walking unsteadily across the ice, flapping their wings to keep their balance.

'What road are we looking for?'

Mersiha scrutinised the map and a photocopied sheet of directions. 'Elkhorn Avenue. We have to go through three sets of traffic lights.' They drove down the main street, which was lined with quaint gift shops and charming restaurants and cafés, all with a rustic feel. Through shop windows they saw displays of wooden howling coyotes, silver jewellery, Indian rugs, pottery and headdresses. The tourists on the sidewalks were mainly young and dressed casually: ski jackets, jeans and sunglasses. Mersiha directed him to the rental agent's office and they parked outside. It was surprisingly warm when they climbed out of the Bronco, especially considering the time of year. Like Mersiha, he'd expected the town to be deep in snow.

They went into the office where an overweight middle-aged woman was typing a letter on an old battered typewriter. She looked up and smiled. 'Is Mr Hellings here?' Freeman asked.

'Not right now,' the woman said, 'I'm expecting him any minute. Are you Tony Freeman?'

'That's right. We've come to pick up the keys.'

The office door opened and a small balding man appeared, polishing a pair of wire-framed spectacles. 'Oh, Sam, this is Mr Freeman,' the woman said.

'Good to see you,' said the new arrival, shaking Freeman's hand firmly. He took off his suede jacket and hung it on the back of a chair while the woman handed Freeman a bunch of keys and a photocopied map.

'Is there anywhere around here I can hire a portable phone?' Freeman asked.

Hellings grinned. 'Most of our guests prefer privacy,' he said. 'We don't get much call for phones.'

'I guess so. But I could sure do with one to keep in touch with my office.'

'I'll see what I can do,' Hellings said. 'Come around tomorrow afternoon.'

'Will do,' Freeman agreed. He studied the map. The route had been highlighted with a fluorescent marker pen. He handed it to Mersiha. 'There you go. You can navigate.'

'Does this mean I get to yell at you and blame you for not following my directions?'

'Ha ha. Get in the car.'

'You should visit the supermarket first,' the woman said. 'There's milk in the refrigerator, but that's all.'

Freeman waved goodbye and headed for the Bronco. The supermarket was marked on the map and they bought steaks, coffee, eggs, bacon, bread and vegetables. Mersiha was quiet, and several times Freeman caught her looking off into the middle distance, frowning and biting her nails.

The cabin was at the end of a long, winding track that crossed a bubbling stream and followed the treeline for almost a mile. It was built of pine logs with a deck at the rear which overlooked the wooded hillside. There was a stone chimney at the side of the cabin and by the side of the track was a stack of cut wood that was almost as high as the Bronco. There was an axe embedded in a tree-trunk on the ground, but Freeman clearly wouldn't need to use it – there was enough firewood for an entire winter. The cabin's shutters were open and they could see red and white gingham curtains gently moving in the wind. 'It's beautiful,' he said as he parked. Mersiha seemed strangely subdued. She walked slowly up the flight of wooden steps that went up to the deck from which the main door led off. She held out her hands and Freeman threw her the keys. 'Wow. Look,' she said, pointing above his head. High above was a brightly coloured hot-air balloon moving across the sky. The only sound was the distant roar of its propane burners.

'Yeah, we'll see about doing that, if you like,' he said. He carried the bags up the steps as Mersiha opened the door. The cabin was furnished with big leather sofas with Indian rugs on the wooden walls and floors. On a rugged carved sideboard was a Panasonic stereo system, a big-screen television and a video recorder.

The kitchen led off the main room. There was a huge fridge-freezer and Mersiha helped transfer the provisions. 'Think we've enough food?' Freeman asked, but she just shrugged. He ruffled her hair and she smiled, but her heart didn't seem to be in it. 'We could barbecue, if you wanted,' he offered. 'There's one on the deck.'

'Sure.'

'Are you all right?' She nodded and Freeman didn't press it. There were three bedrooms upstairs and he let Mersiha have first choice. She selected the smallest of the rooms and dropped her bag at the end of the single bed.

Later they cooked the steaks outside over glowing charcoal and Freeman boiled sweetcorn and potatoes on the massive electric stove in the kitchen. They decided against eating on the deck. As the sun went down cold air came spilling down the hillside and Freeman had to light a fire in the grate. The food tasted all the better for the mountain air, he thought, but Mersiha didn't seem to derive much enjoyment from the meal. She washed up and then told him she wanted an early night.

'Sure,' he said. 'It's probably the altitude. They say it makes you tired until you get used to it.'

'Yeah, it must be that.' She stood up on tiptoe and kissed him on the forehead, then hugged him tightly. 'I love you, Dad,' she whispered.

Freeman patted her on the back, frowning. She was behaving like someone who was about to leave on a long journey, and he was suddenly worried. She broke away and went upstairs. He sat down to read as he heard her turn on the shower. She seemed to stand under the water for ages, as if trying to scrub away a lifetime of dirt, but eventually the flow of water stopped and he heard her pad to her room. After a while he climbed the stairs. The door to her bedroom was ajar and he saw her sitting in front of the dressing-table mirror, a hairbrush in her hand. She seemed frozen, the brush suspended in mid-air, a faraway look in her eyes. She jumped when he pushed the door open, then smiled, albeit tensely.

'Let me do that,' he said softly, taking the brush. He brushed her air with long, slow strokes, watching her in the mirror. 'You can tell me anything, you know that.'

She nodded. Her eyes seemed to be brimming with tears, though it could just have been a trick of the light. 'I know,' she said.

'I mean anything. You're my daughter. There's nothing, absolutely nothing, that you could tell me that would ever change that, Mersiha.'

'I know,' she repeated as he continued to brush her hair.

'I'll always love you, no matter what. You'll always have my support, one hundred per cent.'

She reached around behind her back and held his hand, keeping her eyes on his reflection. 'Dad, it's all right, I know.'

Freeman put the brush on the dressing table and leaned against it so that he could face her. He stroked her hair and she smiled up at him. The white hairs caught his eye and he held one between his finger and thumb. 'Don't pull it out!' she said quickly.

'I wasn't going to.' He ran it through his hand and

then let it fall back into place. 'Have you always had them?'

'No. Not always. Stjepan used to say . . .' She fell silent and avoided his eyes.

'Stjepan said what?'

'All my hair used to be the same, black,' she said, still not looking at him. 'Then they started to go white when I was twelve.' Mersiha began to tremble. 'Stjepan said . . . he said that every time I killed a Serb, one of my hairs would turn white. So that I'd never forget.' She looked up suddenly, and this time there was no mistake. Tears were streaming down her cheeks. She stood up and flung herself at his chest, hugging him with all her might. Freeman held her in his arms and told her that everything was all right, that she was safe and that he loved her. As he comforted her he couldn't stop himself trying to count the white hairs. There were more than a dozen.

The telephone jerked Katherine awake. She groaned and stuck an arm out of the quilt, groping around until she found the receiver. It was Mersiha. 'Hiya, kiddo. What time is it?'

'It's seven o'clock, so it must be nine where you are,' she said. 'Are you still in bed?'

'I was just getting up. How come you're up so early?'

'The mountain air, I guess. Plus, I'm still on Baltimore time.'

'How's the cabin?' Katherine kept her eyes closed, trying

to block out the sunlight that was streaming through the gap in the curtains.

'The cabin's great. Dad and I are going snowshoeing.'

'Snowshoeing. Be careful, won't you?'

Mersiha tutted. 'Of course. What are you doing today? Shopping?'

'Food shopping, young lady.'

'Yeah, yeah, yeah. Do you want to speak to Dad?'

'No.'

'No?'

'I was joking, kiddo. Put him on.'

Katherine heard Mersiha whisper that she was still in bed, then Tony came on the line. 'Kat?'

'Snowshoeing, huh?'

'Hiking, but we'll take the snowshoes in case we go above the snowline.'

'Just be careful, okay?'

'Cross my heart.'

'I miss you, Tony.'

'I miss you too.'

'No, I really miss you.'

'That's nice.'

'Not from where I'm lying, it's not.'

'We'll be back soon.'

'Yeah, I know. Take care, honey. Oh, do you have a number there?'

'Not yet, but the agent says he might have a portable for me this afternoon. I'll call you if he comes through.'

'I'd feel better knowing that I could get you in an emergency.'

'We'll be fine. There's not a flake of snow around the cabin, I promise.'

'That's good to hear. Make sure you eat well. And be careful.' She yawned and she heard Freeman laugh.

'Go back to sleep, Kat. I'll call you again soon.'

'Bye, honey.' She dropped the receiver back on its cradle. Thirty seconds later she was asleep.

Bzuchar Utsyev slept until almost midday. He didn't shower or shave, just dragged on his clothes and headed downstairs. Vincenti was cooking up a batch of spaghetti sauce in a huge stainless-steel pot and he looked up when Utsyev walked into the kitchen. 'Coffee, boss?' he said.

Utsyev wasn't sure when Vincenti had started calling him 'boss', but at least he seemed respectful when he said it. He'd quickly adapted to working as part of Utsyev's team, and seemed eager to help, but Utsyev still resented him for allowing the girl to get close to Gilani. 'Yeah, coffee.'

'Black, two sugars,' Vincenti said. He must have asked one of the crew, Utsyev realised. He was sharp, all right. Maybe too sharp. Time would tell whether or not young Vincenti would get taken on a picnic or not.

'Where's Kiseleva?' he asked.

'With Nikko in the car outside.'

Utsyev nodded. He'd told the two men to cover the house, just in case. He sat down at the large oak table that dominated his brother's kitchen as Vincenti poured the coffee. 'So, when's your man gonna call?' he growled.

'Jeez, I dunno, boss. I don't wanna call him again because . . .'

'I don't wanna hear no becauses, Vincenti. I just wanna know who killed my brother.'

'I'll call him after lunch.'

As if on cue the telephone rang. Utsyev indicated with his head that Vincenti should answer it. Vincenti turned down the heat under the pan before picking up the phone. Typical Italian, thought Utsyev, concerned more about his stomach than the job at hand. He sipped his coffee. It was good. At least Italians could make a decent cup of coffee.

Vincenti grunted and scribbled on a notepad, then hung up. Other than to say his name when he'd answered the phone, he hadn't uttered a word. He grinned at Utsyev. 'Got it,' he said.

'The suspense is fucking killing me,' Utsyev said coldly.

'Sorry, boss.' He read his notes. 'Guy called Freeman owns the HK-4. Anthony Freeman.' He handed him the paper. 'That's his address.'

'So it's not a woman?' Utsyev said, frowning.

'Anthony Freeman, that's what he said.'

'I know that name.' Utsyev tapped the piece of paper against his chin. 'Freeman. Freeman. Freeman.' He repeated the name like a mantra. 'Shit, now I remember. He's the guy who owns CRW.'

'The company that Mr Sabatino was interested in? Yeah, you're right. Tony Freeman.'

Utsyev stood up. 'Let's go and see Mr Freeman.'

Vincenti glanced at his spaghetti sauce, a look of intense disappointment on his face, but he didn't say anything. He followed Utsyev outside.

Kiseleva was asleep, drooling against the window of the limousine. He jerked awake as Utsyev rapped on the glass. 'Come on, we've got work to do,' Utsyev growled.

As he climbed into the back of the car with Vincenti, Utsyev had a thought. 'Hey, this CRW guy that was working with my brother. The coke-head. What was his name?'

'Anderson,' Vincenti said. 'Maury Anderson.'

'Yeah, that's the guy. Let's go pick him up first.'

Freeman sat on a rock and fitted the snowshoes to his boots. 'Can you manage?' he asked Mersiha, who was grappling with the fasteners on her own shoes.

'Yeah, no problem,' she said. 'They're just like tennis racquets, aren't they?' She stood up and held her arms out to the side. 'All done.'

'Let's see you walk, then,' he said. She waddled across the snow, the shoes making hissing sounds as they brushed the surface. Freeman was impressed. 'You've done this before,' he said.

'My father taught me, years ago.' She looked suddenly embarrassed as if she regretted mentioning her real father. She turned her back on him and walked away. Freeman fumbled with his straps and hurried after her, throwing the rucksack over his shoulders.

Mersiha stopped and let him catch up. 'Your dad taught you well,' he said, trying to let her know that it was okay, that he didn't mind her talking about him. In fact, the more she talked about her family, the better he felt.

'Yeah,' she agreed. 'We went hiking a lot in the hills. He loved walking and stuff but he was a doctor so he didn't get much free time. A doctor in Bosnia wasn't like a doctor in the States. It didn't pay so well and he had to work really hard. I hardly saw him except in the evenings. But we went for a week's skiing holiday when I was ten, the whole family. He taught me to ski and to snowshoe.' She looked up at the snow-covered hillside. 'Race you to the top?'

'Winner cooks dinner?'

'Okay.' She frowned. 'Wait a minute, don't you mean the loser cooks dinner?'

Freeman raised an eyebrow. 'You heard what I said.'

'But that's not fair!'

'Pumpkin, life isn't fair.'

Maury Anderson opened his front door to find Vincenti standing there, a wide grin on his face. 'What the hell are you doing here?' he asked.

'Mr Utsyev wants to see you,' Vincenti said. He stood to the side so that Anderson could see the stretch limo parked at the end of his drive.

'Christ, what are the neighbours going to think?'

'I don't think Mr Utsyev gives a shit what your neighbours think. And I don't reckon it's smart of you to keep him waiting.'

Anderson's eyes narrowed. 'Where's Sabatino?'

'Sabatino's dead.'

'Dead?'

'Look, Anderson, get your arse into the limo and talk to Mr Utsyev.'

Anderson took the door keys from a hall table and locked the door. His wife had gone to visit her mother again, which was the only bright spot in what had all the hallmarks of becoming a very shitty day. What Anderson really wanted just then was a hit of the cocaine he had in his medicine cabinet, but he didn't think that Vincenti would let him go back inside the house. 'What happened to Sabatino?' he asked, but Vincenti ignored him, opening the door of the limo and sliding in. Utsyev looked like death warmed up, unshaven and bleary-eyed, and he smelt of stale sweat and booze. Anderson tried to smile but he was too frightened. He just about managed to bare his teeth. Utsyev waved to Nikko to drive off. 'Where are we going, Mr Utsyev?' Anderson asked. Utsyev said nothing. 'I'm sorry to hear about your brother, he . . .'

Utsyev glared at him. 'Shut the fuck up,' he said.

They drove in silence, with Anderson frantically trying to work out where they were going. He feared for his life and his hands began to shake in his lap.

'My brother was murdered,' Utsyev said eventually.

'Oh Jesus, I'm sorry.' Anderson suddenly realised what the implications were and he began to stammer. 'It wasn't me. I didn't, hey, I'd never, I wouldn't . . .'

Utsyev held up a hand to silence him. 'He was shot. By a girl.'

'Jesus Christ.' Anderson slumped in the seat, his arms folded protectively across his chest. At least Utsyev didn't think that he was responsible for his brother's death. After a while he realised that they were heading towards Tony Freeman's house, but he didn't say anything. He could sense that he was on very dangerous ground. He sniffed and rubbed his nose. God, he wanted coke and he wanted it bad. He caught Utsyev looking at him with undisguised contempt, and he pretended to stare out of the window. He tried not to react when the limo pulled into the driveway of Freeman's house. Freeman's car was there, parked in the garage, but Katherine's wasn't.

'Check the back,' Utsyev said to Kiseleva. He turned to Anderson. 'This Freeman. What's he like?'

'What do you mean, what's he like?'

'Is he a hard man?'

'Tony? No. He's just a regular guy.'

'The gun the girl used is registered in his name.'

'No.'

'Whaddya mean, no?'

'I mean, it's just not like Tony. He hates guns.'

'Yeah, well it was his gun. And he's got every reason for wanting to see my brother dead.'

'But Tony wouldn't do anything like that. He'd fight you through the courts, he'd use lawyers, he wouldn't use a gun.'

Utsyev snorted in disbelief. 'A man will always fight to protect what he thinks he's going to lose,' he said. He climbed out of the car and walked with Vincenti to the front door.

Anderson trailed behind. 'I don't think there's anyone in,' he said, trying to be helpful.

'Yeah? What makes you say that?' Utsyev asked.

'Tony's in Colorado. And his wife's car's not here.'

Vincenti rang the doorbell. When no one answered, they walked around to the back of the house where Kiseleva was waiting. 'Right. Open the door,' Utsyev said.

Kiseleva put his shoulder to the door, but before he could smash into it Anderson told him to wait. 'Tony keeps a spare key under the birdbath. Let me see if it's there.'

He went over to the stone birdbath, tilted it and

triumphantly pulled out a brass key. He tossed it to Kiseleva who used it to open the back door. Buffy was there and she growled menacingly. Anderson spoke to her soothingly, trying to calm her down.

Utsyev went through to the sitting room. Buffy barked and chased after him. 'Buffy, come here!' Anderson shouted, but she paid him no heed. She stood behind Utsyev, growling and snapping at his ankles. Utsyev aimed a kick at her head but she dodged away, still barking. She ran back into the kitchen and barked at Kiseleva.

'Kiseleva, take out the fucking dog, willya?' Utsyev shouted as he pulled the curtains shut.

To Anderson's amazement, Kiseleva pulled a handgun from underneath his jacket, screwed in a silencer, and shot the dog at point-blank range. Buffy didn't even have time to whimper: one moment she was on her feet, barking for all she was worth, the next she was dead on the floor, her skull smashed and bleeding. Anderson felt suddenly sick and he leaned against the wall for support.

'What the fuck have you done?' Utsyev yelled at Kiseleva.

'You said . . .'

'I said take the dog out, shit-for-brains. Take the fucking dog outside. Not blow its brains all over the kitchen floor. Look what you've done!'

'Boss, I thought . . .'

'Think? You don't fucking think. You need brains to think, not the crap you've got between your ears.' He shook his head sadly. 'I've just about had it with you, Kiseleva.'

'Sorry, boss.' Kiseleva put the gun back in its holster as Utsyev picked up a large manila envelope. He opened it and took out glossy colour photographs. He held one out to Anderson. 'Who's this?'

'That's Mersiha. Tony's daughter. She's in Colorado with him.'

Vincenti looked over Anderson's shoulder. 'That's her,' he said. 'That's the girl that killed Mr Sabatino.'

'It can't be,' Anderson said. 'She's only just turned sixteen. She's a kid.'

'Are you sure, Vincenti?' Utsyev asked as he scrutinised the pictures.

'That's her, boss. No doubt about it.' He examined the rest of the photographs. 'That's the dress she was wearing on Thursday night.'

'This is ridiculous,' Anderson said. 'She's a sixteen-year-old girl, she still . . .'

Utsyev slapped him across the face, hard. 'Where are they?' he asked.

'Colorado, that's all I know.'

'Where in Colorado?'

'Tony didn't say. A cabin somewhere. He wanted to spend quality time with her.'

'I'll fucking give them quality time. Did he leave a number?'

'There's no phone in the cabin.'

Utsyev put his face up close to Anderson. His breath was sickly-sweet, like rotting meat. 'If you're lying . . .' He left the threat unfinished.

'Boss, look at this,' Kiseleva shouted from the kitchen. He came back into the sitting room, waving a brochure. 'This was on the fridge.'

Utsyev scanned the brochure and nodded. 'Estes Park,' he said. 'That's where they've gone.' He looked at

Kiseleva. 'Get us on the next plane there. Then call Carelli's people in Denver. They owe us, big time, for that business we took care of for them. Tell Carelli what's happened and say we'd like his help. Then call New York. Tell Jenny to get out there with three of the crew. And Kiseleva?'

'Yes, boss?'

'Don't shoot anyone unless I specifically tell you to, okay?'

'Right, boss,' Kiseleva said contritely.

Mersiha sat on a large flat rock and looked down the hillside to where her father was slowly making his way up towards her. 'Come on, slow coach!' she called.

Freeman looked up, panting for breath. 'Sometimes I think you forget that I'm an old man,' he wheezed.

'You're just out of condition,' she laughed, leaning back and lying on the snow-covered rock. The sky above was a perfect blue, devoid of clouds. The snow was cold against her back but the jacket she was wearing was waterproof and the sensation wasn't unpleasant.

She heard her father's snowshoes crunching up the slope and a few minutes later he was standing over her, blocking out the sun. 'Okay, you win,' he said.

'Race you down?'

Freeman collapsed on to the rock next to her. 'No way,' he sighed, opening his rucksack and taking out a thermos flask. He poured hot coffee into two plastic mugs and handed one to Mersiha as she sat up. They drank together, looking out over the magnificent scenery. To the left was the Roosevelt National Forest and to their right were the towering peaks of the Rocky Mountain National Park, their tops covered in snow, the lower slopes bare rock. Nestled between them was the town. From above it looked almost deserted. A lone car drove down the main street, no bigger than a toy.

Mersiha took off her wool hat and shook her hair free. Out of the corner of her eye she caught her father staring at her, and she knew that he was looking at the white hairs. She put her hat back on again. Freeman sipped his coffee, deep in thought. 'Does this remind you of Bosnia?' he asked.

'Sure. The mountains, the forests, the clean air.' Suddenly images of Sabatino, grabbing her, hurting her, and then struggling for the gun with blood on his chest, flooded back. She shuddered and the coffee spilt over her gloves.

When she'd woken up that morning she'd been bursting with happiness at the prospect of a day in the mountains, but within seconds the fear had hit her, like a cold shower. She'd killed a man, and for that there would be a price to pay. Throughout the day there had been times when the fear had retreated and she'd started to enjoy herself, but it always came back. She looked across at her father, but he hadn't noticed her discomfort. He was bending over his rucksack, searching for the egg sandwiches he'd made. She should never have gone to see Sabatino; she'd been stupid to think that she could have handled a man like him. Now she was going to lose her home and her family, and she was going to hurt the person she loved most in the world. It wasn't guilt she felt. She hadn't felt it when she'd pulled the trigger and she didn't feel it now. Sabatino had attacked her, and if she hadn't shot him he would have raped her and possibly even killed her. No, under the circumstances she hadn't been wrong to kill him, but it had been a mistake.

Freeman straightened up and held out the package of sandwiches. 'Want one?' he asked.

'Maybe later,' she said. Her stomach felt as if it had been screwed up into a tight ball and food was the last thing she wanted. She had half a mind to tell her father everything, but part of her was still clinging to the hope that she might get away with it, that somehow the police had overlooked the gun and that the bodyguards hadn't given them her description. It was a faint hope at best, but at least she didn't have to see the look of hurt in her father's eyes. That would be more than she could bear.

'Okay, let me know if you change your mind,' he said, and took a big bite out of one of the sandwiches. 'Mmmmm, is it me or does food taste better the higher up you are?'

Mersiha smiled. 'It certainly doesn't apply in the coach section of a jet at thirty thousand feet, does it?'

Freeman choked on his sandwich, shaking his head with laughter. He swallowed with difficulty. 'Good point,' he said.

Mersiha lay back again, her stomach churning. Far above was a bird of prey, flying into the wind so that it remained static above the ground. It was hunting. Freeman shaded his eyes to see what she was looking at. 'It's a peregrine falcon,' he said. 'I used to see them all the time in Scotland. See the jay over there? The hawk's after it.'

A bird with dark blue plumage was winging its way over the trees. High in the air, the falcon shifted position. It was waiting until the jay was away from the trees. 'He'll be able to see it better when it's over the snow,' Freeman said.

Mersiha felt suddenly afraid, as if she were the intended victim, as if it were her the hawk was stalking. 'There he goes,' Freeman whispered.

The falcon had tucked its wings in and was diving beak-first towards the jay. It accelerated rapidly. The impact was a blur to Mersiha. The jay didn't even have time to cry out. It fell in a flurry of feathers and blood and the falcon swooped down to collect its prize, ripping the flesh with its beak as it kept a wary eye out for other predators.

'It's horrible,' Mersiha said.

'It's life,' Freeman responded. 'Survival of the fittest.'

'The strong kill the weak.' She looked across at him. 'That doesn't make it right.'

Freeman put down his sandwich. 'Hey, I was talking about animals. I didn't mean . . .'

'I know, I know,' she said before he could finish.

'Killing can never be justified,' he said.

'What about if someone threatens your family? Wouldn't you kill to protect Katherine?'

Freeman smiled thinly. 'Only if there was absolutely no alternative.'

'And if you did? Would you feel guilty?'

'Of course.'

Mersiha chewed her lip. Why didn't she feel guilty about Sabatino? Was there something wrong with her, was something missing, a conscience maybe, or a soul? Why was fear the only emotion she felt – fear of getting caught and fear of losing her family?

'Remember last night, what you said about your hair?'

Mersiha's hand instinctively went up to her head but she stopped herself. 'Sure. Of course I do.'

'Do you want to tell me about it? Do you want to tell me what happened?'

She looked at the falcon. It was ripping something long and red from the jay's guts. It hung from the falcon's curved beak like a rasher of bacon. 'I will, Dad. But not just now, okay?' She cupped her hands around her coffee as if trying to absorb its warmth.

Freeman nodded. 'Whenever you're ready, pumpkin.' They sat together in silence as the falcon fed.

Katherine Freeman opened the front door and dropped the carrier bags on the hall table, sighing gratefully. She took off her coat and checked the answering machine. The red light wasn't flashing. Then she carried the two bags containing food towards the kitchen. 'Supper's here, Buffy!' she called, expecting the dog to come bowling down the hallway, tail wagging and tongue lolling. The silence was a bad sign – Buffy liked nothing better than to go through the rubbish bin looking for scraps, even though she knew she wasn't supposed to. Left on her own, she'd poke through the trash to her heart's content, licking dirty cans and butter wrappers. She'd only be assuaged by guilt when she heard a key in the door. Then she'd go and hide, usually under the kitchen table.

'What have you been doing?' Katherine called, expecting to hear a guilty growl. Still nothing. Whatever she'd done, it must be really bad. She elbowed the kitchen door open, expecting the worse. The dog lay in a pool of congealing blood, one eye wide open and staring, the other lost in a mass of smashed tissue and bone. Her tongue looked impossibly big as if it had inflated and grown too large for her mouth. The groceries slipped from Katherine's arms and spilled on to the floor. A loaf of bread rolled into the puddle of sticky blood. Katherine took a step backwards. She looked around as if expecting to see the dog's killer standing in the corner, then her eyes were dragged back to the dead animal. There was no question that she was dead. Her one remaining eye had turned a milky white and the matted fur was quite still.

Katherine backed out of the kitchen, her breath coming in short gasps. She closed the kitchen door and leaned against it, resting her forehead on the painted wood. She couldn't think why anyone would want to kill Buffy, unless the house had been broken into and Buffy had been defending her territory. She frowned and went into the sitting room. There were some valuable silver pill-boxes on a side table, untouched, and a pair of solid silver candelabra, a present from her mother. The fact that they were still there suggested that the house hadn't been burgled. She closed her eyes. Had the dog died of natural causes? she wondered. All she could remember was the blood, and the grotesque tongue. Perhaps Buffy had had a stroke, like Katherine's father. There was only one way to find out. She'd have to go back into the kitchen.

She took a deep breath and opened the kitchen door. For the first time she noticed the smell of urine and blood, and she put a handkerchief over her mouth and nose. Slowly, taking care to avoid the blood, she knelt down and examined the dog's head. There was a small black hole behind its right ear and most of its lower jaw was missing. There were bone and teeth fragments on the tiles and a strip of matted fur against the cupboard under the sink. It was no accident, and it certainly wasn't natural causes. Buffy had been shot. Without thinking, Katherine reached out to stroke the dog's flank, but she stopped when she felt how cold it was. Her hand came away bloody.

She wiped the blood off on her handkerchief as she went into the hallway to use the phone. She couldn't bear to stay in the kitchen. Buffy had been more than a dog; she'd been a member of the family. She dialled 911 with a shaking hand. A bored woman answered. It sounded to Katherine as if she was chewing gum. 'You've got to help me, someone's shot my dog,' she said.

'Name and address?' Katherine gave the woman her details, becoming increasingly frustrated as the woman insisted on double-checking every spelling. 'Now what happened, ma'am?'

'My dog. Someone's shot my dog.'

'The dog's dead?'

'Yes. Yes, the dog's dead.'

'What makes you think your dog was killed, ma'am?'

'What?'

'How do you know she didn't get run over and crawl into the house to die. I'm sorry, ma'am, but it happens.'

'There's an entry wound in the back of the head. I've been hunting, I know what a gunshot wound looks like.'

'And did you see who killed it?'

'No. She was dead on the floor when I got home.'

'Do you have any idea who did it? Have you had trouble with your neighbours recently?'

'My neighbour is a cardiologist at Johns Hopkins. I don't think he fits the normal profile of a dog-killer.'

The sarcasm was lost on the woman. 'Was anything taken from the house?' she said mechanically.

'Not that I can see, no.'

'And you're in no danger?'

'No,' Katherine said coldly. 'No, I'm not in any danger.'

'Well, I'll have a patrol car call around later today.'

'When?'

'Well, when we have someone available, Mrs Freeman. But to be honest, a dead dog isn't going to rank high on our list of priorities.'

'So what do I do? Do I leave her where she is for your forensic people?'

'You can if you want. I'm not sure that they'll send a forensic team out, though. Not for a dog.'

'But they'll want to find the bullet, won't they?'

'I really couldn't say, Mrs Freeman. It is only a dog, after all.'

'It's not only a dog!' Katherine shouted. 'She wasn't just a dog. She was . . .' She realised she wasn't making any impression on the woman on the other end of the line, and she slammed down the receiver. She knew the woman was right. The police weren't going to be over-concerned about the shooting of a pet, not with the city's human murder toll. Baltimore had one of the country's highest murder rates, much of it drug-related, and barely a day went by without at least one murder. On weekends the toll was more likely to be in double figures.

She went to pour herself a drink, but stopped in her tracks, staring at the photographs spread out on the table. She was sure that when she left the house all the pictures had been in the manila envelope. She picked up one of the photographs, a close-up of Mersiha, and looked into her daughter's eyes. 'What's been happening, Mersiha?' she whispered. 'What the hell's going on?'

She carried the photograph with her as she went back to recheck the answering machine, just in case Tony had phoned. There was no mistake. The red light wasn't blinking; no one had called. She picked up the phone and dialled Maury Anderson's number from memory. He answered on the third ring. 'Maury? It's Katherine. Have you heard from Tony?'

'It wasn't my fault, there was nothing I could do,' he mumbled.

'What the hell are you talking about?'

'They made me, Katherine. You don't know what they're like. Utsyev's a killer. Just keep away from them . . .' The line went dead. His voice had sounded strange, as if his mind hadn't been on what he was saying – the disjointed ramblings of someone having a nightmare. She grabbed her coat and ran out of the house.

The black limousine pulled up in front of the terminal in a space earmarked for handicapped drivers. 'You wanna wait here while I pick up the tickets, boss?' Kiseleva asked, tugging at the red scarf around his neck, but Utsyev was already reaching for the door handle. Kiseleva caught up with him after a few steps like an eager-to-please puppy. Vincenti followed behind, his gaze sweeping left and right, looking for trouble but finding none.

There was no queue in front of the first-class counter and

within minutes they were heading for the departure gate where their plane was ready for boarding. A black family were loading their hand baggage on to the conveyor belt that fed the X-ray machine while a bored security officer was making a young blonde girl remove her hair barrette before going through the metal detector a second time. Utsyev stood in line, tapping the tickets against his leg impatiently.

'Fuck,' Kiseleva cursed quietly.

'What's up?' Vincenti asked, chewing on his unlit cigar.

'Fuck,' Kiseleva repeated.

Utsyev looked at him sideways. His eyes narrowed. 'Are you carrying?' he asked. Kiseleva nodded, shamefaced. Utsyev's face darkened and he glared at the man. 'Are you fucking stupid, or what?' he whispered.

'I forgot, boss, what with the rush to the airport and all.'

The family threaded through the metal detector without incident and the security officer beckoned Vincenti.

'Go see if Nikko's still outside. Give it to him,' Utsyev said, handing him a ticket.

'You can come through, sir,' the security officer said, waving to Vincenti.

'Yeah, yeah,' Vincenti said.

'You're not carrying as well, are you?' Utsyev asked. Vincenti didn't rise to the bait; he just smiled smugly. Utsyev put his face close to Kiseleva's. 'Is it traceable?' he hissed.

'No, boss. Definitely not.'

'So if Nikko's not there, dump it in the men's room. And if you fuck up again . . .' Utsyev left the threat unfinished.

Vincenti went through the metal detector. It beeped furiously. Utsyev shook his head in amazement, but Vincenti pulled a metal keyring out of his overcoat pocket and showed it to the security officer. The officer made him put the keyring in a plastic tray and walk through again. This time he was clear. Utsyev went through without incident and the two men walked to the gate, where they boarded immediately. A stewardess with unnaturally black hair and an equally unnatural smile showed them to their seats and took their overcoats to hang up. Utsyev looked at his watch. The flight was due to leave within minutes.

'He'll make it, boss,' Vincenti said.

'Yeah? He'd better.'

A second stewardess, blonde with a painted-on beauty mark on her right cheek, appeared at Utsyev's shoulder. 'Can I get you a drink, sir?' she asked.

'Bourbon, on the rocks,' he said without looking at her. Vincenti shook his head.

'This is a non-smoking flight, sir,' she said mechanically, pointing at his cigar.

'I'm not smoking,' Vincenti said.

'Smoking isn't permitted, sir,' she said, her smile tightening.

'It isn't lit.'

'I'm sorry, sir.' The smile had now become a tight line.

Vincenti realised there was no point in arguing with her and he handed it over, wet end first. She took it between her thumb and first finger, holding it away from her body as she went back to the galley.

'Stepford wives,' Vincenti said.

'Huh?' Utsyev grunted.

'Robots,' Vincenti explained. 'They're not real women.

They're fucking robots. Have a nice day. Fasten your seat belt. Tea or coffee. Thank you for flying with us. Bullshit.' He picked up a copy of the in-flight magazine and flicked through it.

The stewardess was just handing Utsyev his drink when Kiseleva rushed into the first-class cabin, his face flushed. 'Sorry, boss,' he mouthed as he took his seat at the rear of the cabin. Utsyev looked away in disgust. Kiseleva was a good man in a fight, an enforcer second to none, but if they handed out frequent flyer miles for brains, Kiseleva would never leave the ground.

'So, are you gentlemen flying to Denver on business, or for the skiing?' the blonde asked brightly.

Utsyev bared his teeth in a semblance of a smile. 'We're going to a funeral,' he said.

'Oh,' the stewardess said. 'I'm sorry.'

'That's okay,' Utsyev said. 'I'm not.'

Katherine kept her finger pressed against the doorbell until Maury Anderson opened the front door. She pushed him in the middle of the chest and sent him staggering back into his hall. 'Right, Maury, what the hell is happening? You've got ten seconds to tell me or I'm calling the police.'

'Leave me alone,' he said, throwing his hands up to cover his face as if he feared being struck.

'Someone's been in my house. They shot Buffy.'

'It wasn't my fault,' Anderson said, shaking his head in denial. Katherine could see traces of white powder on his upper lip and his nose was running.

THE BIRTHDAY GIRL

'You're on coke, aren't you?'

'So?' he said defiantly.

She slammed the door behind her. 'What's going on?'

'Stay out of it, Katherine.' He rubbed his bloodshot eyes.

'Stay out of what? You said someone was a killer. Who were you talking about?'

'Utsyev. Sabatino's brother.'

'The guy that's been trying to take over the company?'

'He's dead.'

Katherine was confused. 'Who's dead? Sabatino or Utsyev?'

'Sabatino.' Anderson put his hands over his face and slid slowly down the wall until he was crouching on the floor. 'Mersiha killed him,' he whispered.

'What!' Katherine was stunned.

'Mersiha shot Sabatino.'

'That's ridiculous. She's a child.'

'Thursday night. She shot him with one of Tony's guns.'

'Thursday night? No, she was . . .' Katherine remembered that Mersiha had been out of the house all night, staying with Allison Dooley. But even so, she didn't believe for one minute that her daughter would pick up a gun, never mind shoot a man. 'Why were they around at my house?'

'They wanted Tony. They saw Mersiha's photographs. It was her, Katherine. They recognised her. She went to The Firehouse, she got into Sabatino's office, and she killed him.'

'You don't know what you're saying. The drugs have affected your mind, Maury. You're sick.'

Anderson wrapped his arms around his knees as if he were cold. 'Keep out of it, Katherine. Utsyev is a killer.

385

If you get in his way, he'll blow you away without a second thought.'

Katherine's blood suddenly went cold. 'They've gone to Colorado, haven't they?'

'They know Tony rented a cabin. They've got the brochure.'

'You bastard. They've gone there to kill my husband and daughter. And you told them where they are.' Anderson shook his head. Katherine glared down at him. 'I'm going to the police.'

'To tell them what? To tell them that Mersiha killed Sabatino? You can't. They found the gun. They saw her going into Sabatino's office.'

Katherine paced up and down the hallway. 'If I call the police, they'll be able to protect Tony and Mersiha.'

'You think the police will believe you? Besides, they'll be more interested in Sabatino's murder. You want Mersiha to go to prison?'

'That's the choice, Maury?' Katherine screamed at him. 'That's my fucking choice?' She kicked him in the side and he yelped. She kicked him again, hard. Anderson began to cry like a small boy. She felt nothing but disgust.

She went back to her car and sat for a few seconds, gripping the wheel tightly and rocking backwards and forwards. She half expected Anderson to come after her, but the front door stayed closed. Katherine remembered the reaction of the 911 operator and realised that they'd be unlikely to take her seriously if she told them what she knew. She had no proof. She couldn't identify the men who were after Tony and Mersiha and she doubted that Anderson would help. Besides, what if Anderson had been telling the truth about Mersiha? Katherine suddenly realised that there was a way she could check out Anderson's ludicrous assertion. She drove back to her house as quickly as possible, her mind in turmoil.

She parked next to Tony's car and ran to the study. The combination of the lock on the gun cabinet was written down on a scrap of paper in an envelope he kept in a desk drawer. She knelt down by the cabinet and with trembling hands turned the dial: fifteen to the left, eight to the right, nineteen to the left. She swung the door open and scanned the contents. She sighed with relief as she saw that nothing was missing. All the shotguns were there, and so were the cases containing the handguns. 'You lying little shit, Maury,' she hissed. She opened the case containing the pearl-handled Smith & Wesson, then put it on the carpet beside her. The Colt Python was in its case. It went on top of the Smith & Wesson. She pulled out the black case that contained the Heckler & Koch HK-4 and flicked its catches open. 'Oh no,' she sighed as she lifted the lid and saw that the gun was missing. 'Please God, no.' She touched the spare barrels and clips that had been left behind, but all she could see were the empty pre-cut holes in the foam rubber. If Mersiha had indeed taken the gun, and had shot Sabatino, then there was no way Katherine could go to the police. But she couldn't just stand by and let Utsyev hunt them down. There was only one thing she could do. She'd have to go to Colorado herself to warn Tony.

Mersiha cooked corned beef hash while Freeman carried more wood in for the fire. They ate together sitting by the fireplace. 'I'm going out to call Katherine later,' Freeman said. 'Do you want to come?' They'd visited the rental agent's office after going to the supermarket, but Mr Hellings hadn't been able to come up with a portable telephone. He'd promised to keep trying.

'I'm bushed,' she said. 'I'm going straight to bed. Can I talk to her tomorrow?'

'Of course you can. You'll be all right here alone?'

Mersiha raised her eyebrows. 'I'll be safer here than in Baltimore. I don't expect there are many drive-by killings in Estes Park.'

'Yeah, I guess so,' Freeman said, putting down his plate. 'But make sure the door's locked. I'll take a key with me.'

'Dad, I'm sixteen now. You can leave me on my own, you know.'

'You might be sixteen, but you're still my little girl.'

Mersiha rolled her eyes. 'Puh-leeze,' she groaned.

Freeman stood up and picked up his jacket. 'Okay, I'll go now. I shouldn't be more than half an hour.' He bent down and kissed her on the forehead. 'Sleep well.'

She went to the door with him and made sure that it was locked. It was ironic, she thought, that he was so concerned about her safety while they were in Colorado. The real danger was waiting for her back in Baltimore.

The bleached blonde tapped away on her computer key-board as Katherine looked on anxiously. The airport was almost deserted and it had taken Katherine almost five minutes to find someone at the United Airlines desk who'd help her. The UA flight to Denver had left hours earlier and now the blonde was checking other possible routings. 'I don't have any baggage,' Katherine said, hoping that would help.

The blonde sighed. 'I'm sorry, Mrs Freeman. There's no way you'll get there tonight.'

'No red-eyes?'

'No nothing, I'm afraid.'

'But I have to get to Denver,' Katherine protested. 'It's a matter of life and death.' She instantly regretted the cliché, but couldn't think of any other way of describing her predicament.

'There's an early-morning flight to St Louis that'll connect to a Denver flight. You'll arrive in Denver before ten o'clock, local time.'

'That's no good,' she said. 'Look, can you tell me if a man called Utsyev was on your Denver flight?'

The blonde shook her head. 'We're not allowed to disclose passenger lists.'

'Please.' Katherine reached for her purse and started pulling out bills.

'I can't, I'm sorry,' the woman said before Katherine could even offer her the money. 'I'd lose my job.'

Katherine slammed her hand down on the counter in exasperation. 'What about New York? Surely there's something out of JFK?'

'I can get you to New York tonight, but the first flight out from there to Denver will be tomorrow morning. You'll have to spend the night in New York and you still won't get there any earlier.' Katherine felt tears of frustration well up in her eyes. 'You could charter a plane,' the blonde suggested.

'What, charter a jet, you mean? That would cost a fortune, wouldn't it?'

'Not a jet. A small plane. It'd mean flying through the night, but you'd probably get there before the scheduled flights.'

Katherine clenched her fists in front of her chest. 'How? How do I do that?'

The blonde looked at a slim gold wristwatch. 'It's late, but you could try the general aviation terminal down the road. You'll see it signposted on the way out, past the short-term car parks. There are two there that I know of: Hinson Airways and Bluebird Aviation.'

Katherine beamed. 'Thank you,' she said. 'Thank you.' She ran off, leaving the bewildered blonde shaking her head.

There were no lights on at Hinson Airways but as Katherine arrived at the Bluebird Aviation building a tall man in his early twenties was walking out, a flight bag over his shoulder. He was wearing a leather bomber jacket and carrying a headset. She wound down her window. 'Are you a pilot?' she called.

'Sure am,' he said. 'If you want to arrange lessons, you'll have to come back tomorrow. We're just closing up.'

Katherine got out of her car. 'I want to go to Denver.'

'Denver? Tonight?'

'It's important.'

The pilot frowned and looked at his watch. 'Have you tried the airlines? It's a long flight in a twin. You'd be far better off taking a scheduled flight.'

'I tried that. Look, I'll pay whatever it takes.'

The pilot scratched his head. His hair was cut military style, close-cropped and shaved around his ears. As Katherine got closer she realised he was older than she'd first thought. In his early thirties maybe. 'It'd be uncomfortable. There's no in-flight movie and the lavatory's a plastic bag.'

'What's your name?' she asked.

'Clive. Clive Edwards.'

'Look, Clive. This is an emergency. I can't tell you how important it is, but I'm not worried about comfort or cost or anything. Just get me to Denver.'

'I'm just trying to make it clear that it won't be a pleasant flight. The twin-engined plane we'll be using is noisy and cramped. And you'll have to pay for the return journey.'

'I don't care.'

Clive looked at her and nodded slowly. 'Let me see if I can get hold of a co-pilot,' he said. 'It's way too far to fly single-handed. And I'll have to check out the charts. We're going to have to refuel several times.'

'Whatever it takes,' Katherine urged, locking her car door. She followed him inside.

The runway at Denver International Airport had a light dusting of powdery snow when the Boeing 757 touched down. With no luggage to collect, Utsyev and his two bodyguards walked straight out of the arrivals terminal into the cold evening air. Kiseleva shivered and wrapped his scarf tightly around his neck. Utsyev stamped his feet impatiently. 'Where's the fucking car, Kiseleva?' he spat.

'It'll be here, boss. Maybe you should wait inside while I go look for it?'

'Maybe I should get me a new assistant,' Utsyev said, acidly. 'Maybe it's time you thought about retirement.'

A short, stocky man in a black suit rushed up, sweating despite the freezing temperature. 'Mr Utsyev?' he said. Utsyev nodded. 'I'm Ben Sagalle. Mr Carelli sends his compliments, sir. If there's anything he can do to make your stay in Denver more pleasant, you only have to ask. I'm sorry I wasn't here to meet you off the plane, sir. Your car's this way. Do you have any baggage?'

Utsyev shook his head. 'We're travelling light this trip.'

'I understand, sir. We have the goods your people requested. Please follow me.'

Utsyev nodded approvingly. 'Now this is more like it,' he said to Kiseleva. The car was a black stretch limo, and Utsyev noticed that the bar was stocked with his favourite brand of bourbon. He pointed at the bottle. 'See that, Vincenti? Now that's class.'

Vincenti took out a cigar from his inside pocket and put it in his mouth, unlit. Sagalle closed the door and spoke to the driver. The car pulled smoothly away from the kerb, the windscreen wipers swishing the snowflakes away with crisp, efficient strokes. The partition that separated the driver from the passengers closed with a whisper. Sagalle picked up a metal suitcase and placed it on his knees. He clicked the combination locks open, lifted the lid, and presented the contents to Utsyev. 'With Mr Carelli's compliments.'

Utsyev raised his eyebrows. Sitting in foam rubber were three submachine-guns and several clips. 'Ingram Model 10s, .45-calibre, twelve hundred rounds per minute,' Sagalle said, like a waiter detailing the daily special.

'You can select them to fire on semi-automatic or full automatic, thirty-four rounds in the clip. We prefer them to the Uzi. It's a few inches shorter so easier to conceal. I've included Sionics noise suppressors. I think you'll find them more than up to the job.' Sagalle took one out and handed it to Utsyev. 'We obtained them through a contact in Mexico three months ago. The serial numbers have been removed and they haven't been used in this country,' he continued. Utsyev gave the weapon back and Sagalle replaced it in its foam cut-out. He snapped the lid shut and handed the case to Vincenti. 'My understanding is that more of your people are flying in from New York,' he said.

Utsyev grunted and reached for the bottle of bourbon. Kiseleva beat him to it and poured a large measure into a crystal tumbler. 'They're arriving just after eleven,' he said.

'We've taken the liberty of booking you into the Stouffer Hotel, sir. You can wait for them there. I'll have them met and brought to you. Will you be requiring further manpower?'

'What do you mean?' Utsyev asked.

'Mr Carelli says that we are to help you in any way we can, sir. If you need more men, we'll be more than happy to supply you.'

Utsyev shook his head. 'No. We can handle this.'

Sagalle nodded. 'And transport. We weren't sure where you'd be going so I didn't know if you'd be requiring the use of a limo or whether four-wheel-drives would be more appropriate.' He waited expectantly.

Utsyev looked at Vincenti and then back to Sagalle. 'Close to the Rocky Mountain National Park. A place called Estes Park. What is it, some sort of resort area?'

'Yeah, though it's not really a park. It's a small town catering for tourists – hiking, fishing, skiing, that sort of thing. It's pretty quiet this time of the year. The season doesn't really start until May.' He looked at the flecks of snow which were sticking to the windows for only a few seconds before melting. 'There's no real snow forecast to the north, and this'll be over in a few hours. The forecast for tomorrow is sunny. But if I were you, I'd go in four-wheel-drives, just to be on the safe side. If that suits your plans, I'll arrange it.'

'Can't we fly?'

Sagalle shook his head. 'The nearest airfield would be Boulder, and you'd still have a long drive from there. How many of your men will be coming?'

Utsyev frowned. 'Why do you want to know?'

'Clothing, sir. If you're going to the Rocky Mountain National Park you'll need to wear something less conspicuous than two-thousand-dollar suits and cashmere overcoats.'

Utsyev nodded and took a mouthful of the bourbon. 'Four. Three of them are about his build.' He gestured at Kiseleva with his thumb. 'The fourth is a woman.'

If Sagalle was surprised that one of Utsyev's team was female, he didn't show it. 'I'll have suitable clothing delivered to the hotel tonight with the vehicles, along with a selection of footwear. There'll be four untraceable handguns in the trunk of one of the vehicles.'

Utsyev grunted. Sagalle had clearly thought of everything. Utsyev wondered what it would take to get a man like Sagalle on his team. Probably a hell of a lot more than he paid Kiseleva. 'We'll drive up later tonight,' he said. He rubbed his left temple with his knuckles. 'I ain't feeling so good.'

'That could be the altitude, sir,' Sagalle said. 'You're about five thousand feet higher than in New York. It'll pass in a day or two.'

'I hope I'm not still around in a day or two,' Utsyev growled, and took another pull at his drink. Sagalle looked as if he was about to suggest that alcohol wouldn't help his acclimatisation, but then seemed to think better of it. 'Maybe I'll get some shuteye while I wait for my crew to get here,' Utsyev said.

'That'd help,' Sagalle agreed.

The limousine pulled up in front of a white pyramid-shaped building a dozen storeys high. Sagalle handed Utsyev a business card. 'This is the number of my mobile phone, Mr Utsyev. You can reach me night or day. If there's anything you need, call. I'm at your disposal until this matter has been concluded.'

Utsyev and his two men climbed out of the limousine and watched as it drove away through the gently falling snow. 'Until this matter has been concluded,' Utsyev repeated to himself. He rounded on Kiseleva. 'You hear that? That Sagalle is a class operator. You should fucking learn from him, you hear?'

Kiseleva's lips tightened until they almost disappeared. 'Yes, boss,' he said through gritted teeth.

Freeman drove the Bronco slowly down the track towards the cabin. There were no safety rails on the bridge over the stream so he took extra care to stay in the middle. The powerful headlights illuminated the wooden cabin and he saw that smoke was still feathering from the stone chimney. It was a welcoming sight, but the cabin still looked far more isolated at night than it did during the day. The trees and hillside behind disappeared into the blackness and outside the beams of light he couldn't see a thing. He'd been out longer than he'd expected, because Katherine hadn't been home. He'd left a message on the answering machine, but then decided to keep trying, certain that she wouldn't be out too late. By eleven o'clock he was still getting the machine. Either she'd fallen asleep and had turned the ringer off in the bedroom, or she was out with the girls. He had begun to worry about leaving Mersiha on her own for too long, so he'd left another message saying that he'd call again in the morning.

He parked in front of the cabin and turned the engine off. He sat for a while in the darkness, alone with his thoughts. The daughter who lay asleep in the cabin was a totally different girl to the twelve-year-old who'd pointed a Kalashnikov at him when he was chained up in the basement in Sarajevo, and he'd almost forgotten the circumstances under which they'd first met. He went back in his mind to the time she'd levelled the assault rifle at him and tightened her finger on the trigger. She was quite prepared to kill him. He remembered how he'd been sure that his life was going to end on the cold concrete floor. He'd known then without a shadow of a doubt that she was a killer, yet he'd still been shocked to the core when she'd told him the story of her white hairs. He knew he was getting close to discovering her secrets, that she was preparing to open up to him in way that she'd never done with anyone before, and the prospect thrilled him. But he was apprehensive, too, because he had a feeling that what she was going to reveal to him would change for ever the way he saw her.

He climbed out of the Bronco. When he slammed the car door the noise echoed back from the mountain like a gunshot. He shivered. It was a cold night, cold enough for snow. He looked up at the myriad stars above. There were no lights nearby and the air was so clear that he seemed to be able to see right to the other end of the galaxy. He walked softly across the deck, not wanting to disturb Mersiha if she was asleep, and let himself in. The cabin was creaking as it settled down for the night, friendly groans and cracks like an arthritic old man drifting off to sleep. He tiptoed upstairs to his bedroom. On the way he put his ear to Mersiha's door. She was moaning, then he heard words, but he couldn't make sense of them. He turned the handle and pushed the door open. She was talking rapidly, the words tumbling over themselves, but even if she'd been speaking slowly he wouldn't have understood. She was talking in her native language – harsh, guttural sounds that owed little to English. Her arms and legs were moving listlessly and her head was thrashing from side to side. Freeman walked over to her bed on the balls of his feet and sat down beside her. He couldn't make sense of what she was saying, but she was clearly in distress. He wanted to wake her, but he remembered Art Brown's words – it was better to let her sleep through it. He reached over and took her hand in his. It felt so small, like a child's, and it was damp with sweat. 'It's okay, pumpkin,' he whispered, 'I'm here.'

Her brow furrowed and she began to pant like an over-excited puppy. Sweat was pouring off her face and soaking into the pillow. Freeman watched her anxiously. He'd never seen her as troubled as this, even during her first weeks in America. He wondered if it was because she'd started to open up to him, if by knocking down the walls she'd built up he was in danger of unleashing a torrent of bad memories. He squeezed her hand gently, not hard enough to wake her but in the hope that wherever she was in her dreams she'd know that he was there with her.

Mersiha ground her teeth as if she were in pain and began to breathe through her nose. Suddenly she sat bolt upright, her eyes wide open. She took a deep breath and Freeman realised she was going to scream. He put his arms around her and pressed her to his chest, telling her over and over again that it was all right, that he was there and it had only been a bad dream. Her body was trembling as she sobbed into his shoulder, and he caressed the back of her neck. He could feel the tension at the top of her spine, as if the bones had been replaced with steel rods. 'I'm here, pumpkin. I'm here.'

'I'm sorry,' she said.

'There's nothing to be sorry about,' he said. 'It was only a nightmare.'

'It was horrible.' Her arms slipped around his waist as if she were hanging on to him.

'What was happening?'

'I was at the school.'

It wasn't the answer Freeman had expected. 'The school?'

Mersiha gripped him tighter as if it were the word itself which was causing her pain. 'Mersiha, can you tell me what happened?' He felt her shake her head. 'It might help.'

She sniffed. 'It was when I was little,' she said. 'The year before I met you.'

'You were twelve?'

'Uh-huh. It was spring. The fighting had been going on for two years. I'd almost gotten used to it. I don't think I could remember what it was like before the snipers, you know?' She sniffed again and Freeman thought she was going to stop talking, but she continued. 'We ate all our meals in the dark, with the shutters closed. We never walked when we were outside, we always ran. We ran to get water, we ran to the relief convoys for food, we ran to feed the animals. We ran and we bent over to make ourselves smaller targets. I can remember my mother holding my hand and telling me to hurry because the Serbs would shoot us if we didn't run.'

She released her grip around his waist and brushed tears away from her eyes. 'And you used to run to school?' Freeman said, trying to encourage her to continue talking.

She shook her head. 'No. There was no school. The Serbs kept shelling the building. My mother and father taught me at home.'

'The nightmare. What happened in the nightmare?'

'My father had just left the house with a woman whose daughter was about to have a baby. The baby was coming out the wrong way and the woman said my father had to be there. He went. He always went, no matter how dangerous it was.'

'He was a good man.'

Mersiha nodded. 'He was too good, that's what my mother said. She didn't want him to go. The woman was a Serb and she had two sons, both of them fighting. It could have been one of her sons shooting at us from the hills.'

'Your mother said that?'

'No, she would never say anything bad about anyone. She was like my father – she always thought the best of everyone. But she didn't want him to go outside. It was too dangerous, she said. Stjepan told me the woman was a Serb. Afterwards.'

'Afterwards?'

'After he rescued me from the school.'

The school again. Freeman didn't know what its significance was, but he didn't want to ask her directly. He said nothing as he waited for her to continue.

'We stood to the side of the kitchen door to watch him go, standing in the shadows so the snipers wouldn't be able to see us. I didn't see what happened, but we heard a burst of gunfire. Six shots, maybe more. My mother looked at me in terror and I could tell that she knew he was dead. I dashed out of the door but she grabbed my sweater and pulled me back. I was screaming that we had to go and help him but she told me to go upstairs and hide in a cupboard.' She smiled at Freeman through her tears. 'She wasn't the sort of mother you argued with, you know?'

He nodded. 'I know.'

'I went upstairs and hid, like she said. I knew she was going out to help my father, and I wanted to go with her, but I had to do as she said. I had to obey her. Even in the cupboard in my parents' bedroom I could hear shouts. Men yelling. And screams. My mother screaming. I put my fingers in my ears and hummed. Can you believe I did that? I was humming because I didn't want to hear her scream.'

'You were only twelve,' Freeman said. 'There was nothing you could have done.'

'I closed my eyes and I hummed, trying to shut it all out, trying to pretend it wasn't happening. I don't know how long I stayed that way. It felt like hours but it probably wasn't more than a few minutes.'

She fell silent. 'What happened?' Freeman asked.

'They found me,' she said quietly. 'Two of them. One of them was older than my father. The other was taller and thinner and had a gun in his hand. An automatic. I didn't know anything about guns then, but now I know it was an automatic. At the time all I knew was that it was a big gun. They dragged me out of the cupboard and threw me on the bed. I could hear my mother screaming downstairs, and men shouting. I didn't understand what was going to happen, Dad. I knew what my mother and father did in bed. The house we lived in was quite small and sometimes I'd hear them make love late at night, and I knew all about babies and stuff. But I didn't know that men could do it to a girl, not a girl like me.'

Freeman closed his eyes and swallowed. Part of him wanted it to stop right there because he knew that what he was going to hear would break his heart, but he also knew that he wasn't doing this for himself, he was doing it for Mersiha. She had to get it out in the open so that she could start to heal. 'Where was Stjepan?' he asked.

'He'd left three months earlier. The Muslims had started to fight back and he was one of the first to join up. He kept sending word back to us that he was okay, and occasionally we'd get a letter, but he wasn't around. Most of the time we didn't even know where he was.' She wiped her nose with the back of her hand and sniffed. 'They ripped my clothes off. I tried to stop them but they were so strong. They were laughing and one of them, the old one, kept drinking from a brandy bottle. No one but my parents had seen me naked before, not even Stjepan. I tried to cover myself with my hands, but what could I do? They were too big. The young one slapped me across the face and told me to lie still. Then the old one started arguing about which of them was going to go first. I didn't understand what they meant. There were footsteps on the stairs, heavy footsteps made by men wearing boots. Two more men came into the room, men with rifles. One was chewing on a loaf of bread, the other threw apples to his friends. They carried on eating as they discussed who was going to go first. I was crying, but the more I begged and pleaded for them to let me go, the more they laughed.'

Freeman put his arm around her shoulders. Mersiha bowed her head as she continued her story. 'I tried to get under the blankets but they pulled them off the bed and threw them on the floor. All the time my mother was screaming downstairs. Then her screams got louder and I realised they were bringing her upstairs. They dragged her into the bedroom. She was crying. I'd never seen my mother cry before, no matter how bad things got. Even when she argued with my father she never cried, but when they threw her on the bed next to me tears were streaming down her face. Her face was red from where she'd been slapped and her dress was torn. She saw what they'd done to me and she tried to lie on top of me, to protect me, but they dragged her off. One of them had a knife and he used it to tear her dress off, then her underwear, until she was as naked as I was. The men started to compare us, saying which one they wanted, as if we were pieces of meat being haggled over by housewives, and all the time she was begging them to let me go. She said they could do anything they wanted with her, just so long as they let me go. They laughed. They said they were going to have us both anyway. I kept asking my mother what had happened to my father, but she wouldn't say.

'Two of them held my mother's arms while the young one, the one with the gun, raped her. She was looking at me all the time, telling me not to worry, that it would be all right, that it'd soon be over. She kept reaching for my hand but the men kept hitting her. They kept saying stuff about giving us Serbian children, that we'd have sons and that our sons would go out and kill Muslims. My mother never stopped looking at me.'

'She loved you very much,' Freeman said, his voice faltering.

'The old man raped me first. His breath was foul and he kept trying to kiss me. I begged him to leave me alone and then I pleaded with my mother to get them to stop. I feel so bad about that now, because there was nothing she could have done. I can't imagine how she must have felt. I mean, it was bad enough what was happening to her, but to have me there and to have me . . .'

She began to sob uncontrollably. Freeman had never felt so powerless in his life. He held her in his arms and waited for the crying to subside.

'I was only thinking of myself,' she cried. 'They were raping her and all I could think of was that I wanted them to stop hurting me. I was so selfish.'

'No,' he whispered.

She shook her head. 'She passed out eventually, or maybe they beat her unconscious. I can't remember. The men didn't seem to mind whether she was awake or not. They just carried on raping her. It went on for hours. Hours and hours. Men kept coming into the room, leaning their rifles against the wall and laughing with their friends, then pulling their trousers down and dropping down on top of me. One of them made me sing while he was doing it to me. *Niko, Nema, Sto Srbi Imade.* No one has what the Serbs have. All the time he was on top of me. After a while it stopped hurting, I couldn't feel anything. I was numb. Physically and mentally. I didn't even protest any more, I just kept my legs open because the wider apart they were the less it seemed to hurt. I turned my head to the side and stared at the wall and let them get on with it. I tried to blank it out. I kept thinking of other things. Walking in the hills with my dad. Playing with Stjepan. Eating dinner. Watching television. Horses. I loved horses and imagined I was riding a big horse and that it was carrying me away, taking me to a safe place.

'Eventually it was over and they dragged us off the bed and carried us downstairs. They wrapped my mother in a blanket and they gave me a shirt to wear. I thought they were taking us outside to kill us, but I didn't care. I wanted to die. I wanted it to be all over. I couldn't walk so two men dragged me by the arms. Down the road was a large truck and more soldiers were loading women into it. I recognised some of them, girls I'd gone to school with, friends I'd played with. Their mothers. Their grandmothers. They'd all been beaten and raped.

'They dragged me by my father's body. He was lying in the gutter. He didn't look like my father any more. Half of his face was missing. He hadn't just been shot – they'd gutted him with a knife and stabbed him around the groin. The blood had run down the gutter and into a drain. And they'd stolen his boots. That's the thing I remember. He

404

was lying dead in the gutter and someone had stolen his boots. I remember thinking that they shouldn't have taken his boots because his feet would get cold.'

She leaned her head against Freeman's shoulder and fell silent. He could feel her breath on his neck each time she exhaled. He stroked her hair. There were no words he could say. The only comfort he could offer was physical contact.

'They'd killed all the Muslim men. All of them. I heard stories later of the things the Serbs had done to them before they killed them. They made fathers kill their own sons, they made them do things to each other. They killed them with knives, they smashed in their skulls with rifle butts, they raped wives in front of husbands and then murdered the men in front of their women. Ethnic cleansing, they called it, but there was nothing clean about what they did. My father was lucky. At least he died quickly.'

She paused for breath, then continued as Freeman sat transfixed. 'They threw me in the back of the truck. I sat next to my mother, but she didn't seem like my mother any more. Her eyes were blank, like she wasn't there any more. I put my arm around her shoulders but she didn't notice. Then she started shivering. Another woman gave her a shawl and I wrapped it over her legs. It didn't make any difference. It was cold in the truck, bitterly cold, and we huddled together for warmth and comfort, like scared sheep. No one said anything. It was too terrible to talk about. Too terrible even to think about.' She looked up at Freeman, her cheeks flushed and wet. 'I'd stopped thinking about it, I'd locked it away deep inside, somewhere dark and cold, locked it away so it couldn't get out. Except that it always does manage to get out, when I'm asleep.'

'That's why you have to let it out,' Freeman said. 'If you let it out in the open, it can't hurt you.'

'I hope you're right, Dad,' she said.

He smiled. 'I am, pumpkin. Trust me.' She put her head back on his shoulder and they sat together in silence for a while. 'Where did they take you?' he asked eventually.

'To the school,' she said. 'That was where they kept all the women. There were Muslim women in all the classrooms. They'd boarded up the windows and put metal doors where the wooden ones used to be. Inside were mattresses where there used to be desks. Once a day they fed us and gave us water. We had to go to the toilet in a plastic bucket.'

Freeman remembered the basement where he'd been chained. He remembered how he'd been fed, and how he'd had to use a bucket. And yet his experience didn't even come close to the horrors Mersiha had gone through.

'The only men were the Serb soldiers. All the Muslim men had been killed. We were put in a room with two women. One of them had been a nurse who'd worked with my father, years before. She told us what the school was. I couldn't believe it. I thought I'd died and gone to hell.' She shuddered at the memory. 'It was a baby farm. A Serb baby farm.'

'What?' Freeman said, horrified.

'A baby farm. They wanted to use Muslim women to make Serb babies. We were to be raped until we were pregnant. All day, every day. Soldiers who weren't fighting would come to the school just to rape the women there. We were like a huge brothel, I guess. But the aim wasn't to give pleasure, it was to produce a new generation of Serbian soldiers. And to break our spirit.'

Freeman's mouth was wide open in astonishment. It was like something that might have happened in Nazi Germany, but not in nineties Europe. Not with an organisation like the United Nations sending its people into Bosnia, and the Red Cross handing out food and aid. He could scarcely believe what he was hearing.

'Babies were already being born in the school, but they had been fathered by Muslims so they were taken away and killed. They didn't even shoot them. They'd swing them by their legs and crush their heads against a wall, then bury the bodies where the playground used to be. That's what the nurse told us.

'The soldiers would unlock the door and walk in and rape whoever they wanted. The first few days we tried to fight, but if we put up any resistance a group would rush in and beat us and hold us down on the mattresses. The end result was always the same, and at least if we did what they wanted they didn't hurt us. Not as much, anyway. I hated the men, Dad. I hated them with a vengeance I can't even begin to describe. All the time I was at the school, all the time they were treating me like an animal, I hated them.'

She sniffed and rubbed her eyes again. 'From the moment we arrived at the school, my mother didn't say a single word to me. She'd stopped being my mother. She'd stopped being anything. She was like a zombie. Every time the door opened, she'd just lie down and wait for them to get on top of her. I took care of her, I washed her, I fed her, but it was like caring for a baby. She didn't even acknowledge me.'

'I'm sorry,' Freeman said. The words sounded so futile.

'After two months, my mother was pregnant. Two months, Dad. Sixty days. Thirty or forty men every day.

She started to get sick in the morning and the nurse told her she was pregnant. That night my mother pulled a small piece of brick from the wall and used it to gouge her wrists open. We didn't hear a thing. She just bled to death quietly.'

Tears trickled down Freeman's cheeks. Mersiha reached up and wiped them away with her hand. 'The following morning they dragged her body out. Then I was raped again. And again. And again. It was as if they were punishing me for my mother's suicide. I never got pregnant, though. I guess I was too young. Too young to have children, but not too young to be raped. I thought I'd die in that place. I thought they'd drag my body out like they'd done with my mother.'

'What happened?'

'Stjepan rescued me. Stjepan and his friends. It was about a month after my mother died. We heard shots and we thought they'd started to kill the women, that the Serbs were moving out and didn't want to leave anyone behind. There were screams outside, and shooting, and then the door was thrown open. We were crouched together in a corner. A soldier stood in the doorway and several of the women begged him not to shoot. Not me. I was ready to die. I wanted to die. I wanted it all to be over so that I could be with my mother and father. But he didn't shoot. He said we were free. We thought he was lying, that it was some sort of trick, but he led us outside into the sunshine, the first time I'd seen the sun in three months. Stjepan was there. I rushed to him and jumped up. He caught me and held me to him with one hand. In the other he had a Kalashnikov. I couldn't believe it was him. I thought he was a ghost. I thought God had made him an angel and that he'd come to take me to Heaven. I thought it was God's way of proving to me that He really did exist. But it wasn't. It was Stjepan, come to rescue me. He asked me where our mother was and I had to tell him that she was dead. He wanted to know if I could recognise any of the men who'd hurt us and I said I'd try. I didn't want to tell him there'd been so many that they'd all started to look the same.'

Mersiha's words were coming faster and faster, a torrent that he couldn't have stopped even if he'd wanted to.

'He took me outside. There were about twenty Serbs sitting on the ground, their hands tied behind them, and Stjepan's friends were standing around them. There were dead bodies everywhere, but I wasn't looking at them, I was looking at the faces of the men who were sitting on the ground. They were scared, like dogs. None of them would look me in the eye. I recognised three of them. I'd watched one of them rape my mother and do other stuff to her, soon after we'd arrived at the school. He'd made her say things while he was doing it to her, things about my father. He'd hit her and hit her until she said the things he wanted. Another of the men had laughed and watched. The third had done it to her, then he'd done it to me right afterwards, while another soldier forced her to watch. I pointed them out to Stjepan, and told them what they'd done.'

Mersiha looked down at Freeman's hand. She raised it to her cheek and pressed it against the flesh. It was wet from her tears.

'Stjepan gave me a knife. A big hunting knife. He didn't have to tell me what to do. There was no need. I stood behind the third man, the one who'd hurt my mother and me, and I grabbed his hair and I slit his throat the way the butcher used to kill his pigs. He was the first man I ever killed.' She sniffed softly. 'He was the first thing I'd ever killed. I'd never killed an animal or an insect and I wouldn't even go fishing with my father because I thought it was cruel. I killed him and then I killed the two other Serbs. I remember looking at the blood on my hands and being pleased. I wanted to do it again, I wanted to kill them all, but Stjepan said no. He said that it was only right if there was a reason. Does that make sense?'

Freeman didn't know what to say. 'It made sense to him, pumpkin.' His voice was barely a whisper.

'Stjepan said I had to go with him because there was no one else to look after me. That night he saw that three of my hairs were white. I'd never noticed them before. That's when he told me the story about my hair. One white hair for each killing. To remind me.' She reached up and ran her fingers through her hair as if sorting out a tangle. 'I'm sorry, Dad,' she said.

'You've nothing to be sorry for,' Freeman said.

'You don't understand,' she said, avoiding his eyes.

Freeman frowned, not sure what she meant. 'Is there something else? Something else you want to tell me?'

She shrugged. 'On the mountain today, you said that killing could never be justified.'

He stroked her hair and nudged it behind her ear. 'I was speaking as a father. You know how it works – do as I say, not as I do. I was telling you what I thought was right. I didn't mean to condemn you for something over which you had no control.'

'But that's what you think, isn't it? You don't believe that killing is ever right. That's why you hated going shooting with Katherine's dad, isn't it?'

'If you're asking me do I abhor killing, the answer's yes. But if you're asking me if you did the right thing when Stjepan gave you the knife . . . that I can't answer. I really can't. I can't even begin to imagine what you went through, the anger and hurt you must have felt. If I'd been you, maybe I'd have done the same thing. Maybe I'd have been so angry, that the only way I could have released it would have been to take revenge, to have killed the men responsible.'

'But I did wrong, didn't I?'

Freeman couldn't understand why she kept pushing him. It was as if she wanted to be condemned for what she'd done. 'I don't know, Mersiha. I'm not the ultimate judge of what's right and what's wrong.'

'Who is?'

'God, I suppose.'

Mersiha sneered. 'That's a cop-out, Dad, and you know it. There is no God. Just life and then death.'

'You can't say that.'

'Yes, I can. Oh yes, I can. If there was a God He wouldn't have let my mother suffer like she did, and He wouldn't have let my father die trying to help someone else. And if there is a God, I don't think He has any right to tell me what's right and what's wrong, not after what He allowed to happen in Bosnia.' The tears had stopped and now all he saw was anger in her eyes. 'You don't believe in God, either. You know you don't. You know that if there was a God He wouldn't have let Luke die the way He did. Suffer the children. Yeah, right. Fucking right.'

It was the first time Freeman had ever heard her swear, yet he didn't admonish her. He couldn't. He averted his eyes.

She put her hands up to her face. 'I'm sorry, Dad. I didn't mean that. Please, I'm sorry.' Freeman shook his head. 'Don't hate me, please don't hate me,' she said. She threw her hands around his neck and hugged him.

'I don't hate you, pumpkin. I love you more than anything in the world.'

'I'm sorry. I'm so sorry for everything.'

Freeman had a sudden intuition, a feeling that there was more she wanted to say. He smoothed her hair with the flat of his hand. 'I know it's painful, telling me what happened to you and to your parents, but by talking about it you'll eventually come to terms with it,' he said. 'It's not good to lock things away. When Luke died, I wouldn't talk about it for a long, long time. In fact, if anyone tried to talk about him I used to resent it, as if by speaking his name they were taking something away from me. Katherine and I didn't talk about what had happened, not for the longest time. Even now, she doesn't like talking about it, even though I know she thinks about him constantly.' Mersiha didn't say anything but she squeezed him around the neck. Freeman stared out of the window as he spoke, at the stars millions of miles away. 'I think Katherine still blames me for his death. I've tried to get her to talk about it, but she just brushes me away. She says that she doesn't think it was my fault, that it was just a terrible accident, but I know that deep down she resents me for what happened. I wish she'd just let it out, then maybe I could try to make it better.' His voice began to shake and he forced himself to take several deep breaths. 'Silence makes it worse, pumpkin. Believe me.'

'It wasn't your fault, Dad.'

'Yes, it was. I let him take his seat belt off. I let him sit on my lap. If I hadn't done that, Luke would still be alive.'

'And maybe if Luke was still alive, I'd have died in the camp because you wouldn't have wanted me.'

Freeman was shocked by the statement. 'Oh no, don't ever think that,' he said. 'You've never been a replacement for Luke. Our love for you has nothing to do with losing him. When I told you that the day we were on the boat, I meant it.'

Mersiha nodded slowly. 'Okay,' she said. 'I'm sorry.'

'Katherine and I are now your mother and father, and we'll stand by you no matter what.' He looked at her expectantly, hoping that she'd tell him what else was on her mind. For a second it looked as if she was about to say something, but then he saw the shutters come down behind her eyes. Whatever it was, she wasn't going to tell him just then. She wiped her eyes with the backs of her hands and smiled bravely.

'I feel better now,' she said. 'I'm glad you were here when I woke up.' She slid down under the quilt and smiled up at him.

Freeman kissed her on the forehead. 'Sleep well,' he whispered.

She closed her eyes and snuggled down as if she didn't have a care in the world. Freeman sat looking at her. He wasn't fooled. She'd told him more about herself in one day than she had in the previous three years, but he was sure that she was still hiding something.

The sound of the two engines was mind-numbing, despite the noise-cancelling headset that Clive had given Katherine to wear. Her ears were sweating and it felt as if her head was in a vice. Clive had been right – it wasn't a pleasant way to travel. The small plane was constantly buffeted by pockets of turbulence and at times it felt as if she was on a roller-coaster. The headset crackled. 'Are you okay, Mrs Freeman?' he asked.

'I'm fine,' she answered.

Clive was twisting around in his seat while the co-pilot, a young Hispanic, handled the controls. 'It's just that you were looking a little green back there.'

'Well, first class it isn't,' she said with a smile.

'There's a sick-bag under the seat.'

'I'll be okay.'

'Don't be embarrassed, we all get airsick from time to time.'

Katherine nodded and Clive turned back to scan the instruments. It was pitch dark outside, though there were flashes of lightning far off to the left. Katherine looked down into the darkness below. It was impossible to tell if they were flying over fields, hills or water. She shuddered to think what would happen if anything went wrong and they had to land in the blackness. She looked at her watch for the thousandth time. They'd been in the air for five hours and had already landed once to refuel. Clive had said they were making good time and if the winds stayed favourable they'd arrive in Boulder shortly after dawn. He'd been about to file a flight plan for Denver when Katherine had told him that her ultimate destination was Estes Park. He'd suggested they land at Boulder because it was slightly closer, and because the landing fees would be considerably smaller than at the international airport.

The seat was cramped and uncomfortable and there was

barely any leg-room. Her shoulders ached and she badly wanted to go to the lavatory. Clive had shown her the plastic container that could be used in an emergency, but there was no way on God's earth that she would ever dream of using it. Clive and the co-pilot were talking on the intercom but she couldn't hear anything. Clive was nodding towards the thunderstorm and the co-pilot made a small correction to the right. Katherine looked at the instruments, illuminated by soft orange lights, but she couldn't make any sense of them. Her eyes were hurting and she rubbed them with the backs of her hands. She hadn't eaten for more than twelve hours but she wasn't hungry. Her stomach was churning, partly from the rough ride but mainly because she was so worried about Tony and Mersiha. Utsyev would already have landed at Denver and would be on his way to Estes Park. Her one hope was that he wouldn't be able to speak to the estate agent who'd rented the cabin until their office opened. She still had a chance. She closed her eyes and prayed that she'd get there in time. She promised God anything, absolutely anything, if He'd just make sure that Tony and Mersiha were okay.

Freeman sat on a chair by Mersiha's bed and watched her sleep. She looked angelic with her eyes closed, and he wanted nothing more than to be able to protect her and take care of her. He could understand now why he had seen such hatred in her eyes when they'd first met. She must have hated anyone connected with the Serbs. He realised now how stupid he'd been to accept Anderson's advice to try to sell their equipment to the Serbian forces. He could scarcely believe that he'd actually gone there to help the men who'd been responsible for the atrocities Mersiha had been talking about. At the time he'd convinced himself that the CRW equipment was defensive rather than offensive, but now looking back he knew that he'd let commercial considerations override his moral obligations. He was disgusted with himself for being connected in any way to the suffering of his adopted daughter. Mersiha had been constantly saying sorry, as if what had happened in Bosnia had been her fault, but in fact it was Freeman who should have been apologising.

Mersiha began snoring softly, and he could see from her unlined brow that she was sleeping peacefully. He crept out of her room and went to lie down on his own bed. Sleep eluded him and he lay staring up at the ceiling, determined that he would do whatever he could to make up for the suffering Mersiha had experienced. She would never be hurt again, he promised himself.

Utsyev slept fitfully for a couple of hours and then awoke with a raging thirst. He went to the bathroom and drank from the tap. His head ached as if he had the mother of all hangovers, but he knew that it wasn't the alcohol that was to blame. Sagalle had been right – it was the altitude that was hurting him. Utsyev couldn't understand why anyone would want to live above a thousand feet. The top of the Empire State Building was as high as he ever wanted to go.

He splashed cold water on his face and stared at his reflection in the mirror. He looked terrible, and he knew it. His skin was tired, his eyes were bleary and his hair was dry and lifeless. He looked like a walking corpse. He grinned at the thought, and a mirthless skull sneered back at him from the mirror.

There was a timid knock on the door. Utsyev wrapped a towel around his waist before he answered it. It was Kiseleva, dressed in a red plaid shirt and blue jeans. He looked like a typical redneck, thought Utsyev, and the outfit suited him. Kiseleva held out a bag full of clothing. 'Sagalle dropped these off. And there are two Jeep Grand Cherokee V8s outside.'

'Guns?'

Kiseleva nodded. 'A really sweet Colt .357 Magnum Python, a Smith & Wesson, and a couple of SIG-Sauer P230s with silencers.'

'Good. Are the others here?'

'They're in my room. We ordered sandwiches from room service.'

Utsyev took the bag. 'I'll be there in half an hour. Then we leave. Make sure they're ready.' He closed the door in Kiseleva's face and shook his head in annoyance. Why did Kiseleva think he'd want to know about the catering arrangements?

He showered and shaved before changing into his tourist's outfit: a gingham check shirt as tasteless as the one Kiseleva had been wearing, a pair of stcne-washed denim jeans, a Navy pea jacket and hiking boots. He studied his reflection in the mirror. It reminded him of how he used to dress, back in the Soviet Union; clothes worn for their function rather than their style. His headache had gotten worse and he massaged his temples with the palms of his hands, trying to squeeze out the pain. His stomach felt queasy and he was definitely short of breath. He went down the corridor to Kiseleva's room. They were all there, six of them, sitting on the king-size bed eating club sandwiches and drinking coffee like a group of duck-hunters waiting for first light. A suitcase lay on the floor and Kiseleva opened it to reveal the handguns and ammunition. Sagalle had thought of everything. Utsyev didn't like being in Carelli's debt. He had no choice because he carried no weight in Colorado, but he knew that a price would have to be paid eventually. Men like Carelli didn't do favours from the goodness of their hearts. They made loans, that was all, and the time would come when Utsyev would have to pay the man back, one way or another.

Jenny nodded at Utsyev and raised her cup. 'Do you want coffee, Bzuchar?' She'd tied her hair up and hidden it under a fur-lined hat.

Utsyev shook his head. She was the only one of his team who ever used his first name. It was a privilege she had earned over the years. 'We ready?' he asked. 'Who's driving?' Vincenti raised his hand. So did Kiseleva.

The two Cherokee Jeeps arrived in Estes Park while it was still dark. The town had a deserted feel to it. There were no vehicles on the roads and the only living thing they saw was a young deer walking timidly across a side street. They drove through the town and came to a halt in a deserted parking lot illuminated by a single light. Vincenti climbed out and walked over to Utsyev's vehicle. 'What now, boss?' he asked.

'The rental agent,' Utsyev said. 'They'll have details of Freeman's cabin.'

'They probably won't open until nine,' Kiseleva said at his side. Jenny snorted in the back seat and Utsyev glared at his driver.

'We ain't gonna wait until they open, shit-for-brains. We ain't gonna go in and ask nicely like we were relatives up for a visit or something.'

'Sorry, boss,' Kiseleva said.

'Yeah,' Utsyev said coldly. He turned to Vincenti. 'You know what to do.' He handed over the brochure he'd taken from Freeman's house. 'We'll go out of town. It's gonna look too suspicious two Jeeps parked together like this. I'll see you back here in an hour.' Utsyev gestured for Kiseleva to drive and rubbed his temples again. Jenny leaned forward and held out her hand. Two white painkillers nestled in her palm. He took them gratefully.

Katherine opened her eyes and yawned. The horizon was a red smear and down below was a forest of pines. She looked at her watch and realised she'd slept for almost two hours, despite the noise and discomfort. Her mouth tasted bitter and she swallowed. Clive twisted around in his seat and grinned, handing her a Diet Coke. It was warm but she popped the tab and drank it gratefully.

'We'll be landing at Boulder within the hour,' he said through the intercom.

'Great,' she said, rubbing the back of her neck. She smiled but she had a feeling of impending doom. An image kept flashing through her mind of a big, hulking man in a dark overcoat, hiding in the shadows with a gun, waiting for her husband and daughter. She shuddered.

According to the map, the rental office was set back from Elkhorn Avenue, the main thoroughfare through Estes Park. It was impossible to miss – next to the timber building with a sharply sloping shingle roof was a large billboard advertising the firm's services.

The building stood alone with a small parking lot behind it. Vincenti parked by the rear entrance, next to which stood a line of trash cans like soldiers on parade. He switched off the engine and turned to Ostrovetsky in the front passenger seat, who was managing to make the spacious four-wheel-drive look cramped. 'You go and check it out. We'll wait here,' he said.

Ostrovetsky grunted and got out of the car. Vincenti and the remaining two passengers watched him amble over to the door and bend down to inspect the lock. 'He's a big one,' Vincenti said.

'Used to be a college linebacker,' said the man sitting directly behind him.

'Yeah, he was gonna go pro, until the accident,' said the other man.

'What, he got hurt?'

'Nah. He killed a guy, practically took off his head.'

Ostrovetsky walked back to the Cherokee and Vincenti

wound the window down. Ostrovetsky had to bend down to get his head level with Vincenti's. 'Door's pretty strong. I can force it but it'll make a lot of noise.'

'What about the locks?'

Ostrovetsky held out his right hand. It was huge with thick sausage-like fingers. It wasn't the hand of a lock-picker. 'There's a window we can smash. It seems to lead into a storage room. But I won't be able to get through.' He waggled his massive shoulders and there was no need for further explanation.

Vincenti twisted around in his seat. Utsyev's men grinned at him. There was no doubt that Vincenti was the smallest of the four. 'Great,' he said. 'You go ahead and break the window, I'll climb inside.'

Vincenti started the Cherokee again as Ostrovetsky picked up one of the trash cans with no more effort than if he'd been lifting a tin of beans. Vincenti gunned the accelerator as Ostrovetsky charged forward and slammed the metal container into the window. There was a loud crash followed by the tinkle of falling glass, but it was all over in a few seconds and Vincenti doubted that anyone would have heard. There was no traffic on the road and the nearest neighbour was a ski shop which had a sign on the door saying it was closed until April. Vincenti joined Ostrovetsky by the broken window and they carefully pulled out the remaining shards of glass.

Ostrovetsky made a step with his giant hands and bent down to lift Vincenti through the window. Vincenti wasn't a small man, but Ostrovetsky lifted him with a minimum of effort, as smoothly as a hydraulic ram. Vincenti had to wriggle through and drop face down on to the floor, holding out his hands to break his fall and rolling over on to his side. As he stood up and brushed dirt off his jacket he felt a sharp pain in his right hand and realised that there was a glass splinter in his thumb. He pulled it out and tried the door to the storage room. It wasn't locked and he found himself in a corridor. At one end was the rear door, and he slipped back the bolts and opened it. Ostrovetsky filled the doorway as he stepped inside.

The two of them walked through to the main office. It contained two large teak desks, several metal filing cabinets, a fax machine and a photocopier. On the walls were several posters of the Rocky Mountain National Park and a day-by-day calendar marked up with several different coloured pens. Vincenti studied it but there were no clues as to the whereabouts of Freeman and the girl.

The filing cabinets weren't locked. One of them was labelled 'Cabins' and Vincenti handed half the files to Ostrovetsky. As they went through them, they dropped the files on to the floor. With the smashed window, there was no point in trying to cover their tracks. In fact they wanted to make it seem as much like an opportunistic robbery as possible.

'Got it,' Ostrovetsky said. He handed a photocopied map from the file to Vincenti.

'Perfect,' Vincenti said as he studied it. 'Nice and isolated.'

The small plane taxied to a halt and the co-pilot killed the engines. When the propellers had stopped whirling, Clive helped Katherine out on to the tarmac. 'Are you going to be okay?' he asked.

Katherine rubbed her ears which were still ringing from the prolonged engine noise. 'I just need to rent a car, that's all.'

'There'll be plenty of rental places in the main terminal,' he said. 'Do you want us to wait for you? You're paying for the return flight anyway.'

Katherine shook her head. 'No, you guys go on your own. I'll fly back with my family.'

'Are you sure you don't want the police?' Katherine hadn't told him why she was in such a hurry to get to Colorado, but he'd guessed that something was badly wrong.

'No. Absolutely not. I'll be okay.' She handed her headset to him.

'We probably won't leave until this evening. We'll have to get some shuteye. If you need us . . .'

Katherine stepped forward impulsively and kissed him on the cheek. 'Thanks,' she said. She turned on her heel and dashed towards the terminal.

Freeman woke to the smell of frying bacon and steaming coffee. He pulled on his jeans and a shirt and padded to the kitchen. Mersiha was in front of the stove, her hair tied back, wearing one of his shirts. He smiled at her bare legs and unkempt hair – they reminded him of how Katherine used to cook breakfast for him on Sunday mornings, soon after they were first married, in the good old days before she worried about his cholesterol intake. 'Full Scottish breakfast?' she asked.

'You read my mind.' He watched her as she turned back to the stove. She looked happy and relaxed. It was hard to believe it was the same girl who'd been crying in his arms the previous night.

'How long have we got?' she asked.

Freeman looked at his watch. 'About an hour.' It was six o'clock and the sun had yet to put in an appearance. Most of the stables bordering the Rocky Mountain National Park had closed for the off season, but after thirty minutes' ringing around the day before Freeman had managed to find a small family-owned ranch on the edge of the national park which offered to take him and Mersiha for a trail ride so long as they were prepared to make an early start. It had been several years since Freeman had been in the saddle, and he was looking forward to it.

Mersiha slid a fried egg on to a plate and added bacon, sausage, mushrooms and fried bread. She put the food down in front of him. 'One thousand two hundred,' she said.

'What?'

'Calories.'

Freeman grinned at her. 'I've a busy day ahead of me. Growing boy like me, I need my food.'

She laughed, and it sounded like the real thing to Freeman. 'Dad, I hate to tell you this, but you stopped growing some time ago.'

He shrugged and tucked into his meal. 'Did you sleep okay? After . . . you know . . .' His voice tailed off.

She shrugged noncommittally. 'No more nightmares, if that's what you mean.' She reached over and patted his arm as if apologising for her defensiveness. 'That didn't come out right,' she said. 'I meant I slept just fine. How's the breakfast?'

'Fast disappearing.' She poured him a cup of strong coffee and he nodded his thanks. 'We should call Katherine this morning. After our ride, maybe. I didn't manage to get hold of her last night.'

'Sure.' Her eyes narrowed. 'Dad, about last night?'

Freeman raised his eyes expectantly. 'What?'

'You won't tell her, will you? About what happened to me?'

'Not if you don't want me to, no.'

She sighed with relief, then turned his wrist around so that she could see his watch. 'I'd better change.'

The girl at the car rental desk shrugged as she studied her computer. 'I'm sorry, Mrs Freeman,' she said. 'We don't have any four-wheel-drives.'

'I'll take anything you have,' Katherine said, dropping her gold American Express card and driving licence on to the counter.

'For how many days?'

Katherine lit a cigarette and inhaled deeply. 'Just one.'

'I can offer you a Ford Mustang. How does that sound?'

'What about something bigger?'

'I have a Lincoln Continental.'

'Perfect.'

'There's a telephone in it, but I won't charge you for that unless you use it.'

'Fine.'

'Will you require personal accident insurance?'

Katherine burst out laughing.

The two Cherokee Jeeps drove slowly down Devil's Gulch Road. 'It should be just there, on the right,' Utsyev said.

'Yeah, there's a turn-off,' Jenny said.

'That's it,' Utsyev agreed.

'Maybe it'd be better if one of us went in on foot,' Jenny suggested.

'Do you want to do it?' Utsyev asked.

'Sure,' she said. 'I could play the helpless little lady. Gee, I seem to be lost. Can I have a drink of water, pretty please?' She fluttered her eyelids.

'Maybe,' Utsyev said, not convinced.

'What's the alternative, Bzuchar? They're gonna know something's wrong if we all turn up at once. We're not exactly inconspicuous as a group, are we?'

'I just don't wanna lose them. If we spook them . . .'

'They're less likely to get spooked if they see me,' she interrupted. 'I'll talk my way into the house, then when I've got them covered . . . well, you know the rest. You'll have all the time you want . . .'

'. . . for a picnic,' Utsyev finished, grinning.

'Yeah. For a picnic.'

He nodded his approval. He admired Jenny's guts. She wasn't afraid to make suggestions and to defend them if he didn't see things her way. The rest of his team were nothing more than yes-men most of the time, scared of offending him. When he asked for suggestions they'd look at each other like frightened rabbits, trying to second-guess him rather than telling him what they really felt. Jenny had more balls than any of them. Figuratively speaking. 'Okay,' he said. 'We'll wait here.'

'Someone's coming, boss,' Kiseleva said.

A Ford Bronco drove slowly down the track that led to the Freeman cabin. A man was driving and in the passenger seat was a young girl, laughing and fingering her long black hair. 'It's them!' Utsyev hissed. 'Drive on. Quick.'

Kiseleva accelerated away and the second Cherokee followed. The Bronco turned on to Devil's Gulch Road and drove northward.

'So much for my plan,' Jenny muttered in the back.

'You'll have your chance,' Utsyev said. 'Let's see where they're going.'

The two Cherokees did quick U-turns and drove after Freeman and his daughter, taking care to keep well back. Dawn was only just breaking and there was still very little traffic on the road.

Freeman flicked through the channels on the radio until he found a country and western station. 'Might as well get us in the mood,' he said.

'Do you think they'll let us go up into the snow?' Mersiha asked.

'With the horses you mean?'

'Yeah. I've never ridden in snow before. It'd be really neat.'

'We can ask. If the horses are up to it, I certainly am.' He slowed down, looking out for the stable. The old man on the phone had warned that the entrance was easy to miss. He drove by a store selling Indian crafts, and a run-down bar, and braked sharply as he saw corralled horses off in the distance. A short while later he saw the entrance, little more than a packed dirt track that led to a ramshackle wooden bridge. He drove slowly over the bridge, looking down on a shallow stream which seemed to be frozen for the winter. The track curved by a small wooden cabin and up to a large red-painted barn. He parked the Bronco and Mersiha rushed over to the corral to look at the horses. A black and white gelding walked over to her and she blew softly up its nose, making friends. There didn't seem to be anyone around so Freeman sounded his horn twice. The door to the log cabin opened and a gangly teenager appeared. He was wearing a turquoise shirt, too-tight Wrangler jeans, weathered brown boots and spurs that jingled while he walked. He introduced himself as Matt, their guide. He pulled on a faded denim jacket before leading two quarter-horses out of the barn.

'Can you both ride?' he asked.

'Sure,' Freeman said. 'Mainly English-style, though.'

Matt's upper lip curled. 'Western's pretty different,' he said.

'We've ridden Western before,' Mersiha said quickly.

'Yeah?' Matt sneered.

'Yeah,' she said. She patted the neck of one of the horses he was leading, a dark chestnut gelding. 'What's his name?' she asked.

'Red,' Matt said. 'He's a bit headstrong, so your dad should ride him.'

Mersiha gave Matt a cold smile and in a smooth, fluid movement slipped her foot into a stirrup and swung up into the saddle. Before Matt could react she picked up the reins, kicked the horse in the girth with her heels and urged it on. With no apparent effort she walked the horse forward, then turned it left and rode it in a tight figure of eight. She pulled the reins in and the horse stopped dead, then, keeping her eyes on Matt, she pulled harder and walked the horse slowly backwards, then stopped it in its tracks again. She raised one eyebrow, daring Matt to fault her technique.

Freeman thought that Matt was going to yell at her, but a grin slowly spread across the teenager's face. He looked across at Freeman. 'She can ride all right,' he said.

'She's better than I am,' Freeman agreed. 'Maybe I should take the mare.'

'Okay. Her name's Sarah. You'll have to give her a good kick to get her going uphill, but she's steady as a rock. You want a three-hour trail ride, right?'

'Sure,' Freeman said.

'We can't go too high – there's some deep drifts up there and we had an avalanche over to the west a couple of days ago – but I can show you some of the lower trails.' He looked up into the bright blue sky. 'Got a good day for it, too. It was snowing some in Denver last night, but it looks like it's gonna miss us.' He went over to his own mount, a frisky white Arabian gelding tethered to a post to the side of the barn. The horse's ears pricked up as Matt untied him and climbed into the saddle. 'There are some rules we have to follow,' he said after Freeman had mounted his mare. 'We have to ride single file along the trails, with me leading. If at any time you want to stop, to take a photograph or if you drop something, then we all stop. We don't run the horses, ever. Keep your horse on a very loose rein – that's how we work them here. You have to work with these horses, not against them. Always hold the reins with one hand.' He turned to Mersiha. 'If you see Red's ears go flat then slap him on the neck. It means he's going to kick.'

Mersiha nodded. 'We can't run them at all?'

'No,' Matt said. 'It doesn't matter how good a rider you are, our insurance won't cover it. You stay behind me all the time.' Mersiha's face fell. Freeman knew she was more than capable of controlling a horse at the gallop, whether on an English or Western saddle. 'Okay, let's move out,' Matt said. He headed up a trail that wound its way through the wooded hillside. 'Keep your eye out for deer,' he said over his shoulder. 'Might even see an elk if we're lucky.'

The horses moved at a steady pace and clearly knew the trail. Freeman's horse needed no urging. The only guidance he had to give her was if she walked too close to a tree and he was in danger of banging his leg. Matt was a cheerful guide and pointed out the various types of trees they passed. He showed Mersiha the difference between the Ponderosa pine, with its reddish-brown scaly bark and strong smell of vanilla, and the Limber pine with its shorter needles and edible seeds. The pines predominated on the lower levels of the slopes; at higher elevations were the Englemann and Blue spruces, and higher still were Limber pine that had been deformed by the wind into nightmarish bent and twisted shapes, like arthritic old relatives of the straight, proud trees on the lower slopes.

'You know a lot about the mountains, don't you?' Mersiha asked.

Matt nodded. 'I was born here. Learned to ride when I was four on a horse the size of Red there.' He brought his mount to a sudden halt and raised his arm, motioning for Freeman and Mersiha to stop. He pointed off to the left. Freeman squinted through the trees, wondering what he was looking at. All he could see were patches of packed snow and the evergreen trees, but then he noticed something move behind a juniper bush, something that looked like a medium-sized German shepherd dog but was grey in colour with white fur on its underside and legs. The dog stopped and its ears pricked up as it sniffed the air. It was joined by a second dog, slightly smaller with reddish head and ears. They both stared at the three riders for a few seconds, then disappeared among the trees.

'Coyotes,' Matt explained. 'They usually hunt in pairs. We're lucky – you don't see them much around here.'

'There they go,' Kiseleva said, handing the binoculars to Utsyev. 'Just the two of them, and a guide.'

Utsyev focused the binoculars on the three riders. His lips tightened as Mersiha came into focus. It was her. The girl who'd killed his brother.

'What do you wanna do, boss? Do you want to wait for them?' Kiseleva asked.

'Why wait?' Utsyev snarled. 'We can do them in the woods and bury them where no one will ever find them.'

'What about the guide?'

Utsyev turned slowly and glared at Kiseleva. 'What is this? Are you worrying about innocent bystanders all of a sudden? My brother's body still warm and you're bleating about who gets hurt and who doesn't?'

Kiseleva's head jerked back as if he'd been struck in the face. 'I didn't mean nothing by it, boss. I just thought it might be less trouble to wait for them to go back to the cabin, that's all.'

'The longer we hang around, the more likely we'll attract attention. Let's do it now.'

Kiseleva nodded sullenly and climbed out of the Cherokee. He waved to the men in the second vehicle to get out. A plume of smoke trickled from the chimney of a wooden cabin but no one came out as the men followed Utsyev over to the barn. As they got closer they could see that the paint was peeling from the wood and that the doors were sagging on their hinges. Rusting farm equipment lay around as if the owner of the property had lost interest in his surroundings. A metal notice had been nailed to one of the doors, warning that horse-riding was a dangerous business and that the stables took no responsibility for any accidents. Another notice forbade alcohol on the premises. Behind the barn was a large corral containing a dozen horses. Utsyev turned to look at his men. 'Any of you ridden before?' The men looked at each other, shrugging and shaking their heads. Only Jenny nodded. 'Terrific,' Utsyev said. He walked into the barn. The smell of horse manure was overpowering. Along the right side of the barn were stalls, but they were all empty. To the left was an office of sorts with an old desk on which lay an exercise book containing signatures and addresses. It was open, and against that day's date there were two names: Mersiha Freeman and Tony Freeman. Utsyev cleared his throat noisily and spat at the open page. The phlegm smeared the ink as it dripped down the book.

Kiseleva appeared at his shoulder. 'Get those horses saddled up,' Utsyev told him. Kiseleva looked as if he was about to protest, but Utsyev silenced him by pointing an accusing finger at his nose. 'Don't say a word, just do it. Ask Jenny how.'

Next to the office was a room full of tack, with saddles hanging on thick poles above the names of their horses. Three of the poles were empty. Utsyev scratched his chin. Matching the horses to the proper saddles was going to be a problem. Locating Midnight and Silver probably wouldn't be too difficult, but Montana and Bertha? He wondered if it mattered much whether the horses got the correct saddles or not. Kiseleva sniffed as he looked at the saddles, obviously thinking the same thing.

Utsyev walked out of the barn. Something squelched under his left foot and he looked down. He cursed and used the side of the barn to scrape the dung off his boot. A tall, white-haired man with skin like chamois leather came out of the cabin. He walked with a bow-legged strut towards Utsyev, waving a stick-like arm. 'Can I help you gentlemen?' he called, his voice a throaty growl that suggested too many cigars and cheap whiskey.

'We'd like to hire some horses,' Utsyev said.

'Can't help you just now. I've only got the one guide and he's out on a ride. He's gonna be gone for three or four hours. But I can book you in for a trail ride tomorrow.' He stood in front of Utsyev, his hands on his hips. They were of a similar build, though Utsyev was a couple of inches shorter.

'We want the horses now,' Utsyev said.

'I just said that's not possible,' the man said, frowning.

'I heard what you said.'

Kiseleva stiffened and reached inside his jacket with his right hand, but Utsyev flashed him a warning glance and the hand reappeared. The look that passed across the wrangler's weatherbeaten face was so transparent in its guile that Utsyev almost smiled. 'Maybe I could get another guide over here. I'll just have to use the phone.'

'Why don't you do that?' Utsyev said agreeably.

The old man nodded thoughtfully, then walked slowly back to the cabin. Utsyev motioned with his head for Kiseleva to go after the man. 'And use the fucking silencer,' he warned.

The rest of the men were standing at the edge of the corral, pointing at the horses. Utsyev went over to them. 'Get a horse each. The equipment is in the barn.' He waved Jenny over. 'Make sure these guys put the saddles on the right way, will you? If they do it themselves they'll end up facing the horse's arse.'

Jenny grinned. 'Sure.'

'You'll be able to catch up with them?'

She shaded her eyes with her hand and peered up the slope. 'Shouldn't be a problem. They're just walking along the trail.'

'Okay,' Utsyev said. 'What are you carrying?'

'A P230 and silencer.'

He reached into his jacket and pulled out his Ingram machine pistol and suppressor and gave it to her. 'Take this, I'll take the P230.' They exchanged guns. 'I want you in charge up there,' he continued. 'You tell them what to do and when to do it.'

'You're not coming?'

434

Utsyev patted his chest. 'I'm having too much trouble breathing. It's like I'm always gasping, you know? Like I was breathing through a pillow. And my heart is racing like a fucking train.'

'The altitude,' Jenny said sympathetically. 'Don't worry, I'll take care of it.'

'I know you will,' Utsyev said. 'You're about the only one I can truly rely on these days.' He stepped forward and hugged her impulsively, patting her on the back in a gesture that was devoid of all sexuality. 'Kill them both and bury them up there,' he whispered into her ear. 'But I want you to bring me back the girl's head. I wanna piss in the dead bitch's mouth.' He patted her on the back again, and then stepped back. Jenny went over to the tack-room with the men, and a minute later they all reappeared with rope lassoes. One by one they stepped through the rails of the corral and began catching their mounts. One thing was for sure, Utsyev thought wryly as Ostrovetsky was dragged face down through the mud. These guys would never be mistaken for cowboys.

Jenny showed the men how to catch their horses and lead them into the barn. Kiseleva came out of the cabin and closed the door behind him. 'It's done, boss,' he said.

'Good,' Utsyev said. 'Now listen, and listen good. I want Jenny giving the orders up there, okay? She speaks for me. Make sure the guys know that, will ya?'

'Sure, boss. Where will you be?'

'I'm gonna be at Freeman's cabin. You're to stay up in the mountains until they're dead.' He fixed Kiseleva with a cold stare. 'I mean this, Kiseleva. Jenny gives the orders. If she says jump, I want you all leaping like fucking frogs, right?'

* * *

Freeman gave his horse a good kick in the ribs, but the mare refused to go any faster. She was also reluctant to change direction. If he wanted to go left around a tree and the horse wanted to go to the right, then to the right they went, no matter how much he tugged on the reins. As far as he was concerned, the trail ride was proving to be as challenging as a donkey ride on Blackpool beach. Ahead of him, Mersiha was doing much better. Despite Matt's instructions she was keeping the gelding on a close rein and she seemed to have him under complete control. She looked over her shoulder and grinned. 'How are you getting on?' she called.

'It's the getting off that I'm more worried about,' he shouted back. They followed Matt as he rode through the trees, up a narrow trail that at times almost seemed to disappear. Freeman realised it was probably little used during the off season, though the horses had no trouble knowing where to go.

'Giddy up,' Freeman said. As he expected, there was no response. 'Gee up.' Still nothing. 'Yee ha,' he said hopefully. The mare snorted contemptuously and Freeman settled back in the saddle, the reins loose in his left hand. 'Oh well, I might as well enjoy the ride,' he said. The horse snorted softly in agreement.

Up ahead, Matt had stopped and was standing in his stirrups, looking back down the hill. Freeman turned to see what he was looking at. A group of six riders had just left the stables and was heading towards the treeline. Matt spurred his horse back down the trail. 'What's wrong?' Freeman asked.

'Those are our horses down there,' he said, frowning. 'There isn't another ride going out today. I'm the only guide working.'

Mersiha rode up behind them. 'What's going on?' she asked.

'You two stay here,' Matt said. 'I'll go down and talk to them. It could be they've been sent to join us.'

'I hope not,' Mersiha said disappointedly. 'I thought it was just going to be the three of us.'

Matt headed back down the trail. Freeman's horse immediately started after him, but stopped when he hauled back on his reins with all his might. Mersiha saw that he was having trouble and manoeuvred her horse in front of his to block its way. It worked. The two horses stood together, their breath forming clouds in the cold air. Freeman and Mersiha watched as Matt rode down the trail at a fast trot, ducking to avoid branches.

'Having fun?' Freeman asked.

'Oh yeah, this is great,' she gushed. 'I love Western-style, the saddles are so comfortable. And the horses are so smart. You hardly have to tell them anything. I mean, I love Wilbur and all, but his IQ is well below room temperature.'

Matt met the riders where the trail entered the trees. Freeman could just about see them through the pines. Matt was waving his arm. They looked like they were arguing, then suddenly one of the riders pointed at him and he fell back off his horse.

'Did you see that?' Mersiha cried.

Matt's horse galloped riderless back to the corral. 'They just shot him,' Freeman gasped.

'What? Are you sure?'

Five of the riders rode into the forest. The sixth, the one who'd first pointed at Matt, stood over the fallen guide and pointed at him again. This time Freeman heard a dull crack. 'I'm sure,' he said. 'And now they're coming after us.'

'Oh God,' Mersiha whispered.

'What the hell's going on?' Freeman said to himself.

'Oh God,' Mersiha repeated, her hand covering her mouth.

'Why?' said Freeman. 'Why would they kill him?'

'It's me,' Mersiha said.

'Of course it isn't. Don't be silly.'

'You don't understand. It's me they're after.'

Freeman stared at his daughter. They looked at each other in silence. Freeman could see from the look on her face that she was deathly afraid. 'Oh pumpkin, what have you done?'

She told him. As quickly as possible, she told him what she'd done. How she'd gone to see Sabatino. How Sabatino had tried to rape her. How she'd flashed back to the school. How she'd shot him. How they'd struggled for the gun. How he died. And how she'd run away, leaving the Heckler & Koch behind. Freeman sat stunned. Mersiha looked down the trail, shielding her eyes with her hands. 'They're coming, Dad. We're going to have to go.'

Freeman shook his head as if trying to clear his thoughts. He had barely managed to come to terms with what had happened to Mersiha three years earlier. Now he was faced with the revelation that the daughter he loved had killed a man. A man whom Maury Anderson had described as having Mafia connections. 'Mersiha . . .' he began.

'Dad, we don't have time. We have to go.' She pulled her horse around and headed up the mountain. Freeman followed, in a state of shock.

Jenny put the Ingram back in its sling. The cowboy lay sprawled at the foot of a pine tree, his blood soaking into the carpet of needles. The rest of Utsyev's crew were guiding their horses up the hillside. She smiled. None of them seemed at all at ease on horseback. Jenny had been brought up on a farm in Utah and had learned to ride almost as soon as she could walk. Her first pony was a gentle old mare called Tess. Her father would lead her, holding the reins and encouraging her. It seemed like a million years ago.

The horse she was riding was a jet-black gelding which she presumed was Midnight. He was big and strong and very responsive, and it took the merest pressure on his girth to move him forward and up the hill. The trail was narrow but he had a long stride and happily trotted whenever the ground was level. In a few minutes she'd caught up with the rest of the party. She could just about make out Freeman and the girl in the distance. They were moving up, towards the snowline. Vincenti took out his submachine pistol and pulled on his reins to steady his horse. 'You'll never get them from here,' she said.

'We'll see,' Vincenti said. He held the gun with two hands and sighted on the riders in the distance.

'You're wasting your time,' Jenny said.

Vincenti smiled tightly and pulled the trigger. The Ingram coughed and he kept the gun steady as he sprayed bullets through the trees. All he managed to hit were trees and bushes. Snow trickled from the branches above.

'I told you,' Jenny said. 'You're just wasting ammunition.' She kicked Midnight forward and the men followed her. She drove the horse hard and he seemed eager to obey. Her mount was sure-footed and after a few minutes of hard riding it was clear that they were gaining on Freeman and the girl. She looked over her shoulder. Utsyev's men were strung out behind her. They were having trouble keeping up. She smiled to herself. In New York they were tough guys, killers with diamond-hard reputations, but here in the wilderness they were fish out of water. The trail ducked down into a hollow and for a few moments she lost sight of her quarry. She wasn't worried. There was nowhere for them to go. The Ingram banged against her side. It was heavy and cumbersome and a bigger weapon than she was used to, but it would make short work of Freeman and the girl.

Midnight put his head down as he carried her up out of the hollow. The trail levelled off for a few hundred yards and she encouraged the horse into a canter. He moved fluidly through the trees, breathing gently, a light sheen of sweat on his flanks.

From behind her she heard a cry of pain. She reined Midnight back and stood up in her stirrups, straining to see what had happened. One of the men at the back of the group had fallen and wasn't making any move to get up. His horse had bolted and was running back down the trail towards the stables. Kiseleva got down off his horse and bent over the fallen man. He shook his head but didn't help him up, so Jenny figured he was too badly hurt to move. It didn't matter. There were still five of them and five would be more than enough to take care of one man and his daughter. Midnight stamped his feet, eager to be going, and she patted him on the neck. He needed no encouragement to start up the hill again.

'They're gaining on us, Dad,' Mersiha said. 'You're going to have to move faster.'

'I'm doing the best I can,' her father responded, kicking his horse in the ribs for all he was worth. 'She won't oblige.'

Mersiha looked back down the hill. One of the riders was out in front on a large black horse, only a few hundred yards away. 'Kick her harder,' she urged. Freeman slammed his heels into the mare's side, but she didn't seem to notice. Mersiha turned her horse around and circled her father, slamming the mare's flank with the flat of her hand and shouting at her. The horse increased its pace a little, but not much. Around them were patches of snow lying on the pine needles, and ahead the patches merged together until they formed a single blanket of snow. The trail led up to the snowline and then it was impossible to tell where it went. Mersiha hoped that Red would know where it was safe to tread. She wasn't happy about taking the horses through the snow, but with the riders in pursuit they had no choice but to keep climbing.

*   *   *

Jenny patted Midnight on the neck, encouraging him up a steep incline. She could see that Freeman and the girl had slowed down now that the horses were moving through snow. She heard hooves pounding on the trail behind her and turned to see Vincenti galloping up. His horse was out of control and he was pulling back on the reins, a look of horror on his face. She smiled at his discomfort. He wasn't a man who looked at home in a saddle. Luckily for him the horse came to a stop on its own at the base of the incline. 'What happened back there?' she asked.

'Guy's horse threw him off. Leg's broken by the look of it.' He grinned. 'Kiseleva wanted to shoot him to put him out of his misery.'

'He's a dumb fuck,' Jenny said.

Vincenti peered up the slope. 'I think I can get them from here. How far do you think that is? Two hundred yards?'

'More. But there are too many trees in the way. I told you, you're wasting your time.'

'Just one burst?'

Jenny couldn't help but smile at the man's enthusiasm. 'Go on. I bet you fifty bucks you don't even get close.' Vincenti was already drawing his Ingram from under his jacket. He took careful aim and fired a short burst. Pieces of bark sprayed from trees in the distance. He pulled a face and tried again. To Jenny's surprise Freeman's horse stumbled and fell. Freeman himself was thrown to the side. The other horse bucked, out of control. 'You did it!' she shouted in amazement.

Vincenti held the Ingram up to his face and made a play of blowing the smoke away, gunslinger-style. 'I sure did, ma'am. Now let's go string up the varmints.' Jenny grinned at him. He was a good-looking guy, in an Italian sort of way, and she felt that he was the sort of man she'd like to get to know better once they'd taken care of business. She kicked Midnight and started him walking up the slope. She could see Freeman scrambling to his feet, unhurt, but the horse lay where it had fallen.

As soon as Katherine reached Estes Park she drove up to a filling station and dashed inside. She asked a teenager in stained overalls if he had a Yellow Pages she could look at and he gave her one from under the counter. He was chewing on a toothpick and stared at her as she flicked through, looking for rental agents. 'Can I help?' he asked.

'It's okay, I've found it,' she said, giving him back the directory. She'd recognised the name in the listing. 'Where do I find Elkhorn Avenue?'

The boy grinned. 'You're on it,' he said.

'Great, thanks,' Katherine shouted as she ran for the door.

She found the office, set back from the main road. A police car was parked in front of it and she saw a uniformed officer inside writing in a notepad. She wasn't sure what to do. She didn't know if the police were there because of Sabatino, or if it was just a coincidence. She decided not to take the risk and waited in her car until he left.

She put on some lipstick to try to make herself look a

little more presentable, then went into the office. A balding middle-aged man with wire-framed spectacles was sorting through a stack of files. He introduced himself as Sam Hellings, the owner of the company, and he recognised her name straight away. He seemed upset and she asked him what was wrong. 'We had a break-in last night,' he said. 'They stole some money and trashed the place. They smashed a window at the back to get in and threw our files all over the floor. It's not the money I mind, it's the mess they made. Why do they do that?'

'I don't know,' Katherine said sympathetically. 'Maybe it was kids.'

'I doubt it. Estes Park is quite a small community out of season. I know most of the kids in town and they wouldn't do this. It's not that sort of place. It'll be out-of-towners. Anyway, no use crying over spilled files. What can I do for you?' He smiled amiably over the top of his spectacles.

'I'm supposed to meet my husband at the cabin but I've mislaid my map,' she said.

'No problem.' He went over to his desk and pulled out a photocopied map. He used an orange marker pen to draw the route from the office to the cabin. 'It's about a fifteen-minute drive.'

'Have you seen him recently?'

'Only when he dropped by to pick up the keys. Why, is something wrong?'

Katherine shook her head. 'No, everything's just fine,' she said.

*　　*　　*

Red stumbled over a fallen branch and Mersiha instinctively pulled back on the reins, jerking the horse's head up. She winced as her father's grip tightened around her waist, almost squeezing the breath from her. 'Dad, not so hard,' she gasped, holding the reins to the left and guiding the horse around a snow-covered bush. She risked a look over her shoulder. In the distance she could see one of the riders confidently urging a black horse up a snowy slope. There was no doubt about it – they were losing ground. She kicked the horse with her heels. 'Come on, Red. Faster, boy,' she shouted. Red was doing his best, but he was carrying two people and he was already snorting and panting from the exertion.

'I'm going to get off,' her father said.

'No!' she shouted, and kicked the faltering horse again.

'On your own, you might stand a chance. Stop the horse.'

'No, no way,' she said. The trail forked ahead and she chose the right-hand path which wound down the hill, making it easier for Red.

'It's the only way,' Freeman said.

'Dad, I'm not leaving you,' she shouted.

Red's ears suddenly twisted forward as if he'd heard something. He began to buck and Mersiha pulled in the reins to bring him under control. 'What's wrong, boy?' she asked, pushing him on with her heels. It was as if he was afraid of something ahead of them. Mersiha remembered the coyotes. They wouldn't threaten a horse, surely? Maybe Red was just getting jittery, she thought. It was a pity he didn't realise that the real danger was on the trail behind them.

'Something's spooked him,' Freeman said.

'Yeah, there's something ahead that he doesn't like.' One of Red's rear hooves skidded on a stone and the horse lurched to the left, almost throwing them. As Mersiha fought to control the nervous animal, three slugs zipped by her head and slammed into a tree, kicking off flecks of bark. She wrenched the reins to the right and kicked the horse. Red broke into a run and Mersiha bent forward to dodge a snow-covered branch. Freeman wasn't as quick to react and his head banged into the foliage, covering them both with snow.

As Mersiha shook the snow from her hair, she again heard the roaring sound that had alarmed the horse, louder this time. It wasn't an animal, she realised. It was a mechanical, whooshing sound that was vaguely familiar. 'Easy, Red,' she urged. 'Come on, boy.' She knew that Matt had been right about quarter-horses normally working better on a loose rein, but if she didn't exert her authority the frightened horse would bolt. She yanked the reins tight, keeping more pressure on the right side to turn him that way, and kicked him again and again with her heels, hoping the discomfort would take his mind off what lay ahead. More bullets ripped through the branches of the trees overhead. 'Hang on, Dad!' she yelled, as Red plunged forward. The ground was uneven and covered with a foot or so of snow, but Red managed to break into a canter. Mersiha's backside slapped down on to the saddle and she thrust her feet forward into the stirrups. Her father's arms hugged her waist and she heard him grunting in pain as he tried to maintain his grip with his legs. It was hard enough for her to stay in the saddle – she doubted that her father would be able to hang on for long without stirrups.

She heard the roaring sound again and realised what it

reminded her of: the boiler in the basement of their house. It sounded like the gas central heating boiler bursting into life, only a hundred times louder. 'Come on, Red,' she screamed, kicking him for all she was worth.

'Mersiha, no!' her father yelled. 'He'll fall!'

She ignored him. She knew that if Red hesitated for a second, all would be lost. It was only the force of her will that was keeping him moving forward. That and her insistent kicks. The slightest hesitancy on her part and Red would become uncontrollable. In front of her she saw the trees thin out, and as Red jumped over a fallen trunk she realised that they were heading for a clearing. She wasn't sure if that was a good thing or not. They'd move faster over clear ground, but they'd also be an easier target. She risked another quick look over her shoulder. The closest rider, the one on the jet-black horse, had gained another hundred yards on them and was holding a large gun. It must have had some sort of silencer on because the only sound she had heard was the bullets hitting the trees. The rider aimed the gun and Mersiha ducked instinctively, throwing her face forward into Red's thick mane. The horse jumped through the air, crashed over a bush, and when Mersiha looked up they were out of the trees, the sky overhead a brilliant blue.

Something roared, like a dragon breathing flame, and Red reared up, his nostrils flaring in panic. Mersiha felt her father's grip loosen and then he was gone, pitching backwards into the snow. There was a dull thud as he landed, but Mersiha was too busy trying to control Red to see what had happened to him. The horse dropped forward and then bucked, kicking out with its rear legs as if attacking some unseen foe. Mersiha gripped with her

447

legs and clung on to the reins, but the horse was totally out of control. Red began to spin around, and Mersiha felt her feet begin to slide out of the stirrups. Out of the corner of her eye she saw something huge, something red and green and yellow that billowed in the air like a living thing, and then all she could see was the sky and the snow-covered pines. She gripped harder, but it was too late. One of her feet slipped completely out of its stirrup and as Red bucked again she lost her grip entirely and sailed over the horse's head.

She had been thrown enough times to know how to break her fall and protect her head with her arms, but she was still winded when she hit the ground. She caught a glimpse of Red's flashing hooves and wide, staring eyes and then she curled into the foetal position as the horse jumped over her and thundered away across the snowfield. She lay where she had fallen and gently checked her arms and legs until she was satisfied that nothing was broken. She sat up. It was a balloon. A hot-air balloon. Three men in parkas were standing around the wicker basket suspended below the huge brightly coloured lightbulb-shaped envelope. Another man, bearded and wearing sunglasses, was standing in the basket and holding on to two stainless-steel burners. He was staring open-mouthed at Mersiha. One by one the rest of the men turned to look at her as they grappled with the basket, which was hovering only inches above the glistening snow.

Freeman groaned behind her and Mersiha scrambled to her feet and went over to him. 'Hurry,' she said, pulling him up. 'We have to get out of here.' She heard the thud of approaching horses and there were shouts from within the woods. Red was almost half a mile away, his mane

streaming behind him as he cantered across the snowfield.
'Are you okay, Dad?' she asked as she swung his right
arm over her shoulder. She staggered under his weight
but managed to keep her balance.

Freeman nodded, but he was too out of breath to answer.
He had clearly landed badly. Mersiha hoped that he hadn't
broken anything. She half pushed, half carried him over
to the balloon. One of the men in parkas let go of the
basket and was about to help Mersiha, but the balloon
immediately started to rise into the air and the others
shouted at him to hang on. The pilot let go of the burners.
'What's wrong?' he shouted.

'Help us! You've got to help us!' Mersiha screamed. Her
father stumbled and she grabbed him around the waist. He
was breathing heavily and his eyes were glazed.

'What's going on?' shouted one of the ground crew, a
man wearing a balaclava which covered most of his face.

Mersiha didn't reply. She was too busy trying to keep
her exhausted father on his feet.

'Keep away. We're about to launch her!' shouted the
man in the balaclava. Suddenly his body stiffened as if
he'd received an electric shock, and then four small roses
blossomed on his chest. His mouth worked soundlessly as
the red flowers spread across the green parka. The rest of
the ground crew began shouting and screaming and one of
them pointed over Mersiha's head.

She heard the pounding of hooves behind her and the
crashing of a horse through the vegetation. 'Come on,
Dad,' she hissed. The balloon was only yards away. The
man who'd been shot slumped to his knees, his hands
hanging lifelessly at his side.

A second horse leapt out of the woods and into the

clearing. Freeman seemed to gain his second wind and began to run, his breath coming in ragged gasps. Mersiha tried to block out the sound of the horses' hooves and concentrated on moving through the thick snow. It was like a bad dream. The snow seemed to suck at her feet and each step seemed to be harder than the last. Freeman looked back and began to yell. 'Down, down,' he shouted, and pushed her between the shoulders, sending her sprawling. As she fell she heard a rapid coughing noise and then she smacked down into the snow. When she looked up, spluttering and choking, she realised with horror that the bullets had sprayed across the ground crew. All three were lying in the snow. One had been hit in the head – his face was a scarlet mask. The pilot had vanished, but then his head reappeared and Mersiha realised that he'd ducked down to avoid the hail of bullets. She doubted that the wicker basket provided much protection. As she pushed herself up, she swallowed some snow and spat out the rest. One of the injured men was screaming in pain, his back arched and his feet thrashing against the basket. More horses galloped into the clearing. There was shouting and confusion all around. Mersiha realised that they'd stopped firing because they were afraid of hitting each other as the horses milled about.

A hand grabbed her by the scruff of the neck and she was yanked to her feet like a kitten. It was her father. He pushed her towards the balloon. She lurched forward and grabbed the edge of the basket. 'Come on, Mersiha. Get in!' he yelled.

The pilot was in shock, staring down at the injured men. 'Help her!' Freeman screamed. With shaking hands, the man pulled Mersiha over the edge and into the basket.

Bullets thudded into the snow around his boots as Freeman threw himself after her. The pilot pulled the levers that operated the burners. They burst into life. Even lying on the wicker floor, Mersiha could feel the searing heat. The balloon was close to equilibrium and with the added heat it rose swiftly. Bullets ripped through the basket and one screeched off a metal cylinder. Mersiha realised with horror that the cylinder must contain propane – the fuel that powered the massive burners. If the cylinder exploded there'd be nothing left of the basket or the balloon. She looked up at the pilot anxiously. He'd obviously come to the same conclusion and was keeping the burners full on, blasting hot air into the envelope. The balloon rose quickly. Another bullet tore through the floor of the basket and Freeman crawled towards his daughter, trying to shield her with his body. He wrapped her in his arms and they huddled together, trying to make themselves as small a target as possible.

Jenny glared at Kiseleva. 'Who the hell told you to fire?' she hissed.

'We were trying to stop them, right? You were firing, too.'

'I was shooting at them in the woods. When they were alone. You've just killed three people for no good reason.'

Kiseleva's horse stamped its feet and he pulled back on the reins. 'You killed the cowboy back there,' he said defensively.

451

Jenny fought to control the burning anger that was welling up inside her. 'If you'd held your fire, the pilot wouldn't have panicked. He'd have stayed put. We'd have caught the girl and her father and then we could have dealt with the witnesses.' She looked up at the balloon, high in the air. She could just make out the girl, her black hair blowing in the wind. One of the ground crew moaned and then went quiet. Christ, thought Jenny, this was turning into a massacre. She looked around, wondering what to do next. What she really wanted to do was to put a bullet in Kiseleva's guts, but she'd leave that to Utsyev. There were two metallic-blue snowmobiles at the edge of the clearing. She clicked her tongue and her horse walked towards the machines. They were both two-seater Polaris models. The ground crew had obviously been planning to use them to follow the balloon. Both had ignition keys in place. 'You ever ridden a snowmobile?' she asked Kiseleva, who was still having trouble getting his horse to stand still.

'It's gotta be easier than one of these things,' he said. He pulled back on the reins and the horse tossed its head from side to side.

Vincenti walked his horse over to Jenny. 'I've been on one,' he said.

'How fast will they go?'

He shrugged. 'Sixty in good conditions. Depends on the trail. A darn sight faster than a horse, that's for sure.'

Jenny nodded. 'Show Kiseleva and then go after them.'

Vincenti climbed down off his horse and tethered it to a tree. Kiseleva did the same while Jenny walked her horse along the treeline. The crew could have followed the balloon on the snowmobiles, but there was no way they could have used them to transport it up into the hills.

They'd have needed a vehicle, and a road. Through the trees she noticed a flash of red, and as she rode closer she saw a Jeep Wrangler and behind it a trailer. She slid down off her horse and led it over to the vehicle. There was a large-scale map on the passenger seat, along with a compass and a transceiver. The Jeep was parked on a trail that was little more than packed snow, which wound down the hill through the trees. Only a four-wheel-drive could have made the journey. She dropped the reins and walked back to the snowmobiles, where Vincenti was showing Kiseleva how to start the engines by pulling out the red cut-off toggle on the right-hand side of the handlebars and then pulling a large plastic D-ring attached to a rope, just like starting a lawnmower. Kiseleva pulled hard and the engine burst into life. At the front were two skis with independent suspension. The forward motion was provided by a thick caterpillar belt under the seats. The controls were simple – the throttle lever was on the right handlebar, the brake on the left. There was no clutch. Kiseleva sat down and tweaked the throttle. The snowmobile jerked forward, almost hitting Jenny. He slammed on the brake. 'That's all there is to it?' he asked.

'Just remember to keep it at full throttle over loose snow,' Vincenti said. 'If you stop, you'll sink. Try to stay on trails wherever you can. And if you do run into any problems, just hit the red toggle – that'll kill the engine.' He sat astride the second machine and started it. He waved one of the riders over and told him to sit behind him. Ostrovetsky joined Kiseleva.

One of the members of the ground crew was groaning and trying to crawl through the packed snow. He was leaving a crimson trail smeared behind him. Jenny admired the man's courage: there was nowhere for him to go, no one to save him, but still he didn't give up. He was using his elbows for leverage, dragging his useless legs behind him. Jenny walked up and stood in front of the crawling man, blocking his way. He looked up, his face contorted in agony. She shot him once, in the forehead. Blood and brains and bone splattered over the man's shoulders, and for a second he remained staring at her, the top of his head blown away, before dropping lifelessly forward. She unclipped the transceiver from the dead man's belt and tossed it to Kiseleva. He caught it with one hand and shoved it into his coat pocket.

'I'm going to take the Jeep over there and cut down to the road,' she said. 'There's another radio – I'll use it to keep in touch.'

'What about the horses?' Kiseleva shouted above the growl of the snowmobile.

'What, you want to blow away a few more witnesses, do you, Kiseleva?'

'I just meant . . .'

'Yeah, I know what you meant,' she interrupted. 'The horses can take care of themselves. You concentrate on following that balloon and being there when it lands.'

'Can't we shoot them down?' Vincenti asked.

'I doubt it,' she said. 'They're sure to stay high. And unless you're lucky enough to hit the fuel tanks, the bullets will go straight through without damaging the balloon. It'll leak air, but you'd have to riddle it full of holes before you did any real damage. It's not like it's full of explosive gas like the *Hindenburg*. In fact, it's got a lot in common with Kiseleva.'

'Huh?' Vincenti grunted, not understanding.

'They're both full of hot air,' Jenny finished with a cruel smile. 'Just get on with it, will you? If they get away, Utsyev will have your balls for breakfast.' She turned her back on them and went over to the Jeep to unhitch the trailer.

Mersiha held on tightly to one of the rope grab-handles as the basket swung gently below the balloon. The snow-covered trees seemed to be miles away, picture-perfect like a Christmas card. If it wasn't for the far-off buzz of the snowmobiles and the men with the guns, she'd probably have enjoyed the flight. As it was, she couldn't stop her hands from trembling. Her father was standing on the opposite side of the basket, ashen-faced. She tried to catch his eye but he didn't seem to notice her. She had seen the same blank stare on the faces of men and women in war-torn Sarajevo when she was a child: faces that had seen too much. She reached over and squeezed his hand. He looked at her with unseeing eyes. 'Dad, are you okay?'

He nodded slowly, then seemed to snap out of it. He ruffled her hair and forced a smile. 'I'm fine, pumpkin.'

'Yeah, we're three people hanging in the air, a sitting target for a group of killers armed with automatic weapons, but other than that, we're fine,' said the balloon pilot. He peered over the edge of the basket. The snowmobiles were having to skirt a rocky area and were driving at right-angles to the balloon's path. Mersiha could see that they'd only have to go a mile or so before they'd link up with a trail that would allow them to continue the chase. The pilot pulled on the lever that operated one of the burners and a tongue of flame roared into the neck of the balloon.

'How fast can they go?' she asked.

'Sixty miles an hour,' the pilot said. 'Maybe seventy.'

'And how fast do we go?'

'Depends on the wind. Just now we're doing about twenty.'

It was like a mathematics problem, Mersiha thought, but the end result was that there was no way they'd be able to outrun the snowmobiles. 'My name's Mersiha,' she said, holding out her hand.

The pilot stared at it with a look of surprise on his face, as if she were offering him a dead animal, then he grinned and shook it. His grip was firm, his hand totally encompassing hers. 'Tim,' he said. Tim held out his hand to Freeman, and they introduced themselves, the ice broken. Mersiha was standing next to an instrument panel with circular gauges, mounted on one of the three propane cylinders in the basket. One of them displayed the letters 'ALT'. She guessed it was an altimeter, though she had trouble reading its three needles. If she was doing it right, they were eleven thousand feet high, but the ground didn't seem that far away. She asked Tim how high they were. 'About fifteen hundred feet,' he said. Mersiha frowned at the altimeter and Tim smiled. He explained that it showed the height above sea level and the mountains below were more than a mile high. To work out how high the balloon was above the ground, she'd have to subtract the height of the mountains from the altimeter reading. Tim showed her how to read the remaining two instruments: the variometer, which measured the rate of ascent or descent, and the thermistor, which gave the temperature of the air at the top of the balloon. As a general rule, he explained, if ever it got below one hundred degrees, the balloon would start to descend.

'So it's just like a plane, really?' Mersiha said.

'Sort of, except unlike a plane we can't choose where we go. We have to go with the wind. And those guys down there know that.'

'Have you got a radio?' Freeman asked.

Tim shrugged. 'Sure, but it's back there with the ground crew.' He went quiet, turning his back on Mersiha and Freeman, his hands gripping the edge of the basket so tightly that Mersiha could see his knuckles whiten. She didn't know what to say. There weren't any words that would make it any easier for him. She looked at her father. He shrugged.

'Why did they do it?' Tim asked quietly.

'It's complicated,' Freeman said.

'They killed my friends,' Tim said as he turned around. 'They killed my friends and all you can say is that it's complicated.' His voice rose and for a moment Mersiha feared that he was becoming hysterical.

'I'm sorry,' she said. The balloon had started to drift down and so Tim turned on both burners, giving it a six-second blast of heat. The downward drift stopped and the balloon rose, the variometer showing a climb-rate of fifty feet per minute. 'They think I killed a member of their gang,' Mersiha said.

Tim's mouth dropped open. 'They think you did what?' He shook his head. 'Really?'

Mersiha nodded.

'And did you?'

'Like I said, it's complicated,' Freeman interrupted.

'Are you running from the cops?' Freeman shook his head. 'Because if we get out of this, I'm going straight to the cops.' Tim operated the burners again, keeping the balloon in a steady climb.

'Tim, we'll be right there with you,' Freeman said.

Tim ran a hand through his thick beard. The facial hair and impenetrable sunglasses made it difficult to judge his age. Mersiha thought he could be anywhere between twenty-five and forty years old. 'They're gonna follow us until we land, aren't they?' he asked.

Mersiha nodded. 'I'm afraid so.'

'And they're gonna kill me, too?'

'It looks that way,' Freeman said. 'They don't seem to be over-worried about innocent bystanders.'

Katherine sighed with relief as she drove down the track and saw the Cherokee parked in front of the cabin. 'Thank God, they're home,' she said. She tooted the horn. 'Thank you, God. Thank you.'

She climbed out of her car, expecting to see Tony and Mersiha come dashing out of the cabin. The door remained resolutely closed. It was still early. Maybe they are still asleep, she thought. She yawned and stretched. Her whole body ached and she was bone tired. She climbed the steps to the deck and knocked on the door. There was no answer. She turned the handle. The door squeaked on its hinges. 'Tony!' she called. 'Mersiha! It's me!'

It was only as she stepped inside that she remembered that Tony had hired a Ford Bronco, not a Jeep.

THE BIRTHDAY GIRL

* * *

The snowmobile bucked and kicked between Kiseleva's legs as if it had a life of its own. It was a hundred times worse than the horse, and unlike with a living animal there was nothing he could do to return the pain. The wind tore at his face making his eyes water, and every time the front of the machine dipped down, snow was thrown up over the windshield. He was cold, wet and as mad as hell. He squinted up at the balloon. It seemed closer, but it was hard to tell. The snowmobile's left ski hit a rock and he almost lost his grip. He jammed his feet under the metal foot-rests, and used them for leverage to keep himself on the seat. 'Fuck you!' he yelled up at the balloon. 'Fuck you, and fuck the blonde bitch, too!'

He was operating the throttle with his right thumb, which felt as if it was about to drop off. He shifted his grip and tried to use his palm to keep the throttle in the full-on position, but that made it harder to steer. Ostrovetsky was holding him tight around the waist. Both men had put their guns away. The balloon was way too high and the snowmobile was throwing them around so much they couldn't have hit an elephant at point-blank range. He took a quick look at the fuel gauge. It was over three-quarters full. He had no idea how fast the snowmobiles used up fuel, but the ground crew must have assumed there'd be more than enough to track the balloon throughout its flight.

Kiseleva was looking forward to catching up with Freeman and the girl. He wanted to see their faces as he fired. Maybe he'd do it slowly so that he could hear them scream.

A bullet in the leg first. Then an arm. Then the stomach. It took a long time to die if you were shot in the guts. He'd once pumped a slug into the stomach of a Jamaican drug dealer in Brooklyn and stood over him for almost an hour, listening to him beg for his life and watching him die. It was the first kill he'd really enjoyed. The girl would be a first, though. He'd never killed a girl before. He wondered how he'd feel shooting her. He smiled as he wrenched the handlebars to the left, hauling the snowmobile around a clump of pines. The other snowmobile was a hundred yards ahead of him and he pushed the throttle harder, not wanting to get too far behind. The last thing Kiseleva wanted was to be beaten to the kill.

His ears had already gone numb with the cold and he was gradually losing the feeling in his lips. He ducked his head down behind the small windshield, trying to avoid the chilling wind, but that meant he couldn't see where he was going. He hit a drift, hard, and banged his chin on the handlebars. He cursed and sat up. Blood dripped down his chin but he couldn't take his hands off the controls to wipe it away. 'Fuck the bitch,' he screamed into the wind. The Freeman girl wouldn't be the last woman he'd kill. As soon as he got the chance he'd settle the score with the blonde whore. She had no right to treat him the way she did. Just because she opened her legs for Utsyev didn't mean that she could talk to him like that. He'd pick his time carefully, he'd wait until she was alone, he'd take her somewhere where they wouldn't be disturbed, where he'd have all the time in the world. He'd make her beg before she died. Maybe he'd even screw her first. Yeah, that'd be a real kick. Shoot her in the stomach and then screw her. See how she liked that. Kiseleva gripped the seat with his knees and the vibrations of the engine shivered through his groin.

The two snowmobiles far below made buzzing noises like trapped wasps. Tim leaned over the side of the basket. 'Can you see them?' he asked.

'Over there, to the right,' Freeman said, pointing. 'They just went behind that big rock.'

'We're not going to give those guys the slip,' Tim said. He pulled on the burner lever and sent flames roaring into the balloon. 'How high do you think they can shoot those guns?'

'Difficult to say. But they're machine pistols – they're not accurate beyond about a hundred feet.'

'That's something,' Tim said.

'How long can we stay up?' Mersiha asked.

'Until we run out of propane. The problem is, we were only planning a short flight to test the envelope.' He gestured at the three metal cylinders. 'One of them is empty.'

'How long?' she repeated.

'Three hours, tops.'

'What happens then?' she asked.

'Then we go down,' Freeman said.

Tim shook his head. 'We won't be up for three hours,' he said.

'What do you mean?' Freeman asked, frowning.

Tim gestured with his thumb at a mountain range in the distance. 'There's nothing but forest over that ridge. It's just trees and rocks and more trees. They'd rip the balloon apart if we landed there. Us too.'

'Terrific,' Freeman said. Down below, one of the snowmobiles appeared from behind the rocky outcrop and headed across the snow-blanketed hillside. 'So what do we do?'

Tim pulled the lever again and the burners roared as the balloon lifted. He looked at the thermistor. The needle was hovering around the one hundred degree mark, and according to the altimeter they were two thousand feet above the ground. 'There's a map down there by that tank,' he said to Mersiha. 'Can you pass it to me?'

Mersiha knelt down and handed the folded chart to him. Tim opened it over the instrument pack and took off his sunglasses. He studied the chart and suddenly jabbed at it with his forefinger. 'I've got it,' he said, excitedly. 'I know what we can do.'

Jenny drove slowly down the track, grateful for the Jeep's four-wheel drive. Several times she'd almost skidded into the trees, and in a less rugged vehicle she wouldn't have made it down the steep hillside. The forest was dense and the trail was so winding and tortuous that she could never see more than a few dozen yards ahead. She alternated between accelerator and brake, taking care not to skid as she slid the Ingram underneath the seat. If the trail opened up on to a main road, it made sense to keep the weapon hidden from view. She took off her fur cap and threw it

462

on to the back seat, shaking her long blonde hair free so that it cascaded down her shoulders.

The trail she was driving down wasn't shown on the map, but the position of the balloon's launch site was shown with a black cross, and a series of dotted lines marked its projected course to the east. Several roads intersected with the balloon's course, and a number of possible landing sites were marked on the map, all within ten miles or so of the take-off point. She couldn't see the balloon through the pines, but the map and the compass would allow her to keep track of it once she reached a road. She considered using the transceiver to call Kiseleva and check on his progress, but decided against it. She doubted that he'd be able to control the snowmobile with one hand, and she didn't want to be blamed for him running off the mountain. The way Kiseleva was operating, he wouldn't be on Utsyev's team for much longer. He'd been making a lot of mistakes recently, and Bzuchar wasn't a man who tolerated fuck-ups. She hoped that when Bzuchar decided that enough was enough, he'd let her be the one to pull the trigger. Bzuchar owed her one for the way she'd dealt with Lennie Nelson.

Tim compared the chart with the terrain below and nodded to himself. 'Another four miles, okay?' he said. The snowmobiles were far off to the left, skirting an area of dense pines.

'Are you sure about this?' Freeman queried.

'We don't have any other choice,' Tim said. 'If the three of us stay in the balloon we'll end up in the trees. If I drop you two off, I might just be able to make it. They won't be able to cross the ridge in the snowmobiles, so I'll be okay.'

'But you said you'd crash in the forest,' Mersiha said, the concern obvious in her voice.

Tim shook his head. He pulled on the lever and gently sent the balloon up another hundred feet or so. 'With three of us in the basket, that's true. But with the reduced load, I'll probably make it on my own.'

'Probably?' Mersiha repeated.

Tim smiled and scratched his beard. 'I'll be okay,' he said.

'Probably. You said probably.'

'And they'll see us go down,' Freeman said. 'If they see us leave the basket, we're dead.'

Tim tapped the chart. 'Yeah, but if I can get us to this snowfield here, we'll be hidden by that.' He pointed to a rocky outcrop in the distance.

Freeman looked at the chart, then at the terrain slowly passing below. The sound of the snowmobiles faded for a second and then restarted as the machines rounded the trees and headed up a gently sloping hill. They were maybe five miles away. How fast had Tim said the snowmobiles could travel? Sixty miles an hour? They could be directly under the balloon within five minutes. 'We won't make it,' he whispered.

Tim pulled the burner lever again, keeping the flame burning for a full fifteen seconds. He looked over his shoulder at the approaching snowmobiles. 'We'll be okay, if I can just get us to the other side of those trees there.'

Freeman looked where Tim was pointing. A swath of snow-covered pines cut through the snowfield like a huge wedge. The trees were growing together so closely that it was hard to see the ground between them. There was no way the snowmobiles would be able to get through. They'd have to go around, and that would entail a detour of at least ten miles. Freeman frowned. Tim's plan depended on them getting the trees between the balloon and the snowmobiles, but wind was taking them away to the right of the woods. Down below, the snowmobiles were racing across the virgin snow at full speed. Tim pulled on the lever again, a short burst to maintain their altitude. He leant over his instruments, and then checked his chart. 'I thought you couldn't steer balloons,' Freeman said. 'You said they blow with the wind.' Tim didn't answer. He was staring off into the distance. Freeman gripped his shoulder. 'Tim, come on, man. How are we going to get to the other side of the trees?'

'I'm looking for a current that will take us in the right direction. But I think we're going to have to go lower if we're going to make it.'

'Lower?' Freeman repeated. The balloon was about 2500 feet above the ground, so they had plenty of altitude to play with, but he was reluctant to go any closer to the men with submachine pistols.

'It's the only way we're going to get behind those trees,' Tim said. 'The higher we go, the more we drift to the right.'

'Why's that?' Mersiha asked.

'It's just the way it is,' Tim replied. 'In the northern hemisphere the wind veers to the right with altitude – it's something to do with the turning of the earth. "Right with height" is a balloonist's saying. So if we want to go more to the left, we're gonna have to descend.'

'How low?' Freeman asked.

'No way to tell,' Tim replied, keeping a close watch on his altimeter. 'It's never the same. We just have to go down and have a look-see. There's another problem, though. The lower we go, the slower we go.'

'Is that another balloonist's saying?' Mersiha said, smiling. Freeman could see that she was trying to ease the tension.

Tim grinned back. 'No, kid, that's just a fact. The faster winds are higher up, so we'll slow down as we descend.' He tapped the variometer. It was already showing a descent rate of two hundred feet per minute. The thermistor was showing the temperature of the air at the crown of the balloon at just below one hundred degrees.

'How do we go down?' Mersiha asked.

'Simple. We just go easy on the burners. We have to use them to maintain our height: the air in the envelope cools pretty quickly, especially in these temperatures. Cut back on the heat and we'll fall pretty quickly.'

'Is that how you land these things?' Freeman asked.

'That's part of it, but we have a parachute deflation system to let the air out of the top of the balloon. It's a circle of fabric which I can pull into the balloon using this rip-line.' He ran his fingers down a dark blue line which ran out of the neck of the balloon and was tied to the side of the basket. 'Pull it and air floods out; let go and the parachute reseals. That's how we get the balloon down in normal wind conditions. But if we really want to deflate the envelope, say if we were trying to land in high winds, then there's a Velcro rip which runs around the parachute.' He showed them another line. 'Pulling this rip-line effectively creates a huge hole in the top of the balloon. But we don't use that for normal descents – it's a way of quickly deflating the balloon on the ground.'

Tim pointed at the wedge of pines. 'Once we're over the trees I can use the valley winds to take us around the rocky outcrop. They won't be expecting that, and we should pick up some speed.'

'Then you drop us off? I'm still not sure that's a good idea,' Freeman said.

'You'll be fine,' Tim assured him. 'The winds at ground level aren't much more than five miles per hour. I can take this baby down to a few feet above the ground and you can drop into the snow. The drifts are about six or seven feet – you won't get hurt. I'll hit the burners and go way up. All you have to do is lie still. The guys in the snowmobiles won't have a clue what's happened and they'll chase me as far as the ridge. Then I'll be free and clear.'

'If you can find a place to land,' Mersiha said.

Tim ran his finger across the chart. 'I can make it to here with just me on board.'

'Are you sure?'

Tim smiled, obviously pleased at her concern. 'Trust me,' he said. Below, the buzzing of the snowmobiles grew louder.

Kiseleva took his left hand off the brake lever and fumbled in his pocket for the transceiver. The handlebars vibrated and he gripped tighter with his right hand, trying to steer as straight a course as possible. He was crossing a large snowfield and heading towards a forest of snow-covered pines. The skis slipped sideways as he drove across an incline and he felt the machine slip away from him. He started to fall but before he completely lost his grip he smacked his right hand down on the engine cut-off toggle. It died immediately and the machine came to a halt within a few yards with Kiseleva still hanging on grimly with one hand.

'What the fuck happened?' Ostrovetsky shouted over his shoulder. The other snowmobile continued to race after the balloon, though Kiseleva could see that Vincenti was making a mistake in heading directly towards the trees. They'd have to go round, so it made more sense to approach the forest at an angle and then skirt around it.

'I've gotta speak to the blonde bitch,' Kiseleva said, switching on the transceiver and pressing it to the side of his face. His breath fogged around his mouth as he spoke. 'You there?' There was no reply. His hands were tingling and trembling and his arm muscles ached like they did after he'd done a hundred push-ups. 'You there?' he repeated.

'Yeah, what's the problem?' It was the woman. She sounded as if she were a million miles away, her voice faint and crackling. Even through the static, he could hear the contempt in her voice.

'The balloon's coming down. They're half as high as they used to be. I think they're trying to land. Where are you?'

'Still heading down the hill. The trail's a bitch.'

Yeah, thought Kiseleva sourly, so are you, sweetheart. 'They're coming down on the other side of a valley. There's a sort of forest between two hills.'

'Hang on. I've got a map here. How far away are you from the balloon?'

Kiseleva peered up into the sky. Distances out in the open meant nothing to him. Drop him in the middle of Manhattan and he'd know to a block where he was, and how long it would take to get anywhere in a cab, assuming he was lucky enough to get a driver who could speak a close approximation of English. But out in the hills with everything covered in a thick layer of snow, he didn't have a clue. 'Six miles,' he guessed. 'Maybe seven.'

The transceiver crackled and he had to ask her to repeat herself. 'Yeah, I think I see it. Okay, once I hit the road, I'll get over there. In the meantime, get the hell after them.'

'Yeah, what the fuck do you think I'm doing?' he shouted, but he didn't press the transmit button as he said it. He knew better than to antagonise her.

'Everything okay?' Ostrovetsky asked.

'Everything's just fine,' Kiseleva said bitterly.

'Think we'll make it?'

'Damn right.' He sat down astride the snowmobile and pulled the D-ring savagely, imagining it was the blonde's hair he had in his hand. Nothing happened. He pulled again, harder this time. Still nothing.

'The engine cut-off's still in,' Ostrovetsky said.

Kiseleva glared at him. 'I was just warming it up,' he said. He flicked out the red toggle, pulled the D-ring, and the engine burst into life. 'See?' he said, daring his passenger to argue. He pulled his scarf up over his face and tied it behind his neck as protection against the biting wind. Way off in the distance he could see Vincenti's snowmobile approaching the forest. Kiseleva could see that he'd soon realise his mistake and would have to veer off to the right. He gunned the engine. It was his chance to take the lead. He patted the silenced automatic,

469

snug in its leather holster under his left armpit. Soon, he thought. Soon.

According to the variometer the balloon was descending at about two hundred feet a minute, but to Freeman it hardly felt as if they were moving downward at all. The only sensation of movement was forward, over the forest. Tim had been right. The lower they went, the less the drift to the right. Even so, he could see that they were only clipping the edge of the wedge of pines, and one of the snowmobiles was already moving off to go around the obstruction. Mersiha bit her lip nervously and Freeman squeezed her shoulder. 'It's going to be okay,' he said.

She smiled, wanting to believe him, but they both knew that Tim was cutting it close. Her face began to crumple as if she had only just realised the danger they were in. 'I'm so sorry, Dad,' she said. 'If I hadn't been so stupid . . .'

'Hush,' he said, pressing a finger to his lips. 'You were only trying to help.'

She shook her head fiercely. 'No. You were right. Violence never solves anything. It only makes things worse. And that's what I've done. I've made it worse.' She began to shake.

Freeman pulled her to him and hugged her as she sobbed quietly into his chest. 'It's all right,' he said.

'I promise I'll never do anything like that again. I really promise. On my life.' She crooked her little finger on her left hand and offered it to him. Freeman smiled and did the same. They linked little fingers. He stroked her hair with his other hand and looked questioningly at Tim. The pilot shrugged. Freeman could see from the look on his face that he was worried.

'It'll be touch and go,' he said. 'Literally. Twenty seconds at most. So when I tell you to jump, you'll have to go right away. No hesitation. And once you're in the snow, lie still. Don't sit up to check that she's okay, don't say anything, just lie exactly where you are. I'll hit the burners and hopefully they'll be too busy watching me to realise that you aren't in the basket.' Freeman nodded. He rested his chin on the top of his daughter's head. He could see himself and Mersiha reflected in the twin lenses of the pilot's sunglasses, their faces weirdly distorted. 'It might not be so bad,' Tim said. 'The lower we go, the more distance we'll put between them. So long as they're the other side of the trees, they won't see us.' He fingered the dark blue rip-line. 'When I pull this, we'll drop like a stone.'

'When do we do it?' Freeman asked.

Tim looked down at the pursuing snowmobiles. They were still some distance away. He did a quick calculation in his head. 'Three minutes, maybe four.'

'I'm ready,' Freeman said.

'It might be an idea if you and your daughter sat down in the bottom of the basket, so that they get used to not seeing you standing up.'

Freeman nodded. 'Come on, pumpkin,' he whispered in Mersiha's ear. 'Let's sit down.' She'd begun to shake again, and Freeman didn't think it was from the cold. She slowly slid down against the side of the basket and clutched her knees with her arms. Tears were running down her cheeks though her eyes were tightly closed. Freeman sat down next to her and patted her shoulder, overwhelmed by a feeling of helplessness. Now it was all down to Tim.

Kiseleva remembered Vincenti's warning and kept the throttle full on as he raced across the virgin snow. If the snowmobile sank into the deep drifts they'd never be able to dig it out. Every bone in his body ached, and it required a constant effort to keep the vehicle on course. He'd lost all feeling in his right thumb and his eyes were watering. It felt as if he'd been on the machine for an eternity. He couldn't remember a time when his body hadn't been racked by pain and his ears assaulted by the never-ending drone of the engine between his legs.

Over to his left, the balloon was still descending. Kiseleva looked over his shoulder to see where Vincenti was. The other snowmobile was gaining quickly, now racing on a course parallel to his. He crouched forward over the handlebars to cut down the wind resistance and to give his eyes a respite from the wind. Ice was crusting on his eyelashes and he blinked, trying to clear them. The skis hit a snowdrift and the snowmobile pitched up and then slammed down, knocking the breath from his body. Instinctively he throttled back, but immediately the skis began to sink. He forced the throttle forward and leant back, and the snowmobile powered forward once more. The sound of Vincenti's machine grew louder and he realised that he was about to be overtaken. He cursed. He didn't want to be beaten to the kill. Not after all he'd been through. He could think of only one way he'd be able to get to the balloon before Vincenti – he'd have to go through the trees instead of around them. He kept looking anxiously to his left, searching for a way into the forest. Vincenti drew level. He nodded over at Kiseleva. There was something condescending about the gesture, Kiseleva thought, and he turned away to concentrate on the treeline.

Vincenti pulled away with no apparent effort. Kiseleva couldn't work out how the man managed to get the extra speed from his snowmobile. He had his own throttle pushed as far forward as it would go, yet he was clearly falling behind. He cursed, rocking backwards and forwards as if that would coax extra speed from the vehicle. Suddenly Vincenti veered towards the trees and Kiseleva realised that they'd both had the same idea. Vincenti had seen a gap in the pines which appeared to be the start of a narrow trail. The snowmobile shot into the forest like a rabbit disappearing into its burrow. Kiseleva yanked hard on the handlebars and followed him.

The trail Vincenti was following was peppered with hoofprints, obviously well used by deer and elk. The snow was light and fluffy and considerably less deep than it had been out in the open. Both snowmobiles had to slow down because the trail twisted and turned and in places it seemed to vanish completely. Kiseleva followed closely as Vincenti navigated through the maze of snow-laden trees. He hoped that they'd made the right decision. From the ground there was no way of knowing how deep the forest was, or if the trail actually led anywhere. For all they knew, they could be pursuing a dead end. The snowmobile bucked from side to side on the uneven trail, like a small boat riding out a storm. Kiseleva's arms felt as if they were being torn from their sockets. Ahead, Vincenti slowed and stood up, peering through the trees for the best way to go. His passenger pointed off to the right but Vincenti shook his head. Kiseleva could see why – heading to the right would take them further away from the balloon. He took his thumb off the throttle and the snowmobile slithered to a halt. 'What's wrong?' Ostrovetsky shouted behind him.

'We're waiting for Vincenti to make up his mind.'

Vincenti turned to look at them. He shrugged theatrically, clearly unable to decide which way to go. On all sides the pines seemed to have closed ranks. Kiseleva gestured to the left. That was the only way to go. Vincenti rolled his snowmobile forward, still standing to get a better look ahead. Kiseleva followed, gunning his engine impatiently, the snowmobile lurching forward like a bull preparing to charge a matador. Vincenti managed to negotiate a way through the packed pines, frequently squeezing through gaps so narrow that the handlebars scraped the reddish bark. Kiseleva fumed. They were barely managing a walking pace. 'Come on!' he screamed. 'Get a fucking move on!' Whether Vincenti heard him above the noise of the engines or not, he sat down and accelerated. The trees seemed to have thinned, and while the trail had petered out there was still considerably more room to manoeuvre and he made full use of it. 'About time,' Kiseleva growled to himself. The pines began to flash by as he opened up the throttle. They were still managing only thirty miles an hour, but the nearness of the trees gave the illusion of greater speed. They passed in a blur, often only inches away from the skis.

Several times Vincenti's snowmobile banged into low branches, starting small snowfalls which infuriated Kiseleva

474

as he drove through them. His face and scarf were plastered with wet slush, adding to his discomfort. He was mentally cursing Vincenti when suddenly the snowmobile ahead veered off to the right and pitched over on its side, the rubber caterpillar track whirring around uselessly. The two men were thrown off, the passenger slamming into a tree. Snow poured down in a miniature avalanche, half covering him. Vincenti lay trapped under the vehicle, his leg jammed under one of the skis.

Kiseleva braked. Vincenti was conscious but his leg was bleeding badly. The right ski had buckled. Kiseleva realised that Vincenti must have caught it on something – a concealed rock or root. Whatever had done the damage, the snowmobile clearly wasn't going anywhere. Neither was Vincenti. 'Help me,' he groaned. The engine was still racing – the throttle must have jammed. Vincenti tried to lift himself into a sitting position but the effort was too much for him and he fell back into the snow. 'Hit the engine cut-off,' he pleaded. He was bleeding from his mouth as if he'd bitten his tongue.

'No time,' Kiseleva said. He gunned the throttle and accelerated away, spraying snow over the injured man.

'We could have helped them,' Ostrovetsky shouted.

'Later,' Kiseleva yelled. 'We'll come back for them.' He smiled under his scarf as he picked his way through the trees. He was secretly pleased that Vincenti had screwed up. Now he'd get all the credit for killing Freeman and the girl.

*   *   *

Tim tightened his grip on the rip-line and looked down on Freeman and his daughter, who were crouching on the floor of the basket. 'Okay, get ready,' he said.

'What do we do?' Freeman asked.

'Stay just as you are while I take the balloon down. When I give you the word, slip over the side of the basket. We'll be six feet above the ground so there'll be a bit of a drop, but the snow's soft and fairly deep. You'll be fine. When we get down low we'll be in the shelter of the trees so the wind speed will drop dramatically. We'll probably be down to a walking pace. Just remember what I said – lie still and don't move until the snowmobiles have passed.'

'Can you see them?'

'No. They're the other side of the forest somewhere. You can still hear them off in the distance. I don't know how much time we'll have so when I say go, you go.'

Freeman forced a smile. 'Ready when you are,' he said. He put his arm around Mersiha's shoulders. 'Are you okay, pumpkin?'

She nodded and wiped her eyes with the back of her hand.

'This is it,' the pilot said. He pulled the rip-line and almost immediately Freeman felt the balloon drop. His stomach turned over and he took deep breaths to fight the nausea.

'Six hundred feet to go,' Tim said.

Kiseleva pushed the throttle as far forward as it would go and the snowmobile leapt forward and burst out of the forest in a shower of snow and broken twigs. The balloon was only a few hundred yards away, its envelope partially deflated and falling fast. The pilot was standing up, peering over the side of the basket. Kiseleva powered the snowmobile along the treeline, his heart pounding. The pilot looked up and saw them. He let go of the line and began frantically to throw out bags of ballast, trying to stop the balloon's rapid descent. There was no sign of Freeman and the girl. Kiseleva assumed they must be sitting down in the basket, braced for the landing. He grinned and swung the snowmobile to the left, heading directly for the balloon. Behind him, he felt Ostrovetsky draw his gun from inside his jacket. The balloon's descent was visibly slowing. Now it was only fifty feet or so above the snowfield. The pilot was screaming or shouting. Kiseleva couldn't make out the words – it sounded like the roar of an animal in pain. He stopped throwing out ballast and pulled on the levers below the burners. Flames shot up into the envelope, but Kiseleva could see that he was too late – the descent was continuing, albeit slowly.

He angled the snowmobile so that they could get a clear shot and Ostrovetsky let rip with his Ingram. The first burst missed the basket but hit the envelope, rippling the fabric but passing harmlessly through. 'Slow down!' Ostrovetsky shouted above the noise of the engine. Kiseleva jammed on the brake and took his thumb off the throttle and the snowmobile skidded sideways across the snow. Ostrovetsky fired again, the shots muffled by the silencer and sounding like nothing more sinister than rapid handclaps. The bullets caught the pilot in the chest and he fell backwards, his outstretched hands grabbing at the rip-line.

'Yes!' Kiseleva yelled. 'We've got them!'

* * *

Mersiha screamed as Tim staggered back against the side of the basket. His sunglasses slipped from his face and clattered on to her head. Freeman looked up in horror as wet, sticky blood trickled down the front of his daughter's jacket. Blood was pouring from Tim's throat and chest, and as he looked into his eyes he saw them glaze over, like water transforming into ice. His lifeless body pitched forward, and as he fell Freeman felt the balloon suddenly drop.

The rip-line had become wrapped around Tim's wrist and his weight had dragged open the parachute deflation system. Hot air was flooding out of the envelope and they were only seconds away from slamming into the ground. 'Stay down!' Freeman shouted to Mersiha as he scrambled to his feet. He stood up and tried to pull the line free, but as soon as his head emerged above the side of the basket, bullets whipped through the air and he ducked. He threw himself at Mersiha, wrapping himself around her, trying to protect her as best he could. A bullet screeched off one of the propane cylinders and he flinched. The pilot's face lay awkwardly against the bottom of the basket, blood oozing from his open mouth. His backside was up in the air, his knees under his chest, as if even in death he was trying to avoid the hail of bullets.

Freeman looked up through the skirt at the bottom of the envelope, past the burners, and up through the hole at the top of the balloon. He could see the brilliant blue sky and, high up, a bird circling. The basket began to spin crazily. Freeman hugged Mersiha tight and closed his eyes, waiting for the end.

The wicker basket and its occupants slammed into the snow with a dull thud that Kiseleva felt as much as heard. The envelope settled around it like a feather-soft quilt. He pulled his gun out from its underarm holster and checked that the safety was off. Ostrovetsky climbed off the snowmobile, his boots sinking into the snow, covering the balloon with his Ingram. Kiseleva put a hand on his shoulder. 'No. They're mine,' he said.

Ostrovetsky was about to argue, but Kiseleva silenced him with a baleful stare. He stepped off the snowmobile and crunched towards the downed balloon. After the roar of the snowmobile and the thump of the crash-landing, the quiet was intimidating. He could hear a myriad of small sounds as he made his way through the snow. The propane burners were clicking as they cooled, the brightly coloured envelope crackled in the wind, the basket creaked, and somewhere high up in the sky a bird cried.

The closer he got to the basket, the deeper the snow. It was up to his knees, the icy cold soaking through his jeans and chilling his skin. Now that he was no longer astride the hot engine, the cold was spreading quickly through his body. He shivered. He pulled the scarf off his face and wiped his mouth with the back of his hand. The basket had fallen on its side, the open end pointing away from him. He stopped and listened. There were no human sounds. No crying. No pleading. No whimpering.

Kiseleva was suddenly disappointed. He waded through the snow as quickly as he could, lifting his feet high with each step and holding his hands out to the side for balance. It would be all too easy to stumble and fall, but the urge to see Freeman and the girl was overpowering and he pushed forward. He was panting, his breath a white fog around his face. He skirted around the basket, keeping his gun at the ready, his finger aching on the trigger. He swallowed apprehensively, the desire to kill forming a hard knot in his stomach. 'Don't be dead,' he whispered. 'Please don't be dead.'

The deflated envelope was billowing in the wind and being dragged away from the basket. Kiseleva froze in his tracks as he thought he saw a movement at the edge of the basket. He held the gun with both hands, fighting the shivering that threatened to spoil his aim, but the movement wasn't repeated. Small black dots began to swim across his vision and he blinked, trying to clear his eyes. He moved crab-like across the snow, taking careful, measured sideways steps, bending at the knees to keep his centre of gravity as low as possible. He saw a head, its mouth a red slash almost hidden in a beard. The pilot.

As he moved around another face came into view. It was Freeman, his eyes closed, his head back as if he'd been punched on the chin. Kiseleva frowned. He took another step to the side, and as he moved he saw Freeman's head slump forward. Kiseleva smiled grimly. At least the father was still alive. For a while, at least. But what about the girl? He licked his lips in anticipation. She must have been right at the bottom of the basket. Another couple of steps and he'd be able to see right inside – there was nowhere to hide. It'd be like shooting fish in a barrel. He lifted his left leg up and placed his foot carefully to the side. It crunched through the crisp snow and as he transferred his weight he sank up to his knee. He leaned over and craned his neck. He caught a glimpse of black hair and pale skin and he jerked back, his breath coming in ragged gasps. He cursed himself for his stupidity. What the hell was he scared of? She was just a girl. An unarmed girl. He took another step and for the first time got a good look at her. She was lying awkwardly across her father's legs, her hair in disarray, her eyes closed. Her face was almost as white as the snow, but she was still alive – he could see her chest slowly rising and falling. Kiseleva grinned. 'Now you're mine,' he whispered. He took another step forward, wanting to get as close as possible. He wondered which one to shoot first, the girl or the father. God, it would be so much better if they were conscious. He wanted them to beg for their lives, to plead and cry.

He kicked the edge of the basket, gingerly with the tip of his toe at first, then harder. There was no reaction. 'Freeman,' he said. 'Freeman. Wake up.' Neither the man nor his daughter showed any reaction. There was no alternative – he was going to have to do it while they were unconscious. He aimed the gun at Freeman's head. Like fish in a barrel, he thought again. He tightened his trigger finger. That was when Mersiha opened her eyes.

The fall had knocked the wind out of Mersiha, but it wasn't as bad as she'd feared. The half-deflated envelope had contained enough hot air to restrict the downward plunge and the thick snow had absorbed much of the impact. Her father hadn't been so lucky. He'd banged his head against one of the propane tanks and was unconscious, and he didn't react when she shook his arm. Mersiha had heard only one snowmobile and she listened for a while, wondering what had happened to the other one. All she could see out of the basket was the snowfield and a strip of blue sky. She strained to hear what was going on outside. She heard a bird cry out, and far off in the distance something that sounded like a car. Maybe someone had seen them crash. Maybe they'd be rescued. Her hopes were dashed when she heard a crunching noise, as if a bite had been taken out of a crisp apple. Someone was walking towards the balloon.

Mersiha looked around for something to use as a weapon, but there was nothing she could use against men with guns. Something rustled behind her and she flinched, then realised that it was only the balloon moving in the wind. Outside, she heard another footfall. She pinched her father's arm. He moaned but still he wouldn't wake up. Mersiha's heart began to race. She had a sudden urge to rush out of the basket, to go down fighting rather than being shot like a trapped animal. In front of her, the large stainless-steel burners clicked as they cooled. She realised how lucky they'd been that the tanks hadn't been hit. The pilot lights still flickered blue. If the propane had escaped they'd have died in an inferno. She grimaced. Burned to death or shot – did it really matter? The end result was going to be the same. Away to the left, she heard another footfall. She focused her attention on the unseen man, turning her head slowly from side to side as she listened and tried to pinpoint his position. She imagined that she could hear his breathing, rapid and shallow.

Tim's arm was lying across her left foot and she pulled it away, but the movement caused a shifting in the balance of the basket and it squeaked. She stopped. The approaching man stopped, too. Mersiha closed her eyes and played dead. If he thought that they'd died in the fall, maybe he'd just go away. She tried to keep her breathing as still as possible.

The man started to move again. Only one man, Mersiha realised, though there had been two on each of the snow-mobiles. The urge to open her eyes was almost irresistible. She could picture the man standing at the open end of the basket, a gun in his hand, watching her and waiting for the moment when he'd pull the trigger and end her life. She didn't want to die with her eyes closed, she thought. Better to see the face of her killer. Better to look into his eyes so that he'd feel her hatred and contempt. She opened her eyelids a fraction. Still there was nothing to see but the snow and the sky. Her father's head moved, slumping forward. His breathing seemed heavier and more laboured. Mersiha closed her eyes again. Another footfall. Definitely louder this time. How close would the man get, she thought? Would he try to touch them, to see if he could find a pulse, or would he just shoot them where they lay? Something rocked the basket, a light tap at first and then a hefty kick. Mersiha trembled.

When the man spoke, his voice seemed only inches away. 'Freeman,' she heard. 'Freeman, wake up.' When her father didn't reply, the man crunched through the snow, then there was silence. Mersiha opened her eyes.

The man was standing less than six feet from the open

end of the basket, his gun levelled at Freeman's face. 'No!' she screamed. The gun began to swing in her direction. She cowered in the bottom of the basket, trying to push herself away from the weapon. The propane burners were between her and the gun but the man had only to move to the side to get a clear shot. He smiled evilly, showing yellowing teeth. His hair and eyebrows were crusted with melting ice, and he had a soaking-wet red scarf around his neck. He was shivering, either with the cold or with excitement, but the hand holding the gun was steady. The pilot lights in the burners flickered as a gust of wind blew into the wicker basket. Mersiha tore her gaze away from the man with the gun and stared at the huge burners, a frown on her face. Suddenly she realised what she had to do. She screamed as she threw herself forward, her hands clawing as she groped for the metal levers. The man took a step back, confused by her attack, as if he thought she was trying to get at him. Before he could aim his gun again, Mersiha grabbed the lever that operated the left burner. She pulled it with all her might. The propane hissed as it escaped and then roared as it ignited, sending a tongue of bright yellow flame shooting out of the basket, engulfing the man. Mersiha was so close to the burner that the heat was scorching, but she kept it full on, turning her head away and closing her eyes tight.

The man screamed, and when Mersiha opened her eyes he'd dropped his gun and was staggering back, his hands clutched to his face, his jacket in flames. His screams chilled her. His hair caught fire and immediately her nostrils were filled with the stench of burning hair and flesh. The man turned to run but his feet were trapped in the snow and he twisted awkwardly, falling to the side, still screaming.

Mersiha knew she had only seconds in which to act. She scrambled out of the basket and looked for the gun. For a wild moment she couldn't find it; then she realised it had sunk into the snow. The second gunman was still sitting on the snowmobile, his attention focused on his injured colleague. Mersiha sank up to her knees in the snow as she dug frantically with her hands like a dog trying to uncover a buried bone. The man she'd burned was screaming and rolling over and over, trying to extinguish the flames, then suddenly he stopped moving and his screams turned to whimpers. Mersiha's fingers touched hard metal and she pulled the gun free from the snow. She had no time to check if the safety was on or off as she struggled to her feet and fired. She was surprised at how quiet the gun was with its silencer, no louder than a cough. The first shot went wide. The man on the snowmobile turned towards her, a look of disbelief on his face. Mersiha took another step forward and fired again. The man made no sound, but she knew she'd hit him because his shoulder jerked backwards and blood sprayed across the snow. The look of surprise on the huge man's face turned to one of pain. He had a large machine pistol in his right hand and he swung it around, gritting his teeth as he tried to aim. It was obviously a heavy weapon, best suited to a two-handed grip. Mersiha took no chances. She dropped flat on the ground and fired, just as her brother had taught her years earlier. He'd drummed into her that she had to fire at the widest point, the place where she had the most margin for error – the chest. She hit him dead centre. The man tumbled backwards off the snowmobile, the gun falling uselessly from his hand. Mersiha got to her feet, ignoring the snow that covered her clothes, and waded towards the snowmobile. The man lay still, but Mersiha wasn't prepared to take any chances – she shot him again in the chest. His legs jerked once and then were still. Blood continued to bubble from the holes in his chest and soaked into the snow around him, like raspberry-flavoured slush. Behind her, the burnt man stopped whimpering, like an exhausted baby who had finally dropped off to sleep.

Mersiha went back to the basket and knelt down beside her father. She stroked his forehead. 'Dad?' she whispered. His eyelids flickered. She shook his shoulder, hard. 'Come on, Dad. Wake up.' There was no reaction, so she grabbed a handful of snow and rubbed it on his face. Freeman snorted and coughed. 'Dad, we have to go. Come on.'

Mersiha tucked the gun into the back of her trousers under her jacket and helped her father out of the basket and over to the snowmobile. Freeman stared blankly at the bloody corpse in the snow.

'We have to get away from here,' she said. 'The other snowmobile's still around.'

Freeman stood and listened, his head on one side. 'No,' he said. 'We'd hear them if they were coming. Something must have happened to it.'

Mersiha bent over the snowmobile. It had sunk into the snow and she could see that there was no way to pull it out. They'd have to go down the mountain on foot. She took his hand. 'Come on.'

Maury Anderson poured himself a glass of cold water from his kitchen tap and carried it through to the sitting room.

He'd read somewhere once that a glass of water helped. He caught a glimpse of his reflection in the mirror above the sideboard containing his wife's golf trophies, and he flinched. He looked terrible, like a man who'd been involved in a dreadful accident.

He'd used up all the cocaine in the house, except for one line which he'd arranged into a neat row on the glass coffee table. He knelt down and put the glass of water to one side, careful not to disturb the line of white powder. He used a rolled-up dollar bill to sniff the cocaine, one nostril at a time. It felt good, but the kick was nowhere near as good as when he'd first started using the drug. Now it was a need, not a pleasure. He sat back on his heels and blinked as the drug crossed into his bloodstream.

His life was over, he knew that. He'd betrayed his wife, he'd betrayed his friend, he'd betrayed the company he worked for. Everything he'd ever held dear was spoiled. Finished. Over. No matter what happened in Colorado, whether or not Katherine managed to save Tony and Mersiha, no matter what he said or did, his life was worthless. Less than worthless.

The glass of water would help. He wished he could remember where he'd read that. It was one of those stupid facts that lodged at the back of his mind. It was something to do with the way a bullet behaved in a liquid. He took a mouthful of the water and pursed his lips, then slipped the barrel of the gun in. It was his wife's gun. She had always been scared of being left in the house on her own and insisted on keeping it in her bedside cabinet, always loaded, always ready for the inner-city robber she was sure would one day drive out from Baltimore to steal everything she had. Everything he'd worked so hard to give her.

Without the water in his mouth, the bullet might pass through the back of his head, not killing him but leaving him a hopeless vegetable. With the water, his head would explode, with absolutely no chance of survival. At least he'd be able to do one thing right. He began to cry as he pulled the trigger.

'I see the road,' Freeman said. He pointed and Mersiha nodded. In the distance a ribbon of asphalt ran through the woods, glistening wetly. They'd left the snowline behind and were now walking over gravelly soil carpeted with pine needles. The gun was pressing against the small of her back, but she didn't want to remove it, partly because she wasn't sure yet if they were safe from their pursuers, but also because she didn't want to remind her father of what had happened up on the snowfield. They were both breathing heavily and the backs of Mersiha's legs were aching from the strain of walking downhill.

'Dad, what are we going to do?'

'We've got to go to the police, pumpkin. You know that.' Mersiha slipped and almost lost her footing, but Freeman grabbed her by the arm and steadied her. 'Careful,' he warned.

They started down the hill again, moving from tree to tree because the ground was getting progressively steeper as they neared the road. 'Dad? Do we have to go to the police?'

'Those men killed the balloon crew. And if they'd caught us, we'd be dead, too.'

'But after what I did to Sabatino . . .' She left the sentence unfinished.

Freeman said nothing for a while, and Mersiha turned to look at him. His face was in torment and she looked away quickly, knowing exactly what he was thinking: she'd killed a man, she'd done it deliberately, and she'd done it with his gun. The deaths on the snowfield were clearly self-defence, but the police might look differently on what had happened in Sabatino's office. 'He tried to rape you, pumpkin.' Her father's voice sounded oddly flat. They went down the rest of the way in silence, concentrating on keeping their footing on the treacherous hillside. They had to skirt the highway for a hundred yards before finding a place where they could drop safely down on to the asphalt. They were on a sharp bend, so they dashed across the road to a place where they'd be more visible. 'Which way's the town?' Mersiha asked.

Freeman frowned up at the sky, trying to get his bearings. The sun was almost directly overhead and didn't help much. 'I'm not sure, but it'll be too far to walk anyway.'

A truck sounded its horn angrily and they stepped back. Freeman tried to flag it down but it sped by. Either the driver hadn't seen his frantic waving or he couldn't be bothered to pick up a couple of hitchhikers. They stood together, shivering. Freeman hugged his daughter, trying to supply warmth and comfort. Mersiha felt suddenly small and defenceless in his arms, and she rested her head on his chest. She could hear his heart beating, strong and regular like a metronome. His arms began to slide down her back and she pulled away, fearful that he'd find the hidden gun. 'What's wrong?' Freeman asked.

'Nothing. I thought I heard a car coming.'

Freeman lifted his chin and listened. 'I can't hear

anything. But I'm sure there'll be something soon. Don't worry.'

'Should we start walking?' She was scared that he'd try to hug her again.

'Let's rest for a while. There's no point in walking if we don't know which way to go. If we start to get too cold, we'll walk. Okay?'

'Okay,' she agreed.

There was a large rock at the apex of the bend which had been painted with yellow-green warning stripes, and they sat on it. 'Are you feeling okay?' Freeman asked.

'I'm tired. And a bit wet.'

'I meant . . . you know.'

Mersiha knew exactly what he meant. She'd killed two men and he wanted to know how she felt about it. How she was dealing with it. But she also knew that he wouldn't want to hear the truth. He wanted her to say that she was shocked, distraught, remorseful, the way people normally felt when they'd taken someone's life. What he didn't want to hear was the truth – that she felt absolutely nothing. They'd attacked her. She'd killed them. End of story. She wrapped her arms around her legs and put her chin on her knees as she explored her inner feelings, trying to see if she was missing something, but she knew she was wasting her time. There was nothing, just contempt and hatred for the men with the guns. She thought about the ground crew, riddled with bullets and dying in the snow, and she thought about Tim, dead but with his eyes wide open. She was sorry that they were dead, sort of, but it wasn't the sort of grief she'd felt when her parents had died. She looked at her father. He was waiting patiently for her to answer his question. She shrugged and saw the hurt in his eyes.

He was about to say something else when they both heard the growl of an engine. Mersiha jumped down off the rock and waved her arms in the air. She jumped up and down. 'It's a car!' she shouted as Freeman slid down.

In the distance they saw a red Jeep Wrangler, a blonde woman at the wheel.

Jenny Welch didn't believe in God – she'd seen enough men crying for salvation before she'd blown them away to know that there was no saviour – but she definitely believed in fate. And the fact that Freeman and the girl were standing by the side of the road waving their arms and shouting for her to stop didn't surprise her in the least. They were fated to die. And fate had decreed that it would be at her hand. She couldn't think how they'd managed to get away from Kiseleva and the snowmobiles, but maybe that was fate, too. She smiled and gently applied the brakes, coming to a stop on the bend. 'You guys want a lift?' she asked brightly, winding down the window. She knew that there was no possibility of them recognising her – she'd never got close to them on horseback and she'd had her hair tucked up inside her fur hat.

'Are you going into town?' Freeman asked.

'Sure am. Get in.'

Mersiha climbed into the back seat. There were red stains on the front of her jacket.

'What happened?' Jenny asked, pointing at the marks.

Mersiha looked guiltily at her father. 'Ketchup,' he said. 'We had breakfast at Burger King.'

'Yeah, I've done that before,' Jenny laughed. 'You take one bite and everything shoots out the other side.'

Freeman got into the front passenger seat and Jenny drove off. 'So, were you guys hiking?' she asked.

'Sort of,' Freeman said. He sat back and rubbed his eyes. He sighed deeply.

'You sound exhausted,' Jenny said.

'Bad day.'

'You wanna tell me about it?'

Freeman shook his head. 'Just a bad day.'

Jenny studied Mersiha in the driving mirror. She was beautiful, despite the strain on her face. She had a lovely jawline and high cheekbones, and huge eyes that seemed about to burst into tears. It wasn't the face of a killer, but she could see how Bzuchar's brother could have allowed her to get close to him. Jenny smiled to herself. Time and time again she'd managed to get to targets for exactly the same reason – people assumed that she was too pretty and too feminine to be a threat.

'Do you live around here?' Mersiha asked.

'No. I'm a tourist. You?'

'We're on vacation too,' Freeman said.

'Skiing?'

'Horse-riding,' Mersiha replied.

'Yeah? I'm allergic.' Jenny smiled at her in the mirror. 'If I so much as see a picture of a horse, I start sneezing. So, where do you guys wanna go?'

Mersiha put a hand on her father's shoulder and he looked around. Something unspoken passed between them. 'Our cabin,' he said eventually.

'Yeah? Where's that?'

'You can drop us in town. We'll get a cab.'

'A cab at this time of year?' Jenny laughed. 'I don't think so. I'll take you right to the cabin. Just tell me how to get there.'

'Are you sure?' Freeman asked.

'Hey. What else have I got to do? I'm on vacation, remember.'

'Thanks, that's really nice of you.'

Jenny smiled. 'Just show me the way.'

Mersiha said nothing as Jenny drove. Freeman made small-talk about horse-riding and where the best places to ski were. Jenny had to admire the man's guts. He'd been pursued through the mountains, shot at, seen several men killed, escaped, temporarily at least, in a balloon, yet he chatted away as if he'd done nothing more strenuous than a little window-shopping. He seemed a pleasant enough guy, the real fatherly type. Not like her own father, she thought. He didn't have the predatory look in his eyes which her father had developed once she'd gotten beyond the age when she could ride Tess. She shivered as she remembered the late-night visits, the promises of the things he'd buy her if she did what he asked, the threats if she ever told.

'Cold?' Freeman asked.

'No. Someone walked over my grave,' she said, smiling. Not her grave, she thought savagely. Her father's grave. Well, not really a grave at all, just a lime-filled hole behind the barn where he'd never be found.

'That's the track where we turn off,' Freeman said.

'I see it.' In fact she'd already seen it but hadn't let on. She indicated and waited for a mini-van full of skiers to drive by before turning on to the track. Mersiha reached over and put her hand on her father's shoulder. He patted her hand. Jenny was suddenly jealous. It was a father–daughter relationship the like of which she'd never experienced. Total trust and understanding, not after-dark fumblings and threats.

'Wait!' Freeman said sharply.

Jenny slammed on the brakes. 'What? What's the matter?'

'Look,' he said.

Jenny looked. There were two vehicles parked in front of the cabin. Bzuchar's Jeep Cherokee and a white Lincoln Continental. 'What's wrong?' she asked, even though she knew what he was thinking. She turned off the engine.

Freeman turned around in his seat and looked at Mersiha. 'We have to go to the police,' he said. Mersiha nodded silently.

'Why? What's happened?' Jenny asked.

'I can't tell you,' he said. 'Please, just do as I say.'

Jenny shrugged. She turned the key, but not all the way. She cursed, and tried again. 'God, that's twice it's happened today. There's a loose connection to the battery or something. My husband was going to get it fixed but . . .'

'Come on, come on,' Freeman said urgently.

'I'll have to open the hood,' she said. 'Can you look at it for me?'

Freeman swallowed nervously. Jenny made a show of trying again. Nothing. She smiled brightly. 'It's easy to fix, really. It took my husband less than a minute.'

'Dad . . .' Mersiha said apprehensively. 'Let's go.'

'It's better we drive than walk, pumpkin,' he said, climbing out of the Jeep.

He pulled the hood open and peered inside. 'Why don't you help your dad?' Jenny suggested.

Mersiha nodded and clambered out to join her father. 'Stay in the car. We're not hanging around here,' he said.

'But she said . . .'

'I don't care what she said. Do as I say.'

They looked up as they heard the sound of a bullet being chambered. Jenny stood at the side of the Jeep, the submachine pistol in her hands. Freeman looked as if he was going to run and Jenny pointed the Ingram at him. 'I think you'd both better do as I say, don't you?' Without being asked, Freeman and Mersiha raised their hands. Jenny smiled. 'There's no need for that. I don't think you're going to give me a hard time, not when I've got firepower like this.' She gestured with the gun for them to walk to the cabin. Freeman and Mersiha lowered their arms and walked together down the track. He put his arm around her shoulders. It was a touching scene, Jenny thought. But not touching enough for her to spare their lives.

Freeman's shoulders slumped as if he'd given up all hope, but Jenny wasn't fooled – she could see that he was heading for the pile of cut wood and that his hand was swinging a little to the side. 'Freeman, if you even try to reach for that axe, I'll shoot your daughter,' she said. Freeman instantly pulled his hand back as if he'd been stung. Jenny kept her distance as she shepherded them between the two vehicles and up on to the deck. 'Open the door,' she told Mersiha.

Katherine Freeman dabbed at her eyes with a handkerchief, but the man on the sofa was unmoved. 'You can't kill them,' she said.

'I can do whatever I want,' Utsyev said. 'I'm the one with the gun, remember?'

'She's just a girl. A sixteen-year-old girl.'

'She killed my brother. She blew his face away.'

'She must have had a reason.'

Utsyev chuckled. It sounded like the rustling of long-dead leaves. 'And that makes a difference, does it?'

Katherine sniffed. She blew her nose loudly. 'How do you know it was her?'

'She used your husband's gun. And my men saw her going into my brother's office.'

Katherine shook her head. She began to cry again. 'Please don't hurt her. She's only a child.' Utsyev said nothing.

They heard steps on the deck outside. Katherine started to get to her feet but Utsyev held a finger to his lips and pointed the gun at her head. Katherine twisted around on the sofa. The door opened. It was Mersiha. Behind her was Tony, his hand on her shoulder. Katherine jumped up, shouting for all she was worth. 'Run, Tony! Run! He's going to kill you!' The door continued to open, revealing a tall blonde woman holding a large gun.

Utsyev threw back his head and laughed. Freeman and Mersiha stepped into the middle of the room and the woman closed the door behind them. Katherine hugged her husband and then pulled Mersiha to her. 'Are you all right?' she said.

'What are you doing here?' Freeman said.

'I came to warn you,' she answered. Freeman shook his head, sadly.

'Who's she?' Jenny asked Utsyev.

'The wife,' he said.

'The wife?' she repeated. She tossed back her hair. 'That means we can kill three birds with one stone.'

Freeman stood in front of Katherine and Mersiha and stared at Utsyev. The man looked ill. His skin was deathly pale and his eyes seemed rimmed in black as if he hadn't slept for a long time. He had his back to a window and the light behind his close-cropped grey hair formed a halo around his skull. Freeman instinctively knew that there was no way he could talk the man out of what he intended to do. He was a stone-cold killer, with eyes that held no human warmth at all. There was no point in pleading for their lives. As if reading his mind, Utsyev aimed the gun at Freeman's stomach. 'You won't get away with it,' Freeman said.

'We'll see,' Utsyev countered.

'Let me do it, Bzuchar,' Jenny said eagerly.

'Quiet.' He narrowed his eyes at Freeman. 'Suppose someone killed your daughter? Wouldn't you want revenge?'

Freeman looked him straight in the eyes. 'I'd want justice. Not revenge.'

'How very fucking civilised of you . . .'

'He was going to rape me!' Mersiha blurted out.

Utsyev looked at Katherine. 'See – she doesn't even deny it.'

'If your brother was trying to hurt her, of course she'd defend herself.'

'She went there with a gun!' Utsyev screamed. 'She went to see my brother with a fucking gun and she shot him dead.'

He was waving his gun around and Freeman could see that he was close to firing it.

Katherine moved to stand by her husband. 'Don't hurt her,' she pleaded. 'If it's revenge you want, then kill me. Kill me!'

'Katherine, no!' Mersiha shouted. 'Don't beg. Please don't beg. It won't work.'

Utsyev was breathing heavily, his chest heaving as he glared at them. He aimed the gun at Katherine, then swung his arm sideways. 'I'm going to shoot the little bitch first.' He squeezed the trigger, but before he could fire Freeman moved in front of his daughter.

'No!' he said. 'You can't.'

Jenny stepped forward and slammed the butt of her gun against Freeman's temple, knocking him to the ground. 'We can do what the fuck we want,' she said. She turned to Utsyev. 'Let me, Bzuchar. Let me kill him.'

'You always had a thing about father figures,' Utsyev said evilly. He grinned and waved his gun at Freeman. 'Go ahead.'

Jenny brought her gun to bear on Freeman as he knelt on the floor, holding his hands to his bleeding temple. Katherine screamed and threw herself at Jenny, grabbing hold of the weapon and kneeing her in the stomach. The air burst from Jenny's throat and she doubled over. Bullets sprayed across the wall over the fireplace, shattering a mirror and screeching off the light-fittings. Katherine and Jenny fell on to the sofa, still fighting over the gun. It fired again and the television exploded.

Freeman staggered to his feet and headed unsteadily towards them. 'Katherine!' he shouted.

Utsyev fired his silenced gun and Freeman felt his right

hand explode. He held it up to his face in astonishment. It was covered in blood and a chunk of flesh was missing from his palm, close to the base of the thumb. As he stared at the wound the pain hit and he gasped. He staggered backwards, his left hand holding his right wrist. Utsyev's gun coughed again and Freeman felt a bullet slam into his right leg. He fell sideways and crashed to the floor. Utsyev stood over him, grinning. 'How does it feel, Freeman?' he hissed. 'How does it feel to die?'

On the sofa, Katherine was screaming. Freeman looked over at her. She was flat on her back with Jenny on top, the submachine-gun between them. It went off again and bullets ripped into the ceiling. Bits of wood and plaster floated around them like a light snowfall.

Freeman saw Mersiha standing at the end of the sofa. She was looking right at him, as if there were no one else in the room. Her hand moved behind her back and reappeared with a gun. He saw her flick the safety catch off with her thumb. She was still looking directly at him. Katherine screamed again. Jenny was forcing the barrel of the Ingram down towards her face, her finger still on the trigger. Freeman looked back at Mersiha. She had the gun up but she was still looking at him. He knew what she was waiting for. His permission. His approval. Katherine screamed again. Mersiha's mouth opened a fraction. She licked her lips nervously. Her eyes darted over to look at Katherine and Jenny fighting on the sofa, then back to Freeman. He knew without a shadow of a doubt that unless he said it was okay she wouldn't fire the gun. She'd made him a promise and only he could release her from it. It was up to him. Slowly, almost imperceptibly, he nodded, looking deep into her eyes as he did so.

Mersiha whirled around, both hands on the butt of the gun, and fired, two shots. Jenny was knocked backwards over the sofa, her blood smearing down the wall as she fell against it. Utsyev roared like a bull and swung his gun around. Freeman lashed out with his left leg, catching the man just below the knee and knocking him off balance. Mersiha fired again and put two bullets in his chest. He fell to his knees, then keeled over backwards. Mersiha let the gun drop to the floor.

Katherine rolled off the sofa, coughing and spluttering. She gasped when she saw Freeman on the floor, bleeding from his hand and leg. She crawled over to him and hugged him so tightly that the breath was forced from his body. 'I love you, Tony,' she whispered, her breath warm against his ear.

'It's okay,' he said.

'No,' she said, firmly. 'I mean I love you. I really love you.'

She looked at him long and hard with a burning intensity that left him in no doubt what she meant. He returned the look. 'It's okay,' he repeated. She struggled to find the right words to say, but Freeman shook his head. 'Don't say anything,' he said. 'Just hold me.' Katherine burst into tears. She held him in her arms.

Mersiha knelt down beside Freeman and she and Katherine helped him to his feet.

Utsyev had lost all feeling below the waist, and a cold numbness was spreading across his upper body. He could feel his lifeblood oozing out of his chest, and knew that he was dying. He could hear his brother's voice, calling to him from the distance, calling for him to come and play. It was Gilani as a child, a small boy who wanted nothing more than to play in the fields and catch fish in the river. Utsyev could feel himself slipping away, but something was holding him back. There was something he had to do. One last thing.

He concentrated on his right hand until he could feel the hard metal between his fingers, and then he forced himself to open his eyes. The pain returned and the room felt as if it was spinning. His eyes closed and the blackness enveloped him, but he fought against it, pushing it away, telling himself that all he had to do was this one thing and then he could go and play with Gilani. His eyes flickered open and he looked down over his bleeding body to where Freeman was being held up by his wife and daughter. He felt himself start to slip away again. The hand that lay by his side felt as if it belonged to someone else. He was controlling it, he was raising the hand with the gun, but it felt as if he were watching the action from somewhere else. From somewhere outside the body. He pointed the gun at them, his hand wavering. Freeman passed through the sights, then the woman, then the girl. He aimed between Mersiha's shoulder-blades and fought to keep the gun steady as his finger tightened on the trigger. He concentrated all he had left on the index finger of his right hand. At the last moment, Freeman saw him. His mouth opened to shout a warning, but it was too late. Utsyev fired, then the gun fell from his hand as he died.

* * *

Freeman screamed as Mersiha pitched forward as if she'd been punched in the back. 'Dad . . .' she moaned as her legs gave way. He grabbed her, but she was a dead weight in his arms.

'No!' Katherine shouted as Freeman laid her gently down on the wooden floor. 'No!'

'Get me something to stop the bleeding,' Freeman said, cradling Mersiha's head in his lap. Blood was still pouring from his hand and leg but his own injuries didn't concern him. All he could think about was Mersiha.

'What?'

'Anything. A cloth. A towel. Anything.'

Katherine ran past Utsyev's unmoving body to the kitchen.

'Dad, it hurts,' Mersiha whispered.

'I know, pumpkin. I know. You'll be all right.'

Katherine returned with a towel. She knelt down by Freeman. 'Press it against her back,' he said, lifting her. She positioned the towel over the entry wound and then Freeman laid her down again so that her weight would keep it in position.

Katherine stood up, wringing her hands. 'What are we going to do?' she asked helplessly.

Freeman shook his head. They were miles from anywhere and there was no phone in the cabin. Mersiha shivered. He pulled a rug along the floor and wrapped it around her. She smiled up at him. 'Am I dying, Dad?' she asked quietly.

Freeman stroked her hair. 'No,' he said softly. 'Of course you're not dying.' He looked up at Katherine, his face a pained mask.

'I'm sorry, Mom,' Mersiha said.

It was the first time she'd ever called Katherine 'Mom'. Katherine knelt down beside her, tears in her eyes. 'Shh,' she said. 'Don't try to speak.' She looked at Freeman. 'We need help,' she said. 'We have to get her to a hospital.'

'We can't move her. She'll bleed to death in the car.'

'The car!' Katherine said. 'God, I'm so stupid. There's a phone in the car!' She ran out of the cabin.

Freeman put his hand on Mersiha's forehead. She felt cold. When he took it away he left behind a bloody palm-print. 'I'm sleepy,' she said.

'Try to stay awake, Mersiha. Everything's going to be okay.'

'Can't I sleep, Dad?' Her voice was barely discernible.

'No. Try not to.' Blood was seeping through the front of her jacket. Freeman was frightened to open it. He couldn't face seeing the damage done by Utsyev's bullet.

'Dad?'

'Yes, pumpkin?'

'Will you sing to me?'

'Of course I will.' She shivered in his arms and closed her eyes. He shook her and she moaned softly. 'What shall I sing?' he asked.

'You know,' she breathed.

Freeman knew. With tears streaming down his face, he sang 'Happy Birthday' to her.

*   *   *

Freeman stood at the edge of the cliff, looking out over the jagged granite rocks and the white-topped waves of the North Sea below. He never tired of the coast's rugged beauty. It brought home to him the power of the sea. It was nature at its most brutal, a far cry from the soft beaches of the east coast of America. A massive wave crashed down on the rocks, sending salty spray across his face. He wiped the water away with his left hand. His right hand had healed nicely, though it was still a little stiff and he couldn't move his thumb more than a few degrees. The young doctor at the hospital in Aberdeen had said that he'd eventually regain full use of it, though he'd probably always feel a twinge or two during the winter months. The same went for his leg. He still had to walk with a stick and he became tired if he walked any distance, but that he could live with. He smiled as he remembered telling the doctor that he knew it would be all right eventually because he'd been shot in the leg before. The doctor had thought Freeman was joking until he'd seen the old scars.

He heard Katherine walk up behind him and he smiled as she slid her arms around his waist. 'Maybe we should build the house right here,' she said, putting her head on his shoulder. 'Then you'd have the view without going outside.'

'Wouldn't be the same without the wind and the rain,' he said, waving his walking stick at the raging sea. They stood in silence together, Katherine pressing herself against his back as they looked out over the waves. 'You don't mind?' he said eventually.

'Mind what?'

'Leaving America? Leaving the company?'

Katherine thought about her answer before replying. 'No. As long as I'm with you, I don't care where we live.' She squeezed him around the waist.

'Good,' he said. They'd talked about it back in the States and they'd both agreed that there were too many bad memories in America. Too many tainted places. But he still wanted reassurance that he'd done the right thing. After they'd returned to Maryland they'd sold their house and put all their belongings in storage. Walter Carey had been surprised when Freeman had said that he wanted to leave CRW, but the bank had appointed a team of professional managers and all the signs were that the company would survive. Katherine sold half of her block of CRW shares, and the proceeds would provide enough of an income for them to live on, for a while at least. Maybe in time they'd start up a new business, build something together, but he was in no hurry. All he wanted to do for the time being was to take life slowly, one step at a time.

'Is there room for me in there?' Mersiha asked. She was standing on the path that led to the cliff-top, her arm in a denim sling that Katherine had made to match her Levi jeans. 'I mean, God forbid that I should intrude into this tender moment.'

Katherine laughed and waved her over. Mersiha moved slowly. She was still getting used to walking again after a month in hospital in Colorado and another six weeks in Johns Hopkins in Baltimore. The surgeons had done an incredible job. The bullet had ripped through her left lung and exited through her shoulder, and she'd been on a ventilator for several days in a shock-trauma unit. She was still pale, and the muscles of her arm had atrophied while the shoulder healed, so she required regular physical therapy, but every day Freeman thanked God that she was alive. She was recovering slowly, but like Freeman she'd bear the scars, physical and mental, for ever.

'Are you going to stand here all day?' she asked.

'Maybe,' Freeman said.

'That's okay, then,' she said. She sighed. The three of them stood looking out to sea, the wind and spray lashing their faces. Freeman breathed in the salt air. It had been important to get away from America, to start again. It wasn't that he feared retribution. The police hadn't been over-concerned about solving the murders of the Utsyev brothers, as both were known criminals, and they had been more than happy to accept that the Freemans were innocent bystanders caught up in a gang war. As far as they were concerned, the case was closed. Freeman had reported the Heckler & Koch stolen, but the gun was never found. It was over, and now they could put it all behind them. Eventually he planned to build a house in the north of Scotland, a new house, for a new life. But first, all he wanted to do was to spend time with the two people he loved most in the world, and to get to know them. To really get to know them.

Now available from Hodder & Stoughton

Stephen Leather's cracking new thriller:

THE DOUBLE TAP

The assassin – the world's most successful contract killer. Ice-cool, accurate, elusive – with an uncanny ability to change his appearance. An anonymous professional with a unique calling card: one bullet in the head and one in the chest for each of his targets.

The Judas goat – An ex-member of the SAS, Mike Cramer is the perfect sacrificial bait. The FBI discover the next name on the assassin's hit list and Cramer is set up to take his place. Even armed and protected by top SAS marksmen, Cramer must face a bullet at point blank range. And no one has ever been fast enough to escape the assassin.

The wild card – Cramer's past has caught up with him. Ex-IRA extremist Dermott Lynch is now serving his own cause. He blames Cramer for his lover's death and he's out for revenge.

As Cramer trains for the most dangerous mission in his career, Lynch hunts down his sworn enemy. And the unknown assassin silently closes in on his target.

The players are in position for the final deadly game . . .

Turn over to sample the suspense . . .

Cramer didn't look around as the man in the Barbour jacket joined him at the edge of the sea wall. 'Nice day for it,' said the man amicably.

Cramer's upper lip curled back, but still he didn't turn to face the visitor.

'What do you want, Colonel?'

'A chat. You've got time for a chat, haven't you?'

Cramer shrugged listlessly. 'I'd rather be on my own, if that's all right with you.'

'But you're not on your own, are you, Sergeant Cramer. There's an IRA active service unit armed to the teeth heading your way.'

'You'd best be going then, huh?'

The Colonel shook his head sadly. 'This isn't the way to do it, Joker.'

The nickname made Cramer smile. It had been a long time since anyone had used it.

Cramer drew back his jacket so that the Colonel could see the Browning in the holster. He looked over his shoulder. The men on the beach were still heading in their direction. Lynch and O'Riordan were standing in the car park, talking. 'You should go, Colonel. This is going to get messy.'

'Hear me out, Joker. This isn't the way to do it. I'm offering you a chance to do something worthwhile with your last few weeks?'

Cramer frowned, then looked away. 'I'm listening.'

'Over the last two years there've been a series of assassinations around the world. Businessmen, politicians, criminals, all killed by one man. A professional killer who'll hit anyone if the price is right. He's never been caught, and we have no idea who he is.'

'We? We as in the SAS?'

'The FBI, Interpol, MI6, the SVR, Mossad.'

'All the good guys, huh?' Cramer's voice was loaded with sarcasm.

The Colonel ignored the interruption. 'He likes to get in close, this killer. He always uses a handgun. We've dozens of witnesses, but we don't know what he looks like.'

Cramer frowned. 'That doesn't make sense.'

'Oh, we've dozens of descriptions all right. He's short. He's tall. He's thin, he's overweight, he's balding, he has a beard, blue eyes, brown eyes, pale skinned, tanned. The only thing we're sure of is that he's white and male.'

'A master of disguise,' said Cramer, smiling at the cliché.

The Colonel shrugged. 'He uses contact lenses, he grows facial hair as and when he needs it. He puts on weight, he takes it off. Maybe he even has plastic surgery. There isn't anything he won't do to get close to the target.'

Cramer turned around slowly. The men in the car park had started walking again. They'd soon be at the sea wall. He looked anxiously at the Colonel, but he seemed unfazed by the approaching killers. 'What do you want from me?'

'Do you know what a Judas Goat is?'

Cramer shook his head.

'Say you're trying to trap a tiger. You can trample through the jungle all you want, you'll not see a hair of it. You're in his territory. You're wasting your time trying to hunt it. So what you do is take a young goat, a kid, and you tether it in a clearing. Then you sit back and wait. The tiger seeks out the bleating goat, and BANG! One dead tiger.'

'A Judas Goat?' repeated Cramer. 'Sounds more like

bait to me. That's what you're offering me? The chance to be bait?'

'I'm offering you the chance to go up against the most successful assassin in the world, Cramer. To the best of our knowledge he's never failed. Never been caught, and never failed. Wouldn't that be more of a challenge for you? Those bastards down there might call themselves an IRA active service unit, but we know better, don't we? They're psychopathic thugs with guns, that's all. Sure, you'll die with a gun in your hand and the blood coursing through your veins, but there's no honour in being gunned down like a rabid dog. Sheer weight of numbers, that's the only advantage they'll have. They'll just keep firing until you're dead. You'll get a couple of them, maybe more, but look at the company you'll be dying in. Hell's fucking bells, Joker, you wouldn't give those bastards the time of day and yet you want to die with them?'

Cramer said nothing. He stared out to the horizon and took several deep breaths. The Colonel waited for him to speak. 'Why does he take risks?' Cramer asked eventually. 'Why does he always do it close up? There are easier ways to kill. Safer ways.'

The Colonel nodded. 'The FBI reckon it's because he enjoys it. He wants to see his victims as they die. He's a serial killer, but a serial killer who gets paid for his work. It's not a question of whether or not he'll kill again, it's when. He'll keep on killing until we stop him, because he's not doing it for the money. He's doing it for the thrill.'

'And you want this guy to try to kill me?'

The Colonel turned to look at Cramer. He shook his head slowly. 'No,' he said softly, his voice barely audible above the sound of the waves crashing against the sea wall. 'We're pretty sure that he'll succeed.'

Cramer's mouth opened but he was lost for words.

'The man has never left any physical evidence behind,' said the Colonel. 'No fingerprints, no blood or tissue samples, nothing. If we catch him close to you with a gun in his hand, it's not enough. It's not even attempted murder, it's just possession of a weapon and for all we know he might have a licence for it. Even if he points the gun at you, what have we got? Threatening behaviour? Maybe attempted murder. If we're lucky he'll go away for five years. No, he has to pull the trigger. Once he's done that, we've got him.'

Cramer nodded, finally understanding. 'And if he pulls the trigger, I'm dead?'

The Colonel nodded. 'But you'll have a chance. You'll be armed, if you see him coming for you you'll be able to shoot first. It's a better chance than the Judas Goat gets.'

'He'll kill me,' said Cramer flatly.

'But you'll die with honour. In battle. Against a real professional. Isn't that a better way to die? Better than being shot by these thugs?'

Cramer stared out to sea. 'Is that how you'd like to go, Colonel?'

'If I had the choice, yes.' The Colonel's voice was flat and level. It sounded to Cramer as if he was telling the truth. 'It's your call, Joker. If you want it to happen now, I'll just walk away.'

The Colonel looked towards the men on the beach. They were about a quarter of a mile away, still walking in their direction. The other two men had reached the end of the sea wall and the youngster was walking down the road behind them, the newspaper held in both hands. 'You don't have much time,' said the Colonel. He tapped his stick on the floor and the cracks sounded like gunshots.

Cramer chuckled coldly. 'That's the truth,' he said. He paused. 'How do you know he'll come for me?'

'We know who one of his intended victims is going to be. I'll explain later, but we're looking for someone to take his place.' He paused. 'Well?'

Cramer rubbed his chin and then sighed. 'Okay.'

'You're sure?'

Cramer narrowed his eyes and studied the Colonel. 'What? Now you're trying to talk me out of it? I said I'll do it. I'll do it.'

The Colonel put his hand on Cramer's shoulder and squeezed. 'Thank you.'

Cramer shook his head. 'I'm not doing it for you, Colonel. I'm doing it for me. But first we've got to take care of them.' He nodded down the sea wall where the two IRA men were walking quickly towards them. The one in the raincoat was holding both hands to his side, clutching something. A weapon, probably an assault rifle. The men on the beach had broken into a run, guns at the ready.

The Colonel took a small transceiver out of his coat pocket, pressed the transmit button and spoke rapidly into it. Cramer couldn't make out what the man had said, but seconds later he heard the roar of two massive turbines and a huge red, white and blue Westland Sea King helicopter appeared from behind Ireland's Eye. Its main rotor dipped forward and it sped through the air towards them. 'Damn you, Colonel,' Cramer shouted above the noise of the engines. 'You knew I'd accept, didn't you?'

The Colonel said nothing as the helicopter circled and

then dropped so that it was hovering only feet above the harbour wall, the rotor wash flattening the water below. He motioned with his stick for Cramer to get in first. Cramer took one last look over his shoulder, deafened by the turbines. The bearded man had pulled a Kalashnikov out from under his raincoat and was holding it, seemingly unsure whether or not to fire. For one moment they had eye contact and Cramer could feel the hatred pouring out of the man, then a hand reached out of the belly of the Sea King and half pulled, half dragged him inside.

STEPHEN LEATHER

THE CHINAMAN

'Will leave you breathless' – *Daily Mail*

The Chinaman understood death.

Jungle-skilled, silent and lethal, he had killed for the Viet Cong and then for the Americans. He had watched helpless when his two eldest daughters had been raped and killed by Thai pirates.

Now all that was behind him. Quiet, hardworking and unassuming, he was building up his South London take-away business.

Until the day his wife and youngest daughter were destroyed by an IRA bomb in a Knightsbridge department store.

Then, simply but persistently, he began to ask the authorities who were the men responsible, what was being done. And was turned away, fobbed off, treated as a nuisance.

Which was when the Chinaman, denied justice, decided on revenge. And went back to war.

'As real and hard and tough as today's headlines. I couldn't put it down' – *Jack Higgins*

HODDER AND STOUGHTON PAPERBACKS

STEPHEN LEATHER

THE VETS

Hong Kong. The British administration is preparing to hand the capitalist colony back to Communist China with the minimum of fuss.

But Colonel Joel Tyler has other plans for the British colony, plans which involve four Vietnam War veterans and a spectacular mission making use of their unique skills.

Vietnam was the one thing the four men had in common before Tyler moulded them into a team capable of pulling off a sensational robbery.

But while the vets are preparing to take Hong Kong by storm, their paymaster, Anthony Chung, puts the final touches to an audacious betrayal. At stake is the future of Hong Kong . . .

'The plot blasts along faster than a speeding bullet' – *Today*

'His last thriller was praised by Jack Higgins who couldn't put it down. The same goes for this' – *Daily Mail*

HODDER AND STOUGHTON PAPERBACKS

STEPHEN LEATHER

THE LONG SHOT

The plan is so complex, the target so well protected that the three snipers have to rehearse the killing in the seclusion of the Arizona desert.

Cole Howard of the FBI knows he has only days to prevent the audacious assassination. But he doesn't know who the target is. Or where the crack marksmen will strike.

Former SAS sergeant Mike Cramer is also on the trail, infiltrating the Irish community in New York as he tracks down Mary Hennessy, the ruthless killer who tore his life apart.

Unless Cramer and Howard agree to co-operate, the world will witness the most spectacular terrorist coup of all time . . .

'*The Long Shot* consolidates Leather's position in the top rank of thriller writers. An ingenious plot, plenty of action and solid, believable characters – wrapped up in taut snappy prose that grabs your attention by the throat . . . A top-notch thriller which whips the reader along at breakneck speed' – *Yorkshire Post*

HODDER AND STOUGHTON PAPERBACKS